Glenn Cooper graduated with a degree in archaeology from Harvard and got his medical degree from Tufts University School of Medicine. He has been the Chairman and CEO of a bio-technology company in Massachusetts and is a screenwriter and producer. He is also the bestselling author of *Library of the Dead* and its sequel *Book of Souls*.

THE TENTH CHAMBER

Abbey of Ruac, rural France: A medieval script is discovered, and sent to Paris for restoration. There, literary historian Hugo Pineau finds therein a description of a painted cave with the secrets it contains — and a map showing its position close to the abbey. Hugo, aided by archaeologist Luc Simard, goes exploring. They discover a vast network of prehistoric caves deep within the cliffs. At the core of the labyrinth lies the most astonishing chamber of all — as the manuscript chronicled. They set up camp with a team of experts to bring their find to the world. But they are drawn into a dangerous game as one 'accidental' death leads to another. Someone will stop at nothing to protect the enigma of the tenth chamber . . .

GLENN COOPER

THE TENTH CHAMBER

Complete and Unabridged

CHARNWOOD
Leicester

First published in Great Britain in 2010 by
Arrow Books
The Random House Group Limited
London

First Charnwood Edition
published 2011
by arrangement with
The Random House Group Limited
London

British Library CIP Data

Cooper, Glenn, 1953 –
    The tenth chamber.
    1. Manuscripts, Medieval- -France- -Fiction.
    2. Rock paintings- -France- -Fiction. 3. Literary
    historians- -France- -Paris- -Fiction. 4. Archaeologists- -
    France- -Paris- -Fiction. 5. Suspense fiction.
    6. Large type books.
    I. Title
    813.6–dc22

    ISBN 978–1–44480–538–3

Published by
F. A. Thorpe (Publishing)
Anstey, Leicestershire

Set by Words & Graphics Ltd.
Anstey, Leicestershire
Printed and bound in Great Britain by
T. J. International Ltd., Padstow, Cornwall

This book is printed on acid-free paper

Acknowledgements

First and foremost, thanks to Simon Lipskar who I consider more than an agent, but a partner in the craft and enterprise of writing. This book is better, no much better, for his participation. And thanks too, to Angharad Kowal, for her fine representation in the UK. As usual, my first reader, Gunilla Lacoche, kept me going with her encouragement. The fascinating and multi-talented Polly North gave me my very first book on the star-crossed medieval lovers, Abélard and Héloïse and inspired me to include them in my story. Miranda Denenberg was kind enough to let me read her excellent dissertation on the interpretation of prehistoric cave art which was a wonderful jumping off point to the vast literature on the subject. Laura Vogel, amazing psychiatrist and lover of literature, helped me put more character into my characters, and for that I am extremely grateful. My fantastic editors at Random House, Kate Elton and Georgina Hawtrey-Woore are doing more than publishing my books, they are helping build my career, and that has not gone unnoticed. A toast to my pantheon of archaeology mentors, some gone, all remembered, particularly the incomparable John Wymer, my late father-in-law. And finally, for Tessa, who continues to be my bedrock.

Prologue

The Périgord Region, France, 1899

The two men were breathing hard, scrambling over slippery terrain, struggling to make sense of what they had just seen.

A sudden late-summer rain burst had caught them by surprise. The fast-moving squall moved in while they were exploring the cave, drenching the limestone cliffs, darkening the vertical rock faces and shrouding the Vézère River valley in a veil of low clouds.

Only an hour earlier, from their high perch on the cliffs, the schoolmaster, Édouard Lefevre, had been pointing out landmarks to his younger cousin, Pascal. Church spires far in the distance stood out crisply against a regal sky. Sunbeams glanced the surface of the river. Wholesome barley fields stretched across the flat plain.

But when they emerged blinking from the cave, their last wooden match spent, it was almost as if a painter had decided to start again and had brushed over his bright landscape with a grey wash.

The outbound hike had been casual and leisurely but their return journey took on an element of drama as torrents of water cascaded onto the undercliffs, turning their trail muddy and treacherous. Both men were adequate hikers and both had decent shoes but neither was so experienced they would have chosen to be high on a slick ledge in pelting rain. Still, they never considered returning to the cave for shelter.

'We've got to tell the authorities!' Édouard insisted, wiping his forehead and holding back a branch so Pascal could safely pass. 'If we hurry we can be at the hotel before nightfall.'

Time and again, they had to grab on to tree limbs to steady themselves and in one heart-stopping instance Édouard seized Pascal's collar when he thought his cousin had lost footing and was about to plunge.

When they arrived at their car they were soaked through. It was Pascal's vehicle, actually his father's, since only someone like a wealthy banker could afford an automobile as novel and sumptuous as a Type 16 Peugeot. Although the car had a roof, the rain had thoroughly drenched the open cabin. There was a blanket under the seat that was relatively dry but at the cruising speed of twelve miles per hour, both men were soon shivering and the decision to stop at the first café they came to for a warming drink was easily taken.

The tiny village of Ruac had a single café which at this time of day was hosting a dozen drinkers at small wooden tables. They were rough stock, coarse-looking peasants, and all of them, to a man, stopped talking when the strangers entered. Some had been hunting birds, their rifles propped up against the back wall. One old fellow pointed through the window at the motor car, whispered something to the bartender and startled cackling.

Édouard and Pascal sat at an empty table, looking like drowned rats. 'Two large brandies!' Édouard ordered the bartender. 'The quicker the better, monsieur, or we'll be dead of pneumonia!'

The bartender reached for a bottle and twisted out the cork. He was a middle-aged man with jet-black hair, long sideburns and calloused hands. 'Is that yours?' he asked Édouard, gesturing out the window.

'Mine,' Pascal answered. 'Ever seen one before?'

The bartender shook his head and looked like he was inclined to spit on the floor. Instead he asked another question. 'Where've you come from?'

The patrons in the café hung on the conversation. It was their evening's entertainment.

'We're on holiday,' Édouard answered. 'We're staying in Sarlat.'

'Who comes to Ruac on holiday?' the bartender smirked, laying down the brandies.

'A lot of people will come soon enough,' Pascal said, offended by the man's tone.

'What do you mean by that?'

'When word spreads of our discovery, people will come from as far as Paris,' Pascal boasted. 'Even London.'

'Discovery? What discovery?'

Édouard sought to quiet his cousin, but the strong-willed young man was not going to be hushed. 'We were on a naturalist walk along the cliffs. We were looking for birds. We found a cave.'

'Where?'

As he described their route, Édouard downed his drink and gestured for another.

The bartender scrunched his forehead. 'There's lots of caves around here. What's so special about this one?'

When Pascal started talking, Édouard sensed that every man was staring at his cousin's lips, watching each word fall off his tongue. As a teacher, Édouard had always admired Pascal's powers of description, and now, listening to him waxing away, he marvelled again at the miracle they had stumbled on.

He closed his eyes for a moment to recall the images illuminated by their flickering match lights and missed the bartender's quick nod to the men seated behind them.

A metallic clunk made him look up. The bartender's lip was curled.

Was he smiling?

When Pascal's blond head started spraying blood, Édouard only had time to say, 'Oh!' before a bullet ripped through his brain too.

★　★　★

The café smelled of gunpowder.

There was a long silence until the man with the hunting rifle finally said, 'What shall we do with them?'

The bartender started issuing orders. 'Take them to Duval's farm. Chop them up and feed them to the pigs. When it gets dark, take a horse and drag that machine of theirs far away.'

4

'So there *is* a cave,' one old man said quietly.

'Did you ever doubt it?' the bartender hissed. 'I always knew it would be found one day.'

He could spit now without soiling his own floor. Édouard was lying at his feet.

A gob of phlegm landed on the man's bloody cheek.

1

It began with a spark from a mouse-chewed electrical wire deep within a thick plaster wall.

The spark caught a chestnut beam and set it smouldering. When the old dry wood broke out in full combustion the north wall of the church kitchen started spewing smoke.

If this had happened during the day, the cook or one of the nuns, or even Abbot Menaud himself, stopping for a glass of hot lemon water, would have sounded the alarm or at least grabbed the fire extinguisher under the sink, but it happened at night.

The abbey library shared a common wall with the kitchen. With a single exception, the library did not house a particularly grand or valuable collection, but it was a part of the tangible history of the place, just as much as the tombs in the crypt or the markers in the cemetery.

Alongside five centuries of standard ecclesiastical texts and Bibles were chronicles of more secular and mundane aspects of abbey life: births, deaths, census records, medical and herbal books, trading accounts, even recipes for ale and certain cheeses. The one valuable text was a thirteenth-century edition of the *Rule of St Benedict*, the so-called Dijon version, one of the first translations from the Latin to Old French. For a rural Cistercian abbey in the heart of the Périgord, an early French copy of their patron saint's tome was special indeed, and the book had pride of place in the centre of the bookcase that stood against the burning wall.

The library was a generously sized room with tall leaded windows and a grouted stone floor of squares and rectangles which was far from level. The central reading table required shims to prevent it from wobbling and monks and nuns who pulled up to the table had to avoid shifting their weight lest they bother their neighbours with clopping chair legs.

The bookcases which lined the walls and touched the ceiling were centuries old, walnut, chocolatey in colour and polished with time. Billows of smoke poured over the top of the cases on the afflicted wall. Had it not been for Brother Marcel's enlarged prostate the outcome that night might have been different. In the brothers' dormitory, across the courtyard from the library, the elderly monk awoke for one of his usual nocturnal visits to the water closet and smelled smoke. He arthritically shuffled up and down the halls shouting 'Fire!' and before all that long, the SPV, the volunteer fire brigade, was rumbling up the gravel drive to the Trappist Abbey of Ruac in their venerable Renault pumper.

The brigade served a coterie of Périgord Noir communes along the River Vézère. The chief of the brigade, Bonnet, was from Ruac and he knew the abbey well enough. He was the proprietor of a café by day, older than the others on his crew, with the imperious air and ample gut of a small-business owner and a high-ranking officer of the SPV. At the entrance to the library wing he blew past Abbot Menaud who looked like a frightened penguin in his hastily donned white robe and black scapular, flapping his short arms and muttering in guttural spasms of alarm: 'Hurry! Hurry! The library!'

The chief surveyed the smoke-filled room and ordered his crew to set the hoses and drag them inside.

'You're not going to use your hoses!' the abbot pleaded. 'The books!'

'And how do you suggest we fight this fire, Father?' the chief replied. 'With prayer?' Bonnet then shouted to his lieutenant, a garage mechanic with wine on his breath, 'The fire's in that wall. Pull that bookcase down!'

'Please!' the abbot implored. 'Be gentle with my books.' Then, in a flash of horror, the abbot realised the precious St Benedict text was in the direct path of the encroaching flames. He rushed past Bonnet and the others and snatched it off the shelf, cradling it in his arms like an infant.

The fire captain roared after him melodramatically: 'I can't do my job with him interfering. Someone, take him out. I'm in charge here!'

A group of monks who were gathered around took hold of their abbot's arms and silently but insistently pulled him away into the smoke-tinged night air. Bonnet personally wielded an axe, drove the spiked end into an eye-level bookshelf, right where the Dijon version of the Rule had been a few moments earlier, and yanked back as hard as he could. The axe ripped through the spine of another book on its way to the wood and sent scraps of paper fluttering. The enormous bookcase tilted forward a few inches and spilled a small number of manuscripts. He repeated the maneouvre a few times and his men imitated him at other points along the wall.

Bonnet had always struggled with reading and harboured something of a hatred for books so for him, there was more than a little sadistic pleasure in this venture. With four men simultaneously hooked on, they wrenched their axes in unison and the large bookcase leaned, and in a torrent of falling books that resembled a rock slide on one of the local mountain roads, reached its tipping point.

The men scrambled to safety as the case crashed down onto the stone floor. Bonnet led his men onto the back of the fallen case which rested atop piles of volumes. Their heavy boots crashed onto, and in Bonnet's case, through the walnut planking as they made their way to the burning wall.

'Okay,' Bonnet shouted, wheezing through his exertions, 'Open up this wall and get some water on it fast!'

★ ★ ★

When the dawn came, the firefighters were still hosing down the few remaining hot-spots. The abbot was finally let back inside. He shuffled in like an old man; he was only in his sixties but the night had aged him and he appeared stooped and frail.

Tears came when he saw the destruction. The shattered cases, the masses of soggy print, the soot everywhere. The burned wall was largely knocked down and he could see straight through into the kitchen. Why, he wondered, couldn't they have fought the fire through the kitchen? Why was it necessary to destroy his books? But the abbey was saved and no lives were lost and for this, he had to be grateful. They would move forward. They always did.

Bonnet approached him through the rubble and offered an olive branch. 'I'm sorry I was harsh with you, Dom Menaud. I was just doing my job.'

'I know, I know,' the abbot said numbly. 'It's just that . . . oh well, so much damage.'

'Fires aren't dainty affairs, I'm afraid. We'll be away soon. I know a company that can help with the cleanup. The brother of one of my men in Montignac.'

'We'll use our own labour,' the abbot replied. His eyes were wandering over the book-strewn floor. He stooped to pick up a soaking wet Bible, its sixteenth-century boards and leathers already possessing the ever-so-faint sweet smell of rekindled fungi. He used the folds of his habit sleeve to blot it but realised the futility of the act and simply placed it on the reading table, which had been pushed against an intact bookcase.

He shook his head and was about to leave for morning prayers when something else caught his attention.

In one corner, some distance from the piles of pulled-down books, was a distinctive binding he

10

failed to recognise. The abbot was a scholar with an advanced degree in religious studies from the University of Paris. Over three decades, these books had become his intimates, his comrades. It was akin to having several thousand children and knowing all their names and birthdays.

But this book. He'd never seen it before; he was certain of that.

One of the firefighters, an affable, lanky fellow, watched closely as the abbot approached the book and stooped to inspect the binding.

'That's a funny-looking one, isn't it, Father?'

'Yes, it is.'

'I found it, you know,' the fireman said proudly.

'Found it? Where?'

The fireman pointed to a part of the wall that was no longer there. 'Just there. It was inside the wall. My axe just missed it. I was working fast so I threw it into the corner. Hope I didn't damage it too badly.'

'Inside the wall, you say.'

The abbot picked it up and straight away realised its weight was disproportionate to its size. Though elaborate, it was a small book, not much larger than a modern paperback and thinner than most. Its heft was a result of waterlogging. It was as soaked and saturated as a sponge. Water leaked onto his hand and through his fingers.

The cover was an extraordinary piece of leather, distinctively reddish in hue with, at its centre, a beautifully tooled depiction of a full-standing saint in flowing robes, his head

11

encircled by a halo. The binding was embellished with a fine raised split-cord spine, tarnished silver corners and endbands, and five silver bosses, each the size of a pea, one on each corner and one in the middle of the saint's body. The back cover, though untooled, had five identical bosses. The book was firmly held closed by a pair of silver clasps, tight around wet leaves of parchment.

The abbot sorted through first impressions: thirteenth or fourteenth century, potentially illustrated, highest quality.

And hidden. Why?

'What's that?' Bonnet was at his side, thrusting his stubbled chin forward like the prow of a ship. 'Let me see.'

The abbot was startled by the intrusion into his thoughts and automatically handed over the book. Bonnet dug the thick nail of his forefinger into one of the clasps and it easily popped open. The second clasp was more stubborn but only slightly. He tugged at the front cover and just as he seemed to be at the point of discovery, the board stuck firm. The waterlogging made the covers and pages as adherent as if they'd been glued together. In frustration he exerted more force but the cover stayed put.

'No! Stop!' the abbot cried. 'You'll rip it. Give it back to me.'

The chief snorted and handed the book over. 'You think it's a Bible?' he asked.

'No, I think not.'

'What then?'

'I don't know, but there are more urgent

things this morning. This is for another day.'

However, he was not cavalier about the book. He tucked it under his arm, took it back to his office and laid a white hand cloth on his desk. He placed the book onto the cloth and gently touched the image of the saint before hurrying off to the church to officiate at the Prime service.

★   ★   ★

Three days later, a hired car pulled through the abbey gates and parked in a visitor space just as its dashboard GPS unit was informing the driver he had arrived at his destination. 'Thank you, I know,' the driver sniffed at the female voice.

Hugo Pineau got out and blinked from behind his designer sunglasses into the noon sun which hovered over the church tower like the dot on an i. He took his briefcase from the back seat and winced with each step on gravel, irritated because his new leather soles were getting a premature scuffing.

He dreaded these obligatory visits to the countryside. Ordinarily he might have been able to pawn off the job to Isaak, his business development manager, but the wretch was already on his August vacation. The referral to H. Pineau Restorations had come directly from the Archbishop of Bordeaux, an important client, so there was no question of snapping to and providing first-class service.

The abbey was large and fairly impressive. Set in a verdant enclave of woodlands and pastures, well away from the D-road, it had clean architectural lines. Though the church tower dated to the tenth century or earlier, the abbey, as it existed today was primarily built in the twelfth century by a strict Cistercian order and up to the seventeenth century periodically it had been expanded in stages. Of course, there were twentieth-century accoutrements in the realm of wiring and plumbing but the complex was remarkably little changed over hundreds of years. The Abbey of Ruac was a fine example of Romanesque architecture fashioned of white and yellow limestone quarried from the nearby outcroppings prevalent above the Vézère plain.

The cathedral was well proportioned, constructed in a typical cruciform plan. It was connected, via a series of passageways and courtyards, to all the other abbey buildings — the dormitories, the chapter house, the abbot's house, the manicured cloister, the ancient caldarium, the old brewery, dovecote and forge. And the library.

Hugo was escorted by one of the monks directly to the library, but he could have found it blindfolded; he'd sniffed enough days-old fires in his career. His mild attempt at small talk about the fineness of the summer day and the tragedy of the blaze was politely deflected by the young monk who delivered him to Dom Menaud and bowed goodbye. The abbot was waiting amidst the piles of sodden, smoky books.

Hugo clucked knowingly at the sight of devastation and presented his card. Hugo was a small, compact man in his forties with no excess body fat. His nose was broad but otherwise his features were chiselled and quite handsome. He looked elegant, perfectly coiffed and urbane in a closely fitted and buttoned brown sports jacket, tan slacks and an open-necked white shirt made of the finest Egyptian cotton which shimmered against his skin. He had the musky scent of good cologne. The abbot, on the other hand, wore traditional loose robe and sandals and gave off the odours of a sausage lunch and sweaty skin. It seemed like a time warp had brought the two men together.

'Thank you for coming all the way from Paris,' Dom Menaud offered.

'Not at all. This is what I do. And when the archbishop calls, I run.'

'He is a good friend to our order,' the abbot replied. 'We are grateful for his help and yours. Very little was burned,' he added, gesturing around the room. 'It's all water damage, and smoke.'

'Well, there isn't much we can ever do about flames but water and smoke: these can be rectified — if one has the correct knowledge and tools.'

'And money.'

Hugo laughed nervously. 'Well, yes, money is an important factor too. If I may say, Dom Menaud, I am pleased I can converse with you so normally. I haven't worked with Trappists before. I thought there might be, well, a vow of silence that was followed here. I imagined having to pass notes back and forth.'

'A misconception, Monsieur Pineau. We endeavour to maintain a certain discipline, to speak when needed, to avoid frivolous and unnecessary discussion. We find that idle chat tends to distract us from our spiritual focus and monastic pursuits.'

'This concept suits me fine, Dom Menaud. I'm eager to get to work. Let me explain how we do business at H. Pineau Restorations. Then we can survey the task and set ourselves an action plan. Yes?'

They sat at the reading table while Hugo launched into a tutorial on the salvage of water-damaged library materials. The older the book, he explained, the greater its water absorbency. Material of the antiquity of the abbey's might absorb up to two hundred per cent of its weight in water. If a decision was taken to address, say five thousand water-laden volumes, then some eight tonnes of water must be removed!

The best method for restoring soaked books was to freeze them followed by a process of vacuum freeze drying under carefully controlled conditions. The outcome for parchment and paper might be excellent but, depending on the specific materials and the amount of swelling, bindings may have to be redone. Fungicidal treatments were essential to combat the spread of mould growth but his firm had perfected successful approaches to killing the microbes by introducing ethylene oxide gas into the drying cycles of their industrial-sized freeze-drying tanks.

Hugo answered the abbot's well-reasoned questions then broached the delicate subject of cost. He prefaced the discussion with his standard speech that it was invariably more cost-effective to replace volumes that were still in print and apply restoration techniques only to older irreplaceable ones. Then he gave a rough estimate of the typical price tag per thousand books and studied the abbot's face for a reaction. Usually at this stage of his sales pitch, the curator or librarian would start swearing but the abbot was impassive and certainly did not spew oaths.

'We'll have to prioritise, of course. We can't do everything but we must salvage the sacred history of the abbey. We will find a way to pay. We have a roofing fund we can tap. We have some small paintings we can sell. There's one book, an early French translation of St Benedict we'd be loathe to part with but . . . ' He sighed pathetically. 'And you can help too, Monsieur, by offering us a price that reflects our ecclesiastical status.'

Hugo grinned. 'Of course, Dom Menaud, of course. Let's have a look around, shall we?'

They spent the afternoon poking through the piles of wet books, making a rough inventory, and setting up a ranking system based on the abbot's assessment of historical value. Finally, the young monk brought them a tray of tea and biscuits and the abbot took the opportunity to point out one small book wrapped in a hand cloth. It was set apart from the others at the far end of the reading table.

'I'd like your opinion about this one, Monsieur Pineau.'

Hugo thirstily slurped at his tea before putting on another pair of latex gloves. He unwrapped the towel and inspected the elegant red-leather bindings. 'Well, this is something special! What is it?'

'In truth, I don't know. I didn't even know we had it. One of the firemen found it inside that wall. The cover was stuck. I didn't force it.'

'A good decision. It's a cardinal rule unless you really know what you're doing. It's very saturated, isn't it? Look at the green smudge on the edges of the pages here and here. And here's a spot of red. I wouldn't be surprised if there are coloured illustrations. Vegetable-based pigments can run.'

He applied light pressure to the front cover and remarked, 'These pages aren't going to come apart without a good freeze-drying but I might be able to lift up the cover to see the flyleaf. Are you game?'

'If you can do it safely.'

Hugo retrieved a leather clutch from his briefcase and unbuttoned it. It contained an assortment of precision tools with points, wedges and hooks, not unlike a small dissection or dental kit. He chose a tiny spatula with an ultra-fine blade and started working it under the front cover, advancing it millimetre by millimetre with the steady hand of a safe cracker or a bomb defuser.

He spent a good five minutes freeing the entire perimeter of the cover, inserting that spatula a centimetre or so all around, and then with gentle traction, the cover peeled away from the frontispiece and hinged open.

The abbot leaned over Hugo's shoulder and gasped audibly as together they read the boldly written inscription on the flyleaf, rendered in a flowing and confident Latin script:

Ruac, 1307
I, Barthomieu, friar of Abbey Ruac, am two hundred and twenty years old and this is my story.

2

Midway between Bordeaux and Paris, from his first-class compartment of the TGV, Luc Simard was waging a pitched battle between the twin interests that perpetually consumed him: work and women.

He was seated on the right-hand side of the carriage in the row of singles, working on revisions to one of his papers under peer review at *Nature*. The flat green countryside whizzed past his tinted windows but the scenery went largely unnoticed as he struggled to find the right English phrase to frame his amended conclusions. As recently as four years ago, when he was living in the States, this language block would have been inconceivable; he found it remarkable how rusty these skills became when they went unused, even for a bona fide bilingual speaker such as he.

He had noticed the two lovely ladies, seated side-by-side on the left of the carriage a couple of rows ahead who kept turning, smiling then chatting among themselves just loud enough for him to hear,

'I think he's a movie star.'

'Which one?'

'I'm not sure. Maybe a singer.'

'Go ask him.'

'You.'

It would have been breathtakingly easy to

gather up his papers and invite them to the café car. Then, inevitably, an exchange of numbers before they disembarked at Montparnasse station. Maybe one of them, maybe both, would be available for a late drink after his dinner with Hugo Pineau.

But he absolutely had to finish the paper then fully prepare a lecture before he returned to Bordeaux. He didn't have time for this impromptu meeting and had told Hugo as much, but his old school chum had begged — literally pleaded with him — to make time. He had something to show him and it had to be done in person. He'd promised that Luc wouldn't be disappointed and in any event, they'd have a blow-out dinner for old time's sake. And, oh yes, first-class travel and a good room at the Royal Monceau, courtesy of Hugo's firm.

Luc settled back to his paper, a study of population kinetics among European hunter-gatherers during the Glacial Maximum of the Upper Paleolithic. It was incredible to think that as late as thirty thousand years ago there'd only been some five thousand humans in all of Europe, if his team's calculations were correct. Five thousand souls, a number precariously close to zero! If these few hearty ones hadn't found sufficient refuge from the numbing cold in the protected havens of the Périgord, Cantabria and the Ibérian coasts then neither of these giggling young ladies — or anyone else — would be there today.

But the women were relentless with their

whispering and their glances. Apparently they were bored or maybe he was simply too ruggedly irresistible, with his thick black hair spilling over his collar, the heavy two-day growth on his jaw, the pencil dangling like a cigarette from his lips, the cowboy boots extending rakishly from his tight jeans into the aisle. In some ways he looked like a much younger man, but his need for reading glasses balanced the image nearer to the forty-four-year-old professor he was.

One more furtive smile from the prettier of the two girls, the one on the aisle, broke down his wavering resistance. He sighed, put away his papers, and in three long strides he was standing over them. All he needed to say was a friendly, 'Hello.'

The girl on the aisle bubbled over, 'Hi. My friend and I were wondering who you are.'

He smiled. 'I'm Luc, that's who I am.'

'Are you in films?'

'No.'

'Theatre?'

'Not that either.'

'What then?'

'I'm an archaeologist.'

'Like Indiana Jones?'

'Precisely. Just like him.'

The girl on the aisle peeked at her friend then asked, 'Would you like to have a coffee with us?'

Luc shrugged and thought briefly about his unfinished work. 'Yes, of course,' he answered. 'Why not?'

3

General André Gatinois was taking a brisk stroll through the Père Lachaise Cemetery, his habitual lunch-time routine on fair days. Keeping lean into his fifties was proving nettlesome and he found it increasingly necessary to skip lunch and walk a few kilometrers instead.

The cemetery, the largest in Paris, was the most visited and arguably the most famous in the world, the resting place for the likes of Proust, Chopin, Balzac, Oscar Wilde and Molière. Much to Gatinois's irritation, it was also home to Jim Morrison, and he personally complained to the cemetery administrator whenever he noticed another addled Doors fan had spray-painted a To JIM sign complete with arrow on a piece of masonry.

The cemetery was only a kilometre or so from his office on Boulevard Mortier in the 20th arrondissement, but to maximise the amount of time in greenery, he had his driver take him to the main cemetery gate and wait there until he was done with his constitutional. The number plates on his official black Peugeot 607 guaranteed the police wouldn't bother the idling chauffeur.

The cemetery was huge, some fifty hectares, and Gatinois could vary his route endlessly. On a sunny late-summer day, the masses of leaves overhead were just starting to turn and were rustling pleasantly in the breeze. He walked amidst a throng of visitors, although his fine blue suit, military-style hair and stiff posture set him apart from the jeans and sweatshirts of the scruffy majority.

Lost in thought, he found himself somewhat deeper than usual in the grounds so he picked up his pace to make sure he'd be back in time for his weekly staff meeting. A particularly large ornate tomb on a knoll made him slow and stop for a moment. It was open-walled, Byzantine, housing side-by-side sarcophagi adorned by a medieval man and a woman in marble repose. The tomb of Héloïse and Abélard. The twelfth-century star-crossed lovers who so defined the notion of true love that, for the sake of national homage, their bones were sent to Paris in the nineteenth century from their original resting place in Ferreux-Quincey.

Gatinois blew his nose into his handkerchief. Eternal love, he scoffed. Propaganda. Mythology. He thought of his own loveless marriage and made a mental note to buy a small gift for his mistress. He was tired of her too, but in his position, he was obligated to subject each dalliance to a full security check. Although his colleagues were discreet, he felt somewhat constrained: he couldn't chop and change too frequently and still maintain his dignity.

★   ★   ★

His driver passed through the security cordon and let Gatinois off in an internal courtyard

24

where he entered the building through a huge oak door as venerable and solid as the Ministry of Defence itself.

La piscine.

That's what the DGSE complex was nick-named. The swimming pool. Although the name referred to the nearby Piscine des Tourelles of the French Swimming Federation, the notion of swimming laps, working your tail off but remaining in the same place, often seemed apt to him.

Gatinois was somewhat of an anomaly within the organisation. No one inside the Directorate-General for External Security held a higher rank, but his unit was the smallest and in an agency where opacity was a way of life, Unit 70 was the most opaque.

Whereas his departmental peers within the Directorates of Strategy and Intelligence com-manded vast budgets and manpower, stood toe-to-toe with their counterparts in the CIA and other intelligence agencies worldwide and held star status within their ranks, his unit paled in comparison. It had a comparatively small budget, only thirty employees and Gatinois worked in relative obscurity. Not that he ever lacked for resources — it was just that the amount of funding he required was dwarfed by the Action Division, for example, with their global network of spies and operatives. No, Gatinois achieved what he required on a fraction of what other groups needed. In truth, much of his unit's work was accomplished by contractors in government and academic labs who had no

25

idea what they were actually working on.

Gatinois had to be content with the knowledge, reliably passed to him by his superior, the DGSE director, that the Minister of Defence, and indeed the President of France himself, were often more interested in updates about Unit 70 than any other matter of state intelligence.

Unit 70 had its suite of rooms in a nineteenth-century block within the complex. Gatinois favoured it over the other modern cookie-cutter buildings and always resisted relocation. He preferred the high ceilings, intricate mouldings and wainscoting of the quarters even though the toilets were bulkier than their modern equivalents.

His conference room had grand proportions and a brilliant crystal chandelier. Following a brief visit to his personal bathroom to adjust his grooming, he swept in, nodded to his staff and took his place at the head of the table where his briefing papers awaited.

One of his rituals of self-importance was to keep his people waiting in silence while he scanned their weekly status report. Each department head would deliver a verbal summary in turn, but Gatinois liked to know what was coming. His principal aide, Colonel Jean-Claude Marolles, a short, haughty man with a careful little moustache, sat to his right, rolling the barrel of his pen back and forth between thumb and forefinger in his typical skittish fashion, waiting for Gatinois to find something to criticise.

He didn't have long to wait.

'Why wasn't I told about this?' Gatinois asked, peeling off his reading glasses as if he intended to fling them.

'About what, General?' Marolles replied with a touch of weariness that set Gatinois off into a rage.

'About the fire! What do you mean, 'about what?''

'It was only a small fire at the abbey. Nothing at all happened in the village. It doesn't appear to have any significance.'

Gatinois was not satisfied. He let his unblinking eyes settle on each of the men around the table in turn until he found Chabon, the one in charge of running Dr Pelay. 'But, Chabon, you write here Pelay told you that Bonnet himself attended the fire and mentioned that an old book was found inside a wall. Is that your report?'

Chabon replied that it was.

'And what was this book?' he asked icily.

'We don't know,' Chabon replied meekly. 'I didn't think it had relevance to our work.'

Gatinois welcomed the opportunity for histrionics. He took his inspiration from the chandelier, which reminded him of a burst of fireworks. Often, their work had the quality of watching paint dry. It was easy for them to get complacent. It was easy for *him* to get complacent. It had been a solid six months since the last noteworthy breakthrough and his frustration at the torpid pace of his assignment and his long overdue advancement to a larger ministry job was ready to boil over.

He started softly, seething, and let his voice rise in a smooth crescendo until he was bellowing loud enough to be heard down the corridor. 'Our job is Ruac. Everything about Ruac. Nothing about Ruac is unimportant until I say it's unimportant. If a kid gets chicken pox I want to know about it! If there's a power cut in the café I want to know about it! If a goddamn dog shits on the street I want to know about it! An old book is found in the wall of Ruac Abbey and the first reaction of my staff is that it's not important? Don't be idiotic! We can't afford to be complacent!'

His people looked down, absorbing the pounding like good soldiers.

Gatinois stood up, trying to decide whether he ought to stamp out and leave them sitting there contemplating their fates. He leaned over and slammed his fist onto the polished wood. 'For God's sake, people, this is Ruac! Pull your fingers out and get to work!'

4

H. Pineau Restorations had its offices on Rue Beaujon, off Avenue Hoche just blocks from the Arc de Triomphe. It was a high-rent district that Hugo had chosen for its prestige value. To keep costs manageable he leased only a small suite of rooms for his staff headquarters. He lived in the 7th arrondissement with an elegant view of the Seine, and on a nice day, he would walk to the company puffing away on a cigarillo. He encouraged clients to come by so he could show off his tasteful assortment of antiques and pictures, not to mention his stunning red-headed secretary.

As a pure-bred cosmopolitan, he couldn't bear to be separated from the heartbeat of Paris for more than the briefest time and he always felt a little blue when he had to visit the guts of his operation, housed in a low-slung metal building on a drab industrial estate near Orly Airport. There, the company took delivery of all manner of paintings, fine arts, books and manuscripts from across western Europe and beyond, and it was there he kept a staff of thirty, busily employed, patiently and lucratively erasing the effects of flood waters, fire and other human and natural disasters.

Hugo sprang out of his office when he heard Luc's baritone voice resonating in the reception area.

'Right on time!' Hugo shouted, gripping his friend in a bear hug. Luc was a head taller, muscular and tanned from vigorous outdoor labour. Hugo seemed pale and boyish in comparison, trim and effete. 'There, you've finally met Margot. I told you she was beautiful!' And then to his secretary he said, 'And you've finally met Luc. I told you he was beautiful!'

'Well, he's managed to make both of us uncomfortable,' Luc said, smiling. 'Margot, you're a strong woman to put up with this guy.'

Margot nodded saucily in agreement. 'My boyfriend plays rugby so I've got some insurance against his bad behaviours.'

'And this is Isaak Mansion, my head of business development and my right-hand man,' Hugo said, introducing the man in a suit and tie who had appeared at his side, a fellow with short curly hair and a neatly trimmed beard.

Isaak warmly greeted Luc and said slyly, 'You don't know why you're here yet, do you?'

'Quiet!' Hugo said playfully. 'Don't ruin my fun. Go away and make us some money!'

In his office, Hugo sat Luc down and made a show of opening a fresh bottle of bourbon and pouring generous measures into a pair of Baccarat crystal glasses. They clinked and sipped a toast.

'The place looks good, you look good,' Luc observed.

'How long since you were here, five years?' Hugo asked.

'Something like that.'

'It's pathetic. I saw you more when you were living abroad.'

'Well, you know how it is,' Luc mused. 'Never enough time.'

'You had a girlfriend last time we met, an American.'

'Things blew up.'

Hugo shrugged. 'Typical,' and then without missing a beat, 'God, it's good to see you!'

They talked for a while about friends from their university days and Hugo's complicated social life when Margot knocked discreetly at the door and informed Hugo that the police were on the line again.

'Shall I leave?' Luc asked.

'No, stay, stay. This won't take long.'

Luc listened to one side of a conversation and when Hugo hung up he sighed. 'It's always something. We had a break-in at my plant last night. My watchman was beaten silly. He's in hospital with a cracked skull. They ransacked the place.'

'Anything stolen?'

'Nothing. The idiots probably didn't even know we restore books. What's the last thing an ignorant crook is interested in? Books! And that's what they found, lots of them. Poetic justice, but they made a mess.'

Luc commiserated about the stress his friend seemed to be under but finally raised both palms towards the ceiling and said, 'So? What's the deal? What's so special I've got to drop everything and drag my ass to Paris?'

'I need to pick your brain.'

'About what?'

'This.'

31

Hugo went to his credenza and picked up a small muslin-wrapped parcel. They sat together on the sofa. Hugo cleared a space on the coffee table where he made a show of slowly unwrapping the book. The leather looked redder and more lustrous than the day Hugo had first seen it at the abbey. The haloed saint on the cover was more vividly three-dimensional. The silver bobs, corners and endbands along with the dual clasps had a touch of their period shine. And of course, the book was much lighter now, bone dry. 'I got this in a few weeks ago. It suffered a lot of water damage but my people sorted it out.'

'Okay . . . '

'It's from the Dordogne, the Périgord Noir, your stomping ground.'

Luc raised his eyebrows in mild interest.

'Ever hear of a little village called Ruac?'

'On the Vézère, right? I may have poked around it once or twice. What's there?'

Hugo proceeded to tell Luc about the abbey and its fire, employing a touch of drama and showmanship, purposely building to a storyteller's climax. After he had finished with a boastful account of the excellence of his company at manuscript restoration he said, 'I'd like you to thumb through it and give me a first impression, okay?'

'Sure. Let's have a look.'

Luc held the thin light book in his calloused hands, opened the cover, took note of the fourteenth-century date on the flyleaf and started turning the pages.

He let out a low whistle. 'You're kidding me!' he exclaimed.

'I thought you'd be interested,' Hugo said. 'Carry on.'

Luc paused on each page only long enough to register a first impression. Although he couldn't read the text, he could tell the scribe had a competent, practised hand. The manuscript was done in a stylistically boxy script, two columns per page, employing a rust-coloured ink that retained a lovely coppery glint. There were prickings around the edge of the pages that had been employed to keep the lines straight and true.

But it wasn't the text that interested him. What had him captivated were the bright and bold illustrations decorating the borders of several pages.

Particularly the iconic ones, the images which were his life's blood.

The black bulls. The roe deer. The bison.

Wildly animalistic and beautifully rendered in blacks, earthy-reds, browns and tans.

'This is unmistakable polychromatic cave art,' he murmured. 'Upper Paleolithic, very similar in execution and style to Lascaux but these aren't from Lascaux or any site I've seen.'

'And you've seen them all, I imagine,' Hugo said.

'Of course! This is what I do! But you know, what's far more incredible is the date here: 1307! The absolute first credible mention in recorded history of cave art is from 1879 at Altamira, Spain. This is five centuries earlier! I'm not saying that man hadn't laid eyes on these caves earlier than the nineteenth century but no one ever thought to write about it or reproduce any images. Are you certain this is really from 1307?'

'Well, I haven't subjected it to forensic dating, but the vellum, the bindings, the ink, the pigments all cry out fourteenth century.'

'You're sure?'

Hugo laughed and parroted back, 'This is what I do!'

Luc buried himself back in the book. He sought out one particular page and rotated the manuscript for Hugo to see.

Hugo snorted, 'I knew that would interest you. It's quite the image, quite evocative! Ever seen anything like that before?'

In the margin was a primitive outline, a standing human form, not much more than a glorified stick figure rendered in thick black brushstrokes. Instead of a head the figure had the beak of a bird and at its midsection, a long slash of ink, a huge erect phallus.

'Yes! I have! Not identical but very similar. There's a painting in Lascaux of a birdman just like this. Some kind of mystical figure. Complete with the cock. Incredible.'

He flipped to another page and pointed at the marginalia, lavishly rendered in rich pigments — lush greens, earthy-browns and bursting reds. 'And look at all these drawings! These plants.' And another page. 'These are vines of some kind.' And another. 'These are grasses. It's like a natural history!' And finally he turned to one of the last pages. 'And this, for God's sake, Hugo, this is a map!'

Along the margins of the page was a winding blue line snaking through a swathe of greens, browns and greys, some apparent topography. The landscape was dotted with small painted symbols: a tan tower, a meandering blue line — surely a river — a cluster of grey-roofed dwellings, a tree with crazily angled branches, a paired array of wavy blue lines against a grey background and near it, a tiny black X, unlabelled, floating without context.

Hugo agreed. 'It struck me as a map too.'

Luc finished his bourbon but waved Hugo away when he tried to refill the glass. 'So, now you'd better tell me what this says. You're the Latin scholar. I never progressed much past *veni, vidi, vici.*'

Hugo smiled and replenished his own glass then said with theatrical flair, 'Well, the inscription on the flyleaf says, 'I, Barthomieu, friar of Abbey Ruac, am two hundred and twenty years old and this is my story.''

Luc wrinkled his nose in puzzlement. 'Go on . . . '

'And the first line on the first page says, 'In the ever-lasting memory of the greatest man I have ever known, Saint Bernard of Clairvaux.''

Luc ran his finger over the saint's halo on the cover. 'This guy?'

'Presumably.'

'Any relation to the dogs?'

'As it happens, yes, they're named after him, but as I've since learned he's a bit more famous than that.'

'So tell me the rest.'

35

'I can't.'

Luc was losing his patience. 'Why not?'

Hugo was enjoying himself. 'I can't read it.'

Luc was finished with the game. 'Look, spit it out and don't be a jerk. Why can't you read it?'

'Because the rest of it's in code!'

5

For Luc visiting the Périgord was like coming home. It was green and fertile and always seemed to welcome him like a mother's arms. From his earliest boyhood days at the family vacation cottage at Saint-Aulaye where he spent his summers wading at the village beach along the Dronne, Luc was happiest when he was in that countryside.

The undulating terrain, the steep river gorges, the limestone cliffs, the sun-splashed terraces extending beyond the wine-producing slopes, the dense patches of woodlands, the plum trees and holm oak abundant in the sandy soil, the ancient villages and sandstone towns that dotted the winding by-roads — all these things stirred his soul and kept drawing him back. But none were as important as the ghosts of the Périgord's distant past, faraway souls that came to him as if in a waking dream, shadowy figures darting through the forests always just out of reach.

His childhood visions of early man prowling the land, fueled by field trips to the dark painted caves of the region and the novel, Jean Auel's, *The Clan of the Cave Bear*, which the precocious eleven-year-old had practically inhaled, set him on an academic path that took him to the University of Paris, Harvard and now the faculty at Bordeaux.

Luc had picked up Hugo from the main

Bordeaux train station, Gare Saint Jean, and from there they headed west in his banged-up Land Rover. For Luc the route was automatic; he could almost close his eyes. The Land Rover, once dubbed the Gland Rover by a waggish English grad student, had a few hundred thousand kilometres on the clock. By day, when an excavation was running, it ferried students and equipment to the dig site on its unforgiving shock absorbers and by night, beer-stoked, hormonally charged young diggers to and from the local cafés.

They arrived before lunch at the abbey and sat with Dom Menaud in the study of his abbot house, a dusty book-filled room more resembling a professor's apartment than a cleric's. Hugo performed the introductions and offered a quick apology for their casual clothes. The creature of fashion he was, he was chagrined to be taking a meeting dressed for a hike.

Hugo had corresponded with the abbot about the status of the restorations and a timetable had been set for the return of all the volumes. But now, Dom Menaud was particularly anxious to see the Barthomieu manuscript for himself and when Hugo produced it from his bag he grabbed at it like a greedy child offered a chocolate bar.

The abbot spent a full five minutes in silence, pawing through the pages, studying the text through his bifocals before shaking his head in wonder. 'This really is quite remarkable. Saint Bernard, of all people! And why did this Barthomieu feel it necessary to hide behind a cipher? And these fantastic illustrations! I'm delighted and puzzled and at the same time, I admit, somewhat apprehensive about what it all means.'

'We don't disagree,' Hugo said with a counter-balancing lack of emotion, always the professional before his clients. 'That's why we're here. We're keen to find explanations and Professor Simard has graciously volunteered to help.'

The abbot turned to Luc, his hands resting protectively on the manuscript. 'I appreciate, that, professor. One of the Brothers did an Internet search for me. You have an illustrious background for such a young man. A baccalaureate in Paris from my alma mater, a doctorate from Harvard, a faculty appointment there and most recently, a prestigious professorship at Bordeaux. Congratulations on your accomplishments.'

Luc bowed his head in appreciation.

'Why Harvard, if you don't mind my curiosity?'

'My mother was American, my father French. When I was young I attended boarding school while my parents lived in the Middle East, though we came back to France for summers. When they divorced, it was natural to split the baby, where I'm the baby, you see. I went to an American high school to be with my mother then Paris for my university studies to be near my father then to Harvard to be near my mother again. Complicated, but it worked out.'

'But most of your research has been done in this region?'

'Yes, at least ninety per cent, I should think. I've had my hand in many of France's important paleolithic sites of the last couple of decades, including the Chauvet Cave down in Ardèche. For the last several seasons, I've been extending some old trenches originally dug by Professor Movius from Harvard at Les Eyzies. I've been busy.'

'Not too busy for this?' the abbot asked, pointing to the book.

'Certainly not! How can I turn my back on a great intrigue?'

Dom Menaud was nodding and staring down at the cover. 'Saint Bernard of Clairvaux is a very important figure in our order, are you aware of that?'

Hugo acknowledged he was well aware.

The abbot who was wearing his simple monk's habit suddenly pursed his lips in concern. 'As excited as I am to have a document associated in any way with him, we should be aware of some sensitivities. We don't know what this Barthomieu has to say. Saint Bernard was one of our great men.' He proceeded to unfold a finger for each point: 'He was a founder of the Cistercian order. He was a participant in the Council of Troyes which confirmed the Order of the Knights Templar. He preached the Second Crusade. He established almost two hundred monasteries throughout Europe. His theological influence was immense. He had the ear of popes and famously was the one who denounced Pierre Abélard to Pope Innocent the Second.' When Luc's expression didn't register recognition, the

40

abbot added, 'You know, the famous romance between Abélard and Héloïse, the great tragic love story of the middle ages?'

'Ah yes!' Luc said. 'Every schoolboy's forced to read their love letters.'

'Well, later in Abélard's life, long after his physical tragedy, as it were, Bernard made his life quite difficult again, but it was over a theological matter, not an affair of the heart! Well, to be sure, it's just an interesting footnote. But nevertheless, for his great works, Bernard was not only canonised, but the Pope made him a Doctor of the Church in 1174 within a mere twenty years of his death! So, what I'm saying, gentlemen, is that even though this Barthomieu is dedicating a tract to the Saint almost two hundred years after his death, we have to be mindful of Bernard's reputation. If I am to allow you to investigate this matter, I insist you exercise appropriate discretion and inform me of every finding so I may communicate to my superiors and take instructions. In this, as in all things in life, I am only a servant.'

★   ★   ★

From the rough map in the book, Luc had decided the best place to start their search was on the southern edge of Ruac, which was situated on the eastern bank of the Vézère. Ruac was an ancient village that, unlike many of its neighbours, completely lacked tourist attractions, and so it remained quiet throughout the year. There were no museums or galleries, only a single café and no signposts directing visitors to prehistoric caves or rock shelters. There was one main cobbled street lined by lemon-coloured stone houses — a good number still with their original lauzes roofs made of impossibly heavy slabs of mottled-grey rock, once common to the region, now rapidly vanishing, replaced by more practical terracotta-tiled roofs. It was a neat tidy enclave with modest gardens and poppy-stuffed flower boxes, and while Luc slowly drove through its heart, looking for a place to park, he made some idyllic comments about its unspoiled authenticity. Hugo was unmoved and flinched at an old heavy-haunched woman who scowled at the car as it squeezed past her on the narrow lane. At the end of a row of houses, as Luc was pondering which direction to take, a goat tethered near a tool shed within a small low-walled pasture spectacularly relieved itself and Hugo could no longer hold in his sentiments.

'God, I hate the country!' he exclaimed. 'How on earth did you persuade me to come with you?'

Luc smiled and turned towards the river.

There wasn't a convenient place to park, so Luc pulled the Land Rover onto a grass verge on the outskirts of the village. Through the woods, the river was unseen but faintly heard. He left a cardboard sign on the windscreen indicating they were on official University of Bordeaux business, which may or may not prevent ticketing, depending on the officiousness of the local gendarmes. He helped Hugo adjust his rucksack and the two of them delved into the forest.

It was hot and the air hummed with insects. There was no trail but the undergrowth of bushes, ferns and weeds wasn't too thickly tangled. They had few problems weaving through the stands of horse chestnuts, oak and beech trees which formed an umbrella-like canopy, blocking the midday sun and cooling the air. It wasn't completely virgin territory. A pile of crushed lager cans under a false acacia tree bore witness to recent nocturnal pursuits. Luc was peeved at the violation. An otherwise perfect image of hanging clusters of creamy flowers against a verdant background was spoiled by the litter and he grumbled that on their way back they should stop and clean up. Hugo rolled his eyes at the boy-scout sentiment and trudged onwards.

As they drew closer to the river, the sound of flowing water filled their ears until they broke through a heavy thicket and were suddenly on a ledge, a good twenty metres above the river. There was a splendid view across its wide, sparkling expanse towards the fertile valley on the opposite bank. The vast plain, a patch-work of asymmetrical fields of wheat and beans and grazing cattle seemed to fade and disappear into the hazy horizon.

'Now where?' Hugo asked as he uncomfortably adjusted his rucksack.

Luc pulled out the copy of the map and pointed. 'Okay, I'm going on the assumption that this cluster of buildings represents Ruac, because this tower, here, is perfectly compatible with the

Romanesque tower of the abbey. It's obviously not drawn to scale but the relative positions make sense, see?'

Hugo nodded. 'So you think we're somewhere around here?' He stuck his finger on a map point near the meandering blue line.

'Hopefully. If not, we're in for a very long day. So I say we start walking along the cliffs that way until we find something that looks like this.' He was tapping his finger on the first set of wavy-blue lines. 'I don't think we can rely on this odd tree he's drawn. I'd be surprised if it's still there after six hundred years!' Then he laughed and added, 'And please be careful and don't fall. It would be tragic.'

'Not so much for me,' Hugo said glumly, 'but the two women who cash my alimony cheques would go into mourning.'

Because of the geography of the steep-sided valley, the precipice they were perched upon was lower than the cliffs downstream. As they hiked, the surface they were traversing turned into heavily wooded undercliffs — above them, the limestone face soared another twenty metres over their heads. It was not a treacherous hike. The ledge of the undercliffs was broad enough and stable and the view down into the river was postcard lovely. Nevertheless, Luc was aware his friend was a novice at outdoors pursuits so he kept the pace leisurely and opted for the safest possible footings for Hugo to match step-by-step.

He knew this stretch of cliffs, but not well. It had been fifteen years since he explored this section, but even then it had been a casual survey, a time-filler with no specific motivation. The entire river valley was riddled with prehistoric caves and shelters and it was a well-accepted certainty that important sites, perhaps even spectacular ones, remained to be discovered. Some would be found by professional archaeologists or geologists, others by cavers looking for new thrills, still others by hikers or even, as had happened before, the family dog.

Before today's expedition with Hugo, Luc had gone back and checked his old journals about the Ruac cliffs. The notations were sparse. He'd spent a day or two poking around the area during the summer following the award of his doctorate. His scribbled notes spoke of buzzards and black kites soaring on the thermals and the pleasures of a good packed lunch, but there was not a single mention of an archaeological find. Looking back, what he remembered most of that summer was the lightness that came from finishing one part of his life and starting another. His student days were done; his professorship had not yet started. He could still conjure up the bliss of that liberty.

In researching the trip, Luc discovered that a colleague from Lyon had done a helicopter survey of the stratified oatmeal-coloured rock surfaces of the Vézère valley several years earlier. This was potentially of greater use than the notes he had made years before, and Luc had him email a file of photographs and maps. He studied them intently, side-by-side with the Barthomieu map, peering through a photographer's loupe for any useful clues — waterfalls, crevasses, cave mouths — but like the archaeologist from Lyon, he saw nothing of particular interest.

An hour into their hike, the two men paused for some bottled water. Hugo slipped the rucksack from his shoulders and squatted on his haunches with his back up against the rock face to avoid getting dirt on the seat of his khakis. He lit a cheroot and his face registered the first pleasure of the afternoon. Luc remained standing, squinting into the afternoon sun. He pulled the crude map from the back pocket of his jeans, had another look then folded it back up.

Hugo pouted. 'I hadn't appreciated how futile this would be until I got up here. We can hardly see the rocks below us! It's almost impossible to make anything of the rocks above us! I suppose if there were a big fat cave entrance right off this ledge, maybe we'd find it. You never told me how ridiculous this was going to be.'

Luc shrugged off his friend's comments. 'The map is the key. If it's for real then perhaps we'll find something. If it was from this guy's imagination then we're getting our sun and our exercise for the week, that's all. Plus some male bonding.'

'I don't want to bond with you,' Hugo said irritably. 'I'm hot, I'm tired, my new boots hurt and I want to go home.'

'We've just started. Relax and enjoy. And did I tell you your boots are splendid?'

'Thank you for noticing. So what's the map

telling you, professor?'

'Nothing yet. Like I said,' Luc explained patiently, 'once he's steered us to the general area by orienting us to the position of the abbey, the village and the river, the only landmarks are this peculiar tree and a pair of waterfalls. Since the tree's bound to be long gone, if we find waterfalls, then maybe we're on the right track. If not, we're probably going to come up empty. What do you say we keep moving?'

As the afternoon progressed, their trek became more difficult. Periodically, the ledge they were travelling on would taper and disappear and Luc had to find a new reliable ledge higher or lower on the cliff face. The ascents and descents weren't so difficult as to require anything remotely like technical climbing but he nevertheless worried about Hugo's abilities to keep his footing. On a couple of occasions he instructed his friend to pass his rucksack up on a short rope before Hugo would begin his search for foot and hand holds up the vertical face. Hugo grumbled and generally made a nuisance of himself but Luc lightly deflected his groans and kept them forging ahead on their slow, steady pace.

Down below, a group of kayakers, their boats, in bright primary colours like children's playthings, paddled downstream. A flock of black kites very high in the pale-blue sky swooped by in the opposite direction. The sun was getting lower and the rich flood plain was taking on the hue of good beer. Luc checked his watch. If they turned back soon they'd be able to make it back to the car in daylight, but he decided to press on

47

for a little while longer. They were approaching a promontory. Once they got beyond it he was hoping they'd be able to get a look at a long stretch of rock face. That would be their go/no-go point.

Unfortunately, when they got to the promontory the ledge dwindled to non-existence and the only way to progress was a scramble up a craggy ledge covered in scrubby bushes. It wasn't an easy decision. Hugo was irritable and tired and Luc knew that the extra climb would delay their return. But the adventurer in him always had to know what was on the other side, so he parked Hugo on the ledge, left his own rucksack behind and said he'd be back in a quarter of an hour or so. Hugo, no longer concerned about staying clean, moodily sat cross-legged on the trail and bit into an apple.

The climb wasn't too challenging but Luc was happy to have ditched his friend so he could move at his own pace. The peak of the promontory was a flat expanse of limestone about three-quarters up the cliff face. The view over the valley was magnificent, almost demanding a photograph, but the sun was low and time was precious so he left his camera hanging around his neck and moved a little further downstream to get the lay of the land beyond.

Then he caught sight of something that made him let out an involuntary throaty sound of surprise.

Just below him on a broad ledge was a solitary large juniper tree growing out of the scrub. Its enormous dry and rough twisted trunk the colour of charcoal ash fanned out and gave way to a jumble of corkscrew branches that jutted out in every conceivable direction. Its greenery was minimal, a few coniferous tufts here and there, like an old dog with mange.

Luc scrambled down the slope as quickly as he safely could and ran to it. When he was close enough to touch it, he pulled the map out again, looked up into its impossible jumble of branches and nodded his head. The match was uncanny — even after six hundred years! If any tree was going to live for centuries in this kind of barren terrain it would be the indomitable juniper, the ultimate survivor, with the odd specimen living for two millennia or more.

At that moment Luc decided they wouldn't be turning back.

He knew Hugo would complain bitterly, but it didn't matter. They were going to be camping tonight. If there wasn't a good spot further on, they could always come back and sleep under the protection of this ancient tree.

★ ★ ★

Hugo did complain.

It was certainly *a* tree, he agreed, but he thought it was an article of extreme faith that it was *the* tree. He was sceptical to the point of being obnoxious. Finally Luc told him flatly that he was carrying on and if Hugo wanted, he could go back, take the Land Rover and find a hotel.

Hugo had no appetite for either course of action. He groused equally about sleeping rough

49

and finding his way back to the car on his own. In the end he gave in and meekly followed Luc along the new ledge in search of, as he put it 'mythical waterfalls and unicorns.'

They were running out of daylight. The temperature was dropping and the sky had turned a dusky, rose-like pink. Hugo, resigned to spending an uncomfortable night under the stars, demanded a break for his aching shoulders. They stopped on a secure shelf and guzzled water. Then Hugo unzipped his fly and urinated over the edge. 'There's your waterfall,' he said without a trace of humour.

Luc had his rucksack off too. He leaned back and rested his head against the cliff, about to make a schoolboy comment in reply, when instead he said, 'Hey!' He felt the dampness on his scalp. He wheeled around and laid both hands on the rocks. They were wet. Stepping back as far as he could without going over the edge, he looked up and pointed at a wide dark stripe. 'Look! It goes all the way up. It's our waterfall!'

Hugo looked up too, unimpressed. 'If that's a waterfall, I'm the Pope.'

'It's been a dry summer. After a rainy spring, I'll bet it turns into a proper waterfall. Come on before we lose the light. If there's a second one, I'll buy dinner.'

They walked into the fading light for the better part of another hour. Now, instead of looking, Luc constantly touched the rock face to feel for moisture.

Dusk was overtaking them. Luc was about to

call a halt when they both heard it at the same time: a trickle, like a running tap. A few paces ahead, the rocks were soaking wet and water was seeping onto the ledge, puddling and flowing down towards the river. It was more a water dribble than a waterfall, but as far as Luc was concerned they were on the right track. Even Hugo perked up and agreed to push on until the sun completely set.

Luc pulled out the map one more time and pointed to the two waterfalls and the X that marked the cave. 'If this part of the map is to scale then the cave is nearby, but it's impossible to know if it's below us or above us. I think we have about fifteen minutes of light before it's going to be pointless.'

They consumed the entire quarter of an hour, using Luc's small powerful LED torches to make up for the lack of natural light. There were good sightlines above them. To explore the rock face underneath, Luc would periodically drop to his belly and shine the light over the edge, sweeping the surface with the beam of his torch. Aside from the normal stratigraphy and fissures there was nothing remotely suggestive of a cave opening above them or below.

Now it was simply too dark to continue. They were on a broad enough shelf to camp for the night so they didn't have to back-track — which was just as well since both of them were hungry and tired.

Hugo crumpled and set his rump down hard on his pack. 'So, where's dinner?'

'Coming up. You won't be disappointed.'

In short order Luc produced an excellent meal on his portable gas stove: peppered fillet steaks and pan-fried potatoes, crusty bread, some creamy local chèvre and a bottle of decent Cahors, which he reckoned was worth the weight he carried all day.

They ate and drank into the evening. The moonless sky slipped through the darkening shades of grey until it became a virtually sightless black. Perched on the ledge they seemed alone on the edge of the universe. That, and the full-bodied wine, moved their conversation to a melancholy place and Hugo, tucked into his sleeping bag for warmth, was soon morosely lamenting his life.

'How many men do you know,' he asked, 'who've been married to two women but divorced three times? When Martine and I got married again, I have to say, it was a moment of temporary insanity. And do you know what? I was rewarded for those three months of madness with another assault on my wallet. Her lawyer's better than mine but mine is my cousin, Alain, so I'm stuck.'

'Are you seeing anyone now?' Luc asked.

'There's a banker named Adele who's as cold as frozen peas, an artist named Laurentine who's bipolar, I think, and . . . '

'And who?'

Hugo sighed. 'I'm also seeing Martine again.'

'Unbelievable!' Luc half-shouted. 'You're a certified idiot.'

'I know, I know . . . ' Hugo's voice drifted off into the night and he finished his wine then poured some more into his aluminium cup. 'What about you? Are you prouder of your record?'

Luc rolled out his foam mattress and laid his sleeping bag over it. 'No, sir, I'm not proud. One girl, one night, maybe two, that's been my history. I'm not wired for relationships.'

'You and what's her name, that American girl, definitely were a couple a few years ago.'

'Sara.'

'What happened?'

Luc slithered into his sleeping bag. 'She was different. It's a sad story.'

'You left her?'

'On the contrary. She dumped me, but I deserved it. I was stupid.'

'So you're stupid, I'm an idiot, and both of us are sleeping on a ledge one step away from an abyss, which pretty much confirms our intelligence.' He zipped up his bag and declared, 'I'm going to sleep now and put myself out of my misery. If I'm not here in the morning, I went for a leak and forgot where I was.'

In a remarkably short time, Hugo was snoring and Luc was on his own, trying to pick out a star or a planet through cloud cover and wine-induced mistiness.

In time, his eyes fluttered closed, or so he thought, because he was aware of swift black shapes moving above him, perhaps an incipient dream. But there was something familiar about the wild unpredictable zigzags, the jet-plane speed, and then it came to him in one sobering thought: bats.

He hurriedly unzipped his sleeping bag, grabbed his torch and aimed the beam overhead. Dozens of bats were darting around the cliffs.

He trained the light on the rocks and waited.

Then, a bat flew straight into the cliff and disappeared. Then another. And another.

There was a cave up there.

Luc woke Hugo and steadied the man as he struggled to get oriented and upright. As he stepped out of his sleeping bag Hugo was sputtering, 'what? what?' in total disorientation.

'I think I've found it. I'm going up. I can't wait till the morning. I need you to keep an eye on me, that's all. If I get in trouble, get help, but I won't get in trouble.'

'You're mad,' Hugo finally said.

'At least partially,' Luc agreed. 'Shine the torch there. It doesn't look too bad.'

'Christ, Luc. Wait till tomorrow.'

'Not a chance.'

He directed Hugo where to aim his torch and found a good hand-hold to start the ascent. The distinct strata of the rock face formed a staircase of sorts and he never really felt in imminent danger, but still he took it slowly, aware that night-climbing and wine were not an ideal combination.

In a few minutes he was at the spot where he thought the bats were disappearing, although he wasn't positive. There was nothing resembling a cave mouth or shelter in sight. He had a good enough purchase on the cliff that he was able to remove his own torch from his jacket pocket for a closer inspection. Just then, a bat flew out of

54

the cliff and zoomed past his ear. Startled, he paused for a moment to catch his breath and make sure his foot hold hadn't slipped.

There was a crack in the rock face. No more than a few centimetres wide. After he transferred the torch to his left fist he was able to slide his right hand into the crack until his fingers disappeared to the knuckles. He pulled down and felt a wobble. On closer inspection the wobble was coming from a flat rock wedged in the wall. In an instant it dawned on him. He was staring at a dry wall of flat stones installed in the cliff face, so artfully crafted that it simulated the natural strata.

He wiggled the stone out with some effort and when it came free he carefully placed it on its side on a narrow shelf, calling down to Hugo in warning to step aside in case it fell, for it was deadly enough, the size of a coffee-table book. The next several rocks came out more easily but he ran out of places to balance them so he started pushing them back into the widening opening instead. Before long he was looking at a hole large enough to ram his body through.

'I'm going in,' he called down.

'Are you sure that's a good idea?' Hugo pleaded.

'Nothing's going to stop me,' Luc defiantly replied before reaching over and wedging his head and shoulders into the gap.

From the ledge below, Hugo watched as Luc's shoulders disappeared, then his torso and finally his legs. He called up, 'Are you all right?'

Luc heard him but didn't answer.

He was inside the mouth of the cave crawling on all fours until he realised the vault was capacious enough to stand upright. He shone his torch ahead then swung it from side to side.

He felt his knees weaken and he almost lost balance.

Blood was rushing in his ears.

There was the sibilant fluttering of a bat colony.

Then he heard his own cracking voice rasp, 'Oh my God!'

6

Luc was aware of motion.

He felt surrounded, in the middle of a pack, a stampede.

It was at once suffocating and disorientating, compounded by the way he was hyperkinetically moving his torch, bouncing angles of light off the tawny walls and stalactites in an effort to take it all in, flitting from image to image, creating a stroboscopic jumble in the black confines of the cave.

To his left was a charging herd of horses, huge beasts boldly rendered in charcoal that overlapped one another, their mouths open in exertion, their manes thick, their pupils piercing black discs afloat in pale ovals of unpigmented rock.

To his right were thundering bison with upraised tails and cloven hooves, all energy and menace, and unlike the horses which were done in stippled black, their massive bodies were fully shaded in bold swathes of black and reddish-brown.

Above his head was a single giant black bull in full motion, running headlong into the cave, two legs off the ground in a full gallop. Its head was lowered, presenting its horns in aggression and its nostrils were flared and its scrotum swelled.

Ahead, to his left and right, were massive stags with racks of antlers half as large as their bodies, their heads turned up, their eyes rolled back and their mouths open in bellowing posture.

And there was more, much more, fantastic creatures he strained to see in the dimming reach of his torch beam — a crush of lions, bears, roe deer, colour, so much colour, and was that the trunk of a mammoth?

Although there was a sense of velocity all around, his feet were firmly rooted to the ground. He must have stood on the same spot for an immeasurable length of time before he became conscious of the pleading shouts coming from below.

He also became aware that he was shaking febrilely and that his eyes were wet. This was more than a moment of discovery. This was Carter at the Valley of Kings, Schliemann at Troy.

In the mouth of the cave alone were dozens of the finest prehistoric paintings he had ever seen, nearly life-size animals done in a confident, masterful, naturalistic style. The great Lascaux Cave had a grand total of some nine hundred beasts. Within his limited sightlines he already saw nearly a quarter as many. And this was the tip of the iceberg. What lay beyond the limits of his torch?

Luc fully realised the weight of the moment — this was potentially even more important than Lascaux or Chauvet. Luc had never shown any interest whatsoever in mapping out his future. He'd always let things just happen in his professional and personal lives. He let himself be carried along by the stream of fate. But in an instant both exhilarating and frightening, he knew he'd be spending the rest of his life here, in this cave on the outskirts of Ruac.

He stepped back towards the fresh air, stuck his head out and had to snap his eyelids shut when Hugo's beam hit him full-on.

'Thank God you're okay!' Hugo shouted. 'Why didn't you answer me?'

All Luc could say was, 'You need to come up.'

'Why? What have you found?'

'This is Barthomieu's cave!'

'Are you sure?'

'Yes, it has to be. Climb the same route I took. Carefully. And think about this: your life, my friend, will never be the same again.'

7

Time became a curious commodity.

At once it crawled to a dead stop and raced ahead at warp speed. That night was both the longest and the shortest in his life and in the future, when Luc spoke about it, people would wrinkle their brows in non-comprehension, which would prompt him to say, 'Trust me, that's what it felt like.'

He had given Hugo stern instructions to stand still and keep his hands in his pockets while he twice made the climb down to the ledge to retrieve their rucksacks. When he finished, he aimed his torch over his head to provide a reflected cone of light and delivered a solemn little speech. 'This is now an archaeological site, a national treasure. We have a responsibility to science, to France and to the world to do this right. We don't touch anything. You only step where I step. You don't light any of your foul cigars. If you don't know what to do, ask.'

'Christ, Luc, I'm not an idiot.'

Luc playfully swatted him. 'I thought we already established you were. Let's go.'

It didn't take long to prove incontrovertibly, that this was the cave of the manuscript. They quickly found three distinctive paintings — a horse, a stag and a stippled bull — that were identical in every respect to Barthomieu's illustrations.

Luc trod delicately towards the interior of the cave, training his beam on the guano-encrusted floor before taking each successive step, making sure he wasn't crushing something precious under his boot. Above their heads, bats were squealing incessantly in ear-splitting, high-pitched urgency. The atmosphere was noxious, not intolerable but undeniably unpleasant. Hugo took his handkerchief and pressed it over his mouth and nose to shield himself from the caustic ammonia sting of the bat urine.

'Is this going to kill me?' Hugo complained, shivering in the cool dampness.

Luc was uninterested in any distraction and only said, 'The handkerchief's a good idea.'

Every couple of paces Luc removed the lens cap from his Leica and flashed a series of shots, checking the images on the LCD screen to assure himself he wasn't imagining the whole thing.

'Look at the quality of these horses, Hugo! The understanding of anatomy. The capture of motion. This is highly sophisticated. See the crossed legs on this one? That's a full realization of perspective. It exceeds the artistry at Lascaux. It's absolutely incredible. And these lions! Look at the patience and wisdom on their faces.'

The ammonia must have served as smelling salts. Hugo was now completely sober and he asked seriously, like a student, 'How old do you think these are?'

'Hard to know. Lascaux was painted about eighteen thousand years ago. This seems more advanced. There's a full palette of pigments in use here too: charcoal, graphite, clays, red and yellow iron oxide, manganese, so if I had to guess, I'd say it's more recent.'

The end of the first chamber seemed to be demarcated by a fanciful painting of a mammoth with a trunk so gigantic it reached below its legs. Beyond that, they came to a narrower, uphill part of the cave, not so strictured they had to crawl, but a fairly tight squeeze. There was a single adornment within this channel — at eye level a pair of human hands done in finger stencilling. In this instance, red ochre had been blown by mouth onto outstretched hands, leaving pale, almost flesh-coloured negatives on the rock.

'The hands of the artist?' Luc asked reverentially. He was about to explain the technique when he was distracted by something ahead illuminated by Hugo's wandering torch. 'Look, there! My God, look at that!'

The cave opened up into another bulbous chamber, larger than the one they had left.

They were standing in the middle of something quite wondrous.

There were dozens, literally dozens, of charging black and brown bison, each no more than a metre in length, their legs in motion, their manes and beards flowing, their eyes bright circles swimming in black chunky heads. The herd was immense and since it spanned the walls on both sides, it behaved like a stereoscopic gimmick, giving Luc and Hugo the impression they were running with the herd. It wasn't an impossible stretch to hear the thunder, to experience the ground shaking between them and feel hot plumes of breath escaping from their bearded mouths.

'This is completely unique, totally . . . ' Luc started to mumble and then he saw the human figure to his left, a sole hominid in a bovine sea.

Hugo saw it too and shouted through his handkerchief, 'It's our man!'

The primitive figure, which had been aptly reproduced in Barthomieu's manuscript, stood with his bird-like head, spindly arms extending into four-fingered hands, long, simply rendered oblong body, stick legs with exaggerated canoe-shaped feet and that big, erect knife of a penis, pointing like a weapon at one of the charging bison. Above the heads of the beasts was a swarm of barbed spears zeroing in. One appeared to have found its mark. It was sticking into a bison's belly, spilling concentric circles of disembowelment.

Luc quickly snapped a dozen pictures then let his camera swing back against his midsection. 'One, solitary man against a herd. The world's first hero, wouldn't you say?'

'He seems excited by his own work,' Hugo joked.

'It's a sign of virility, not arousal,' Luc said seriously, continuing forward.

'Yes, professor,' Hugo countered, 'whatever you say.'

The cave seemed to be generally linear, a series of chambers burrowing into the cliff like plump segments of an insect. Each chamber contained further marvels, a prehistoric bestiary of succulently drawn game. Luc was lapping it all up, a cat at a trough of cream and eventually, it was up to Hugo to declare that surely it was dawn outside. And besides, he said, the ammonia had got to him. He had a headache and was fighting nausea.

Luc was reluctant to leave until he had completed at least a cursory examination of the entire complex, however daunting the task. There always seemed to be one more nook, one more chamber and gallery, each graced with creatures as fresh as the day they were painted. However, the deeper they got, the more they had to compete with bats, frantically unappreciative of the light.

Luc persuaded Hugo to bear with him a little longer, to explore one more chamber, one more gallery until they came to what appeared to be a dead end, a completely unpainted cul-de-sac, thick with bat droppings, almost choking them with stench. Luc was about to declare their night at an end and perhaps surrender to exhaustion and his own ammonia-sickness when his beam caught a small opening to his right, a hole through the wall that was just large enough to crawl through, if one had the temerity.

Luc removed his rucksack and left it behind. Hugo knew it was pointless to try to stop him. He refused to follow, though he had no desire to stay on his own because the ceiling was moving with roosting bats, stimulated by the intrusion and occasionally taking to flight. He could almost feel leathery wing tips brush his face and he struggled to control his breathing. He couldn't bear training his light on the roiling mass overhead and he was equally unwilling to be in the dark so he shone his torch in the direction of the hole. The best he could do was plead with Luc to hurry up while he kept his face tightly covered by cloth. He shuddered when Luc's soles disappeared into the blackness.

Luc gingerly crept through several metres of hard narrowness. He had the uncanny sensation of crawling through a birth canal.

Suddenly he was able to stand inside a small vault, the size of a modest sitting room. He shone his torch in sweeping arcs and blinked in awe at what he saw. While he was wetting his lips to call Hugo, he realised he was merely in an anteroom, of sorts. A larger chamber was just ahead, an igloo-shaped dome that literally left him gasping for air.

'Hugo, you must come!'

In a minute, Hugo emerged on all fours to join him, grumbling and growling, but when he stood he let out an enthusiastic 'Christ!'

The entire antechamber was festooned with hands stencilled in red ochre, 360 degrees of hand prints, lefts and rights, all the same size, giving the room the appearance of a planetarium with the hands as stars.

Luc beckoned him, 'Come here!'

The walls of the final chamber were lavishly painted — that was hardly a surprise — but there were no animals. Not a single one.

Luc said, 'I was wondering, what about those other pictures in Barthomieu's book — what about the plants? Look!'

They were in a garden, a paradise. There were panels of green vines with stellate leaves, shrub-like plants with red berries, and on one wall a veritable sea of tall ochre and brown grasses, each stalk individually drawn, all of them bent in the same direction, as if a wind was bearing down. And standing in the middle of this savannah was a life-sized man rendered in black outline, a much-larger version of the bird man from the bison hunt, arms extended, hugely priapic, facing the direction of the unseen wind with his beak open. Calling, perhaps calling.

'It's our hero,' Luc quietly said, fumbling with his lens cap.

★   ★   ★

There was no question the time had come to leave. There was nothing left to explore and Luc and Hugo were physically and mentally spent, both suffering from over-exposure to the foul air. There were only so many ways that Luc could repeat that what they were experiencing was unprecedented. The animals were superbly naturalistic and in many ways unique for their quality and abundance but there was nothing remotely comparable to this depiction of flora in Paleolithic art.

After yet another expression of wonder from Luc, Hugo was getting impatient. 'Yes, yes, so you've said, but we've really got to get out of here now. I can feel my life slipping away.'

Luc was staring eye-to-eye with the bird man, and wanted to speak out loud to him, but for

Hugo's sake, he played out the conversation in his head: *I'm coming back soon. You and I are going to get to know each other very well.*

He wasn't sure what made him look down, but in the dimmest periphery of his torch light there was something he couldn't ignore beside his left foot.

A small edge of black flint against the cave wall.

He knelt over it and swore. He had left his trowel in his rucksack, which was in the previous chamber.

He had a Bic pen in his breast pocket, removed its cap and started picking away at the earth and guano with the plastic prong.

'I thought you said, touch nothing,' Hugo complained.

'Don't worry. I'm an archaeologist,' Luc replied. 'This is important.'

In short order he had pecked away enough of the surrounding earth to expose a long slender blade of chipped flint, almost double the length of his index finger. It was leaning against the wall on its end, almost as if it had been purposefully balanced there. Luc lowered his head almost close enough to kiss it and blew the remaining dirt from its exposed surface, then excitedly he put his camera on macro mode and flashed away.

'What's the big deal?' Hugo asked.

'It's Aurignacian!'

'Oh yes?' Hugo replied, unimpressed. 'Can we please go now?'

'No, listen. This central spine, here, this flaking pattern and this hourglass shape, this tool is definitely Aurignacian. It was made by the very first Homo sapiens in Europe. If, and I stress if, it's contemporaneous with these paintings, this cave is about thirty thousand years old! That's over ten thousand years older than Lascaux, and it's more advanced than Lascaux in every artistic and technical criteria! I simply can't understand this. I don't know what to say.'

Hugo tugged him by the sleeve of his jacket. 'You'll think of something over breakfast. Now, for God's sake, let's go!'

★ ★ ★

The morning sun had turned the Vézère river into a sparkling ribbon. The air was fresh and birdsong rained down on them. It felt cleansing to breathe clean cool air.

Before they left the cave, Luc carefully rebuilt the dry wall, taking pains to conceal the entrance as effectively as the original wall builders, whoever they were, had done. He was bone-tired but giddy and a small voice inside his head warned him, that under these circumstances, they needed to be especially cautious along the ledge.

Nevertheless, they made steady progress retracing their route and it wasn't too long before the old juniper tree came into view. Hugo needed to readjust his rucksack and the broad shelf under its rough, peeling trunk was a safe place to stop.

Luc dreamingly sipped what was left of his bottled water as he stared out across the river.

Had the night really happened? Was he ready for the position he found himself in? Was he prepared to have his life irrevocably altered, to become a public person, the face of this mad discovery?

His reverie was interrupted by an almost trifling sound, a suggestion of rough scraping coming from the direction they had come. It was out of sight, behind bushes and jutting rock. He almost shrugged it off, but his senses were pricked enough that he couldn't let it pass. He excused himself and backtracked several metres. As he was about to make his way around the jutting stones he thought he heard another faint scrape, but when he got a clear view of the ledge they had just traversed, there was nothing there.

He stood for a short while, trying to decide whether to backtrack further. There was something about that scraping that unsettled him; he felt a current of concern — or was it fear? — trickle through his body. But then Hugo called, loudly declaring he was ready to move, and the feeling passed. He quickly rejoined him under the juniper and said nothing of it.

★　★　★

It was late morning when they wearily arrived at the Land Rover, and true to his word, despite the phantasms of the night, Luc had insisted they stop and pick up the litter.

He saw the damage first and swore loudly, 'Shit, Hugo, would you look at that!'

The driver's side window was smashed and

rounded pellets of safety glass filled the seat. And the cardboard University of Bordeaux sign was torn in half and tucked under the wiper blades as a clear taunt.

'Friendly locals,' Hugo sneered. 'Shall we return the beer cans to their rightful place?'

'I'm not going to let this spoil my mood,' Luc insisted, through gritted teeth. He began sweeping up the glass with the torn pieces of cardboard. 'Nothing's going to spoil my mood.'

Before putting the car in gear, he rummaged through the glove box and started swearing.

'I thought nothing was going to spoil your mood,' Hugo said.

'My registration's gone. Why the hell would someone steal my logbook?' He snapped the cover closed and drove off muttering.

★   ★   ★

In the centre of Ruac, they stopped at the small café, nameless, just a sign: CAFÉ, TABAC. When Hugo attempted to lock the car, Luc pointed to the smashed window and ridiculed him, but before they went inside he cautioned, 'Be careful what you say. We have a big secret to protect.'

The café was dimly lit, six tables with plastic tablecloths, only one of them occupied. The owner was behind the bar. He had leathery skin, a full head of white hair and a salt and pepper flecked moustache. His gut was round and protruding. Two diners, a young man and an older woman stopped talking and stared as if a couple of spacemen had arrived.

70

'Serving?' Hugo asked.

The owner pointed to one of the tables and gruffly laid down two paper menus before retreating towards his kitchen, shuffling his heavy legs across the floorboards.

Luc called after the fellow about the location of the nearest gendarmerie. The owner slowly turned and answered with a question: 'Why?'

'Someone broke my car window.'

'While you were driving?

'No, I was parked.'

'Where were you parked?'

In the face of this interrogation, Luc glanced incredulously at Hugo before blowing the guy off. 'It doesn't matter.'

'Probably somewhere illegal,' the old man mumbled under his breath loud enough for them to hear. Then, with more volume, 'Sarlat. There's a station in Sarlat.'

Hugo sniffed at the air. He knew that odour anywhere. His bread-and-butter aroma. 'Was there a fire nearby?' he asked the old man.

'Fire? You smell something?'

'Yes.'

'It's probably my clothes. I'm the local SPV chief. That's what you smell.'

Hugo shrugged and began eyeing the pretty raven-haired woman at the corner table. She was no more than forty. There was a natural curl and bounciness to her hair and she had pouty lips and nice bare olive legs showing beneath a clingy dress. Her companion was younger by at least a decade, with the thick shoulders and ruddy complexion of a farmer, and since it was unlikely

71

this was her boyfriend or husband, Luc guessed that Hugo would therefore be unimpeded from being Hugo.

True to form, Hugo said, 'Nice day,' in her direction with a grin and a nod.

She replied with a small facial gesture that, if it was a smile, lasted no longer than a second. To put the period on the sentence, her scowling companion purposely tapped her forearm and reengaged her in conversation.

'Friendly place,' Hugo said to Luc. 'They're having omelettes. So will I. Let the natives lead the way, I always say.'

Luc excused himself and came back in a few minutes to find that Hugo had ordered beers. 'Was it clean?' Hugo asked.

'Not really.' He laid his mobile phone on the table. 'Here's to us,' Luc toasted with the beer Hugo had ordered.

They kept their voices low while they hungrily tucked into three-egg cheese omelettes and pommes frites.

'You know I'll have to drop everything,' Luc said wistfully. 'All my projects have to end. None of them will ever be finished.'

'Well, that's obvious,' Hugo replied. 'But you're okay with that, no?'

'Of course! I'm just feeling overwhelmed all of a sudden. You never prepare for something like this.'

'I'm happy for you,' Hugo said expansively with a touch of playful sarcasm. 'You'll be busy and famous, I'll return to my grubby business life and only emerge from time to time to bask in your reflected glory. Please don't forget your old friend down the line. Maybe you'll name it, Pineau-Simard, or if you must, Simard-Pineau, and toss me a bone once in a blue moon when you're on the chat shows.'

'Don't be so fast to disappear behind the curtain,' Luc laughed. 'You've got a job.'

'Oh yes?'

'The manuscript. You're the manuscript guy, remember?'

'Surely it's of less importance now.'

'Not at all,' Luc insisted, whispering. 'The manuscript is part of this. When it's time to tell the story to the world, we'll have to understand its role. There's some kind of important historical context that can't be ignored. The book must be decoded,' he whispered.

'I suppose I can make some enquiries,' Hugo sighed.

'To whom?'

'Ever hear of the Voynich manuscript?'

Luc shook his head.

'Well, to make a very long story a very short story, it's a bizarre, possibly fifteenth-century manuscript that was acquired by a Polish rare-books dealer named Voynich in 1910 or thereabouts. It's a fabulous thing, really, the craziest collection of fanciful illustrations of herbals, astronomical signs, biological processes, medicinal concoctions, even recipes, and it's all written in a beautifully weird script and language that's defied a century of deciphering efforts. Some think it was written by Roger Bacon or John Dee, both mathematical geniuses of their

73

day who dabbled in alchemy circles, others think it's a giant fifteenth- or sixteenth-century hoax. Anyway, I bring it up because, to this day, amateur and professional cryptographers have tried to break the code. I've met some of these people at seminars and conferences. They're real characters with their own language. You should hear them go on about Beaufort ciphers and Zipf's law and other crap, but I can contact one of the less loony ones and see if he'll look at our book.'

'Okay,' Luc nodded. 'Do it. But be very discreet.'

The couple at the other table got up to leave without any attempting to pay. The young man pushed through the door first. Following behind, the woman glanced over her shoulder, looked directly at Hugo, and repeated that fleeting almost-a-smile before the door closed and she was gone.

'Did you see that?' Hugo asked Luc. 'Maybe the countryside isn't so bad after all.'

Three men came in, two of them farm hands from the look, their hands dirty, shoes crusted with dirt. The third, an older man, was clean and well dressed in a suit without the tie. The café owner nodded to them from behind the bar and addressed the older man loudly by name. 'Good day, Pelay. How are you?'

'The same as I was at breakfast,' he said gruffly, but while he was answering, he gawked unselfconsciously at Luc and Hugo.

The trio occupied a rear corner table, talking among themselves.

74

Luc felt distinctly uncomfortable. Since the café owner seemed to be communicating with the men behind them with his eyes, Luc felt as if he was in the children's game, piggy in the middle. Every time Luc turned his head to look behind, the men glanced away and resumed their chat. Hugo seemed oblivious to the little drama, or perhaps, Luc, thought, *he* was being overly sensitive.

The owner called over their heads. 'Hey, Pelay, do you want some bacon later?'

'Only if it's from Duval,' the man answered. 'I only eat bacon from Duval.'

'Don't worry, it'll be from Duval.'

Luc noticed the owner flip the Open sign in the window to Closed.

He heard a chair sliding, wood on wood.

He had the vivid sense of hard stares on his back.

The owner started clattering glasses, arranging them noisily on a shelf.

Luc didn't like the prickly way he was feeling and was about to turn to confront the imagined stares when he heard the squeal of brakes.

A blue and white gendarmerie van jerked to a stop behind his Land Rover and Luc gladly sprang to his feet. 'I called them about my car,' he told Hugo. 'Come out when you're done.' He took the opportunity to glower at the men in the corner but they refused to meet his gaze.

The owner stepped around the bar and gruffly slapped down the bill. 'I'm closing now anyway.'

Luc glanced at it contemptuously, threw some euros on the table and said to Hugo, 'Don't be so quick to change your mind about the countryside.'

8

Luc stared at the phone long and hard before lifting the handset and punching the number he had found on her web page.

It wasn't easy making the call, in fact it was entirely out of character, but this was, after all, an extraordinary circumstance.

He needed the best people and in her field there was no one better. He simply refused to compromise.

He was in his office on the Bordeaux campus, watching a fast-moving Atlantic storm soak the quadrangle. The familiar, insistent UK dial-tone blared into his ear and then, just like that, he heard the soft roundness of her voice.

'Hello, Sara?'

'Luc?'

'Yes, it's me.'

There was silence on the line, prompting him to ask if she was still there.

'I'm here. I'm just trying to decide whether to hang up on you.'

★   ★   ★

It had been two years since they first met.

She'd spent that summer in Paris working on her book, *A Palynological Perspective of the Magdalenian to Mesolithic Transition*, which hadn't been destined for the bestseller lists, but would further cement her growing credentials.

He was at Les Eyzies, doing survey work and opening the first tranche of what would become a multi-year campaign.

They'd been an 'item' as she called it, for two years. He'd heard her lecturing in her bad French at a Pleistocene conference at the University of Paris and afterwards he had sidled up to her at the drinks reception. Later, she would tell friends she saw him coming, smoothly manoeuvring through the assembly like an assassin, and hoped the darkly handsome guy was heading her way. He disarmed her with effusive compliments about her work in perfect American English. They had dinner that night. Dinner the next night too.

She'd told her friends, even told her mother back in California, that she'd fallen; she'd drunk the Kool-Aid and gone back for more. That they spoke the same language professionally was nice though hardly the basis for her attraction. She knew his reputation but beyond that, there was something wild and untamable about him which she took as a challenge. He was almost ten years older than her and she wanted to believe he'd sown enough wild oats to be able to settle into something resembling monogamy. She poured energy into the relationship like a boiler-operator on an old coal-fired steamer, shovelling, constantly shovelling. He'd announced so many times in his taunting way that this was the longest affair of his life that she was sick of hearing it. She bridged the geographic gap between her position in Paris and his in

Bordeaux by living on the train. She'd been expecting an invitation to join him on his dig that summer but it never materialised and she heard through the rumour-mill about a special friendship with a comely Hungarian geologist on his team.

So, out of mounting concern over the paucity of texts and calls, she hired a car and one Friday afternoon, arrived unannounced at his dig. Judging from the strained expression of pleasure on his face at seeing her, and the sidelong glances from the Hungarian who, regrettably for Sara, was a real stunner, the rumours were true. Her visit only lasted until early the next day. Sometime around three in the morning she angrily broke it off, spent the rest of the night at the furthest edges of his bed and let him sleep when she slipped away at dawn. Within months she had accepted a faculty appointment at the Institute of Archaeology in London and there she completely faded from his life.

★ ★ ★

'Please don't hang up. This is important.'

She sounded concerned. 'Are you all right?'

'No, no, I'm fine, but I need to talk to you about something. Are you in front of a computer?'

'Yes.'

'Can I send you some material to look at while I hold the line?'

She hesitated then gave him her email address.

He heard her breathing into the mouthpiece as

78

he attached some files and sent them on the way. 'Got it?' he asked.

'Yes.'

'Open photo 93 first.'

He waited, staring at his copy of the picture, still mesmerised by it, and tried to imagine her at the moment of download. Two years wasn't such a long time. She couldn't have changed much. He was glad he finally had an excuse to call.

She sounded startled, as if someone had dropped a stack of china behind her back. 'God! Where's this from?'

'The Périgord. What do you think?'

It was a picture of the dense herd of small bison with the bird man in their midst.

'It's magnificent. Is it new?'

He enjoyed the excitement in her voice. 'Very new.'

'You found it?'

'Yes, I'm happy to say.'

'Does anyone know about it yet?'

'You're among the first.'

'Why me?'

'Open Number 211 and 215 next.'

They were taken in the last of the ten chambers, the Hall of the Plants, as Luc had come to call it.

'Are these for real?' she asked. 'Was this photoshopped?'

'Unmanipulated, unretouched, au naturel,' he replied.

She was quiet for a moment then said in a hushed voice, 'I've never seen anything like it.'

'Didn't think you had. Oh, and one more

thing. I found an Aurignacian blade in direct association with the paintings.'

'Oh, boy . . . ' she whispered.

'So, I need a plant expert. Want to come and play?'

9

Gatinois sat rigidly at his antique chinoiserie desk keeping his ankles, knees and hips fixed at ninety degree angles. He never slouched, not even at home or at his club. It was the way he was brought up, one of the social artefacts of a merchant family vaguely clinging to its aristocratic heritage. At the office, the sight of his erect posture contributed to his carefully cultivated image of imperiousness.

He had in his hand a dossier entitled: 'Proposal to Mount a Major Excavation at Ruac Cave, Dordogne, by Prof. Luc Simard, University of Bordeaux'. He had read it, sedulously, poring over the photos and absorbing the implications unfiltered by static from his staff.

After nine long years running Unit 70, this was his first bona fide crisis and it was stirring up mixed emotions. On one hand, it was a disaster, of course. The Unit's sixty-five-year mission was threatened. If a major security breach occurred, there'd be hell to pay. His head would certainly roll, but not only his. Could the Minister of Defence survive? The President?

But the fear of bad outcomes was tempered by the perfumed whiff of opportunity. Finally, he would be front-and-centre in the Minister's mind. His instincts were telling him to stir the pot. Get his superiors agitated, keep things hot. Then, if he was ultimately successful in keeping the lid on Unit 70, he'd surely be recognised.

Finally, a plum senior staff position at the Ministry was within his grasp.

He ran his finger over the clear acrylic cover of the dossier. Was this his path to heaven, or hell?

Marolles came as summoned, standing at attention, his moustache twitching, waiting to be recognised.

Gatinois motioned for him to sit.

'I've read it. Cover to cover,' the general said evenly.

'Yes, sir. It's certainly a problem.'

'A problem? It's a disaster!'

The small man nodded solemnly. 'Yes, sir.'

'Tell me, in the history of this unit, has anyone ever been inside that cave?'

'No, no. I've checked the archives and Chabon queried Pelay. It's been sealed since 1899. Certainly, *we've* always let sleeping dogs lie. And, to the best of our knowledge, no one from the outside has rediscovered it.'

'Until now,' Gatinois added coldly.

'Yes, until now.'

'What do we know about Luc Simard?'

'Well, he's a professor of archaeology at Bordeaux — '

'Marolles, I've read his biography. What do we *know* about him? His personality. His motivations.'

'We're working up a profile. I'll have it to you within the week.'

'And what can we do to stop this before it starts?' Gatinois asked with a calmness that seemed to surprise the colonel.

Marolles took a deep breath and delivered an unfavourable assessment. 'I'm afraid the project has already attained a positive momentum within the Ministry of Culture. It will undoubtedly be approved and funded, I'm sorry to report.'

'Who's your source?'

'Ah, one bright spot in a dark sky,' Marolles said hopefully. 'My wife's cousin works in the relevant department. He's an unctuous fellow named Abenheim. He's always poodling up to me at family gatherings, making sly references to his belief I work in clandestine services. I've tried to avoid him.'

'Until now, perhaps?'

'Exactly.'

Gatinois leaned forward and lowered his voice conspiratorially, as if someone else were in the room. 'Use this man. Suggest to him that someone within the DGSE is interested in Simard and his work. Imply something negative but say nothing specific. Tell him to keep you informed of everything, to insinuate himself into the project as much as possible. Tell him if he does well that certain people within the state apparatus will be grateful. Keep it on that kind of level.'

'I understand, sir.'

Gatinois leaned back, straightening his back to its usual position. 'At the end of the day, you know, Bonnet will probably sort this out. He's a ruthless bastard. Perhaps all we'll need to do is sit back and watch the carnage.'

10

Luc had bypassed the usual channels and had gone straight for the top. The stakes were too high. If feathers were ruffled at his own university and with regional bureaucrats at the Department of Dordogne, then so be it.

The cave had to be protected.

He used the full weight of his academic position and his friendship with an important senator from Lyon to secure an immediate face-to-face meeting at the Palais-Royal with the Minister of Culture and her top antiquities deputies including the Director of the National Centre of Prehistory, a respected archaeologist named Maurice Barbier, who fortunately maintained a cordial relationship with Luc. The participation of Barbier's Deputy Director, Marc Abenheim, was less fortunate. Luc had butted heads with Abenheim for years, and the two men had a mutual dislike for one another.

Working from a lavishly illustrated dossier replete with his photos, Luc requested an emergency protection order, an accelerated permitting process, and a sufficient allocation of ministry funds to secure the cave and begin its excavation.

Heeding advice from his senator friend, he glossed over the enigmatic Ruac manuscript to keep the high-level assembly focused on one issue at a time. And taking further advice, he liberally used the term, 'Spectacular New National Monument'.

The importance of having another Lascaux and Chauvet from the perspective of international prestige and local economic development wasn't lost on the group. Maurice Barbier was moved to a state of excitement that appeared to border on illness. Red-faced and nearly trembling, he declared that an emergency order would have to be immediately drawn up designating the cave a Historic Monument. A commission would be established to determine correct procedures and methodologies and to select the leadership of the excavation campaign.

At this, Abenheim, who had been silently scowling during Luc's presentation, piped up and began to make the case for direct Ministry involvement, the implication being that he ought to head such a commission and personally take charge of the excavation of this new cave. Luc simmered at the unctuous performance. Abenheim was of Luc's generation, a couple of years older, certainly as well credentialed in academic archaeology but, unlike Luc, he was not a field man. Luc viewed him as an autocratic bureaucrat, more like a pale, scrawny accountant than an archaeologist. Luc loved shovels and picks and the sun on his back. Abenheim, he imagined, had an abiding affinity to telephones and spreadsheets and fluorescent-lit government offices. Abenheim, for his part, undoubtedly saw Luc as a glory-seeking swashbuckler.

Barbier deftly deferred any discussion of leadership and urged the group to consider for now only the larger issues at hand.

The Minister took charge and crisply gave her assent to the protection order and the granting of emergency funds. She instructed Barbier to forward his recommendations on a commission and asked to be kept informed of all developments. And with that, the meeting was over.

Luc left the room whistling cheerfully through the marble corridors of power. Outside in the sunshine, he yanked off his necktie, tucked it into his pocket and went to meet Hugo near the Louvre for a celebratory dinner.

⋆ ⋆ ⋆

For a bureaucracy as Byzantine as the Ministry of Culture, the follow-through was executed at break-neck speed. Luc breathed easier when Barbier informed him two weeks later that the newly formed Ruac Cave Commission had designated Luc as the director of the excavation, with only a single dissenting vote. 'You don't have to guess who that was,' Barbier joked, but urged Luc to try to keep Abenheim well informed and happy, if only to make Barbier's life easier.

Then Barbier added in a tone panged with jealousy, 'You'll be made a Knight of Arts and Letters, you know. It's only a matter of time.'

Luc replied sardonically, 'If I have to wear a suit and tie for that, I'm not so keen.'

⋆ ⋆ ⋆

Within a week a military-style operation was loosed upon the Vézère valley. A detachment from the French Engineers Corps backed up by the local gendarmerie accompanied Luc to the Ruac cliffs where a massive bank-grade titanium gate was bolted into the rock face over the mouth of the cave. Power cables were dropped from the top of the cliff, closed-circuit cameras were installed, a prefab guard hut and Portaloos were placed in the woods above the site and sturdy aluminium cliff ladders with railings were hung over the edge providing easier access than trekking along the ledges.

When the convoy noisily rumbled through Ruac, Luc could see faces suspiciously peeking through lace curtains. Outside the café, the white-haired owner halted his sweeping, leaned on his broom and scowled into Luc's slow-moving Land Rover with an irritable flicker of recognition. Luc resisted the boyish impulse to shoot the old man the finger but he did, as he would later regret, lay down a wickedly obvious wink.

After the cave was shuttered and padlocked, Luc had his first restful sleep since the night of discovery. He'd been sick with worry over the threat of leaked information, vandalism and looting. That was behind him now.

The work could begin.

Yet, it was well into the autumn before a full-scale campaign could begin. One couldn't just snap one's fingers. There was a team to assemble, schedules to clear, equipment to sort out, accounts to establish, accommodation to arrange.

87

That last task, as mundane as it was, proved difficult. Luc was determined to find local accommodation, preferably in Ruac. Nothing frustrated him more than losing valuable time commuting to a dig. He was advised to contact the Mayor of Ruac, a Monsieur Bonnet, to see if there were houses that might be rented. Failing that, permission to set up caravans and tents in a farmer's field with some access to water would suffice. He wasn't against roughing it. In fact, camping improved the camaraderie in these kinds of enterprises. The lack of creature comforts usually begat a useful sort of bonding.

It was, to say the least, unpleasant to learn at the last possible moment that the mayor and the white-haired owner of the café were one and the same.

Bonnet pointedly sat Luc down at the identical plastic-clad table as before and wordlessly listened to his pleas with his meaty arms tightly folded as if he was keeping his guts from spilling out.

Luc employed every rhetorical arrow in his quiver: the mayor would be helping his café, his town, his country. His diggers would be good and respectful neighbours. He'd arrange for a personal tour of this marvellous new cave; if there was a Madame Mayor, she could most definitely come too. Surely, the mayor must be curious what all the fuss was about? Surely. As Luc doggedly pressed ahead with his one-sided conversation the mayor's unshaven jaw remained fixed.

Luc wished he could have taken that wink back.

When he was done, Bonnet shook his head and spat out, 'We like our peace and quiet in Ruac. No one here is interested in your precious cave. We're not interested in your studies. We don't want tourists. There's no place for you to stay, monsieur.' With that, he got up and left for the kitchen.

'That went well,' Luc muttered to himself on his way out the door.

A couple of dull-looking teenagers held their ground on the pavement, forcing Luc to step off into the road. They sniggered over his forced detour.

He was in the mood for a dust-up, and had a fleeting vision of beating the daylights out of them. But he held his tongue and his temper and angrily climbed into his Land Rover. At least his window hadn't been smashed again, he thought bitterly, as the village disappeared in his rear-view mirror.

Thankfully, Abbot Menaud came to the rescue. There was a level, well-drained field on abbey grounds located behind the old stables, tucked enough out of the way that the monks and the archaeologists would hardly notice each other. He wanted no compensation, although he added a humble request to visit the cave when it wasn't terribly inconvenient.

★   ★   ★

On a windy Sunday in October, the Ruac Cave team began arriving one by one at the abbey campsite. Luc had been there for a week with two of his graduate students, Pierre, a Parisian originally from Sierra Leone, and Jeremy, a Brit with a broad Manchester accent. They made an unlikely pair, Pierre, black as onyx, tall and athletic and Jeremy, colourless and puny, but they shared a schoolboy sense of humour and were grateful to be involved in something historic. They worked tirelessly setting up the camp and preparing a good welcome for the team.

Caravans were dispersed in a giant circle, like an Old-West wagon train protecting itself from attack. Each senior team member would have his or her own caravan, junior members would double-up and grad students would triple-up. Undergrads would have to make do with tents on the periphery. The caravans had reasonably comfortable bunks and the deluxe ones had small sitting areas with built-in desks. There was no electricity but each unit had a couple of mantle lamps. It was all very well thought-out and properly hierarchical.

But in the spirit of egalitarianism, Luc insisted on having the same-sized unit as his deputies. He carefully considered where to put Sara. Too close would send one message, too far away, another. He opted to assign her a caravan two away from his.

In the centre of the circle they erected a kitchen shed and pantry and beside it they raised a large canvas ridge tent with picnic tables for group meals in inclement weather. The final structure was a Portakabin building containing the excavation office and laboratory, complete with a generator to run the computers and a satellite dish for Internet. Near it, they dug a large fire pit for the obligatory evening campfires and ringed it with wine-crate seating.

One section of the dilapidated barn was assigned to male portable latrines. Another section was for the women. Two sets of cold-water showers were rigged, the best they could do under the circumstances.

That was it — for better or worse, this was going to be their village, but Luc was quite sure that once the team laid eyes on the cave, no one would be grousing about living conditions.

★　★　★

On the dawn of the day, Luc admitted to himself he was nervous about Sara's arrival. As a rule, he thought more about work than emotions. So, what was making him jittery? He had legions of ex-girlfriends. When he reconnected with old flames by happenstance or design it was usually all very light-hearted. But that morning, sitting at his desk, drinking his coffee, he felt a gnawing hollow-ness. Their 'item' years seemed far-away and washed-out like an over-exposed photo. He remembered certain things clearly enough, mostly about the way she looked, even the way she smelled, but forgot others, mostly about the way he had felt.

Always a slave to punctuality, she was among the first to arrive, and when Pierre knocked on Luc's door to let him know Sara Mallory was there, he felt a quivering in his belly, schoolboy nerves.

She looked small and light and lovely.

She was apprehensive too, and frosty. He could tell by the way her peach-glossed lips were pressed together in a forced smile. He greeted her and pecked both cheeks in an official manner, as if they had never been intimate. Her skin was fine, almost translucent, showing the pink blush of capillaries under the surface. Before he backed away he got a whiff of her hair. No chemical fragrance; the scent was hers alone and he remembered the way he used to enjoy pulling out the clip and letting her light-brown hair spill over her chest where he nuzzled its tan silkiness against her breasts.

'You look well,' he said.

'So do you.'

She had her own style. She turned a masculine black leather motorcycle jacket feminine with a turquoise silk scarf that matched her eyes. Her suede skirt and calf-length boots fit tight over maroon tights.

'How was your flight?'

'Uneventful.' She looked at the ground. 'Can I put my bags somewhere?'

He paced the circle, waiting for her to come out of her caravan. The midday sun was bright but at this season it failed to warm the earth much. She hadn't changed clothes; he was glad of that. She looked good, very like the Sara he had known.

'Is it okay?' he asked.

'Better than most.'

'We have good funding for a change.'

'So I understand.'

He smiled and gestured towards the abbey. 'Before the others arrive, I want to show you the original manuscript.'

Dom Menaud was happy to once again retrieve the book from its resting place in an inlaid rosewood box on his desk. But the old monk seemed uncomfortably fussy around Sara's prettiness and he quickly excused himself for Sext prayers.

Left behind, they sat in opposing armchairs. Luc watched her turn pages, taking delight in every raised eyebrow and facial twinge. She held the book on her lap. The tightness of her skirt pinned her legs demurely together.

She finally looked up and said, 'Everything about this is extraordinary.'

'As advertised?'

She nodded. 'And you still haven't had it translated?'

'We're working on it. What do you make of the plants?'

'They're somewhat stylised. Not exactly *camera lucida*. I have some ideas but I'd rather not commit yet. I need to see the cave paintings first. Is that okay?'

'Of course! I didn't mean to put you on the spot. We're just at the beginning of a long process.'

She closed the book and handed it back avoiding his eyes and suddenly said, 'Thank you for including me on the team. It was good of you.'

'The entire commission was supportive. You've developed quite the reputation.'

'Still, you could have gotten someone else.'

'I didn't want someone else. I wanted you.'

He regretted the poor choice of words but he couldn't take them back. Her response was an icy, mute stare.

Through the abbot's window Luc saw a taxi approaching. Relieved, he said, 'Ah, another arrival.'

★ ★ ★

By nightfall the entire group of principals had checked in. The last to show up was the Israeli, Zvi Alon, who drove his own rental car, and after being shown his caravan, complained that he had no need for all that space.

Also there for the occasion, at the insistence of the Minister of Culture, was the culture editor from *Le Monde*. In exchange for exclusive access to the opening day of the excavation, the publisher had agreed to embargo their reportage until clearance arrived from the ministry.

Luc felt the evening required a touch of ceremony so after a dinner of a thick lamb stew he assembled everyone around a dancing fire, broke out several bottles of decent champagne and delivered a short welcome address in English.

Holding his glass aloft, he declared he was honoured to be their leader. He lauded the French government and the CNRS, the French National Centre for Scientific Research, for acting expeditiously, and he was pleased to have the full commitment for a probationary year of study with the likelihood of a further triennial programme after the preliminary report was filed.

He made the introductions. Team Ruac, as he called them, consisted of the best and the brightest in their disciplines, an international group of geologists, cave-art gurus, lithics, bone, and pollen experts, conservationists and cavers known to each other through years of collaboration and debate. There was even a bat expert, a diminutive man named Desnoyers, who shyly bowed at his introduction then disappeared to the periphery like a small roosting winged mammal.

Finally, Luc acknowledged his cadre of students, many from his own programme at Bordeaux, and instructed Pierre and Michael to pass out Team Ruac fleeces with the official logo of the excavation — a stylised bison.

Just then, there was a commotion from near the stables and a short fat man, led by a lantern-shining aide, called out, 'Hello! Hello! I'm sorry I'm late. It's Monsieur Tailifer, the Council President from Périgueux! Where is Professor Simard? Is it too late to address the group?'

Luc welcomed the hyperventilating politician from the local préfecture, gave him some champagne and a crate to stand on then politely listened as he subjected the gathering to an overly long, overly flowery, overly obvious speech.

Afterwards, Luc and Monsieur Tailifer chatted by the fire and drank another glass. The politician waved off an invitation to visit the cave saying he was far too claustrophobic to do any spelunking but he would be an excellent 'above-ground' advocate for their work in the area. He mentioned he was already thinking about a future tourist attraction, a 'Ruac II' facsimile cave for the mass public, similar to Lascaux II, and wanted to know what Luc thought about that. Luc patiently observed that they hadn't yet begun to study 'Ruac I' but in the fullness of time, many things were possible.

When Tailifer asked how they had come to camp on the grounds of the Abbey, Luc told him about his amusingly rude treatment by the Mayor of Ruac and hearing this, the politician clucked knowingly.

'He's a disgrace, that Bonnet, a jerk, if I may say, but please don't quote me,' he spat heatedly. 'I don't know him well, but I do know him. You know why they say he and his village are so unfriendly?'

Luc did not.

'The legend is that the town got filthy rich from piracy! You never heard that? No? Well, that's probably a fairy tale but it's a fact there was a famous hijacking in the Périgord in the summer of 1944 during the war. The Nazis had a very rich cargo on a military train, huge deposits looted from the Banque de France, art work, antiques and such, all headed to Bordeaux for transfer to German naval authorities. The Resistance struck the main railway line, near Ruac, and made off with a fortune, maybe two hundred million euros in today's money, and some very famous paintings, including, it's rumoured, Raphael's *Portrait of a Young Man*, all on their way to Goering personally. Some of the loot made it to de Gaulle in Algiers and was put to good use, I'm sure, but a lot of that money and the art disappeared into thin air. The Raphael was never seen again. There've always been rumours that the good people of Ruac developed their charming ways because they're still covering up for the theft, but you know how these stories go. Still, don't ever ask anyone in that village about the Resistance and the train robbery or you might get shot yourself!'

Tailifer's aide reminded him of their next engagement and the man hurriedly finished his drink, handed Luc his empty glass and excused himself.

Luc tried to find Sara in the crowd but was buttonholed by the Palaeolithic art expert, Zvi Alon, and Karin Weltzer, the Pleistocene geologist, who wanted to talk about the next day's logistics. Luc couldn't decide who was pushier, the bald, bullet-headed Israeli or the pugnacious German woman in bib overalls. While he was calming both of them down and giving assurances their needs would be well met, he noticed that Sara and the young Spanish archaeologist, Carlos Ferrer, were chatting.

He was about to join them when the *Le Monde* editor, a phlegmatic senior journalist named Gérard Girot, approached Luc to catch his personal thoughts on the momentous occasion. Luc politely accommodated him and the man began scribbling furiously in his notebook.

Out of the corner of his eye, Luc saw Sara and Ferrer slip the light of the camp fire for the darkness.

He still had champagne in his glass and he found himself gulping it down.

11

They looked more like astronauts than archae-ologists.

The ecosystem of a cave sealed for centuries was a finely tuned affair. The mélange of conditions — the temperature, the humidity, the pH and the gaseous balance of the chamber courtesy of the bats — all contributed to an environment that, in this particular case, had fortuitously yielded the excellent preservation of wall art.

The worst thing Luc could do was disrupt that equilibrium and start a chain reaction of destruction such as had occurred elsewhere. At Lascaux, years of unfettered access by scholars and tourists had led first to a scourge of green mould and more recently to white calcite patches, the result of excess CO_2, which now threatened the paintings. Presently Lascaux was sealed to allow the scientific community the opportunity to find solutions.

At Ruac, better an ounce of prevention from the start.

While Desnoyers, the bat man, was arguably the most popular team member, Luc considered the conservationist, Elisabeth Coutard, to be the most important. There'd be hell to pay for an early mould problem or other environmental catastrophe.

Just after dawn on Monday, Luc, Coutard,

Desnoyers and the cave expert, Giles Moran, stood in single file on the cliff ledge beneath the cave mouth. They were poised to ascend the iron stairs that the engineers had sunk into the limestone face. Close behind, Luc's grad students Pierre and Jeremy were laden-down with packs of Moran's patented cave-floor mats, rubberised semi-rigid sheets designed to protect any delicate treasures that might lie underfoot.

Moran had a tough nubbin of a body, ideal for wiggling through the tightest cave passages. He'd be responsible, for not only the protection of the cave and safety of the explorers, but for the detailed laser-guided mapping of the chamber architecture.

Coutard was a statuesque, almost courtly woman who curled her long white hair into a practical bun. She back-packed several pieces of her most delicate electronic gear and Luc lugged the rest.

Desnoyers had an infrared light strapped to his forehead, night-vision goggles and when he walked, he rattled with assorted traps dangling from his belt.

They were clad in hooded white Tyvek coveralls, rubber gloves, miners' hats and disposable respirators to protect against toxic gases and shield the cave from their germs. After the entry team posed for an archival photograph of them stretched out on the ladder like Everest climbers Luc unlocked the heavy gate and swung it open.

The expedition had officially begun.

The early-morning light softly illuminated the

100

first few metres of the vault. Luc took immense pleasure watching Coutard's reaction to the frescoes and when he switched on a series of tripod lamps, vividly illuminating the entire first chamber, she stopped dead in her tracks, like the biblical pillar of salt and said nothing, absolutely nothing. She simply breathed in and out through her mask, transfixed by the beauty of the galloping horses, the power of the bison herd, the majesty of the great bull.

Moran behaved more like a surgeon, glancing about quickly to get his bearings then setting to work on his patient, carefully laying the first ground mats. Desnoyers scuttled onto one of them. He trained his night scope on the ceiling. '*Pipistrellus pipistrellus,*' he said, waving his arm matter-of-factly at a few darting shapes overhead, but then he got excited and piped up, '*Rhinolophus ferrumequinum!*' and started to step off the mat to follow a larger flapping form into the darkness. Moran sharply admonished him and insisted he wait for the placement of more mats.

'I take it he's found something delightful,' Luc remarked to Coutard.

She replied with a beautiful, heavy sigh, overcome with emotion, seemingly surprised at the effect it was having on her. Luc patted her shoulder and said, 'I know, I know.' The touch brought her back to the here and now. She collected herself and got to work deploying an array of environmental and micro-climate monitors: temperature, moisture, alkalinity, oxygen, carbon dioxide, and the all-important culture media for bacteria and fungi. Baseline readings had to be taken before the others could begin their work.

Drawing on lessons from the past, a protocol had already been established. The fieldwork would be limited to two fifteen-day campaigns per year. Only twelve people at a time would be allowed inside the cave and they would work in shifts on an alternating schedule. Those who weren't inside the cave would have analytical tasks back at the base camp.

Much of that first shift was devoted to laying protective mats along the entire length of the cave and installing Coutard's analytical gear at various points.

Moran used his LaserRace 300 to measure the linear length of all ten chambers of the cave at 170 metres, a tad shorter than Lascaux or Chauvet.

Packs of mats were lowered from the cliff top in a continuous line of student manpower, akin to sandbaggers at a levee. Luc was obliged to wait for each section of mats to be laid before he could revisit deeper chambers. In a way, he already missed the blissful freedom of his first day of discovery, when he could roam freely and let each wave of adrenalin carry him along. Today he was more a scientist than explorer. Everything had to be done according to protocol.

His head was swimming with a million technical and logistical issues — this was a monumental project, larger in scope than anything for which he'd previously been responsible. But seeing the paintings again, the elaborate bestiary and the bird man, all so fresh and richly coloured, so magnificently rendered, made thoughts about project details disappear like snowflakes settling on a warm upturned forehead. Alone in the Chamber of the Bison Hunt, he was startled by the sound of his own respirator-muffled voice. He was telling himself, 'I'm home. This is my home.'

Before breaking for lunch Luc checked in with Desnoyers for an assessment of the bat situation. 'They don't like people,' the small man said, as if he agreed with them. 'It's a mixed population but mostly Pips. Large colony, not enormous. I'm quite sure they'll leave on their own accord and set up elsewhere.'

'The sooner the better,' Luc said and when the bat man answered with a stony face, Luc added, 'So what do you think of the paintings?'

The bat man replied, 'I hadn't really noticed.'

★   ★   ★

In the early afternoon, the second shift assembled on the ledge in anxious anticipation. Then Luc led the rest of the principals and the *Le Monde* journalist on a guided tour, acting like an artist at his own gallery opening. Every gasp, every murmur, every cooing sent a pleasant ripple up his back. 'Yes, it is extraordinary. Yes, I knew you'd be impressed,' he said over and over.

Zvi Alon caught up with Luc in between the Chamber of the Bison Hunt and a passage they were calling the Gallery of the Bears, where three large brown bears with expressive, open mouths and squarish snouts overlapped one another. 'Listen, Luc,' he said excitedly, 'I can't buy your assertion this is Aurignacian. It can't be that early! The polychromatic shading is too advanced.'

'I'm not making an assertion, Zvi. It's only an observation from a single flint tool. Look at the outline of these bears. This is charcoal, no? We'll have radiocarbon dates soon enough and we won't have to speculate about the age. We'll know.'

'I know already,' Alon gruffly insisted. 'It's the same age or later than Lascaux. It's too advanced. But I still like it. It's a very good cave.'

Luc left Sara alone till the last of the tour. They were nearly at the end of the cave, the unadorned Chamber 9. He sent the others back to start their work but kept Sara at his side. Everyone else looked bulky and shapeless in their protective suits. Her extra-small Tyvek garment somehow fit perfectly. She looked incongruously elegant, not couture, certainly, but unaccountably stylish.

'How're you doing?' he asked.

'Well.' Her eyes were starry from the art. 'Really well.'

'I've got a private tour for you. Ready to get on your hands and knees to see the tenth chamber?'

'I'd crawl a mile for that. But just so I'm prepared, are there a lot of bats?'

'No. They don't seem to like it there. I'll have to ask our friend Desnoyers why.'

She stole a glance at the undulating colony

overhead. 'Okay, let's start crawling.'

Moran's padded mats made the passage easier on the knees. He led, she followed and he was quietly amused she had to follow his rump so closely. They emerged in the tenth chamber and stood upright. Luc could tell that Sara was dazzled by the exuberant display of humanity on the dome-shaped walls. Stencilled hands everywhere, bright as stars on a moonless night. 'I saw your pictures, Luc, but, wow.'

'It's a warm-up. Come on.'

The last chamber was rigged with a single tripod lamp giving off a stinging halogen flare. He saw her buckle and instinctively grabbed her around the waist for support. She pulled away whispering an irritated, 'I'm okay,' then firmed her knees. She slowly began turning with little foot movements, eventually making a full circle. She reminded Luc of a music-box ballerina his mother had when he was young, which pirouetted on a mirrored base to the sound of an oriental melody. Finally, she spoke again. 'It's so green.'

'Beyond being the first depiction of flora in Upper Paleolithic, it's the only known use of green pigment from this era. It must be malachite but we'll have to see. The browns and the red berries are iron oxides, undoubtedly.'

'The grasses,' she marvelled. 'They're completely compatible with the dry steppes we'd expect in the Aurignacian period during the warm seasons. And look at this fantastic beaked man standing in the grass like a giant scarecrow.'

'He's my new best friend,' Luc said drily.

'What about the other plants?'

'Well, this is what's so interesting. The manuscript illustrations are more realistic than the cave paintings but there appear to be two varieties,' she said moving first to her right. 'This panel is a bush with red berries. The leaf pattern is fairly impressionistic and imprecise, see here? And here? But the bushes in the manuscript clearly have five-lobed leaves in a spiral array on the stem. I'd have to say *Ribes rubrum* if pressed. The redcurrant bush. It's indigenous to western Europe.' She moved to her left. 'And these vines. Again, the manuscript has a clearer rendering. The long stems and the elongated, arrow-head-shaped leaves, *Convolvulus arvensis* is my best guess, but it's only a guess. The European bindweed. It's an awful bugger as far as weeds go but it's got pretty little pink and white flowers in the summer. But, no flowers here, as you can see.'

'So, grass, weeds and redcurrants, is that the verdict?'

'Hardly a verdict,' she said. 'A first impression. When can I get to work on the pollen?'

'First thing in the morning. So, are you glad you came?'

'On a professional level, yes.'

'Only professionally?'

'Jesus, Luc. Yes. Only professionally.'

He awkwardly turned away and pointed towards the Vault of Hands. 'You first. I'll get the light.'

★　★　★

Celebration hung heavy in the air like the smell of gunpowder after fireworks. The air was chilly but as there was no threat of rain people were taking their meals on folding chairs and wine crates out in the open. Luc spent a last few minutes with the journalist, Girot, before the man departed for Paris. Before he left, they warmly exchanged business cards and Luc sought one more assurance the piece would be embargoed until further notice.

'Don't worry,' Girot said. 'A deal's a deal. You've been great, professor. You can trust me.'

Alon sought out Luc and pulled up a chair. He had passed on the cook's main course of rosemary lamb chops and roasted potatoes and opted instead for bread and butter and some fruit. Luc looked at his plate. 'I'm sorry, Zvi, are we not accommodating your dietary needs?'

'I don't keep kosher,' he replied, 'I don't like French food.'

Luc smiled at his bluntness. 'So? The cave?'

'Well, I think you've found one of the most remarkable sites in prehistory. It's going to require a lifetime of study. I only wish my life span were longer. You know, Luc, I'm not an emotional man, but this cave moves me. I'm in awe of it, whatever its age. Lascaux's been called the Paleolithic Sistine Chapel. Ruac is better. The artists here were masters. The colours are more vivid, which speaks to excellent pigment technology. The animals are even more natural-istic than Lascaux or Altamira or Font de Gaume or Chauvet. The use of perspective is highly advanced. These were the da Vincis and

107

Michaelangelos of their time.'

'I feel the same way. Look, Zvi, we have a chance to study this right and maybe make a breakthrough on the subject that you've written about so eloquently: why did they paint?'

'You know I've had strong opinions.'

'That's why I chose you.'

Without a trace of self-consciousness, Alon said, 'You made the right choice. I've been hard on Lewis-Williams and Clottes for their shamanistic theories, as you know.'

'They've both commiserated with me,' Luc replied. 'But they respect you.'

'I've always felt that they place far too much emphasis on observations of modern shamanism in Africa and the New World. This whole business of the cave wall being a membrane between the real world and the spirit world and the shaman being some paleolithic Timothy Leary with hallucinogens and a skin full of pigments — it's hard to swallow. Yes, these people of Ruac and Lascaux were Homo sapiens, just like us, but their societies were in a continual state of transformation, not static like modern stone-age cultures. That's why I can't accept extrapolations from modern ethnography. There may not have been neurological differences between our brains and theirs but, by God, there were cultural differences which we simply cannot understand. You know where I stand, Luc. I'm old school, a direct descendant of Laming-Emperaire and Leroi-Gourhan. I say let the analysis of the archaeology speak for itself. Look at the types of animals, the pairings,

108

the clusters, the associations. Then you can divine the common mythological stories, the significance of clans, try to make some sense of it all. Think about it, for a period of at least twenty-five thousand years, a huge span of time, they used a core set of animal motifs: horse, bison, deer, bulls with a smattering of felines and bears. Not reindeers, which they ate, not birds, or fish — okay, one here, two there — and not trees and plants, at least not until now. They didn't paint whatever they fancied. There were reasons these motifs exist. But . . . '

He stopped speaking, removed his glasses and rubbed his rheumy eyes.

'But?' Luc asked.

'But Ruac is disturbing me.'

'In what way?'

'I've become more of a statistician than an archaeologist, Luc. I'm up to my neck in computer models and algorithms. I can tell you more about the correlation between cave position and left-facing horses than any man on the planet. But today! Today I felt more like an archaeologist which is good, but also I felt like someone who knows nothing, which is unsettling.'

Luc agreed with him and added, 'There's a lot of ground-breaking material here. It's not just you who's going to have to reevaluate beliefs. Everyone is. The Chamber of Plants alone. And if it's Aurignacian, which I accept you don't buy into, then what?'

'Yes, the plants, of course they're something totally new. But it's more than that. The whole gestalt of the place is getting to me. The bird men, particularly. One with the bison, one with the vegetation. I looked at them and that goddamn curse word, shaman, kept popping into my head.' He slapped Luc's knee. 'If you tell Lewis-Williams I said that, I'll kill you!'

'My lips are sealed.'

Pierre trotted over and towered over them. 'Got a minute, Luc?'

Alon's knees cracked when he stood up. He raised up on his toes and steadied himself with an arm on Luc's shoulder to whisper some hot-breathed words in his ear. 'Would you let me go back to the cave tonight, alone, just for a few minutes? I need to experience it on my own, with just one small light, like they did.'

'I think we need to stick to protocol, Zvi.'

Alon nodded sadly and went on his way.

Luc turned to Pierre. 'What's up?'

'A couple of people from Ruac village are here to speak with you.'

'Do they have pitchforks?'

'They brought a cake.'

★ ★ ★

He'd seen them before. The couple from the café in Ruac.

'I'm Odile Bonnet,' the woman said, 'and this is my brother Jacques.'

Odile clearly noticed the look of recognition on Luc's face.

'Yes, the mayor is our father. I think he was rude to you before so — well, here's a cake.'

Luc thanked her and invited them to his caravan for a brandy.

She had the flashing smile and sultry looks of a golden-era film star past her peak, not his type, a little on the easy side and too much of the peasant in her, but definitely Hugo's kind of woman. Even though it was chilly, she liked to show a lot of leg. Her blank-faced oafish brother didn't seem as pleased to be there. He stayed quiet, a bit of a cipher, probably roped into coming along, Luc figured.

She sipped the brandy while her brother swallowed his in large gulps, like beer. 'My father is not a modern man,' she explained. 'He likes the quiet old ways. He doesn't like tourists and outsiders, Germans and Americans in particular. He's of the opinion the painted caves, especially Lascaux, have changed the character of the region, with the traffic and the postcard shops and the T-shirts. You know what I'm saying.'

'Of course,' Luc said. 'I completely understand his position.'

'He reflects the views of the majority in the village which is why he's been mayor for as long as I can remember. But I — my brother and I — are more open-minded, even excited about your discovery. A new cave! Right under our noses! We've probably hiked by it dozens of times.'

'I can arrange a tour,' Luc replied enthusiastically. 'I can't tell you how much I want the support of the village. Yes, it's a national treasure, but first, it's a local treasure. I think local involvement from the beginning will help

111

shape the future of Ruac Cave as a public institution.'

'We'd love to see it, wouldn't we, Jacques?' He nodded automatically. 'We'd also like to volunteer. We can do anything you'd like: Jacques can dig or move things around — he's strong as a farm animal. I can file, I can draw well. Cook. Anything.'

There were a couple of sharp raps on Luc's caravan door and it swung open. Hugo was there, hoisting a magnum of champagne with a red bow around its neck. 'Hello!' Then, seeing Luc was with someone, he added, 'Oh, sorry! Shall I come back?'

'No, come in! Welcome! Remember that nice couple from the café in Ruac? Here they are.'

Hugo climbed in and immediately shifted his attention to the woman, and when it was established the man with her was her brother, he joked the champagne was for her. They chatted for a while then Odile uncrossed her legs and announced they'd have to be off.

'The answer is yes,' Luc said to her. 'I'd welcome your help at the campsite. Cave work is going to be very restricted but there's lots to do here. Come anytime. Pierre, the guy who showed you in, will set you up.'

This time her parting smile to Hugo was unambiguous. Luc felt the kind of humming sometimes experienced around a high-voltage line.

'If I'd known she'd be here I would have come yesterday,' Hugo said. He looked around the cramped caravan. 'This is where the famous Luc

112

Simard, co-discoverer of Ruac Cave, is staying? Not exactly Versailles. Where am I sleeping?'

Luc pointed to the spare bunk at the far end that was piled high with Luc's laundry. 'There. Have some brandy and don't you dare complain.'

★　★　★

Zvi Alon button-holed Jeremy in the kitchen where the student had gone to brew a cup of tea.

The bald man blurted out, 'Luc gave me permission to visit the cave on my own for a short while. Let me have the key.'

Jeremy was thoroughly intimidated by Alon and his tough reputation. His bony knees were practically knocking. 'Of course, professor. Do you want me to go with you to unlock it? It's tricky going down in the dark.'

Alon held out his hand. 'I'll be fine. When I was your age I was commanding a tank in the Sinai.'

★　★　★

Luc started filling Hugo in on the first day's activities but as he was speaking, he sensed his friend was restless. Suddenly Luc stopped talking and demanded, 'What is it?'

'How come you're not asking me about the manuscript?'

'Has there been progress?'

'I don't suppose you've ever heard of a Caesar cipher?'

Luc impatiently shook his head.

'Well, it's a pathetically easy code that Julius Caesar used for secret messages. It practically requires your foe to be illiterate since it's so easy to break, just a shift of say three letters to the right or left. Most of his enemies couldn't have even read the plain Latin so it worked fine for him. Over time code breakers and code writers competed for rather more sophisticated methods.'

Luc was red-faced with testiness.

'Okay, okay, well according to my guy from Brussels, one of the Voynich geniuses, our manuscript was coded with something called the Vigenère cipher which by itself is pretty remarkable since it wasn't thought to be invented until the sixteenth century. It looks like our Barthomieu or a colleague was a few hundred years ahead of his time. I won't bore you with the details but it's a far more complicated variant of the Caesar cipher with an additional requirement of requiring secret key words for deciphering.'

'If you don't cut to the chase, I'm going to kill you with my bare hands,' Luc shouted.

'This morning, before I left Paris, my Belgian geek told me he was close to cracking a few pages. He thinks there are probably at least three sections, each with its own key word. He was crunching numbers, or whatever it is that computer people crunch, and he told me he'd email me when he had something definitive. Is there someplace I can check my mail?'

Luc practically grabbed him by his jacket.

114

'The office. Let's go.'

As they passed the camp fire, Luc pointed at a woman and said to Hugo, 'By the way, that's Sara.'

Immediately he wished he'd kept quiet because Hugo sprinted towards her and introduced himself as one of Luc's oldest friends not to mention the co-discoverer of the cave.

'I've heard of you,' she sparkled. 'I can't believe we never met back when, you know, Luc and I . . . '

'And I've heard of you too!' Hugo exclaimed. 'So lovely, so intelligent. Luc, come over here!'

Luc approached, shaking his head in anticipation of what was coming. 'Don't be making trouble, Hugo.'

'Trouble? Me? It's just that, well, Sara, I'll be blunt. I met a lady tonight and I'd like to ask her out but a double-date might be less of a challenge for her. How about you and Luc joining us sometime this week? I'm only here for a couple of days.'

'Christ, Hugo,' Luc groaned.

'I'd love to,' Sara said, taking Luc aback but making Hugo smile knowingly.

'Then it's settled. All I need to do is ask this lady and we're set. Luc will tell you what I think about the countryside. This should make it more palatable.'

★ ★ ★

Luc switched on the office lights. The floor of the sturdy little building was vibrating along with the

115

rumbling generator. He logged onto the web and let Hugo enter his own email portal.

The dapper man puffed out his chest and proudly announced he had twenty new messages, several from female friends, then spotted the important one. 'Ah, it's our code breaker!'

He opened the email. 'Fantastic! He says he's got six pages done. The secret keyword for the section was NIVARD, whatever that means. He's sent the deciphered passages as an attachment and says he'll start working on the next section soon.'

'What does it say?' Luc demanded.

'Hang on, let me open it. I don't think he even read it. He's only interested in the code, not the text! Besides he says it's in Latin, which for our Belgian friend is just one more cipher, a boring one.'

Hugo scanned the document getting a feel for the language.

With Luc standing over his shoulder he slowly started to read on the fly. He soon cast off the dispassionate tone of a translator. The language was too volatile and Hugo began to ardently channel the old monk's words.

I am certain to meet a horrible and painful death. Unlike a martyr who dies for his beliefs and piety, I will die for the knowledge I possess. There has been blood and there will be more. To lose a friend is not an easy thing. To lose a brother is terrible. To lose a brother who has also been a friend for nigh on two hundred years is unbearable. *I buried your bones, dear Nivard. Who will bury mine? I am not a saint, O Lord, but a pitiful soul who loved his knowledge far too dearly. Did it crowd out my love for You? I pray not, but it is for you my God to judge. For my sins I will pay in blood. I cannot confess to my Abbot for he is dead. Until they come for me I will write my confession. I will conceal its meaning in a cipher devised by Brother Jean, a scholar and a gentle soul who I miss terribly. The knowledge contained in my confession is not meant for every man and when I am gone it will disappear. If it is ever found again, it is because Christ has seen fit to make it manifest for reasons known only to Him. I am a scribe and book binder. Should the Lord give me time to finish it, I will bind the book and I will dedicate it to Saint Bernard. If the book is burned so be it. If it is torn asunder so be it. If it is found by another man in its intended hiding place and the words untangled, then I say to that man may God have mercy upon your soul, for the price you will pay will be great.*

Hugo stopped to blink and wet his lips.
'Is there more?' Luc asked.
'Yes,' he whispered. 'There's more.'
'Then for God's sake, keep going.'

★ ★ ★

Alon drove his rental car the way he did

117

everything in life: pugnaciously. He accelerated hard, braked hard and navigated the short distance from the camp in over-revved lurches. A gravel parking lot had been established near the top of the cliff and when he got there he braked aggressively, his tyres spraying up pebbles. Clouds blurred the edges of the crescent moon and the night sky had tendrils of black, like the veins on the back of one's hand. The temporary guard shelter that had been erected before the gates were installed was long gone. The CCTV images and telemetry data from the cave entrance and chambers now fed directly to the camp office.

He locked the car and zipped his bomber jacket to his throat. Convections of chilly air rolled over the valley. He felt around in his pocket for the key to the gate of the cave. It was large and heavy, a satisfying implement, almost medieval. He would have preferred complete authenticity, a flickering oil-fed lamp, but the small flashlight in his hand would have to do. He aimed it at the path and headed towards the cliff ladder.

He was eager to spend half an hour on his own, wandering the passages in the minimal light. He'd apologise to Luc in the morning in his own way, plead temporary insanity, but he had to do this. Luc would officially disapprove but the incident would pass, he was sure. The cave was calling out to him. He needed to have a private conversation with it. He'd write about the night. It would shape his thinking, maybe even shake some long-held, stubborn beliefs.

'Damn the shamans,' he whispered out loud, the thought escaping his lips. *Could I have been wrong?*

He slowed his pace as he neared the ladder. It was a long way down and at his age he was no longer a mountain goat.

A flurry of footsteps! Running.

He startled and spun but never made it full around.

He didn't see the log that bashed his head, never felt himself being dragged to the edge and at the last moment, at his passage through the membrane, he never heard the urgent fluttering of a pair of black-shouldered kites taking to wing, spooked by the sound of his body crashing through the oaks.

12

Clairvaux Abbey, France, 1118

On a crystalline winter morning the great woods surrounding the new monastery were silent. The fields were calm, the flat horizon at peace.

Inside a frigid room with no more than a straw mattress, a piss pot and a basin glazed with ice, the young abbot had cast off his rough blanket because he felt his body burning, despite the cold. His skin was slick, as if freshly dunked in water. The hacking cough that had kept him up all night was quiet for now, but he knew that any minute it would return to rack his body and pound his head. He tried to breathe through his nose to prevent another spasm.

When, as a privileged youngster, Bernard became ill, a gentle-woman would attend him — an aunt or a cousin. But he had banned females from the congregation and as a consequence he was forced to rely on the not-so-tender mercies of men. His feverish lamentations turned to his beloved mother, dead so long. He still had a fading memory from early childhood, lying in bed with a raw throat, being soothed with a song, a honeyed drink and her pretty face. He was a man now, twenty-eight years old and the head of Clairvaux Abbey. For him, there was no mother and no gentle hand. He had to bear his illness stoically and trust in the benevolence of Christ for deliverance.

If his mother had survived to old age surely she would have swelled with pride at how her pious plan had unfolded. At birth she had offered each of her children — six sons and one daughter — to God, and had fully devoted herself to their Christian upbringing.

By the time Bernard had completed his education, his mother was gone. His tutors had identified him as a special talent, a young man who, in addition to noble birth and natural intellect, had a sweetness of temper, a keen wit and the kind of immense charm which blesses a man infrequently. Despite a brief flirtation with the secular seductions of literature and poetry, there was never a serious doubt that Bernard would become a minister of God.

Certainly, the path of least resistance would have taken him to the nearby Benedictine abbey in Fontaines, but he shunned that option with vehemence. He had already aligned himself philosophically with the new men of the Church — Robert of Molesme, Alberic of Cîteaux, the Cistercians who felt the strict observance of the Rule of Saint Benedict of Nursia had been forsaken by corrupted abbeys and their clergy. These Cistercians were determined to strip away the excesses of flesh and spirit that had infected the Benedictines. They would reject fine linen shirts, breeches, furs, sheets and bedspreads. Their abbeys and cloisters would never be embellished by gargoyles and chimeras. They would take their bread hard, without lard or honey. They would charge no burial dues, take

121

no tithes, they would build their communities away from cities, towns or villages and ban all women to avoid all worldly distractions. And they would interrupt their prayers and meditations only by the kind of hard physical labour necessary for subsistence.

With this spartan ideal firmly in mind, the young Bernard was praying one day in a small wayside church, asking God for his guidance, and when he arose, he had his answer. Transfixed by the clarity of his decision, he persuaded his brothers Barthomieu and André, his uncle, Gaudry and soon, thirty-one other Burgundian nobles, to venture with him to Cîteaux, leaving the Kingdom of France for the Holy Roman Empire and leaving old lives for new. Two other brothers Gérard and Guy were away as soldiers though in time they would join him too. Only the youngest, Nivard, was left behind.

'Farewell, Nivard,' Bernard had called to this favourite brother the day the party rode off. 'You will have all the lands and estates for yourself.'

The boy cried out tearfully, 'Then you are taking Heaven and leaving me only the earth! The division is too unequal!'

These words greatly moved Bernard and there would be a pit in his stomach until the day when he and Nivard were finally reunited.

In the year 1112, Cîteaux Abbey was still all wood and no stone. It had been established fifteen years earlier but the abbot, Stephen Harding, a flinty Englishman, had not received new novices for some time. He was overjoyed by this influx of humanity and he welcomed

Bernard and his entourage with open arms.

That first cold night in the lay dormitory, Bernard blissfully lay awake, the crowded room resonating with the snores of exhausted men. In the days and weeks to come, the harder the travails the greater his pleasure and in the future he would tell all novices at his gate: 'If you desire to live in this house, leave your body behind; only spirits can enter here.'

His abilities were so exceptional and his labour so vigorous that within two years, Stephen had decided Bernard was more than ready to initiate a new sister abbey. He made him abbot and sent him off with his brothers André and Gérard and twelve other men to a house in the diocese of Langres in Champagne.

On a flat clearing, they built a simple dwelling and embarked on a life of extreme hardship, even by their own tough standards. The land was poor, they made their bread from the coarsest barley and in the first year they had to make do with wild herbs and boiled beech leaves. But they persevered and built up their monastery. They named it Clairvaux.

Because of Bernard's charisma, disciples flocked to Clairvaux and by the time he became ill there were over a hundred monks in residence. He missed the union of sleeping with his fellows in the long open dormitory but it was just as well he had agreed to move to a small abbot chamber adjacent to the church. His month-long coughing fits would have deprived the monks of what little sleep they had.

Gérard was always the most robust of the six

brothers. Other than a sliced thigh, a proper soldier's trophy, he had never suffered a sick day in his life. He fussed over his frail brother and tried to have him keep down soups and infusions but Bernard was slipping away, a slack bag of bones. Too listless to lead the men at prayer, he delegated the authority to his prior but still insisted on being helped to the church to attend services and observe the hours.

One day, Gérard took it upon himself to ride off to inform the powerful cleric, William of Champeaux, Bishop of Châlonsen-Champagne, about the state of Bernard's health. William openly appreciated Bernard and acutely recognised his potential as a future church leader. On report of his illness, he obtained the permission of the Cistercian order at Cîteaux to govern Bernard for a year as his superior. The decree in hand, he ordered the young abbot to be relieved of all clerical duties and freed from the harsh observances of the order until his body was healed. Bernard was taken by horse cart south, to the warmer climes of a richer and more comfortable abbey where a few years earlier his middle brother Barthomieu had been dispatched. And thus, Bernard of Clairvaux came to reside at the Abbey Ruac.

Ruac was a Benedictine community sluggishly shedding the excesses which Bernard had railed against. It was not yet fit to be part of the Cistercian order. Although new nuns were no longer admitted, the abbot, a benevolent old sort, did not have the heart to cast the old ones out. Nor did he cast away the wine cellar or the

124

brewery or empty the plentiful larder and granary stores. Barthomieu and some other new men had been sent to Ruac as a vanguard of reform, but they began to relish the comforts they found there having endured hard years at Clairvaux. In truth, they were more changed by Ruac than Ruac changed by them.

On arrival, Bernard was too ill to notice the ecclesiastical shortcomings of his new environs, let alone protest them. He was given a one-room stone house on the outskirts of the abbey with a hearth, a comfortable bed, a reading table with horse-hair chair and an abundance of thick candles. His brother Barthomieu stoked the fire and hovered at his bedside like a worried lover, and an elderly nun, Sister Clotilde, plied him with fresh food and wholesome drink.

At first it seemed Bernard might not survive. He lapsed in and out of consciousness, intermittently recognised his brother, weakly blessing him anew each time, and called the nun 'mother', which seemed to please her no end.

On the twentieth day, Bernard's fever broke and he became aware of his surroundings.

He propped himself to a sitting posture as his brother adjusted his coverlet. 'Who brought me here?' he asked.

'Gérard and some of the monks from Clairvaux.'

Bernard rubbed the grit from his eyes and artfully concealed chastisement as compliment. 'Look at you! You look well, Barthomieu!' His older brother was fleshy and robust, his complexion pink as a pig, his hair in need of updated tonsuring.

'I'm a little fat,' Barthomieu said, defensively patting his middle through his good linen robe.

'How is that?'

'The abbot here is not so strict as you!'

'Ah, I have heard that said about me,' Bernard said. His down-cast eyes made it impossible to tell if he rued the austerity he had imposed on his community or Barthomieu's dismissiveness. 'How is your life here, brother? Are you serving Christ fully?'

'I believe I am, but I fear you will look upon my contentment with suspicion. I do love it here, Bernard. I feel I have found my place.'

'What do you do beyond prayer and meditation? Have you a vocation?' He recalled his brother's aversion to manual labour.

Barthomieu acknowledged he was more inclined to indoors pursuits. His abbot had freed him from planting and harvesting. There was a small scriptorium at Ruac turning out copies of *The Rule of St Benedict* for a tidy profit and he had been apprenticed to a venerable monk with a practised hand. He was also adept at caring for the ill, as Bernard had come to witness first-hand. He assisted Brother Jean, the infirmarer, and spent a good hour a day scuttling around the infirmary, making sure the fires were ample, lighting the candles for Matins, cleaning the bowls that had been used for bloodletting, washing the feet of the sick and shaking their clothing of fleas.

He hoisted Bernard to his feet, let the skeleton

of a man lean on his back as he held the piss pot for him. He enthusiastically commented on the improved flow and colour of his brother's urine. 'Come,' Barthomieu said when he was done, 'take a few steps with me.'

Over the weeks, the few steps turned to many and Bernard was able to take short walks in the spring air and start attending mass. The old abbot, Étienne, and his prior, Louis, were both entrenched in the ancient Benedictine ways and were, as they admitted to each other, rather fearful of the esteemed young man. He was a fire-brand, a reformer, and their provincial minds were no match for his intellect and powers of persuasion. They hoped he would see fit to be a humble guest and let them keep their casks of wine and the likes of dear old Sister Clotilde.

⋆　⋆　⋆

One day while strolling in the meadow by the infirmary, Barthomieu pointed to the low building and remarked, 'You know, Bernard, there is a cleric here, sent to Ruac by confidants to recover from a horrific injury, who is the only man I ever met who is your equal in discourse, knowledge and learning. Perhaps when he is stronger, you may wish to meet him, and he, you. His name is Pierre Abélard and, though you will vigorously disapprove of certain aspects of his tempestuous life, you will surely find him more stimulating than your dull brother.'

The seed planted, Bernard wondered about this Abélard. As spring turned to summer and

127

his strength increased, each time he walked the perimeter of the abbey, he would peer into the arched windows of the infirmary hoping to catch a glimpse of the mystery man. Finally, one morning after Prime prayers, Barthomieu told him that Abélard had requested a visit. But before it took place, he felt his brother was obliged to hear Abélard's story, so that neither man would need to suffer embarrassment.

In his youth, Abélard had been sent to Paris to study at the great cathedral school of Notre-Dame under the same William of Champeaux, now Bernard's superior. Before long, the young scholar was able to defeat his master in rhetoric and debate and at the age of only twenty-two had established his own school outside Paris where students from all over the land elbowed each other to be at his side. Within ten years, he himself would occupy the chair at Notre-Dame and by 1115 he had become its canon. Bernard interrupted at this point and remarked that yes, of course, he had heard of this brilliant scholar and wondered what had become of him!

The answer: a woman named Héloïse.

Abélard met her when she was fifteen, young and petite, already skilled and renowned in classical letters. She lived in Paris in the gilded home of her uncle, the wealthy canon Fulbert. Abélard was so smitten he arranged for her uncle to give him lodgings for the ostensible purpose of rendering private tutoring to the sharp-minded girl.

Who seduced whom would become a matter of debate but no one could deny that a passionate affair did ensue. Abélard giddily ignored his teaching duties and indiscreetly allowed songs he had written about her to be sung in public. Tragically, their affair culminated in a pregnancy. Abélard had her sent away to his relatives in Brittany. There she delivered a child she called Astrolabe after the astronomical instrument, a name that spoke volumes about Héloïse's striking modernity.

The child was left in the care of her sister and the two lovers returned to Paris where Abélard began to tensely negotiate a pact with her uncle. He would agree to marry her but he refused to make the marriage public lest his position at Notre-Dame be compromised. Fulbert and he almost came to blows over disagreement on this point. In turmoil, Abélard convinced Héloïse to remove herself to the nunnery at Argenteuil, where she had gone to school as a girl.

She went against her will, for she was an earthly person with no inclination towards a religious life. She sent Abélard letters questioning why she had to submit to a life to which she had no calling, especially a life that required their separation.

It was 1118, a few months before Bernard had arrived at the Abbey Ruac. Her uncle was incensed that Abélard had seemingly dealt with the inconvenience of his niece by sending her off instead of publicly taking a stand for an honest union. Fulbert could not let the matter rest peacefully. He bade three of his sycophants to accost Abélard in his rooming house. Two held him down on his bed and one used a knife to crudely castrate him like a farm animal. They plopped his severed testicles into his wash basin and left him moaning in a coagulating pool of blood.

Abélard hoped to die but he did not. He was a freak now, an abomination. In agony he contemplated his fate: did not God Himself reject eunuchs, excluding them from His service as unclean creatures? Fever set in and the numbing asthenia of blood loss. He languished in a dangerously precarious state until William of Champeaux, that perennial protector of fine minds, intervened and sent him to Ruac to be attended by the noted infirmarer, Brother Jean. And in that peaceful countryside, after a long physical and spiritual convalescence, he was ready to meet Ruac's other notable invalid, Bernard of Clairvaux.

Bernard would long remember their first encounter. He waited outside the infirmary that summer morning and there emerged a dangerously thin, stoop-shouldered man with a domed forehead marked with worry lines and a shy almost boyish smile. His gait was slow and shuffling and Bernard winced in empathy. Abélard was forty, an old forty, and despite his own infirmity Bernard felt robust compared to this poor soul.

Abélard extended his hand, 'Abbot Bernard, I have so wanted to meet you. I know well your esteemed reputation.'

'And I too have wanted to meet you.'

'We have much in common.'

Bernard arched an eyebrow.

'We both love God,' Abélard said, 'and we both have been nursed back to health by Sister Clotilde's green soups and Brother Jean's brown infusions. Come, let us walk, but pray not too swiftly.'

From that day forward, the two men were constant companions. Bernard could scarcely believe his good fortune. Abélard was more than his equal in matters of theology and logic. Through debate and discourse, he was able to exercise his mind as well as his body. As they took the air, they discussed Plato and Aristotle, realism and nominalism, the morality of man, matters concrete and abstract. They verbally sparred, swapping roles of teacher and student, lost in argument for hours at a time. Barthomieu would sometimes look up from his chores and point out the infirmary windows towards the two men walking the meadow, gesticulating. 'Look, Brother Jean. Your patients are thriving.'

Bernard was keen to talk about the future — his desire to reengage in church matters, his ardour for spreading Cistercian principles. Abélard, for his part, refused to look forwards. He insisted on dwelling in the present as if he had no past and no future. Bernard let him be. There was no profit in insisting on candour from this pitiful soul.

★ ★ ★

One morning, some distance from the abbey on a favourite high outlook over the river, they stopped to take in the view. Both men sat on

131

rocks and fell silent. The first warmth of spring and the first petals of the season combined to make heady fragrance. Abélard suddenly said, 'You know of my past, do you not, Bernard?'

'I know of it.'

'Then you know of Héloïse.'

'I know of her.'

'I would like you to know her better, for if you know her, you will know me better.'

Bernard gave him a look of non-comprehension.

Abélard reached into his habit and pulled out a folded parchment. 'A letter from her. You would honour me to read it and give me your thoughts. She would not object.'

Bernard began to study it, hardly believing it was the product of an eighteen-year-old woman. It was a love letter, not low in any way, but lofty and pure. He was moved by the melody of her words and the passion in her heart. He had to stop after some minutes to clear a tear from his eye.

'Tell me what passage is that?' Abélard asked.

Bernard read it aloud. 'These cloisters owe nothing to public charities; our walls were not raised by the usuries of publicans, nor their foundations laid in base extortion. The God whom we serve sees nothing but innocent riches and harmless votaries whom you have placed here. Whatever this young vineyard is, is owing only to you, and it is your part to employ your whole care to cultivate and improve it; this ought to be one of the principal affairs of your life. Though our holy renunciation, our vows and our manner of life seem to secure us

132

from all temptation.'

Abélard nodded sadly. 'Yes, please finish it.'

When he was done, Bernard folded it and returned the letter. 'She is a remarkable woman.'

'Thank you. Though we are married, she can no longer be my wife. I am dead inside, the joy for ever gone. Nevertheless, I aim to dedicate the remainder of my life to her and to God. I will live as a simple monk. She will live as a simple nun. We will be as brother and sister in Christ. Though I will live with the perpetual misery of my fate, through our love of God we will be able to love each other.'

Bernard touched the man's knee. 'Come, brother. It's a fine day. Let's walk further.'

They wandered downstream, the river far below. The summer had seen heavy rains and run-off from the banks turned the river muddy-brown and turbulent, but on their wide ledge the ground was dry and firm. Their sandals snapped against their heels with each step. They approached the furthest point along the cliffs they had ever travelled but the weather was perfect and both of them had the energy to carry on. There was no need for talk; competing with the sounds of the wind rustling through the foliage would have been a shame. High on the cliffs they felt privileged to be in the realm of the hawk, the realm of God.

In time, Bernard said. 'Look! Let's rest here.'

On a wide ledge with a marvellous view over the valley, there was a gnarled old juniper tree seemingly growing out of the rocks. Its twisted branches provided a zone of cool shade. They sat, resting their backs against the rough trunk and continued to revel in silence.

'Shall we go back?' Abélard asked after a spell.

Bernard stood up and surveyed the path forward, shielding his eyes from the sun, searching the top of the cliffs. 'I have a notion that it may be possible to return to the abbey by continuing on, finding a gentle climb to the top and walking through the meadows to the north of the church. Are you feeling fit enough?'

Abélard smiled. 'Not as fit as you, brother, but adequate for the enterprise.'

The path forward was somewhat more difficult and their sweaty feet started slipping on the soles of their sandals. Just as Bernard was doubting the wisdom of proceeding, they heard a wonderful splashing sound. Around the next bend was a small waterfall, the sunlight making it sparkle like a ribbon of gemstones. The water lashed the ledge and cascaded over the cliffs.

They thirstily cupped handfuls of pure cold water into their mouths and decided it was perhaps a sign the way forward was propitious.

The going was slow and the ledge a bit treacherous but they were committed to finding their shortcut and both were silently glad their bodies were up for the task. Months earlier, they had been so feeble they could hardly rise from their beds. They were thankful and trudged on.

A second waterfall graced their path allowing them to drink their fill again. Bernard wiped his hands dry on his habit and craned his neck. 'Just there,' he pointed. 'If we go a little further I believe that is a place we can safely climb to the top.'

At the chosen spot, Bernard put hands to his hips and asked Abélard if he was prepared for the ascent.

'I am ready, though it does seem a long way up.'

'Don't worry. God will keep us attached to the firmament,' Bernard said cheerfully.

'If one of us is to fly, pray it be me, not you,' Abélard replied.

Bernard led the way, searching for a route that best approximated a stairway. Sweating heavily, his chest heaving from exertion, he pulled himself up to the next level and stopped dead in his tracks. 'Abélard!' he cried. 'Take care on that loose rock there but come! There is something marvellous!'

There was a gaping hole in the cliff face, as wide as a man's bed, as tall as a child.

Bernard extended a hand to help the older man up. 'A cave!' Abélard exclaimed, gulping air.

'Let us have a look at it,' Bernard said excitedly. 'At least it will cool us down.'

Without fire, they had to rely on sunshine to see anything within the vault. A yellow glow extended only a few feet before tapering into blackness. After crawling inside they found they were able to stand easily. Bernard took a few tentative steps forward and saw something at the edge of the light. 'My God, Abélard! See there? There are frescoes!'

Running horses.

Charging bison.

The head of a huge black bull overhead.

The creatures disappeared into the darkness.

'A painter has been here,' Abélard sputtered.

'A genius,' Bernard agreed. 'But who?'

'Do you think it is from antiquity?' Abélard asked.

'Perhaps but I cannot say.'

'The Romans were here in Gaul.'

'Yes, but these do not appear as any Roman statue or mosaic I have ever seen,' Bernard said. He looked out over the valley. 'Whatever its age, it is a spot of majesty. The artist could not have found a better tablet to paint upon. We must return with illumination to see what lies deeper.' He clapped his hands on Abélard's shoulders. 'Come my friend. What a marvellous day this has been. Let us get back to the abbey for mass.'

★   ★   ★

Bernard encouraged Barthomieu to return to the cave with he and Abélard, and in turn, Barthomieu recruited Brother Jean who was learned about and fascinated by the natural world. The four men set off from the abbey in the morning after the Terce service. They aimed to return by the Sext service at noon. They would have to hurry, but if they missed Sext, they would do penance. The world would not end. If Bernard had been the abbot at Ruac, attitudes would not be so lax, but that bright day he felt more explorer than cleric.

The men arrived at the cave by mid-morning, with the giddiness of boys on a lark. Barthomieu was buoyed by his brother's improved vigour and good cheer. Jean, a tubby, good-natured healer, the oldest of the group by a few years, was eager to see these frescoes for himself. Bernard and Abélard for their part, happily nurtured their growing bond.

They brought good torches with them, lengths of larch with ends wrapped in fatted rags. On the ledge below the cave, Jean knelt down, not to pray but to open his pouch of fire-making materials: a flint, an iron cylinder which was the broken shaft of an old abbey key and some powdery linen char cloth, prepared and dried in his own special way.

He worked fast, sparking the iron on the flint and had the kindling going in moments. After his torch was lit, the others set theirs blazing too. Soon, four men were standing in the mouth of the cave, hoisting burning torches, staring wordlessly at some of the finest art they had ever seen.

Inside, they completely lost track of the hours; by the time they would return, Sext would be long over and they would be fortunate to attend the next service at Nones. By the light of hissing torches, they marvelled at the menagerie. Some of the animals such as the bison and mammoths seemed fanciful, though the horses and bears were realistic enough. The weird priapic bird man startled them and set their tongues clucking. And when they came to crawl through the spider hole at the rear of the cave they were dazzled by the red-stencilled hand prints that encircled them in a small chamber.

From the first moments, they had been discussing who the artist or artists might have been. Romans? Gauls? Celts? Other distant barbarians? Lacking an answer, they turned to the question of why. Why bedeck a chamber with hands? What purpose would be served?

Jean wandered into the last chamber and exclaimed, 'Now, brothers, here are things I can better understand! Plants!'

Jean inspected the paintings with a keen eye. He was an avid herbalist, one of the most skilled practitioners in the Périgord, and his abilities as an infirmarer were unrivalled. His poultices, rubs, powders and infusions were legendary, his reputation reaching all the way to Paris. There was a long history of herbalism in the region and knowledge of plants and medicaments was carefully passed down from father to son, mother to daughter and in the case of Ruac, monk to monk. Jean had a particular gift at embellishment and experimentation. Even if a poultice for wheezing worked well enough, might it not work better with the addition of stalk of cranesbill? If loose bowels could be staunched by the usual brews, might the infusions be made more potent with the added juice of poppies and mandrake?

With his companions hovering over his shoulder, Jean pointed his torch at the paintings of bushes with red berries and five-sided leaves. 'To my eye, that is the gooseberry bush. The juice of those berries is good for various lassitudes. And these vines, over here. They look to be in the family of possession vines which are said to remedy the ague.'

Barthomieu was inspecting the large bird man on the opposite wall. 'Have you seen this creature, brothers?' He poked a finger at the figure's erect cock. 'He is as felicitous as the other one. That said, even I know the type of vegetation surrounding him. It is meadow grass.'

'I agree,' Jean sniffed. 'Simple grass. It is of limited value as a medicament although I will use it from time to time to bind a poultice.'

Bernard slowly moved around the chamber, inspecting the walls for himself. 'I almost tire of saying it but I have never seen a place as singular in all of Christendom. It seems to me . . . '

There was a crunch underfoot and Bernard lost his balance. He fell, dropping his torch and scuffing his knees.

Abélard hurried over and held out his arm. 'Are you all right, my friend?'

Bernard started to reach for his torch but retracted his hand as if a serpent was about to strike back and crossed himself. 'Look there! My God!'

Abélard lowered his torch to better see what had so startled Bernard. Against the wall was a heaped-up pile of ivory-coloured human bones. He quickly drew the sign of the cross against his chest.

Jean joined them and began an inspection. 'These bones are not fresh,' he observed. 'I cannot say how long this poor wretch has lain here but I believe it is no short time. And look at his skull!' Behind the left ear hole, the back of the vault was crushed and deeply depressed. 'He met a violent end, may God rest his soul. I wonder if he is our painter?'

'How can we ever know?' Bernard said. 'Whoever he is, it is incumbent upon us to assume he is a Christian and give him a Christian burial. We cannot leave him here.'

'I agree, but we will have to return on another day with a sack to carry his remains,' Abélard said. 'I would not wish to disgrace him by leaving some of his bones here, scattering others there.'

'Shall we bury him with his bowl?' Barthomieu exclaimed like a child.

'What bowl?' Jean asked.

Barthomieu stuck his torch out until it was almost touching the limestone bowl, the size of a man's cupped hands, which was lying on the floor between two piles of foot bones. 'There!' he said. 'Shall we bury him with his old supper bowl?'

★   ★   ★

Long after the bones were interred in the cemetery and a mass for the dead held in the church, Jean revisited the flesh-coloured stone bowl he kept on his reading desk by his bed. It was heavy, smooth and cool to the touch and cradling it in his hands he could not help but wonder about the man in the cave. He himself had a heavy mortar and pestle which he used to grind his botanicals into remedies. One day on an impulse, he retrieved his mortar from the infirmary bench and placed it alongside this man's bowl. They were not so different.

His assistant, a young monk named Michel, was watching him suspiciously from his corner perch.

'Do you not have work to occupy yourself?' Jean asked irritably. The hatchet-faced youth was incapable of minding his own affairs.

'No, Father.'

'Well, I will tell you how to bide your time until Vespers. Change all the straw in the infirmary mattresses. The bed bugs have returned.'

The young monk shuffled off with a sour expression, whispering under his breath.

Jean's cell was a walled-off space within the long infirmary. Usually, by the time he would slip off his sandals and lay his head on the straw, he would be asleep, oblivious to the snores and moans of his patients. Since the day he visited the cave, however, he had slept fitfully, dwelling on the images on the walls and the skeleton in the chamber. Once, in a dream, the skeleton rearticulated, rose and became the bird man. He awoke in an unpleasant sweat.

On this night he lay awake staring at the small candle he left burning on his desk between the two stone bowls.

A compulsion overtook him.

It would not be quieted easily.

It would not wane until he dragged Barthomieu, Bernard and Abélard out with him into the dewy meadows and succulent woodlands that surrounded the abbey.

It would not wane until they had collected baskets overflowing with meadow grasses,

141

gooseberries and possession vines.

It would not wane until Jean had mashed the berries, chopped and ground the plants in his mortar then boiled the stringy pulp into an infusion.

It would not wane until the night the four men sat together in Jean's cell and one-by-one swilled down the tart, reddish tea.

13

'That's it?' Luc exclaimed.

Hugo had stopped translating. He closed the email attachment and turned his palms upward in a gesture of apologetic futility. 'That's all he's decoded so far.'

Luc impatiently stamped his foot, shaking the portable building. 'So they made a tea from these plants. Then what?'

'Hopefully, our Belgian friend will have more for us soon. I'll send an encouraging message. I'd hate for him to get distracted by something like a *Star Trek* convention and lose interest.'

'There was a skeleton, Hugo, and artefacts! But now, no surface finds in the tenth chamber or anywhere else. What a loss!'

Hugo shrugged. 'Well, they probably did what they said they were going to do. They gave the pre-Christian cave man a Christian burial!'

'It's like finding an Egyptian tomb cleaned out by grave robbers. An in situ skeleton from the period would have been of immense value.'

'They left the paintings for you, don't forget that.'

Luc started for the door. 'Send an email to your friend and get him to hurry up with the rest of the manuscript. I'm going to talk to Sara about the plants.'

'If I were you, I'd do more than talk.'

'Oh for God's sake, Hugo. Grow up.'

Sara's caravan was dark but Luc still rapped on the door. There was a muffled 'Who is it?'

'It's Luc. I've got some important news.'

After a few moments, the Spaniard Ferrer opened the door, shirtless, and cheerfully said, 'She'll be right with you, Luc. Want a drink?'

Sara lit a mantle lamp and appeared at the doorway, flushed with embarrassment like a caught-out teenager. Her blouse was one buttonhole off and when she noticed it, all she could do was roll her eyes at herself.

Ferrer gave her a peck on the cheek and took off, remarking without a touch of bitterness that business came first.

Luc asked if she'd be more comfortable if they talked outside but she invited him in and lit the lamp in the sitting area. Its hissing sound broke the silence. 'Seems like a nice fellow,' he finally said.

'Carlos? Very nice.'

'Did you know him before Ruac?'

She frowned. 'Luc, why is it I'm feeling like I'm being interrogated by my father? This is a little awkward, wouldn't you say?'

'Not for me. I'm sorry it's awkward for you. That wasn't my intention.'

'I'm sure.' She sipped from a bottle of water. 'What did you want to talk about?'

'Our plants. I think they were put to specific use.'

She leaned forward, unwittingly exposing glistening cleavage. 'Go on,' she said, and as he repeated the story gleaned from Barthomieu's manuscript she obsessively twirled strands of hair over and over, tightly enough to make her finger blanch. It was a nervous habit he'd forgotten until just now. During their final night together she'd done it a lot.

He wasn't sure if it was his presence that was causing her stress or Barthomieu's story. Either way, when he was done and they had both made eager comments about the work that lay ahead, he told her to take it easy and get a good night's rest.

From her quizzical expression, he suspected his tone carried more admonishment than advice.

★   ★   ★

The second day of the excavation quickly unspooled and knotted up like a tangled fishing line.

Zvi Alon was a no-show for breakfast. His car was found parked above the cliffs. The cave gate was locked and undisturbed. Jeremy anxiously came forward to tell Luc about Alon's request for the key the night before, to which Luc angrily denied he'd granted the man permission.

In a panic, the team began searching the undercliffs and found nothing at all. Then Luc made a command decision and ordered the morning shift to begin work inside the cave while he contacted the authorities.

Given the profile of the Ruac excavation a lieutenant, named Billeter from the local

145

gendarmerie, personally responded to the call. When he ascertained the matter to be complex, he summoned his superior officer from the Group Gendarmerie of the Dordogne in Périgueux, Colonel Toucas, and mobilised a police boat from Les Eyzies to motor up the Vézère.

By mid-morning, Luc was radioed in the cave and informed that Toucas had arrived. The colonel was a rather loutish-looking man, slightly overweight, bald, with big facial features and dangling, creased ear lobes. His moustache was clipped too short for the wide expanse between his nose and upper lip, leaving a naked line of skin, and like many men with a paltry head of hair, he compensated with a goatee. But he had an incongruously smooth, elegant voice and a rather cultured Parisian accent. Luc would have had more confidence in him if they'd been speaking over the telephone.

They met at Alon's rental car. The two had only begun to talk when the young Lieutenant trotted over and excitedly informed them that a body had been found near the river bank.

Luc would not make it back to the cave that day.

His first duty was to take a boat to identify the corpse. The task left him queasy and shaken. Alon was bloodied and broken. A sheared-off tree branch had gruesomely impaled his lower abdomen. The stuttering fall had bashed his face and twisted his arms and legs into bizarre angles like the limbs of the old juniper tree high on the ledge. Even though it was cool and dry, insects

146

had already staked their claim.

There were statements to be taken. Luc had to surrender his office to Toucas and his men to conduct their interviews. Late in the afternoon it was Jeremy who was the last to be questioned and he emerged from the Portakabin as drained of blood as Alon's remains. Pierre was waiting for him. He goodheartedly swung his long arm around Jeremy's shoulder and took him away for a drink.

The mood around the camp was grim. After dinner Luc felt compelled to address the group. Toucas had informed him that pending an autopsy, it seemed probable that Alon had slipped while attempting to climb down in the dark; there was no reason to suspect otherwise. There was a straight line from the ladder to the body's resting place. The trauma he suffered was consistent with a great fall. Luc passed the assessment along to the sombre group.

After reflecting on Professor Alon's contributions to their field he led a minute of silence and concluded by beseeching everyone to accept that access to the cave beyond protocol-defined hours was strictly prohibited and that he alone would control the keys. One would remain on his keychain, the duplicate would be locked in his desk.

Luc hardly ate. Hugo took him back to his caravan, fed him a liquid diet of bourbon and played New Orleans jazz on his battery-operated MP3 player until Luc eventually fell asleep in his clothes. At that, Hugo switched off the music and listened to a hooting owl until he too drifted off to sleep.

★   ★   ★

Despite the tragedy, work at Ruac continued. Alon would have to be replaced but that hole in the team would not be filled until the next season. They forged ahead with the plan for the first campaign. The focus of the initial excavations would be two chambers: the cave floor at the entrance chamber, or Chamber 1, its official designation, and the Chamber of Plants, Chamber 10.

Space was tight within Chamber 10 and Luc restricted access to only a few people at a time. That core group included Sara, Pierre, Craig Morrison, the lithics expert from Glasgow and Carlos Ferrer, their authority on microfauna, the diminutive bones of small mammals, reptiles and amphibians. Luc felt he was making a devil-may-care statement by teaming Sara with the Spaniard, but his gut fluttered every time he saw them working next to one another, their bodies almost touching. Fortunately Desnoyers had been correct. The bat population started thinning almost immediately. There were a few stubborn hold-outs flapping around the rear chambers but the team was greatly relieved the ceiling had ceased moving.

Sara was concentrating on a one-by-one-metre square of earth bordering the south-west wall of Chamber 10 where Luc had discovered the flint blade. The upper layers were encrusted with modern guano, complicating her work since bat droppings were rich in the pollen she was seeking. Her goal for the first season was to find

148

a guano-free layer and make a preliminary assessment of the types and frequency of pollen and spores. In an ordinary dig her remit as paleobotanist would have been to assess the flora and climate during the period of study. The paintings in the tenth chamber were a constant reminder that Ruac was far from ordinary.

About ten centimetres from the surface the earth turned from black to tan and the guano petered out. The transition zone was at the level where the bottom of Luc's upright blade had rested before its removal.

The Chamber 10 group stood and watched as Pierre cheerfully scraped away the last of the black earth from the square metre. After a series of photos, they decided to go deeper.

Before proceeding, they changed into fresh suits, boots and masks and swapped out all their trowels, brushes and spatulas to avoid contaminating older levels with younger pollen. Sara climbed into the square to do the honours and began trowelling a section for sample collection. She had barely begun when she said 'Oh wow!' and stopped working.

Ferrer was bending over her back and started yammering in his hyper way, 'Look, look, look!'

'Is that flint?' Pierre asked.

Morrison asked to step in and switch places with Sara. The six-and-a-half foot white-haired Scot folded himself into a crouch and whipped out his specimen brush. The object was smooth and yellowish but it was not stone. 'Not my shop, I'm afraid,' he said. 'Looks like bone. All yours, Carlos.'

Ferrer brushed away some more dirt and picked around the object with a dental tool. 'No, no, it's not bone. More champagne tonight. It's ivory!'

After they'd carefully exposed the entire object, leaving it in place for photography, Pierre ran to fetch Luc who was working at the furthest point in Chamber 1.

'What are you so excited about?' Luc asked him.

Even though he was wearing his mask, Luc could tell by the crinkling around his eyes that Pierre had a huge, childlike smile on his face. 'I'm in love, boss.'

'With whom?'

'It's not a whom, it's a what.' Pierre was having fun with him.

'All right, with what?'

'The prettiest little ivory creature you've ever seen.'

When he got to Chamber 10, Luc gushed. 'Well done! It's a beautiful thing. It completes the picture. Now we can say that Ruac has everything, even portable art. I wish Zvi had seen it. It looks Aurignacian, just like our blade.'

It was a carved ivory bison about two centimetres in length, as polished and smooth as a river pebble. The animal could have been stood upright on its flat-bottomed feet. Its thick neck was holding its head high and proud. Both small carved horns were intact. The right eye hole was visible and its flank was inscribed by parallel lines, an attempt at depicting fur.

Sara said, 'When we've got it plotted and

150

photographed, I'll take my first pollen sample right under it.'

'How long until you know something?' Luc asked.

'I'll start when I get back to the lab this afternoon. Tonight, hopefully, for something preliminary.'

'Then it's a date. I'll see you in the lab tonight.' He thought he heard Ferrer snort at him from under his mask but he couldn't be certain.

The snort mutated into a shout of sorts and a rat-a-tat of Spanish. Sara called Luc back. Ferrer's bone-finding eyes had spotted something all of them had missed. A few centimetres away from the ivory statuette was a speck of brown and Ferrer was on his hands and knees with a dental pick. 'Jesus,' he moaned. 'I think we were kneeling on it.'

'What is it?' Luc demanded.

'Wait, wait, let me work.'

It was a small thing, not tiny in the realm of the micro-fauna that Ferrer was accustomed to handling, but quite small, about half a centimetre in length, less than a quarter centimetre in width. Because of its size it didn't take him long to expose the bone.

'So?' Luc asked, hovering over the square like an expectant father.

'You're going to have to get some better champagne, my friend. It's a fingertip, a distal phalanx.'

'What species?' Luc asked, holding his breath.

'It's human! An infant's fingertip! We struck gold!'

★ ★ ★

Sara collected her pollen samples and the rest of the team trowelled and picked away at the square of earth in search of more human bones. By quitting time they had come up empty but they'd already hit the jackpot. Human bones from the Upper Paleolithic were rare as hen's teeth. The find was the talk of the camp and Ferrer passed the little bone around in its plastic specimen box like the relic of a saint. None of them were expert enough in hominid infant bones to assign a definitive age, let alone a genus and species. Outside academics would have to be consulted.

At nine that evening, Luc came around to the Portakabin and found Sara working at the lab bench. Odile was with her doing accounts at Jeremy and Pierre's shared desk.

Odile had quickly found a niche for herself keeping the paperwork for the groceries and household supplies, pretty much the same job she did by day for her father. Her brother was spending less time at the camp, only an hour in the evenings, helping the chef chop vegetables and the like.

Sara and Odile were chatting in French and giggling like girls when Luc noisily entered, sagging the floor with his cowboy boots.

Odile piped down and quietly resumed her work. Sara let him know she was almost ready to examine specimens under the binocular micro-scope. She'd worked through dinner, wet-sieving the material and chemically preparing the samples with hydrofluoric acid to digest the silicate minerals.

He watched her slender fingers thin-prep the first glass slide, pipette a drop of glycerol and mount a cover slip.

She adjusted the light and started scanning under low power and declared with relief that it looked like 'good stuff'. Under higher power she moved the slide back and forth and exhaled deeply. He hadn't realised she'd been holding her breath. 'You can't make this up.'

'What is it?'

Her voice was raspy with excitement. 'There's the usual background of ferns and conifers but I see three abundant and very-unique populations of pollen. Have a look.'

He focused the microscope up and down to get his bearings. He was no expert but he could tell there were three predominant species of microscopic hollow spheres. One looked like hairy rugby balls, another like flat car tyres and the third like four-celled embryos.

'What are they?' he asked.

She looked over at Odile who was working away, oblivious. Odile didn't speak English but Sara signalled discretion with her eyes. 'Let's talk outside, okay?'

They excused themselves and walked towards the campfire which was pleasantly crackling and popping. 'Okay,' he insisted, 'what?'

'The pollen is from the three plants depicted in Chamber 10 *and* the manuscript: *Ribes rubrum*, the redcurrant bush that Barthomieu called goose-berries, *Convolvulus arvensis*, bindweed, or possession weed as Barthomieu called it, and *Hordeum spontaneum*, wild barley grass. The concentrations are staggering!'

Luc chimed in with what he thought might be her next words. 'This tells us that significant quantities of these three plants were carried into the cave! They *were* used for a purpose. We've never seen this kind of activity in the Upper Paleolithic!'

She was beaming. The orange glow of the fire lit half her face. He suddenly remembered how much he used to admire the sharpness of her jawline, the way it set off her long delicate neck. It wasn't the usual erogenous zone but it triggered something and he kissed her on the lips before she could react. He was holding her shoulders and at first he thought he felt the stirrings of a reciprocal kiss but instead there were hands on his chest pushing him away.

She wasn't smiling anymore. She scanned the camp for prying eyes. 'Luc, you and I had our moment. You chose to end it, I got over you, and that's that. I'm not going to do this again.'

He took a slow breath, tasting her lipstick. 'I apologise. I wasn't planning that. It's the excitement, you know, and maybe more, but you're right, we shouldn't go there. You and Carlos seem to have hit it off anyway.'

That made her laugh. 'You know how it is, Luc. The archaeology equivalent to a shipboard romance. Once you disembark, it's over.'

'I admit I know about this syndrome.'

She gave him a canny look and said she wanted to check more samples and write up her findings. As he watched her leave he cursed himself. He wasn't sure if he was angry because he'd kissed her or because he hadn't done more to explain himself, to try to make amends for past transgressions. Either way, he wasn't feeling so good about himself, but he was feeling pretty damned good about Ruac.

And there it was again, his old problem of work and women. No third leg to balance the stool. Maybe he needed a hobby, he thought, but he shook his head when he tried out the laughable image of Luc Simard swinging a golf club.

He'd go find Hugo and have a drink by the fire.

★ ★ ★

Despite Luc's stolen kiss, Sara kept her word and participated in Hugo's double date. For the occasion, Hugo pulled out all the stops and went for the spectacular hill-top setting of Domme, an ancient fortified town, its ramparts still intact. Before dinner at L'Esplanade, the best restaurant in the area, the four of them walked the ramparts and took in sweeping dusk views of the Dordogne River valley.

Odile was taking it all in like a tourist and asked a stranger to take a picture of them with her mobile phone. The wind was playing with her short, filmy dress, a summer frock even though it was a chilly autumn evening. She looked dark and sultry, like a latter-day matinée star. Hugo paid close attention to the wind gusts

155

and was rewarded with glances of her thighs and higher. But when he did, he noticed large blotches of black-and-blue, fresh bruises that looked painful and angry.

Luc was in a polite gentlemanly mode, engaging Sara in neutral thoughts about the remnants of the town's original thirteenth-century architecture. Later, when Hugo button-holed Luc to mention Odile's bruises, Luc shrugged and informed his friend that it was clearly not their business.

The dinner itself was lavish and Hugo splashed out for some expensive bottles. Everyone drank liberally, except Luc who gladly accepted the role of designated driver and the discipline that went along with it. After all, until the excavation ended in a week's time, he was Sara's boss, and bosses had a certain responsibility of behaviour.

Hugo had no such duty. He and Odile sat next to each other, watching the sunset from their valley-facing table. They ogled each other, made suggestive jokes and touched each other's arms whenever they laughed. Sara joined in the jollity as best she could, but Luc could sense an invisible barrier, a negative energy field of his own creation.

Hugo was telling a bad joke he'd heard him tell before and Luc's mind drifted instead to a crazy thought: if he could go back in time just once, where would he go? To that night with Sara at Les Eyzies two years ago or to Ruac thirty thousand years ago? The decision was tolled by the arrival of the entrées.

156

Odile didn't seem to be the kind of woman who liked to talk about herself but she responded perfectly well to a man like Hugo who placed himself at the centre of every anecdote and story. She laughed at his jokes and asked leading questions to nudge him along. Hugo was thoroughly enjoying himself and wanted a record of the evening so he snapped photos with his mobile phone and passed it across the table to Sara to take shots of him mugging with his date.

It was only when Hugo stopped talking long enough to chew his beef, that Sara could jump in with a question for Odile. 'So I'm curious. What's it like living in a small village?'

Odile squeezed her lips into an 'it is what it is' gesture and said, 'Well, it's all I know. I've been to Paris before so I know what's out there, but I don't even have a passport. I live in a cottage three doors away from the house I was born in — upstairs in my father's café. I'm growing in Ruac like one of your plants. If you pull me out by the roots, I'll probably die.'

Hugo finished swallowing in time to say, 'Maybe you need some fertiliser.'

Odile laughed and touched him again. 'There's enough manure in Ruac. Maybe just some water and sunlight.'

Sara wondered, 'It must be hard meeting new people in a tiny village.'

Odile wiggled the fingers of her left hand. 'See, no ring. You're right. That's why I wanted to work for you. Not to get married! To meet new people.'

'What's your impression so far,' Luc asked.

'You're all so smart! It's a stimulating environment.'

'For me, also,' Hugo said, refilling her wine glass with a smile that bordered on a leer.

★ ★ ★

On the drive back, Sara was quiet but the two tipsy ones in the back seat were chatting non-stop. In the rear-view mirror Luc spotted a kiss here, a grope there. When they got close to the abbey, he heard Hugo whispering, pleading to come over.

'No,' Odile whispered back.

'What about tomorrow?'

'No!'

'Why, do you live with someone?'

'No.'

'Oh, come on.'

'I'm old-fashioned. Date me some more.'

★ ★ ★

Hugo sat on his bunk, watching Luc strip down to his briefs then brush his teeth.

Hugo remained dressed. 'Aren't you going to bed?' Luc asked.

'I've got to see her,' Hugo moaned.

'Oh for God's sake!'

'Did you see those legs?'

'This is like university redux. You used to go on like this all the time.'

'So did you.'

'I outgrew it.'

158

'Did you?'

Hugo got up and fumbled around for his car keys.

'Look, you had a lot to drink,' Luc admonished.

'I'm okay. I'll go slow and I'll keep my window open. Fresh air's my friend. Are you my friend?' His speech was too slurred for comfort.

'Yes, Hugo, I'm your friend. I should drive you.'

'No, believe me, I'm fine. You've got a dig to run.'

They went back and forth a few times until Luc finally acquiesced and said, 'Be careful.'

'I will. Don't wait up for me.'

★ ★ ★

By the time Hugo got to the village he was sober enough to question his own sanity. All he knew was she lived 'three doors down' from the café. But which direction and on what side of the street?

If this was going to be an exercise in chance involving knocking on doors, the probability of looking like a fool was fairly high. Sorry to wake you, Madame, do you know where the mayor's daughter lives? I'm here to screw her.

The main street was empty, not a soul in sight, not surprising since it was almost midnight. He slowly drove towards the café, counting doors. Three doors down on the same side, the cottage was dark. There was a large motorcycle by the door. Scratch that one, he thought. Probably.

159

He counted off three doors on the other side of the café. That cottage had lights burning on both floors. He stopped to have a better look. What was it she'd said about having an orchard? She'd made the comment at the peak of his inebriation, before dessert. And what kind of orchard — apple, cherry, pear? At this time of year without fruit how would he know? With his assemblage of city skills, he could hardly tell a bush from a tree. He parked on the side of the road and crept along the side of the cottage to get a look at the back garden. The moon was his friend. It was full and provided enough light to see at least a dozen trees laid out in rows.

It certainly looked like an orchard and that gave him hope.

The door was blue, the small cottage lemony sandstone. He knocked lightly and waited.

Then he knocked harder.

The curtains were drawn on the ground-floor windows. One set of curtains in the sitting room was parted just enough to see inside but there was no sign of her or anyone else.

He took a few steps back to look at the upstairs bedroom window. The curtains were back-lit. He picked a few small pebbles from the flower bed and tossed them against the window like a teenage boy trying not to wake the parents.

Again, nothing.

The rational thing to do was get back in his car and drive off; he wasn't even positive this was the right house. But a wave of Parisian temerity swept him back to the door. He tried the knob.

It turned fully and the door unlatched.

160

'Hello?' he called out hopefully. 'Odile? It's Hugo!'

He entered and looked around. The sitting room was neat and pretty, like you'd expect from a single woman.

'Hello?' he called again.

He glanced into the kitchen. It was small and immaculate, no dishes in the sink. He was about to go in for a better look when he noticed mail on the hall table, an electricity bill on top. Odile Bonnet. He felt better.

'Hello, Odile?'

He stood at the base of the stairs and hesitated. Only rapists ascended to a woman's bedroom unannounced and uninvited.

'It's me, Hugo! Are you there?'

There were muffled bars of music. He was sure of it. He followed the sound to the kitchen.

Then he saw it right away, over the kitchen table, big as life.

'Jesus Christ!' he gasped, splaying his arms involuntarily. 'Jesus Christ!'

He looked around to make sure he was still alone and yanked out his mobile phone to hastily shoot a picture.

The music was louder. He thought he ought to turn around and leave, look at the snapshot in the morning and think things through with the sober light of day, but against his better judgement he followed the melody.

There was a door by the pantry. When he opened it, there were stairs leading to a cellar. The music was louder still, guitars, an accordion, a thumping drum — musette music, not his

161

favourite. There was a naked dirty bulb lighting the stairway.

He walked halfway down when the light went off and he was in darkness.

'Odile?'

14

Luc went to breakfast grinning. Hugo's bunk was undisturbed. The scoundrel had clearly succeeded and undoubtedly would soon be peppering him with tales of conquest.

After Luc dispatched the first shift to the cave he embarked with Sara on an old-fashioned field trip, complete with specimen bags and notebooks. In the damp mist of early morning, they started from behind the abbey walls and hiked through a saturated pasture in the direction of the river.

Jeremy and Pierre were by the Portakabin and saw them taking off. 'Where do you think they're going?' Jeremy asked.

'Haven't got a clue,' Pierre answered with a wink. 'The boss looks happy though.'

They walked in silence, inhaling the fertility of the countryside. It had rained hard for an hour or more the previous night and their wellington boots were soon shiny from the wet grass. The sun finally managed to eke out an appearance and when it did, the land began to sparkle brightly, sending both of them reaching for sunglasses.

They made their first find only a kilometre from the campsite. Sara noticed the border between the meadow they were traversing and the forest was speckled, a mixture of greens and yellows. She spotted tall yellow shoots towering above green grasses and started running for them. Luc kept pace with easy, long-legged lopes. The two of them left trails of trodden-down grass in their wake.

'Wild barley,' she said. '*Hordeum sponta-neum*, tons of it.'

To Luc, it looked like run-of-the-mill culti-vated barley but she snapped off a spiky head and showed him two rows of kernels rather than six-rowed cereal grain.

She had pruning shears and he had a pocket knife and the two of them methodically snipped and cut a large bagful of golden heads. 'This was probably the precursor of the domesticated species,' she happily explained while they worked. 'The transition to farmed grain would have happened during the Neolithic, but there's nothing to suppose that Mesolithic and even upper Paleolithic people wouldn't have foraged wild barley for food and even beer.'

'Or other purposes,' Luc added.

'Or other purposes,' she agreed. 'I think that's enough.' She stretched her back. 'One down, two to go.'

He carried the sack of barley and followed her as she plunged into the forest. The thin sunlight didn't warm the woodlands much and it became chillier the deeper they wandered.

She wasn't trying to avoid thickets and brambles; she was searching them out, which made for slow going. Luc trekked along, content to let his mind wander. She'd know what to watch out for; he knew what he wanted to watch — her hips, perfectly tight in khakis. And her shoulders were small and feminine even in that thick leather jacket. He tussled with a growing urge to grab her from behind, spin her and pull her against him. They'd kiss. She wouldn't resist this time. He'd ask for absolution. She was always the one, he'd say. He hadn't known it then but he knew it now. He'd pull her down. His sins would be washed away. The cool wetness of the forest floor would wash them away.

'We're looking for a creeping, tangled vine, climbing up small-to-medium-sized trees,' she said, breaking the spell. 'The leaves look like elongated arrow heads. It's late in the season so don't expect pink-and-white flowers but there could be some late-bloomers.'

There was a trickling sound and their boots began to slurp in mud. Luc wondered if the stream fed into one of Barthomieu's waterfalls. Along the stream bed there was a mixed population of mostly holm oak and beech along with a thick undergrowth of weeds and prickly acacia. His jeans caught on some thorns and when he bent to free himself he heard Latin spilling from her mouth, euphonious, as if she was beginning to sing a hymn, '*Convolvulus arvensis*! There!'

The flowerless bindweed had attacked saplings and juvenile trees just like she'd predicted. Its vines wound tightly around bark in a choking grip, spiralling high over their heads.

There was an abundance of the weed. The problem wasn't quantity but collection. The vines were wrapped so snugly it was impossible

165

to pull them away from the trunks. They were obliged to undertake an exercise that was painstaking and made their fingers ache — cutting and unwrapping, cutting and unwrapping — until they had a second bag filled with stems and leaves.

'Two down, one to go,' she declared.

She was leading again, he was following. The cliffs and the river were ahead. She doubled back towards the meadows. She had studied the topo maps and knew there was a disused train tracks nearby, a long-abandoned spur. Their last target favoured the kind of land that had once been tamed and was now fallow. They were seeking bushes. She was talking about them but he wasn't absorbing the botany lesson. He was aching inside and becoming angry with himself for who he'd become.

His father was a petrochemical executive, stereotypical of men of his generation, with his private clubs, his drinking, his narcissistic arrogance and his insistence on keeping young mistresses despite having a perfectly lovely wife. If it weren't for his fatal coronary, he'd still be at it, drinking and romancing, a pathetic septuagenarian Lothario.

Genes or environment — the eternal question. What accounted for Luc's emulation of his old man? He'd seen the effect his father's behaviour had on his mother. Fortunately, she'd been able to regain her dignity with a divorce, move back to the States and reclaim a life suspended for a quarter century as the brittle spouse of an oil company man, desiccating in the desert heat within the walled confines and country clubs of Doha and Abu Dhabi, pining for her only child who was sent away to Swiss schools.

His mother married again, this time to a wealthy dermatologist in Boston, a man with a mild manner and a soft body. Luc tolerated him but had no affection.

Suddenly, the blindingly obvious question flooded his mind. Why had he driven Sara away? Hadn't it been the most complete relationship of his life? The most satisfying?

And why had he never asked himself why?

The old train tracks ran parallel to the river and were now overgrown. Sara pointed in the direction of a flat linear strip at the edge of a field and made a beeline towards it. Luc quietly trudged along, his thoughts percolating like hot coffee grounds.

The tracks were visible only when they stood directly over them. Sara, with the intensity of a blood hound, sensed that north was a better direction than south. They followed the tracks, adjusting their steps to land on the sleepers. On the river-side of the tracks was a wild hedgerow of hawthorn and Sara told Luc this was as good an environment as any to find what they were looking for.

The clouds blew off and the sun stayed out. Half an hour later they were still walking the rails and Luc began to fret about the excavation. His mobile phone had zero bars and he didn't like being out of touch. They were about to pack it in and reverse direction when she began jumping like a little girl and spouting Latin again, '*Ribes rubrum, Ribes rubrum!*'

The cluster of shrubs growing out of the hedgerow had pale-green five-lobed leaves and, as she explained, the persistence of berries so late in the season was the result of the longish summer and the temperatures which had been mild until recently.

The berries glistened in the sunshine like ruby-coloured pearls. She tasted one and closed her eyes in pleasure. 'Tart, but lovely,' she exclaimed. Luc playfully opened his mouth and she grudgingly obliged him by popping a berry between his lips.

'Needs sugar,' he said, and the two of them began to pick berries until a litre-sized plastic bag was full and their fingertips were stained red.

★ ★ ★

They kicked the cook out of the kitchen hut and commandeered chopping boards, utensils and his largest stewing pot. Emulating the sketchy description in the manuscript, they chopped the vines and grasses like salad greens, mashed them with a make-shift mortar and pestle — a wooden salad bowl and meat pounder — and set them on a boil with added water and crushed redcurrants. The kitchen took on a unique steamy smell of fruit and botanicals and they both stood over the pot, hands on hip, watching the concoction bubble.

'How long do you think?' Luc asked.

'I don't think we should overcook it. It should be more like making tea. That's generally the

168

correct ethno-botanical approach,' Sara said. Then she laughed and added, 'Actually, I've got no idea. This is so crazy, don't you think?'

'Too crazy to talk about it publicly, that's for sure,' he said. 'This is strictly between you and me. How are we going to send it to Cambridge?'

She had a Thermos flask in her caravan, her personal one, a nice stainless steel and glass model used for real tea. After stirring the pot one more time, she turned the gas down a bit and went to retrieve it.

Before she returned, Abbot Menaud came flopping in on his sandals, a little too flushed for a cool day.

'There you are, Luc. I was looking for you. I even rang your mobile phone.'

Luc fished it from his pocket. There were several missed calls. 'Sorry, there wasn't any reception where I was. How can I help you?'

The abbot was momentarily distracted by the peculiar sweet smells in the hut. 'What is that?' he asked, pointing at the stove.

Luc hated to be evasive with a man who had shown so much generosity but he ducked the question anyway. 'Professor Mallory is just cooking something. I'm watching the pot.'

The abbot resisted the urge to sample whatever was simmering as he habitually did in his own kitchen. The reason for seeking out Luc came back to him. There had been a flurry of calls to the abbey, from the young head of the local gendarmerie, Lieutenant Billeter. He had left his number several times and was growing insistent.

169

Luc thanked him and wondered out loud if there had been some development in the investigation of Zvi's accident. When Sara almost bumped into the abbot in the doorway they separated like pole-matching magnets. The old monk glanced at her thermos and muttered as he fled that her dish smelled lovely and that he'd like to try it one day. She held her tongue and Luc sealed the moment with a wink.

Luc returned the lieutenant's call while Sara began straining the hot concoction into a clean bowl.

He expected to hear Zvi's name mentioned in the first sentence, but instead the officer startled him by asking him something unexpected. 'Do you know a man named Hugo Pineau?'

★ ★ ★

There was one steep downhill curve on the road leading from the abbey into the village of Ruac. It wasn't considered a particularly dangerous stretch but sprinkle together a dark night, a downpour, excessive speed and perhaps some wine and one could imagine the result.

The point of impact was a good ten metres off the road, hidden to passing vehicles. It was as if the forest had parted to receive the car then closed itself up after the crash. Just after nine in the morning, a sharp-eyed motorcyclist had spotted some broken branches and found it.

Car and tree were fused into a knot of wood and metal, a broken, caved-in, twisted mass. The force of the impact was enough to lodge the tree trunk well into the passenger compartment, displacing the engine from its mounts. The front tyres were somewhere else entirely. The windshield glass was gone as if vaporised. Although there was a strong smell of petrol, there hadn't been a fire, not that it would have mattered to the driver.

An SPV pumper was hosing the road down to wash away an oil run-off which was trickling downhill. Two gendarmes were keeping the road open to an alternating trickle of north and south-bound traffic.

Lieutenant Billeter and Luc spent a time sombrely talking inside the lieutenant's car. Luc followed the officer to the scene with the shuffling steps of a man going to the gallows. Before he got there, Pierre pulled up in his car and Sara jumped out. After the phone call she had finished in the kitchen, frantically completing the job. Until she arrived, all she had heard was that Hugo had been in an accident.

She saw his eyes and they told the full story. 'Luc, I'm so sorry.'

The sight of his tears set her off and both of them were sobbing when they stepped from the pavement onto the wet verge.

As an archaeologist, Luc routinely handled human remains. There was something clean, almost antiseptic about skeletons; without the unpleasantness of tissue and blood, one could be ultra-scientific and dispassionate. It took a seeker's effort to find emotion in skeletal remains.

Yet, in the compressed span of days, Luc

confronted fresh death not once but twice and he was ill prepared to deal with it, especially this time.

Hugo was badly mangled. How badly, Luc wouldn't know for sure, because he turned his head after a second. That was long enough for him to peer into the driver's side window and identify Hugo's stylish olive jacket and his wiry hair, neatly trimmed and sculpted around a bloody left ear.

From the other side of the wreck, Luc suddenly saw a man looking into the passenger-side window. It was an older face with dark penetrating eyes, the neatly dressed man he had encountered weeks before in the Ruac café.

Luc and the man raised themselves simultaneously and stared at each other over the dented top of the car.

'Ah, it's Dr Pelay,' Billeter said. 'Do you know him, professor? He's the doctor in Ruac. He was kind enough to come out and pronounce the victim.'

'Death was instantaneous,' Pelay told Luc, curtly. 'A clean break of the neck, C1/C2. Not survivable.'

Pelay's face and voice set Luc off. They were hard as rocks without a touch of compassion. Luc wanted Hugo to be attended by someone with a good bedside manner, even in death.

When he straightened fully and attempted to walk away, gravity overtook him. The officer and Sara simultaneously gave support and leaned him up against a gendarmerie van for balance.

'We reached his secretary. She told us he was

staying with you,' Billeter said, searching for something neutral to say.

'He was supposed to go home tomorrow,' Luc said, wiping his nose on his sleeve.

'When did you see him last?'

'About eleven-thirty last night, at the camp site.'

'He left the abbey then?'

Luc nodded.

'Why?'

'To visit a woman at Ruac.'

'Who?'

'Odile Bonnet. We had dinner last night, the four of us,' he said, pointing to Sara. 'He insisted on seeing her.'

'Did she know he was coming?'

'He didn't have her number. I don't think he even had her address. But Hugo was, you know, motivated.'

'He didn't make it to the village. If he left your camp at eleven-thirty, the accident must have happened no later than eleven-forty,' the officer said flatly. 'By the looks of it he was going pretty fast. He didn't brake. There aren't any skid marks. He flew into the trees until he was stopped by a large one. So tell me, Professor Simard, was he drinking last night?'

Luc looked pitiful. He didn't care about absolving himself from the guilt he felt. But before he answered, Sara jumped in protectively. 'All of us except Luc had some wine with dinner. Luc drove back from Domme. By the time we got back I think all of us were sober.'

'Look,' Billeter said, 'the coroner already took

173

samples from the body. We'll know how much he had soon enough.'

'I shouldn't have let him go on his own,' Luc choked. 'I should have driven him.'

The officer had his answer and left them alone.

Sara didn't seem to know what to do or what to say. Tentatively, she put the palm of her hand against Luc's shoulder and he let her keep it there.

Another car arrived, this one from the direction of the village. A couple leaped out, Odile and her brother. She looked at Luc and Sara and started to run towards the crash but one of Billeter's men stopped her and had a word.

She began to scream.

Sara told Luc she should go to her but before she could, one of the firemen strode from behind the pumper and grabbed Odile by the arm. It was her father, the mayor, decked out in his SPV uniform.

Bonnet pulled his daughter away and Sara did the same with Luc, tugging him in the direction of his car. 'Come on,' she said. 'You don't need to be here.'

$\star$ $\star$ $\star$

The afternoon light streamed thin through Luc's caravan windows. Stretched on his bunk, he was more in darkness than light. Sara sat next to him on a pulled-up chair, sharing Hugo's last bottle of bourbon.

174

Luc's tongue was thick and lazy with booze. He pulled his hands from behind his neck and cracked his knuckles. 'Do you have many friends?' he asked.

'What kind of friends?'

'Same-sex friends. In your case, girlfriends.'

She laughed at his overexplanation. 'Yes, quite a few.'

'I don't have same-sex friends,' he said sadly. 'I think Hugo was it for me on that score. Why do you think that is? I mean, you know me.'

'I used to know you.' She had been drinking a bit, enough to be convivial.

'No, no, you still know me,' he stubbornly insisted.

'I think you spend too much time on female friends and your work to have male friends. That's what I think.'

He turned on his side to face her with a revelatory expression. 'I think you're right! Women and work, work and women. It's not healthy. A stool needs three legs, no?' He began to flounder. 'I think Hugo was going to be my third leg. We were reconnecting, really getting on, and now, he's gone. The bastard drove into a tree.' He reached for her with two arms.

'No, Luc,' she said, collecting herself and getting up. 'Your instincts have gone haywire. You need emotional support right now, not physical love.'

'No, I — '

She was already halfway out the door. 'I'm going to get the chef to bring you something to eat and then I'm going to pack up the thermos to make the afternoon express parcel run. I want it to get to Cambridge by tomorrow afternoon. They're expecting it at PlantaGenetics.'

'Are you coming back?' He was pathetic now, like a child.

'When you're asleep!' she said soothingly. 'Shut your eyes and drift off. And yes, I'll come back to check on you. Just to check on you.'

When she was gone he stood up on shaky legs to splash some water on his face from the sink.

He stood over Hugo's empty bunk and began to shake with the helpless rage he'd been suppressing all day. He closed his eyes and saw orange. Violence was needed, some sort of violence. That's what his brain was telling him, so he punched the partition between his sleeping area and sitting area hard enough to seriously crater the particle board. He winced from the pain he'd inflicted on himself and saw blood on the wall. His fourth knuckle had a good deep cut. He wrapped it in a bandanna and sat back on his bed bleeding into the cloth and drinking more bourbon.

Sara protected him that night with a fierce, almost maternal instinct. She discovered his wound, saw the fist-shaped depression in the wall, clucked at him and dressed it. He was not to be disturbed. People could sort out their excavation issues on their own for one day, she insisted, and she posted a note on his caravan door to make sure he'd be left alone.

She stopped back later in the afternoon and wished she'd thought to take the bourbon bottle with her. It was empty, his tray of food was uneaten and he was snoring. She wiggled his boots off and threw the cover over his clothed body.

Later, when it was dark, she came back again. He had hardly moved. She decided to do her evening's work at his desk to keep an eye on him. She kept vigil until quite late, reading her notes and typing on her laptop as the camp ground grew quiet and still.

⋆　⋆　⋆

A beam of light stretched across the darkness of the Portakabin. Luc's desk was in the corner, furthest from the door. The light moved up and down over the desk drawers and settled on the lowest one.

The side drawers couldn't be opened until the centre drawer was unlocked. There was a coffee mug on the desk crammed with pencils and pens. They were removed and the mug was tipped upside down. A small key dropped out.

The key unlocked the centre drawer and when it was opened, the side drawer slid open too. Inside were hanging files, in alphabetical order, covering a myriad of administrative issues.

A hand went straight for the Ds and a hand parted the file labelled DIVERS, for miscellaneous items. Among papers was an unmarked envelope, closed, not sealed.

Inside the envelope was the duplicate key to the titanium gate which sealed and protected Ruac Cave.

15

Ruac Abbey, 1118

Bernard strode back and forth inside his stone house, trying to outpace the black cloud hanging over his head. He couldn't remember when he had been more troubled. The events of the previous evening had shaken him so deeply he felt he might go mad.

The only remedy was prayer and fasting, he was sure of that. He had already vigorously prayed in the church three times at Lauds, Prime and Terce, and in between prayer sessions he had marched straight back to his house and fallen on his knees for bouts of more personal prayer. He had avoided the others. He wanted to be alone.

He thought to ignore the knock on his door but his sense of comity would not abide that. It was his brother, Barthomieu, bowing his head. 'Can we speak?'

'Yes, come in. Sit.'

'You did not have food this morning.'

'I am fasting.'

'We noticed your absence at breakfast and your demeanour in the chapel. There is anger on your face.'

'I am most vexed. Are you not?

Barthomieu lifted his head to look at him squarely. 'I am reflective. I am amazed. I am quizzical, but no, I am not vexed.'

Bernard raised his voice. He could not remember the last time he had shouted. 'I believe you should be vexed! Last night you were powerfully turbulent. Do you not remember?'

'I do remember,' he chuckled. His knuckles were raw. 'I hope it wasn't you I struck, brother! Most unlike me, but it passed.'

'You tried to strike Jean, for God's sake, but you hit a cooking pot instead!'

'Well,' Barthomieu mused, 'the good far outweighed the evil in my humble opinion.'

There was another knock on the door.

'Good Lord, can I not be left in peace?' Bernard exclaimed.

Jean and Abélard were both at the door, and the little stone house became crowded.

'I was concerned about you,' Abélard said.

'We should all be concerned for our souls,' Bernard answered acidly. 'The Devil visited evil upon us last night. Do you have any doubt of this?'

'I have thought of nothing else and I am certain all of us will brood in contemplation. But the Devil?'

'Who else?'

'God, perhaps.'

Bernard threw his arms about so wildly it seemed he was trying to cast them from his body. 'God was not with us last night! God does not want his children to suffer such things.'

'Well, I did not suffer,' Jean insisted. 'Quite the opposite. I found the experience . . . enlightening.'

'I confess, I did not suffer either, brother,' Barthomieu said.

'Nor I,' Abélard concurred. 'Perhaps there were a few moments that might be construed as troubling, but on the whole I would say it was amazing.'

'Did we, I wonder, have the self-same experience?' Bernard cried. 'Tell me what happened to you and I will tell you the same.'

★ ★ ★

Bernard always relied on prayer to firm his actions. He had done so when he had first decided to leave his comfortable life and commit himself to the Cistercians at Clairvaux and he relied on it again.

Following an afternoon of exhausting and contentious debate, Bernard ardently threw himself into Vespers prayers and in the echoing sing-song in the vaulted stone church he found his answer in Psalm 139.

Eripe me, Dómine, ab hómine malo;
a viro iníquo éripe me;
Qui cogitavérunt iniquitátes in corde,
tota die constituébant praelia.
Acuérunt linguas suas sicut serpéntis;
venénum áspidum sub lábiis eórum.

Deliver me, O Lord, from the evil man;
and preserve me from the wicked man;
Who have imagined mischief in their hearts,
and have stirred up strife all the day long.

They have sharpened their tongues like a serpent;
adder's poison is under their lips.

Custódi me, Dómine, de manu peccatóris;
et ab homínibus iníquis éripe me.
Qui cogitavérunt supplantáre gressus meos:
abscondérunt supérbi láqueum mihi.
Et funes extendérunt in láqueum;
juxta iter scándalum posuérunt mihi.

Keep me, O Lord, from the hands of the ungodly;
preserve me from wicked men.
Who are purposed to overthrow my goings:
the proud have laid a snare for me.
And they have spread a net abroad with cords;
yea, and have laid for me a stumbling block by the wayside.

Every time the words *wicked, evil* and *ungodly* fell from his lips he glanced at Abélard, Jean and yes, even his own brother, all huddled like conspirators on an adjacent pew, because he could not reconcile their views with his.

And with the same certainty that told him that Christ was his saviour, he knew that he was right and they were wrong.

He also knew he had to leave Ruac, because they had made their intentions known. They fully intended to partake again of the infusion which they lauded and he reckoned was a devil brew.

★   ★   ★

The following morning, he was off. For his safety and companionship, Barthomieu had persuaded him to have two younger monks accompany him on the long journey back to Clairvaux. One was Michel, Jean's infirmary assistant, who had noticed residual tea and had been pestering his master with questions. Better to send him away for a while to cure his curiosity.

Bernard and Barthomieu hugged, though Barthomieu's grip was the tighter.

'You will not reconsider?' Barthomieu asked.

'Will you reconsider taking that wicked brew again?' Bernard countered.

'I will not,' Barthomieu said emphatically. 'I believe it is a gift. From God.'

'I will not repeat my arguments, brother. Suffice it to say, I will take my leave and may God have mercy upon your soul.'

He kicked the flanks of the brown mare with his heels and slowly departed.

Abélard was waiting by the abbey gate. He called up to the rider. 'I will miss you, Bernard.'

Bernard looked down and deigned to reply. 'I confess I will miss you too, at least the Abélard I knew, not the Abélard I saw two nights ago.'

'Judge me not harshly, brother. There is but one road to righteousness, but many paths converge on that road.'

Bernard shook his head sadly and rode off.

⋆ ⋆ ⋆

That night, three men met in Bernard's now-empty house, lit some candles and talked

182

about their departed friend. Was it possible, Barthomieu asked, that Bernard was right and they were wrong?

Barthomieu was a man of simple vocabulary. Jean was more skilful as a healer and herbalist than an ecclesiastical scholar. It fell on Abélard to frame the debate. They listened to his elegant dissertation on good versus evil, God versus Satan, right versus wrong, and concluded that it was Bernard who was hide-bound and unseeing, not them.

Having satisfied themselves of their rectitude, Jean produced a crockery jug, pulled out the stopper and poured each participant a generous mug of reddish tea.

★ ★ ★

Abélard was alone in his room.

A single candle burned on his table, casting just enough light to write on parchment. For a week, a letter to his beloved had lain begun but unfinished. He reread the opening:

My dearest Héloïse,
I have passed these many days and nights alone in my cloister without closing my eyes. My love burns fiercer amidst the happy indifference of those who surround me, and my heart is alike pierced with your sorrows and my own. Oh, what a loss have I sustained when I consider your constancy! What pleasures have I missed enjoying! I ought not to confess this weakness to you; I

am sensible *I commit a fault. If I could show more firmness of mind I might provoke your resentment against me and your anger might work that effect in you which your virtue could not. If in the world I published my weakness in love songs and verses, ought not the dark cells of this house at least to conceal that same weakness under an appearance of piety? Alas! I am still the same!*

He dipped his quill and began a new paragraph.

Some days have passed since I wrote these words. Much has changed in a short time, though not my love for you which burns ever brighter. God has chosen to bestow a gift upon me which I can scarcely believe, yet its truth is manifest. Oh, though I fear writing these words lest their power should fade by the act of committing them to the page, I believe, dear Héloïse, that I have found a way for the two of us to be together again as man and wife.

16

The last day of work at Ruac Cave came and went.

That final night, there was a celebratory dinner of sorts, though spirits were tamped down by the twin catastrophes that had befallen the excavation, a pair of accidents that sent tongues wagging about curses, ill fate and the like.

After Hugo's funeral in Paris, Luc had returned to Ruac and thrown himself into his work like a whirling dervish, toiling himself into a state of anaesthesia, sleeping only enough to keep going. He became flat and detached, spoke only when spoken to, maintained a professional efficiency with his team but that was the extent of it. Hugo's death had washed away his usual witty charm like waves washed away letters etched on a sandy beach with a stick.

Matters were made worse by the unannounced appearance at Ruac by Marc Abenheim who parachuted in from Paris, hell-bent on exploiting the tragedy. The weedy martinet arrived and demanded everyone leave the Portakabin so he could speak with Luc privately. Then, like an actuary, he challenged Luc on the odds of one excavation having two fatalities in one season.

'What are you driving at?' Luc had spat back.

Abenheim's voice had an infuriating nasal

tone. 'Lack of discipline. Lack of management. Lack of good sense for inviting your friend to stay at an official Ministry dig. That's what I'm driving at.'

It was nothing short of a miraculous act of self-restraint that Luc was able to send Abenheim on his way without a broken nose.

When the officious prat drove off, Luc started fuming openly. He'd kept a damper on his anger during Abenheim's visit but now that he was gone he retreated to his caravan and slammed the door. The first thing that caught his attention was the dent in the wall he'd left the night after Hugo died.

He had a strong urge to punch it again, finish it off by putting his fist right through the blood-stained wall but when he curled his fingers he remembered this was a terrible idea. His cut knuckle had become infected, turned beefy and swollen, and there were red streaks creeping up the back of his hand. He didn't have the time or inclination to find a doctor. One of the students had a bottle of erythromycin left over from a chest infection and Luc had started popping them a few days earlier. He unclenched his aching fist and kicked a chair instead.

As to Sara, if Luc had harboured any designs on restarting something with her, he had suppressed them, forgotten them, or maybe he never had them at all. He couldn't remember.

She gave him space and didn't compel him to deal with his loss. The more he withdrew, the more she rallied, scurrying around the edges of his life, fretting with Jeremy and Pierre about his health and well-being. She knew a little bit about clinical depression.

He'd given her a case once.

The autumn night was cold, drawing people to the fire much the same way that their prehistoric forebears would have gathered. Luc felt he had to address the group one last time, though he didn't have the appetite for much of a speech.

He thanked them for their tireless work and rattled through a list of their accomplishments. They had accurately mapped the entire complex from the first chamber to the tenth chamber. They had photographed every inch of the complex. They had a first radiocarbon date back from the charcoal outline of one of the bison and it confirmed the suspicion that the cave dated to 30,000 BP. They had begun to understand the geological forces that had shaped the formation of the cave. They had comprehensively excavated the floors of Chamber 1 and Chamber 10. In Chamber 1 they had found evidence of a fire pit and an abundance of reindeer bones and signs of a long occupation of the cave mouth. In Chamber 10 they found more Aurignacian blades and flakes, that lovely ivory bear and phenomenally, the fingertip of a human infant. Although it was the only human bone they had unearthed, it was still a miracle find that would be analysed intensively in the weeks to come. Sara Mallory also had a wealth of pollen samples to analyse over the winter. He said nothing of their plant-gathering and kitchen experiments. No one else needed to know about that bit of fringe work for now.

He concluded by reminding everyone that this was just the beginning, not the end. The funding had already come through for three additional seasons and they would meet again in the spring to compare notes they had made during the off-season. He reckoned they'd still be coming to Ruac Cave when they were old and grey, to which Craig Morrison interjected in his Scottish brogue that some of them were already old and grey, thank you very much!

Then Luc raised his glass to the memory of Zvi Alon and Hugh Pineau and begged them all to take care on their journeys home.

The team drank and chatted into the night but Luc withdrew to his caravan. Sara was looking for an excuse to go to him. Checking her email, she found it.

'Hi,' she said gently, when he opened the door. 'Mind some company?'

'Sure, come in.'

The was only one small light on. He hadn't been reading, he hadn't been drinking. It looked like he'd just been sitting and staring.

'I've been really worried about you,' she said. 'We all are.'

'I'm okay.'

'No, I don't think you are. When you get back to Bordeaux, maybe you should see someone?'

'What, like a shrink? You're joking.'

'I'm not. You've been through a lot.'

He upped his volume. 'I said I'm fine!' But he saw her mouth was twitching so he continued, softer, 'Look, when I get back to the university and I get into my usual routine I'll be right as

188

rain, as the Brits say. Really I will. And thanks for caring.'

She let them both off the hook with her news. 'I got an email tonight from Fred Prentice, my contact at PlantaGenetics. They finished their analysis.'

'Yes?'

'It sounds like he's pretty excited but he didn't want to say anything by email — he said there were intellectual property issues and patent rights that needed to be sorted out. He wants us to come to Cambridge personally.'

'When?'

'He suggested Monday. Will you come with me?'

'I need to close up the dig.'

'Pierre and Jeremy and the others are quite capable. I think you should come. It'll do you good.'

Luc mustered a chuckle. 'If the choice is between a psychiatrist and a visit to the UK, I guess I'm in.'

★ ★ ★

Instead of sleeping, Luc broke his own rule and went to the cave for one last visit.

Director's prerogative, he told himself.

Climbing down the ladder in the dark, his miner's helmet illuminating the cliff wall, he had an unpleasant image of the moment Zvi slipped a rung and plunged to his death, but he shook it off and kept descending.

On the ledge, he put on his Tyvek suit in the

189

dark, unlocked the heavy gate and hit the switch. The halogen lights made the cave bright and harsh, so different from the way it would have looked in prehistory.

He slowly walked to the rear towards his favourite place, the tenth chamber. The bats had all but departed and the cave was truly quiet now.

At the furthest point, he stood face to face with the life-sized bird man in the field of wild barley. He had a candle. He lit it with a disposable lighter then killed the electric lights. Zvi Alon had wanted to do this, to experience the cave in this natural way. It was the right instinct.

In the faltering candle light, the barley seemed to wave. The bird man's beak seemed to move.

What was he saying?

Luc strained to hear.

What I wouldn't give, he thought, to be able to stand beside the man who painted these images, to watch him, to understand him, to speak to him.

He blew out the candle to spend some moments in the most complete darkness he had ever known.

17

Ruac Cave, 30,000 BP

The first spear glanced off the tough hide, angering the animal but doing it no harm.

The hunters circled.

The beast was a good-sized male. The fact they had been able to isolate it from the herd so easily, spoke, they believed, to its willingness to be sacrificed. The huge animal had certainly heard them chanting the previous night and had agreed to surrender itself to their purpose.

But it was too noble to go down without a fight.

Tal's only brother, Nago, moved in for the kill.

The bison was backed against the bank of the swiftly flowing river, its hooves sinking into the mud. Its nostrils flared and steamed. It would have to charge. It had no choice.

This is how men died, Tal thought.

He was seventeen, a grown man, already the tallest in his clan, which made his brother suspicious, because for generations, the head man of the Bison Clan was always the tallest. Their father was still head man, but his broken leg had never healed. It stank like rotten meat. At night he groaned in his sleep. There would be a new head man soon. Every clan member knew something was destined to happen to one of the brothers. The smaller Nago could not be their leader if the taller Tal lived. The younger Tal could not be the head if the older Nago lived.

It was not their way.

Nago made sure the butt end of his spear was flush against the bone spear-thrower.

A man could hurl a spear without a thrower and kill a reindeer, but to take down a bison, one needed extra power. They took only two bison a year, once, like now, in the hot season and once in the cold season. It was their right, their sacred calling to do so, but to kill more than one at a time was forbidden.

A single animal gave them enough hide to mend their winter clothes and fashion new ones for the children. One animal gave them enough bones to make digging tools and flaking tools and spear throwers. One gave them enough meat to feed the entire clan for a long while before it became rank.

They had a reverence for the bison, and the bison, they were certain, had a reverence for them.

Nago screamed the kill shout and swung his arm forward.

His spear flew straight and low and struck the bison in the breast, squarely between its front legs but the flint tip must have hit bone because it did not penetrate far.

Shrieking in agony and fear, the animal leaped forward, lowered its head and planted one of its thick horns in Nago's shoulder.

Tal's cries for the other men to converge was drowned out by Nago's howls. It was up to him to save his brother.

Running forwards, he slung his thrower as hard as he could and the spear found the bison's flank. It stuck deep and true but he took no chances. He ran to the beast, grabbed hold of the spear shaft and pushed it deeper and deeper until the animal's front legs buckled and it collapsed on its side, bleeding from the mouth.

Nago was on the ground gasping, his shoulder a mass of blood and torn muscle.

Tal kneeled over him and began to wail. The other men converged, pointing at the wound and whispering to each other.

Tal had seen horn wounds before. They did not close or heal on their own. If Nago had been wearing a hide shirt, perhaps the wound would not have been so deep but owing to the warmth of the day he was bare-chested, his shirt tied around his waist.

Nago was the hunt leader but Tal had to take over as leader now. To slow the blood, he took Nago's shirt and wrapped it as tightly as he could around the wound and told two cousins to carry him back to the camp.

Then he stood over the bison and thanked it for providing for their clan. He had never before been privileged to deliver the bison kill chant but he knew the words and delivered them with feeling. The rest of the men nodded their approval then fell upon the hot carcass to start the ritual butchering.

Tal peeled off and ran as quickly as he could towards the high grasses of the savannah. His father had taught him how to hunt and how to chant. Now it was time to use the knowledge passed to him by his mother.

His mother had been dead for two years. She left the world along with her newborn daughter after a tortuously difficult childbirth. She was not from the Bison Clan. She called her kin the People of Bear Mountain. As a young woman, she had been caught in a flash flood and separated from her tribe. Maybe they escaped or maybe they perished. She never knew. Tal's father, then a young man, hunting with elders, came across her in the forest, cold and hungry and took her in. He liked her, and though it caused jealousy and conflict within the clan, he chose her for his mate.

Her people were healers and she was skilled in making poultices and had the knowledge what leaves, roots and barks to chew for various maladies. When Tal was young, he remembered a bitter leaf that stopped his gums from aching and a tasty bark that cooled his body when it was hot.

As soon as the boy could walk he would toddle after his mother, collecting specimens in the forest and grasslands and helping her carry them back to camp in pouches sewn from reindeer hide.

His memory had always been prodigious. He only had to hear a bird call or a clan chant one time to remember it for ever. He would smell a flower petal, see an animal track or a cluster of leaves just once, or listen a single time to an explanation of a phenomenon — and it would never leave him.

And it was not only his mind that was active.

From the earliest age he excelled with his hands too. He learned how to strike long thin blades off a flint core. Even before he came of age, he was the best tool maker in the clan. He could carve wood and bone as skilfully as the older men and he was adept at making spears that flew straight and shaping perfectly balanced spear-throwers. Nago spent years stewing in anger at his skills but Tal never stopped respecting his brother because he always believed that one day Nago would become head of the clan.

Tal's mother also taught him how to paint. The People of Bear Mountain had a long tradition of adorning rock shelters and caves with the outlines of great animals in charcoal and ochre. She would scratch naturalistic outlines of bears, horses and bison in the mud or hard dirt and the boy would take the stick from her hand and copy them.

When he was older, he would pick up colourful rocks and clays and crush them into pigments that he would smear on his body to the amusement of the adults.

He was never idle. He was perpetually in motion, scurrying to do something.

Now his lungs ached with all-out exertion. He didn't have much time. The blood was draining from Nago's body with each of his strides.

His mother had taught him many poultices. There were ones for colic, ones for the flux, for sores, for boils, for head pain and tooth pain. There were others for wounds, some for old wounds that oozed and stank, like his father's and some for fresh bleeding wounds like Nago's.

195

The key ingredient for staunching fresh blood was a bright-green vine that twisted itself around the bark of young trees. In much the way it choked the trees, his mother had explained, it would choke the flow of blood. He knew where to find it, in a glade near the river.

He also needed a particular kind of berry, known to keep a wound clean. There was a good patch of them growing on bushes, not far from the glade.

And finally, to bind the poultice together and give enough bulk to pack the wound and draw its edges together, he needed a generous amount of yellow grasses. These were all around, ever abundant.

★　★　★

Because the weather was warm, the Bison Clan was in an open-air camp. Two days' journey towards the evening sun was a rock shelter they favoured for the cold months but the only protections they needed during this season were the skin lean-tos, made from reindeer and saplings that were flapping in the afternoon breeze.

Nago was laid out in the shade of one of these shelters. He gritted his teeth in pain. His shirt bandage seeped blood.

Tal ran to him. He had shed his own shirt and had used it to carry the plants and berries he needed to make the poultice.

All twenty-two members of the clan, men, women and children, gathered around but

196

parted when Tal's father limped up. He implored one son to save the other.

Tal set to work. His mother's old limestone mixing bowl was fetched for him and he furiously began cutting the vine down to manageable pieces with a flint blade. One of his aunts crushed the berries between large shiny leaves with the heel of her hands and channelled the juices into the bowl. Tal added the vine segments and mashed them into the berries with a smooth river stone. Then he cut clumps of yellow grass into short lengths and mixed a large handful into the bowl's red mush.

The finished poultice was thick and sticky.

Tal told his brother to be as strong as the bison they had killed. He scooped the poultice into the open wound and pushed more and more into the gaping hole until there was room for no more.

Nago was brave but the exertion of keeping silent overcame him and his eyes fluttered shut.

★   ★   ★

Tal kept vigil that night, and the next, and the next.

He left his brother's side only long enough each day to collect more ingredients to keep the poultice fresh.

He took these brief journeys on his own, not because others did not want to join him, but because he relished being alone. One of his cousins, a girl named Uboas, was particularly keen on following him. And so was her small brother, Gos who tagged along wherever she went.

Uboas was fast and pretty and Tal knew they were meant to be mates, but he still wanted to be by himself. When she refused to return to the camp, he simply outran her, as she outran her brother. When he was free of her, he looked back. In the distance, he saw her reunite with the child and take his hand.

★ ★ ★

Tal was in the glade, cutting vines off a tree when he saw them.

Actually, he heard them first, a low jabbering. Words of some sort. He strained to hear but could not understand.

At the edge of the glade two trees were parted enough to see one, then two.

He had heard of them, the Shadow People, the People of the Night, the Others — his clan had several names for them — but he had never seen them before. And this first encounter was brief, lasting only a few heartbeats.

One was old, like his own father, the other younger, like him. But they were both shorter and thicker than his own kind and their beards were redder and longer. The younger one had a heavy growth, not a wispy one like his own. The older one looked like he had never trimmed his beard with flint as was the custom of the Bison Clan. They carried spears but they were heavy thick ones, good for direct strikes, useless for throwing. Their clothes were rough and fur-bound, bear-skin by the looks of it, uncomfortable in this kind of heat.

And then, after exchanging the briefest of mutual glances, no more than a tacit acknowledgement of Tal's presence, they were gone.

★   ★   ★

Nago's last night was turbulent.

There was no doubt that Tal's poultice had done some good — the wound stayed clean and fresh-smelling and the blood flow had slowed to an ooze. But he had lost so much blood after the goring that no remedy or chant could reverse the outcome.

In his last hours his body grew swollen and the flow of urine stopped. Drops of water spooned into his mouth from a creased leaf just spilled out. As the dawn came, his breathing slowed then stopped.

The moment the women began to howl, the sky opened and a warm rain fell, a sign their ancestors had welcomed the head man's son to their realm. Their camps were burning bright in the night sky but they were too far away for the Bison Clan to hear their songs.

Tal's father laid his hands upon his shoulders and spoke to him in front of all the people. Tal would be the next head man. The old man wearily declared his time would come soon. Once Nago's mourning ritual was done, Tal would need to go to the highest point of the earth to be close enough to their ancestors to hear their chants.

The rain kept falling and soon his mother's limestone bowl, half-filled with unused poultice, was overflowing with rain water.

⋆   ⋆   ⋆

Tal was not afraid to climb.

He was sure-footed and even though the cliffs were wet from the rain he was able to make good progress. He had learned an old climbing trick from an elder years ago and had wrapped his loose hide boots with thongs of leather to keep them snugly on his feet.

Hours of daylight remained before he had to reach the top so his pace was unrushed. He carried two pouches on his belt, one with strips of dried reindeer meat and one with kindling and fire-making tools. When it was dark, he would build a campfire, chant and listen for the responsive song from the heavenly campfires far in the distance. Maybe, if he were pure enough of heart he would even hear a song from the campfire of his mother.

He didn't burden himself with a water skin. He knew there was a waterfall flowing over the cliffs and he would reach it in time to slake his thirst.

Halfway up the cliff he stopped on a safe ledge and turned towards the mighty river. From this great height it did not look so powerful. The earth stretched as far as he could see, an endless sea of grasses. In the distance, two brown shapes were moving through the savannah, a pair of shaggy mammoths. Tal laughed at the sight. He knew they were the largest beasts in the earth but from high on the cliff, it seemed he could pluck them up with his fingers and pop them into his mouth.

At the waterfall, he drank and washed the sweat away.

He looked for a good way to the top and traced a path with his eyes.

He made his way to another safe ledge and when he pulled himself up, he stopped and stared.

A sign!

There could be no doubt!

In front of his eyes was a cleft of blackness in the face of the rock.

A cave! He had never seen it before.

He approached it slowly. There were creatures to fear. Bears. The Shadow People.

He cautiously stepped into the cool blackness and inspected the mouth of the cave to the point where the light of the sun stopped.

The floor was pristine. The walls were smooth. He was the first to enter. He was jubilant.

This is Tal's cave!

I was meant to be the head man!

When it is my time I will bring my clan here!

★ ★ ★

The next day when the sun was high, Tal returned to his camp.

He shouted to his people that he had heard their ancestors chanting and that he had found a new cave in the cliffs. He could not understand why they seemed preoccupied with something else, all of them pointing at the ground by the camp fire. The women were crying.

Uboas ran to Tal and pulled him by his sleeve.

Her brother, Gos, was lying on the ground, spouting mad, nonsensical things, sporadically flailing his limbs about, trying to strike whoever drew closest.

Tal demanded to know what had happened and Uboas told him.

His mother's limestone bowl had been sitting by the fire and the hot sun and warmth of the fire had made the contents hiss and bubble. Gos had wandered by that morning and with his usual curiosity he dipped a finger in and tasted the red liquid. He liked it well enough to taste more, and more, until his chin was red.

Then he became possessed, screaming words that did not fit together. He thrashed and fought, but now was becoming quieter.

Tal sat beside him, put the boy's head on his lap and touched his cheek. The touch calmed him and his little eyes opened.

Tal asked how he felt and told him not to be afraid. He would stay with him until he got well.

The little boy wet his lips with his tongue and asked for water. In time he sat up and pointed at the bowl.

Tal wanted to know what he wanted and the boy's answer shocked those who had witnessed his spell.

He wanted more red liquid.

18

Saturday Night

General Gatinois's mistress was almost at orgasm or at the very least she was announcing in her own way that it was all right for him to think about finishing things up and rolling off.

He got the message and redoubled his efforts. His sweat beaded up and wicked down the fine white hairs of his chest where it mingled with her own dampness.

She was saying, 'Ah, ah, ah, ah,' and suddenly his mobile phone pitched in with a ring tone and cadence remarkably similar to hers.

He reached for the phone which made her angry so she pushed him away and padded off to the lavatory, pink, naked and swearing under her breath.

'General, am I disturbing you?' Marolles asked.

'No, what is it?' Gatinois asked. He really didn't care he hadn't climaxed. It was all too predictable and boring anyway.

'We've been able to hack into the server at PlantaGenetics and obtain the report Dr Prentice intends to deliver to Professor Simard and Professor Mallory on Monday.'

'Yes?'

'It's quite alarming. It's preliminary, of course, but he's made some profound observations. He is clearly on the right track to discover more, should he so choose.'

'Send it to my email. I'm presently not at home but I will be shortly.'

'Yes, Sir.'

'But Marolles, time is short. Don't wait for my review. Let our people know they may proceed.'

Marolles sounded uncomfortable. 'Are you certain, General?'

'Yes, I'm certain!' Gatinois was annoyed by the question. 'And I'm also certain I don't intend to be summoned to the Elysée Palace to explain to the President why the greatest secret in France has been compromised on my watch!'

19

Sunday

The campsite at Ruac Abbey was a melancholy place that Sunday night.

Most of the team had packed up and took off during the morning; Luc and Sara had left at noon to catch a flight to London. A skeleton crew remained to shut down the cave for the season.

For fifteen days, the camp had been a beehive of scientific activity, ground zero in the world of Paleolithic archaeology. It had crackled with excitement, the place to be. Now, it felt empty and a bit sad.

Jeremy and Pierre were in charge of the wind-down and clean-up, commanding a group of four undergraduate students itching to get back to the bars and clubs of Bordeaux. The only senior scientist who stayed to the bitter end was Elizabeth Coutard, who was setting up the environmental monitoring protocol to evaluate conditions within the cave throughout the off-season.

The chef was gone too so the quality of the meals was poor. After an every-man-for-himself dinner, Jeremy and Pierre ambled over to the office to pack boxes taking a couple of bottles of beer with them.

Well into the evening, Pierre caught something

205

out of the corner of his eye. He stiffened and snapped his head towards the computer screen.

'Did you see that?' he asked.

Jeremy looked bored. 'See what?'

'I think there's someone in the cave!'

'Can't be,' Jeremy yawned. 'It's locked.'

Pierre sprang up and hit the surveillance program's replay button, pushing the clock back thirty seconds. 'Come here, look.'

They watched the recording stream forward.

There was a man with a backpack in full illumination.

'Christ!' Pierre exclaimed. 'He's in Chamber 9 heading towards 10! Dial 17! Get the police! Hurry! I'm going down!'

'That's not a good idea,' Jeremy said urgently. 'Don't!'

Pierre grabbed a hammer off the table and ran for the door. 'Just call!'

Pierre's car was already backed up to his caravan so it took him no time to jump in and speed towards the cave. Jeremy listened to the high-pitched whine of his engine fade into the distance.

He nervously glanced at the computer monitor. Either the intruder had left or he was somewhere in between camera angles.

He lifted the telephone handset, punched in the 1 then everything went black.

★   ★   ★

Pierre swiftly climbed down the cliff ladder, using all his athleticism to eat up the rungs, the hammer thrust into his belt.

The gate was wide open, the interior lights were blazing. He'd never gone into the cave without protective gear but now was not the time for caution. He ran into the mouth and pulled the hammer from his belt.

Pierre had been a pretty good footballer in school and he was able to run through the cave at a good clip while maintaining his balance on the uneven matting. He burned through the chambers, the cave art blurring in his peripheral vision. He had the illusion of running through herds of animals, weaving in and out, avoiding hooves and claws.

His heart was in his throat when he got to Chamber 9. There was no trace of the intruder.

He had to be in the tenth chamber.

Pierre had never had an easy time crawling through the narrow passage. His legs were too long to fold into an easy crawl. He tried to be as quiet as he could and prayed he wouldn't run into the man in the middle of the tunnel — a claustrophobic nightmare.

He stood in the Vault of Hands and crept forward. There were sounds of activity within the Chamber of Plants.

The intruder was on his hands and knees, facing the other way, concentrating on wires and bricks of material he was removing from the backpack. He didn't see Pierre coming.

'Who are you?' Pierre yelled.

The startled intruder looked over his shoulder at Pierre, tall and muscular, wielding a hammer, an incongruously menacing sight since Pierre had the frightened look of a cornered rabbit on his face.

The man slowly stood up. He had thick, powerful arms and an untidy speckled beard. The shock of seeing Pierre quickly disappeared, replaced by a cold-as-ice expression.

Pierre got a better look at the paraphernalia on the cave floor, a jumble of wires, detonators, batteries and cakey yellow-brown bricks. He'd seen this kind of gear before, at the mines back in Sierra Leone. 'Those are explosives!' he shouted. 'Who the hell are you?'

The man said nothing.

He lowered his greying head, as if he were politely bowing, but instead he rushed forward and caught Pierre with a head-butt to his chest, knocking him back against the bird man who was standing there with his open beak and his ridiculous cock.

Pierre started swinging his hammer defensively, trying to fend off the man's fists and fingers which were swarming all over his most-sensitive areas, his groin, his eyes, his neck. The man was trying to exact as much pain and cause as much immobility as possible.

The hammer blows weren't slowing the man, because Pierre's sense of humanity was stopping him from smashing him on the head. Instead, he whacked his shoulders and his back but that wasn't enough: the man kept coming.

Then, the man landed a hard punch to Pierre's throat that hurt him mightily and set him into a panic. He coughed and choked and for the first time in his life thought he might die.

In desperation, he swung the hammer one more time, as hard as he could, and this time he aimed for the top of the man's head.

⋆ ⋆ ⋆

There were three men at the campsite, toting shotguns and rifles. They went from caravan to caravan in a frenzy, like a pack of wild dogs, barging in each cabin, and when they found the ones that were occupied, they dragged out frightened students.

Elizabeth Coutard heard a commotion and emerged on her own. She saw a male student being frogmarched at gunpoint.

She ran towards the abbey, her white ponytail bobbing against her shoulders, awkwardly feeling in her pockets for her phone.

She made it as far as the barn.

⋆ ⋆ ⋆

Pierre had only a moment to deal with the horrible sight of this man lying at his feet. He was making guttural noises and oozing blood from a hammer wound to the dome of his skull. The blood was seeping out concentrically making it appear as if he had donned a red skullcap.

Then Pierre felt the worst pain imaginable, a lightning strike to his kidney that took his breath away, making it impossible to scream.

⋆ ⋆ ⋆

Four students huddled with Elizabeth Coutard in the Portakabin. Jeremy was motionless on the floor. The lone woman among the students, Marie, a girl from Brittany, was shaking uncontrollably and Coutard moved to hold her, defying one of the men who menaced them with a raised weapon.

'What do you want?' Coutard demanded somewhat fearlessly. 'Jeremy needs medical attention. Can't you see that?'

One man appeared to be in charge. He ignored her and shouted at the three male students to sit on the floor. They meekly complied and he trained his double-barrelled shotgun at them and assumed a tense at-ready position. Then he nodded in the direction of the women, a pre-arranged sign.

His two compatriots responded by roughly dragging the women out the door, shouting at them like crazed prison guards, 'Move! Move! Come on!'

At the cold campfire, Coutard and Marie were separated from each other's clutches and prodded at gunpoint into separate caravans.

★ ★ ★

The old man with a knife watched Pierre bleed to death on the cold hard floor of the tenth chamber.

Bonnet knew the art of killing. A long blade through the kidney, piercing the renal artery. A victim would go down quickly and die fast from internal bleeding. Slashing a carotid was too

210

messy for his tastes.

He was breathless from wending his way through the cave, crawling through the tunnel and killing a man. His knees were sore, his hips ached. He paused to wipe his knife on Pierre's shirt and let his heart slow down a little. Then he turned his attention to his stricken comrade, turned him over and tried to shake him to consciousness. 'Wake up!' he demanded. 'You're the only one who knows how to set the damned charges!'

He looked at the tangle of wires and high-explosives and shook his head. He didn't have a clue how to rig the charges himself, nor would the others. There wasn't time to summon someone else. All he could do was string together a run of profanities and start shouting into his walkie talkie.

The only response was static; he remembered he was deep inside the cliffs and he swore some more.

Then he noticed the bird man on the wall behind him and instead of marvelling at the image, his reaction was more prosaic.

'Go screw yourself,' he said, turning away.

Then he spat contemptuously on Pierre's body.

20

Sunday Night

They stayed in a small hotel in the heart of the university. The journey from Ruac to Cambridge had involved changing planes, trains and taxis and when they arrived and checked into their separate rooms they were worn out.

Still, Sara agreed to Luc's proposal to take a walk in the chilly night air. They were both fond of the city and Luc had a habit of stopping for a pint at the riverside pub, The Anchor, every time he was in town. Years earlier, the British archaeologist, John Wymer, had dragged him there for a few pints of Abbot Ale after a conference. The details of that night were sketchy but Luc had ended the evening waist-deep in the River Cam with Wymer doubled over in hysterics on the shore. Each return visit to The Anchor for an Abbot was an homage to the eccentric Englishman.

It was late and the pub was Sunday-night-mellow. They sat at a window table, unable to see the river in the inky darkness but happy in the knowledge it was there. They clinked their pint mugs three times, toasting Ruac, Zvi and finally Hugo.

'So, what now?' Sara asked, wearily.

It was a funny kind of open-ended question and Luc wasn't sure what she meant or how to answer it. What now for *you*? What now for *Ruac*? What now for *us*? 'I don't know,' he answered vaguely. 'What do you think?'

'I think it's been a crazy few weeks,' she said. She was drinking the strong beer faster than him. 'I don't know about you, but I need a long hot bath and a few days off to read a trashy novel — anything but think about pollen and cave art.'

'After tomorrow, you mean.'

She agreed. 'After tomorrow. I wonder what Fred found and why he was so mysterious about it.'

Luc shrugged. 'Nothing would surprise me. We'll know soon enough.'

She bore down to the question she was really asking. 'So, after tomorrow what are *you* going to do?'

'The same as always, I suppose. Back to Bordeaux, back to my office, my lab, my papers. We've generated an unbelievable amount of data. It all needs to be sorted out, coordinated.' He looked out the window, trying hard to see the river. 'The Ministry will be expecting a report. We have to plan the official unveiling of the cave, you know. I've got a full voicemail box with French, British and American television companies who want exclusive rights to the first documentaries. Then there's the manuscript. It's not fully translated. I've got to get in touch with Hugo's secretary and figure out how to keep in contact with his Belgian decoder. There's a million things to think about.'

She stared out the window too. It was more comfortable to look at each other's reflections.

213

'We should try to stay in touch. Professionally. You know what I mean.'

Something about what she said or the way she said it made him sad. Was a door opening or closing? Of course he wanted her. She was lovely. But he'd had her before and had forced her away with ruthless efficiency. Why would it be different now?

He escaped from the moment by guzzling his beer and suggesting they ought to get some rest before their morning meeting.

★ ★ ★

The streets in the centre of Cambridge were nearly empty. They walked in silence up Mill Lane towards the street-facing facades of Pembroke College and when they turned onto Trumpington Street Luc noticed a parked car, a football field away, turning on its headlights.

He thought nothing of it until the car accelerated in their direction and crossed into the wrong lane.

The coolness of the night and the quick rush of adrenalin flushed the beer from his brain. Although the next events happened in no more than five or six seconds he had a beautifully clear, almost slow-motion perception of those moments — and that strange clarity almost certainly saved their lives.

The car was heading directly towards them on a murderous diagonal.

As it jumped the kerb three car-lengths from their legs, two wheels on the sidewalk, two wheels off, Luc had already grabbed a fistful of Sara's leather sleeve and was flinging her out of the way with all the rotational force his shoulder and torso could muster. She twirled onto the road like a child's top being released from its coiled string.

He allowed his own body to follow the same path of momentum and at the instant of impact, the fender of the car clipped his hip. The difference of an inch or two, a fraction of a second, or any way one chose to characterise the closeness of it all, was the difference between a bruise and a smashed pelvis.

He tumbled to the road, spun and landed close enough to Sara for both of them to instinctively reach out to each other and try to touch fingertips.

The car scraped and sparked against the limestone blocks of a residential hall of Pembroke College, sheared a gutter downspout, and careened back onto the street where it sped away in a squeal of rubber.

Lying in the middle of the street, Luc and Sara's fingers intertwined.

Both of them asked simultaneously, 'Are you all right?' and both answered, again at the same time, 'Yes.'

★   ★   ★

They wouldn't get to their beds for another four hours.

There were police statements to be given, first-aid to be administered by the ambulance

215

crew who dressed their minor cuts and Luc's road-burn scrapes and a cautionary X-ray of Luc's hip to be shot at the Nuffield Hospital casualty department. The young Asian doctor in casualty seemed more concerned with Luc's red knuckles than his recent injuries.

'This is infected,' she said. 'It's turned into cellulitis, a tissue infection. How long have you had it?'

'A week, week and a half.'

She inspected his hand more closely and saw the scar on his fourth finger. 'Did you cut yourself?'

He nodded. 'I took some erythromycin. It didn't do much.'

'I'll take a culture but I'm concerned about MRSA. Resistant staph. I'm going to give you different pills, rifampin and trimethoprim sulfa. Here's my card, call me in three days for the culture results.'

The police took the incident seriously but Luc and Sara's gut feel of being deliberately targeted was shrugged off by the responding officers who went off looking for a blue sedan and a drunk driver. There were bulletins to put out on police frequencies and CCTV footage from the city centre to review. Luc and Sara would be notified if the culprit was found, etcetera, etcetera.

Mute with fatigue and roughly shaken by their near miss, they found themselves staring at each other in the deserted lobby. He thought about hugging her but didn't want to add more trauma to her night.

She beat him to the punch.

He liked the feeling of her arms around his

216

waist but it didn't last long. In a few moments they were limping off to their separate rooms.

★   ★   ★

Gatinois was almost hoping his phone would ring again to give him an excuse to extricate himself from his brother-in-law. The man, a wealthy blow-hard with a gaudy apartment, was some kind of international currency trader. The fellow had given him the particulars of his job a hundred times but Gatinois shut his mind off whenever his jowly face began to yammer on about weak euros and strong dollars and the like. The idea of making money by electronically shifting pots of currency from here to there struck him as parasitic. What did the man *do*? For the greater good? For his country?

His wife and sister-in-law seemed engaged enough by whatever he was saying, attentively sipping cognac, a final round of drinks after a Sunday night dinner celebrating the man's promotion to chief of one of his bank's divisions.

Gatinois had no doubt what *he* did for his country. Today he'd spent hours on the phone, even made an unprecedented Sunday visit to The Piscine for a personal briefing by his staff.

He'd been absolutely correct about Bonnet's ruthlessness and he liberally reminded Marolles of his prediction. Over the past two weeks he had absorbed each piece of news from Ruac with grim admiration. Now the campsite. The old boy liked his blood.

Well, more power to him.

217

Almost as if he'd willed it to life, his phone began to ring. He gratefully leaped up, and excused himself to take the call in the library.

His wife told her sister, 'He's been on the phone to his office all day!'

The banker seemed sorry his audience had diminished. 'Oh well. I suppose we'll never know what André really does for a living, but he's keeping us all safe in our beds, I'm quite sure of that. More cognac?'

★ ★ ★

Gatinois sank into one of the banker's library chairs. The bookcases were stacked with old leather-bound volumes, touched by the cleaner's feather duster and nothing else.

Marolles sounded weary. 'Bonnet's been at it again.'

'Does he ever rest?' Gatinois asked incredulously. 'What now?'

'There was just an attempt to run down Simard and Mallory on a city street in Cambridge. One of our men saw it with his own eyes. They were only lightly hurt. The driver got away clean.'

Gatinois snorted. 'So his tentacles reach all the way to England! Amazing, really. He's got balls, I'll give him that.'

'What should we do?' Marolles asked.

'About what?'

'*Our* plans.'

'Absolutely nothing!' Gatinois exclaimed. 'This has nothing to do with our plans. Don't change a single operational detail. Not one detail!'

21

Monday Morning

The meeting at PlantaGenetics with Fred Prentice, Sara's biologist friend was set for 9 a.m. The biotech company, founded by a Cambridge University botany professor, was in the business of finding new biologically active molecules from plant extracts. Their labs hummed round the clock with the whirring sound of hundreds of robotic arms bobbing up and down, pipetting specimens extracted from plants collected around the world and sent to Cambridge for analysis.

Sara and Fred travelled in the same botany circles and though they'd never had a chance to collaborate, they followed each other's work and saw each other at conferences. Truth be told, she knew he fancied her. He had once shyly asked her to dinner at a congress in New Orleans. She accepted the invitation because he was a sweet man and seemed lonely, and she was saved from a goodnight kiss by his allergic reaction to a spice in his gumbo.

Sitting in the taxi that morning, both of them looked like B-movie zombies. Luc's forearm and hand were wrapped in a gauze bandage and his hip smarted. Sara had a few Band-Aids here and there. They'd skipped breakfast and met each other in the lobby, both running late. They hurried to get a cab. When they finally got a gander at each other in the back seat they had to laugh.

'How long will it take to get there?' Luc asked the driver.

'Just ten minutes, up the Milton Road to the Science Park. You running late?'

'A little,' Sara said. It was already nine.

'Should you call?' Luc asked.

Sara took the suggestion.

'Hello, Fred, it's Sara,' she said trying to sound cheery. 'Sorry, but we're running a few minutes . . .'

In the distance there was a flash, magnesium-bright. Then a shuddering percussive whump.

A dome of white smoke rose from the top of the trees.

'Jesus!' the taxi driver yelped. 'That can't be too far from where we're heading!'

Sara had her phone to her ear. 'Fred? Fred?'

★ ★ ★

They never made it to the Science Park. Emergency Services had the road blocked off and all traffic was diverted.

All they could do was return to their hotel, turn to the news on the lobby TV and watch live reports on Sky and ITV accompanied by the noise of helicopters overhead and the wail of sirens.

The explosion had devastated a wing at the Science Park. By 11 a.m. a reporter from Sky read out a list of companies located in the

220

building. One of them was PlantaGenetics.

There was talk of a gas leak or a chemical explosion. The possibility that it was a terrorist attack was mentioned. The wing was a smouldering mess. There were multiple casualties. Burns units in Cambridgeshire and beyond were filling up. Blood donors were needed.

Then at noon, Sara's phone rang.

She looked at the caller ID and said, 'Oh my God, Luc, it's Fred!'

★ ★ ★

They returned to the Casualty Department at Nuffield. The night before, the waiting area had been speckled with patients with minor problems.

Today it was a war zone. It was a small hospital, only fifty beds and it was melting down in the crisis.

After fighting their way inside, Luc and Sara eventually got the attention of a nurse to tell her they were friends of one of the blast victims. 'Hang on a minute, luv,' they were told and then they were left hanging for half an hour as people chaotically pulsed around them. After several attempts, a young man pushing an empty wheelchair took pity on them and pulled them through the casualty doors to search the stretcher-choked corridors for their Mr Prentice.

It was quite a scene, a hospital at its breaking point. Luc followed along as Sara gazed at each victim, searching for Fred's face. Past the Radiology Department she found him, his arm

221

and shoulder in an elaborate plaster cast. Both feet were also casted to the calves. He was in his early forties with widow-peaked hair and a complexion as colourless as the plaster. He had the squint of a man who had lost his glasses.

'There you are!' he said to Sara.

'Oh, Fred! Look at you! I was so worried.'

He was sweet and caring as usual. He insisted on exchanging polite introductions with Luc, as though they were meeting at his conference table. 'Thank goodness both of you were late,' he said. 'Otherwise, you'd have been caught up in all this mess.'

He had been in the lavatory. He was embarrassed because his pants had been around his ankles when she rang.

The next thing he remembered he was being stretchered out by a fire crew with unbearable pain in his feet and his shoulder. A morphine jab in the car park cheered him up no end, he assured them, and other than the mental torture of not knowing the fate of several colleagues and friends, he was doing well enough.

Sara held his good hand and asked if she could do anything for him.

He shook his head. 'You came all the way from France to see me. I can't have you leave without hearing what we found.'

'Don't be crazy, man!' Luc exclaimed. 'You've been through hell. We'll talk in a few days. Please!'

'I had a PowerPoint presentation for you,' Fred said wistfully. 'Everything's gone ka-boom. My computer, my lab, everything. Oh well. But, let me at least *tell* you about our results. Maybe we'll be able to reproduce them one day. Our lawyer was upset at me because I analysed your sample without putting the proper paperwork and agreements in place. You see, we obtained some important data and it wasn't clear who would own the intellectual property. She wouldn't let me put any of in a letter or email. It all seemed so critical last week.' His voice tailed off. 'I was told she died this morning — that lawyer. Her name was Jane.'

'I'm sorry, Fred,' Sara said, squeezing his hand.

He asked for water from his bendy-straw. 'Well, that liquid of yours had some really interesting biology. It lit up our screens like a Christmas tree. Where to start? Okay, then, did you have any idea it was swimming in ergot alkaloids?'

'You're kidding!' Sara said. Then when she saw Luc's puzzled expression, she explained, 'They're psychoactive compounds. Nature's LSD. How'd ergots get in there? I gave you the list of plants, Fred.' And then the answer hit her and she blurted out, '*Claviceps purpurea*!'

'Exactly!' Fred said.

She was slowed down by the need to explain things to Luc. 'It's a fungus. It contaminates wild and cultivated grasses, like our wild barley. The fungus produces the ergot compounds. In the Middle Ages tens of thousands of Europeans came down with ergotism from naturally contaminated rye, causing hallucinations, madness, sometimes death. The Aztecs chewed

Morning Glory seeds which contain natural ergots. It was their way of communicating with their gods. Christ, I studied ergotism in grad school! Ergot contamination of livestock grain is still a major problem.'

'I'm a hundred per cent sure it was *Claviceps*-derived,' Fred said with an excited look, seemingly forgetting his circumstances. 'The predominant ergots were agroclavine and elymoclavine.'

She shook her head knowingly. 'Did you find anything else?'

'You bet I did. Ergots were only the beginning. Wait till you hear the rest!'

Luc's mobile phone rang. When he opened it, someone with a hospital badge told him he couldn't use it inside.

Luc excused himself and limped down the corridor towards the casualty department. 'Hello?'

'Is that Professor Simard?'

'Yes, who's this?'

'It's Father Menaud, from Ruac. I need to speak with you.'

'Yes, one moment. Let me get outside.'

On the way out, Luc saw two large men heading towards him, shoulder-to-shoulder, and he thought he heard one of them say 'Oui,' which struck him as out of place in the corridors of the Nuffield Hospital. One was wearing a sweatshirt, the other a padded jacket. Both looked haggard. When he looked at them, he had the impression they deliberately looked away but it happened quickly and he was out the door.

The forecourt to the Casualty Department

224

was crowded with ambulances, police cars and satellite trucks. Luc tried to find a relatively quiet spot.

'How can I help you, Dom Menaud?'

It wasn't a good connection. Syllables were dropping. 'I'm afraid they're all gone. I don't know any other way to tell you.'

Luc was confused. 'I'm sorry, what do you mean, gone?'

'All your people at the camp. All of them are dead. It's a terrible tragedy. Please, professor, come as soon as you can!'

22

Monday

Luc left Sara speechless and trembling at Fred Prentice's side with nothing more than a few hurried words to tell her there'd been an accident in France.

Maybe it was a cruel thing to do to her, to leave so abruptly, but his mind wasn't focused on anything but getting back across the Channel. He hailed a taxi and persuaded the driver to take him all the way to Heathrow for the cash in his wallet. He left his bag at the hotel; it was the last thing he cared about. He used his mobile until the battery went dead then sat in the cab with his hands in his head. The rest of the journey was a long, slashing blur, a journey to hell.

★   ★   ★

Hell was roped off with yellow incident tape.

The abbey grounds were the site of a major gendarmerie investigation. In the parking area, an officer recognised Luc and escorted him through the forensic cordon. In the distance, Luc saw the monks heading to the church. Which office of the day was it? He'd lost track of time. Then he noticed the sun was setting. Vespers. Nothing was going to interrupt the cycle of prayer.

Luc was like a foetus, suspended in murkiness, aware of his own heartbeat, his breathing, but primitively unaware of what was happening outside the womb.

Colonel Toucas was strutting around, very much in charge. By the cold ash of the camp fire pit, he immediately started peppering Luc with questions and confronting him with grim facts. The way he was so energised, almost giddy in the midst of all this calamity, angered Luc and brought him crashing back to the here and now.

But Luc had trouble looking into Toucas's animated face when the policeman started describing the location of bodies, the nature of the wounds. Instead, he found himself staring furiously at the objects that adorned the colonel's sky-blue shirt — his epaulets, his service patches, the dark-blue tie with its emblematic clip.

Luc began to fully absorb the horror. The three male undergraduate students and Jeremy were shot dead in the office, execution style. Marie, the female undergrad, raped and shot in one caravan. Elizabeth Coutard, raped and shot in another.

Finally, Luc was able to look at Toucas's fleshy lips. 'What about Pierre?' he asked in little more than a whisper.

'Who's Pierre?' the officer asked.

After Luc explained who Pierre was and that he was certainly there on Sunday night, Toucas began barking at his men, demanding an explanation for the incomplete body count, haranguing them to make another search of the

227

camp site. Luc offered up the make and model of Pierre's car and an officer was dispatched to locate it.

Toucas all but forced Luc to enter the Portakabin to give an accounting of what was missing. Mercifully, the bodies were covered, but the shrouds couldn't hide all the blood.

'My God,' Luc muttered. 'My God. Who could have done this?'

'Who indeed,' Toucas said. 'We'll find them, you can be sure of that.'

The office was completely ransacked. The computers were gone as were the scientific gear, the microscopes and environmental monitors. The file cabinets and desk drawers had all been emptied out into a great pile and by the looks of it, the intruders had set the pile on fire. About a quarter of the papers were burned through or singed.

'Why would they burn the files?' Luc asked numbly.

Toucas pointed to the charred remnants. 'Perhaps they were using the papers to set the building off and destroy the evidence. The fire must have burned out on its own. These coated file folders don't ignite easily. There's no sign of accelerants. You light a match, start the fire, run away and it dies out. That's what I think happened.'

An officer poked his head in. 'That car isn't around, Colonel.'

'So where is this Pierre? What's his last name, professor?'

'Berewa.'

'What kind of name is that?'

'He's from Sierra Leone.'

'Ah,' Toucas said suspiciously, 'An African.'

'No, a Frenchman,' Luc responded.

Toucas half-smiled. 'Well, we need to find Pierre Berewa. Do you have his mobile number? Can you call him?'

Luc's phone was dead. He used the Colonel's to no avail. Suddenly, he looked at his own desk. The drawers were tipped out. 'We kept the spare key to the cave entrance in that drawer.'

'See if you can find it,' Toucas said. 'But put these gloves on please.' He pointed to a box of latex gloves left there by the forensics squad. 'Fingerprints.'

Luc began rummaging through the files.

'How many keys did you have?' Toucas asked.

'Two. Pierre had my key.'

'Ah, Pierre, again.'

After an exhaustive search Luc declared the spare key missing and said, 'I think we should check the cave.'

'Very well, let's do that.'

Lieutenant Billeter drove. On the way, Toucas took a call, mostly listening. When he was done he turned to Luc in the back seat. 'The coroner tells me there was something interesting about the rape samples from the female victims.'

Luc didn't want to hear but Toucas wasn't attuned to his sensibilities.

'The rapist had abnormal sperm. Short tails, apparently not good swimmers. The doctor used the term, 'immotile'. Maybe this will be helpful, we'll see.'

Luc could see Marie and Elizabeth in his mind. For the first time that day tears began to stream down his face.

★ ★ ★

At the end of the lane, they saw Pierre's red car in the gravel parking area. Luc ran to it, but Billeter warned him off. 'Don't touch anything!'

They peered in but it was empty.

Luc led them down the ladder. On the ledge of the cliff the sight of the gate wide open sent him into fury. 'Someone's been in there! Christ!'

Billeter used his walkie talkie to radio for more men.

'Take us in there, Professor,' Toucas said, unbuttoning his stiff leather holster.

There was still a cardboard box of shoe covers in the cave mouth. Luc hit the universal power switch and the entire cave lit up, front to back.

'We should have protective clothes,' Luc mumbled.

'To protect us?' Toucas asked.

'No, the cave.'

'Under the circumstances, let's not worry about that,' the colonel commanded.

Toucas and Billeter seemed irritably distracted by the cave art, as if it was put there to confuse a crime scene. Luc moved forward cautiously, checking each treasure, fearful he would find graffiti, or some ruinous act. Anyone capable of debasing human life would certainly be capable of that.

'What are these?' Toucas asked, pointing at a Roman Numeral III, affixed to the wall.

'There are ten chambers in the cave. This is the third, The Chamber of the Red Deer.'

'Which is the most important?'

'They're all important. But if I had to answer, I'd say the tenth chamber.'

'Why?'

'You'll see.'

They finally got to Chamber 9. Luc took some comfort in seeing all the art untouched, as perfect as ever.

They entered the tunnel on hands and knees.

When they emerged from the tunnel into the tenth chamber and the Vault of Hands, Luc immediately saw Pierre's long arm in the Chamber of Plants.

He shouted, 'Pierre!' and ran to him.

He was lying face-down.

His black skin was as cold as the cave floor. Billeter went through the motions of trying to find a pulse and declared that rigor mortis had already set in.

'Search him,' Toucas ordered, and Billeter donned gloves and began the task while Luc collapsed on his haunches to watch the nightmarish scene.

Another student murdered.

At the feet of the bird man.

In this mystical place.

He heard Abbot Menaud's words in his head: 'I'm afraid they're all gone.'

Billeter was saying something that he missed. Luc looked up and asked him to repeat it. 'I said he had one key in his pocket. Is this the original or the copy?'

'It's the original. It's my keychain.'

Billeter resumed his inspection. 'There's a stab wound in his right flank. We'll see what the coroner says but that's the probable cause of death.'

'What do these mean, these plants and that man or whatever he is with this erection of his?' Toucas asked.

'I don't know if we'll ever know what they mean,' Luc answered wearily. 'I'm sure people will have theories.'

'What's *your* theory?'

'Right now, I couldn't say. My best student is dead. My people are dead. The women . . . '

Toucas didn't pretend to be empathic. 'This isn't idle chatter, Professor. I'm conducting an investigation! Do you want justice? I'm sure you do! How well did you know this man?' He pointed at Pierre with a jut of his chin.

'I knew him very well. He was with me for four years. He was a good archaeologist. He might have become a great one.'

'Where was he before he was your student?'

'Paris. University of Paris. He was Parisian.'

'From Africa.'

Luc keyed on the accusatory way the man spat that out. 'So what?'

'Did he ever have friends or relatives come visit him here?'

'No.'

'Did he have any bad habits, drugs?'

'No. Not that I know of.'

'Money problems?'

'Beyond what all students face? I wouldn't know. What are you driving at?'

Toucas rubbed his fleshy cheeks with the heels of his hands in a show of fatigue or maybe exasperation. 'A crime has been committed. A great crime. All crimes have motives and opportunities. Why do you think Pierre Berewa was in this cave, professor?'

'I don't know. He shouldn't have been.'

'Well then. We have a motive. There's been a theft. Your equipment is gone, the purses and wallets of the victims were taken. There was a sexual assault. Spontaneous perhaps. The women were there. The perpetrators were men. It happens. And your Pierre had a key to the cave. Maybe . . . ' He stopped long enough to respond to Luc's growing anger. He had risen from his squat and was towering over the colonel, growing red with rage. 'Just maybe, Professor, please listen to me, this student had some shady dealings with bad people. Maybe he was their opportunity. We must keep an open mind.'

'There was another key!' Luc shouted, the words echoing in the chamber. 'It's gone. Maybe Pierre was trying to stop them from — I don't know what.'

'Well, maybe. Of course, there are other explanations. A drug gang. Travellers. Gypsies. Your presence down here wasn't exactly a secret. Scientists are rich. They have fancy gear. I know how crooks think. This was an easy target, whether or not Pierre Berewa was involved.'

Luc was half-listening, half-watching the

233

lieutenant lifting Pierre up by a stiff shoulder to see if anything was under his body. He saw something. An archaeologist's eye. 'What's that?'

'Where?' Billeter asked.

'Near his left hand.'

With Toucas moving in to keep Pierre's shoulder and upper body off the ground, Billeter shone his torch underneath and pulled out a block of brown cakey material, the size of a dozen pencils bundled together.

Toucas put on a single glove to receive it and sniffed at it. 'What is this, professor?'

Luc had no clue and said it wasn't anything to do with his excavation.

'I have some ideas, but I'd rather not say for now. We'll have it analysed. Everything will be analysed, you can be sure of that,' Toucas said.

'You need to know something,' Luc said suddenly.

'Go on.'

'Last night I was in England, in Cambridge. Someone tried to run me over with a car. He got away.'

'And what do the police think?'

'They thought it was probably a drunk driver.'

Toucas shrugged.

'This morning, I was on my way to an appointment with a scientific collaborator. There was an explosion at the office park before I got there. There were many casualties.'

'I heard something on the radio. I've been busy today,' Toucas sniffed. 'Other than the fact you've had a bad run at the tables, Professor, why are you telling me this?'

234

'Because, maybe there's some kind of connection. All these things just don't happen.'

'Why not? Things happen all the time. Conspiracy theorists make a living of stringing random events like different-sized beads into one ugly necklace. This is not what we do in my command.'

'Could you at least talk to the police in England?' Luc asked. He fished a business card from his wallet that one of the Cambridge officers had given him. Toucas took it and slipped it in his breast pocket as if he had no intention of ever looking at it again.

There were faraway calls from inside the cave.

'Despite everything,' Luc said miserably, 'we're going to have to protect the integrity of the cave. We can't have people just walking around with no safeguards.'

'Yes, yes,' Toucas said, dismissively. 'You can help us strike a balance between our needs and yours, I'm sure. A protocol, perhaps.'

A head popped through the tunnel into the Vault of Hands but it wasn't a member of the gendarmerie.

It was Marc Abenheim.

He had a sweet-and-sour look on his officious face. In the face of all this horror, something was pleasing him.

'There you are!' Luc cringed at his nasal smugness. 'I was told you were down here.' He looked around, blinking nervously and sniffed, 'Oh dear!' at the sight of Pierre's body. When he had visited during the excavation, Luc recalled he had trouble making eye contact. Now he was latching on with laser beams. 'I didn't expect to be back so quickly. It's good to see the cave again but not under these circumstances. What a tragedy! The Minister herself sends her condolences.'

'Thank you, Marc. You didn't have to come all the way from Paris. It's a matter for the authorities.'

Abenheim tried not to look at Pierre's body. Luc knew they'd met. He had assigned Pierre to take Abenheim on his obligatory cave tour. 'I'm afraid I did have to come. Can we speak in private?'

They withdrew to the adjacent vault. The bright, almost gaily painted hands all around them were discordant, bordering on absurd, considering the circumstances.

'I seem to be seeing you only on unfortunate occasions,' Abenheim said.

'It seems so.'

'These kinds of things are unprecedented in French archaeology. One excavation, so many deaths. It's a very serious matter.'

'I assure you, Marc, I know that.'

'Professor Barbier is concerned. The Minister is concerned. There's a danger of the image of this spectacular national monument being tarnished by these human tragedies.'

Luc was almost amused that Abenheim was parroting his words from the first ministry meeting — 'spectacular national monument'. 'I'm sure it will be a footnote to every report and popular article about Ruac in the future,' Luc replied. 'That much is unavoidable, I'm sure, but

236

I'm also sure that now is not the right time to think of these matters.'

'The ministry depends on me to think about these matters!'

'What do you want us to do, Marc? What do you want *me* to do?'

'I want you to resign as director of the excavation.'

To Luc, the stencilled hands seemed to be in motion, rotating in a slow clockwise swirl.

He heard himself answering this snivelling son-of-a-bitch. 'Zvi Alon's accident. Hugo Pineau's car crash. This attack on the camp. These are random acts. Horrible random acts.' He stopped for a moment to listen to his own argument. Minutes ago he was trying to convince Colonel Toucas to keep an open mind about connections. In exasperation he asked, 'How will my resignation help explain anything or bring closure to anyone?'

'Random acts? Perhaps. But there's one link, Luc, and we can't ignore it.'

'What link?'

'They all happened under your watch. You have to take responsibility. You have to go. The commission has named me the new director effective immediately.'

23

Ruac Cave, 30,000 BP

Tal had begun calling the red liquid Soaring Water.

No one could say a man was meant to fly. But after drinking Soaring Water, no one could say where a man ended and a bird began.

How often had he looked up at birds on the wing and wondered what they could see and how they felt?

Now he knew.

Fear quickly gave way to exhilaration and a sensation of overwhelming power.

The power to soar on the wind, to see great distances, to feel more deeply, the power to understand.

He would always return from his journeys where they had begun — by the fire. He was sure he had been on remarkable adventures, spanning time and great distances but his people insisted his body had been rooted, restless, to be sure, thrashing, spouting strange utterances, but very much rooted to one spot. And everyone learned how to deal with the aftermath, a turbulent period they called, Tal's Anger.

Throughout the clan, there had been anxiety and worry during his first soaring journey. Tal's fate was fixed by his brother's death. His father was growing weaker by the day and the very existence of the Bison Clan was dependent on his ability to rise to his position and lead them into the future.

His insistence on trying the red liquid was a matter of furious debate. Tal had argued that the boy Gos had been made to drink the liquid by their ancestors to show the clan a new path forward. A grand plan was playing out in front of their eyes. First Tal's father was sickened and weakened by his accident. Then Nago was killed by the sacred bison. Then Gos drank the powerful liquid Tal had prepared to heal Nago.

These were not unconnected events.

Tal argued he was meant to learn from the teachings of the Soaring Liquid. When his father passed, he was meant to be a bold new clan leader.

The Elders counselled otherwise. If Tal were lost, what would become of the clan? The risk was too great. The world was a dangerous place. The Shadow People were lurking in the woods.

In the end, Tal's father made the decision, perhaps his last great one. He was weak in body but strong in mind.

Tal could embark on his quest.

The first time Tal swallowed Soaring Water, Uboas told him she would sit by his side and stay awake as long as it took for him to return. Deep into the night, she stroked his hair, tried to respond to his guttural sounds and touched his dry lips with her water-dipped fingers.

When he finally came back to her, in the bluish dawn, hers were the first human eyes he saw.

He reached out to touch her face and she asked him where he had been and what he had seen.

And this is what he told her.

He felt his body transform. First his hands turned into talons then his face elongated into a hard beak. With a few easy flaps of his arms he was airborne, making lazy passes over the fire, peering down on his own people, circling protectively, getting accustomed to tilting and turning. The whistling wind and the light, effortless travel exhilarated him and made his heart sing. Was he the first in his clan to experience such things, the first man?

In the distance he saw black horses grazing in the savannah and he flew towards them, attracted by their grace and power. He swooped over their broad rippling backs, making them gallop and sweat. He flew among them, eye-to-eye, matching their speed. Of course he had seen horses before. He had crept up to them and pierced them in the flank, spilling their blood. He had eaten their flesh, worn their hides. But he had never seen them before. Not like this.

Their huge brown eyes were clear like puddles on dark stones after a rain storm. There was no fear in those eyes, just a life force as strong as he had ever experienced. He saw his own reflection in those brown globes, the shoulders and arms of a man, the head of a hawk. And then he saw beyond his reflection into the heart of the beast. He felt its freedom and wild abandon. He felt its life force, its determination to survive.

He felt a stirring in his loins and looked down.

He was large and erect, prepared for mating. He felt more alive than ever before.

He arched his neck and soared higher, leaving the horses behind. Something caught his keen hawk's eyes. On the horizon. A dark mass. Moving.

He tilted and rode the wind across the flowing river, towards the vast plain.

Bison.

A huge herd, the largest he could remember, moving as one, thundering the earth with the power of their stampede. Would they let him into their midst?

He lowered his head and dove until he was skimming the ground, following behind, catching up. Haunches and tails, as far as the eye could see. His ears filled up with the sound of churning hooves.

Then they parted.

They were letting him inside.

Bison to the right, bison to the left, he flapped his arms and matched their speed until he was level with the lead beasts, two huge males with heads the size of boulders and horns as long as a man's forearms.

While the horse eyes were full of freedom and spirit, the black bison eyes were brimming with wisdom. He was talking to them, not with words, but with a language more powerful. He was them, they were him. They spoke to him of his ancestors and their ancient ways. He spoke to them of his love and reverence. He told them he was Tal, of the Bison Clan.

They honoured him by letting him run with them. In turn, they demanded he honour them.

And after Tal told her everything, he drifted off to sleep, but when he awoke a short time later, his mood was as dark as the night. He yelled at her to withdraw. He threw off his skins. He was shouting, in blind anger, cursing the night, demanding the sun to rise. When the clan was awakened by his shouts and one of his cousins approached to calm him, he attacked the young man and tried to throttle him before other men pulled him off and held him down.

Uboas was frightened by his wild eyes but she came back to his side and rubbed his shoulders even as he strained against the hands and knees of the men who were restraining him with all their might.

And when his anger finally passed and he returned to his normal self, the men cautiously released him. Talking among themselves they drifted back to their skins. Uboas stayed with him, pressing herself against his now-calm body until the morning.

★ ★ ★

Following his first Soaring, Tal's mind was never more active. He approached his commitment to the Bison Clan with a fury of purposeful activity. His determination was a source of awe and inspiration. It was almost as if he were growing into the role of head man before the clan's eyes. His post-soaring rage scared them, but they also knew that a head man had to be fierce. The

242

world was hazardous and they needed a warrior.

Tal became a font of activity, even more than usual. On one day he was leading a hunt, landing a good reindeer buck with one thrust of his spear. On the next day he was off on his own, collecting plants. Then he was knapping fresh sharp cutting blades and teaching Uboas how to chop the vegetation, crush the berries and place his mother's stone bowl into the embers of the fire until the red liquid bubbled into Soaring Water.

He felt a tug towards the magical place he had found the time he had climbed the cliffs to commune with his ancestors — Tal's cave. Uboas went with him, to watch over him and keep him safe. At the mouth of the cave, he lit a fire and the two of them sat in silence as night came to the valley. He warned her to leave him when the anger started.

Then he soared.

And she watched over him and trembled later in the night when he flew into a rage and charged deep into the black cave, shouting for his ancestors to reveal themselves.

The next morning she fed him chunks of reindeer stomach, roasted over the fire, its contents full of the mashed grasses that had been the animal's last meal. He told her about the soaring and the creatures he had visited as half man, half bird. When he had eaten his fill he rose and paced the mouth of the cave until his legs became strong and sturdy once again.

The pale stone walls of the cave, that outermost zone that caught the morning sun dazzled his eyes. A few steps deeper and all was dark. He thought about his journey. He had been with the bison again. And the horses. And the deer. And the bears. Before his eyes, on the cave walls, he saw the images his hawk eyes had seen, these animals in all their glory and power. They demanded respect. The bison demanded his honour.

He rushed to the fire and grabbed a kindling stick, its end charred black. As Uboas watched, he strode back to the sunny wall and began to draw a long curving line, at eye level, parallel to the ground. The charcoal line was thin and poorly adhesive and the result was not pleasing to his eye, no better than the outlines he had drawn at his mother's knee. He complained out loud. In a flash of inspiration, he poured out the remnants of the Soaring Water from his stone bowl and pressed a hunk of reindeer fat into the concavity. He took another kindling stick with a heavily burned end and twirled it into the fat until it was black and greasy. Then he retraced the curving line and this time it was thick and black and stuck smoothly to the rock surface.

He quietly worked into the morning, dipping fatted kindling sticks and painting in equal measures with his hand and his heart. When he was done he grunted and summoned Uboas to stand beside him.

She gasped at what she saw. A perfect horse, as real and beautiful as any living creature. It was running, its hooves in full gallop, its mouth open, sucking air, its ears pointing forwards. Tal had given it a thick mane that looked so real she was tempted to stroke it to feel its silkiness. It had a captivating oval-shaped eye with a black disc in the centre, a piercing, all-knowing eye. It was the most beautiful inanimate form she had ever seen.

She began to sob.

Tal wanted to know what was wrong and she told him. She was moved by its magnificence but she was also scared.

Of what?

Of this new power that Tal possessed. He was a different man than the one she knew. The Soaring Water had transformed him into a mingler with the world of spirits and ancestors, a shaman. The old Tal was gone, perhaps for ever. She feared him now. Then her real concern erupted in a geyser of tears. Would he still want her as his mate? Would he still love her?

He gave her his answer. Yes.

★ ★ ★

When Tal's father finally died he had become an emaciated bag of bones. He was carried to a hallowed spot, a stretch of the river where the tall grasses and reeds gently sloped to the water, a spot he had come to throughout his life to listen to the voice of the flowing water. His body was quietly left on the slope. From a distance, Tal looked back one last time. It appeared as if the old man was resting. If he were to come back in a day there would only be bones. In three days, nothing.

Tal's elevation to head man simply happened.

There was no ceremony and no words said. It was not their custom. If the clan people had any doubts about Tal's ability to lead them, perhaps there would have been whispers, but the elders who remembered Tal's grandfather, and the one wizened old soul who remembered his great-grandfather, agreed that Tal would be a powerful head man. Yes, he was very young but he was a healer and a soarer who was able to commune with the natural world and the realm of the ancestors. And they very much feared Tal's Anger, that time when he was unapproachable and violently malevolent. And there was furtive talk about a magical cave in the cliffs that no one but Tal and his new mate, Uboas, had ever seen.

One day, Tal announced that he would lead the clan up the cliffs to see for themselves what had been consuming him. Even though the weather was fine the trek was slow because the oldest people had to walk with sticks and Uboas was heavily laden with a child in her belly. They arrived with the sun at its highest, splashing the river with its rays. Tal made a fire on the ledge and lit a torch slathered in bear fat for a rich, slow burn.

He stepped inside the cave and the clan shuffled at his heels.

The light of the torch eased the transition from light to dark. In the hissing glow, his people were stunned. One young woman yelped in fear because she though she was going to be trampled by horses to her left and bison to her right. A small boy became giddy at the sight of a huge black bull floating overhead and he jumped

246

up and down making sure his mother saw what he was seeing.

Tal had been working steadily, preparing this place. With his father's blessing, he had taken Uboas as his mate and the two of them had fallen into a joyous rhythm. When he was not hunting or catching fish or resolving arguments among clan members, he would prepare a batch of Soaring Water and climb to the cave with her. He would drink the tart red liquid, spend the night lost in his dream world and when he came back to her, energised and virile, his loins aching, he would lie with his mate on his father's bison hide laid on the cave floor and thrust his hips until they were both spent. After a sleep, he would rage for a time, like a wild animal until his body was limp and exhausted from demon exertions.

And then he would come back to himself, cleansed, and he would paint.

Drawing upon his childhood pastime of mixing pigments from crushed coloured rocks and clays, he had prepared wonderfully rich paints which, through trial and error, he adapted to adhere to the cool, moist walls.

It was not enough to draw the outlines of the animals as people had done in the past. He saw them in vivid colours and that was the way he wanted to capture them. He chose his spots by the light of his lamps, which in and of themselves were an invention that sprang from his mind. He used his skills as a stone-shaper to fashion a shallow, ladle-shaped lamp from limestone, and in the bowl, he placed lumps of bear fat mixed with juniper twigs, which when lit, gave a yellow, slow-burning flame that Uboas held for him while he worked.

He also considered the topography of the wall. If a bump suggested a horse's rump, then there he drew the rump. If a depression suggested a creature's eye, that is where he placed the eye. And he was always keen to see how the lamp light played against the rock surface. He loved the sense of motion he could achieve with light and shadows.

He would draw the outlines of the animals with fat and charcoal or a lump of manganese but his desire to capture the true colours of the beasts led him to devise ways to deliver ochres and clays to the walls in a way that would faithfully coat the surfaces. When smearing pigments with his hands failed to produce the effect he was seeking, he conceived a radical solution, based on his belief that through his visions, his mission was to breathe life into these cave walls.

Breath.

Uboas tried to stop him the first time he tried the manoeuvre, thinking him mad. In a stone bowl he mixed ochres and clay and added water and spittle to make a slurry then scooped it into his mouth. He chewed at the slurry and sloshed it from cheek to cheek and when it felt the right consistency, he pursed his lips, stood a short distance from the wall and spat the colour out in a mist of fine droplets, using his hand like a stencil to shape the spray to the contour of his outlines. When he wanted to give the animal's hide texture and body, he had the inspiration to blow his paint through a hole punched through leather to concentrate the spray into dots. It was slow, painstaking work, but he was happy, even when Uboas teased him on one day about his red tongue, on another day about his black lips.

The clan people whispered and murmured as Tal led them from painting to painting, from wall to wall. Tal's animals had all the vitality and colour of the animals they knew so well. The horses were black and stippled, the bison, swathed in black, reds and browns, the giant bull, black as night.

He held the lamp in his left hand, touched his proud heart with his right and announced that this was only the beginning of a long journey for the Bison Clan. The cave was vast, too long for them to even imagine, darker and colder than any place in the world. He told them it was a gift from the ancestors and the spirit world to him, and as head man, it was his gift to them to make it their sacred place. He would continue to paint all the important animals for as long as he breathed. And he would teach the young men. From now on, their passage to manhood would take place in the cave. The boys would drink Soaring Water so they could learn to roam freely among the creatures of the land and learn from them. He would teach them how to paint what they saw. This would be the most sacred place in the world and it would belong only to the Bison Clan.

The elders nodded their approval and all the people agreed. Make no mistake, they had loved

Tal's father, but his son was a leader like no other in their long history as a clan.

Tal and Uboas were the last to leave. Just as he was about to douse the lamp with a handful of dirt, Uboas reached into the pouch hanging on her horse-hair belt and pulled something out with her fingers. She gave it to him. A small statue of a bison that she had carved from the ivory tusk of the bison that had killed his brother. He stood it in his hand and held the lamp close to inspect it. He placed his large hand on the top of her head and held it there tenderly until she laughed and told him the old people would fall off the ledge without their help.

The clan dispersed themselves on the ledge waiting for Tal to emerge. He blinked in the harsh sunlight and waited a moment to regain his sight. The boy, Gos, suddenly began pointing out towards the valley, well over the river. Tal's eyes focused on the moving forms, small as ants, but unmistakably two-legged. A tribe was moving through the savannah, stalking a bunch of reindeer seemingly unaware of their presence.

The tiny figures in the distance must have seen something or sensed something because one of them began pointing his spear up at the cliffs. From what Tal could see, the entire tribe, a good ten of them, began pointing their spears and jumping like fleas. Though too far away to hear, they must have started shouting because the reindeer bolted, and they too ran off back towards the green forest.

One of the young men of the Bison Clan, a hot-headed hunter, second only to Tal in his spear-throwing ability, started calling for a war. The reindeer belonged to the clan. They needed to drive the intruders away, once and for all.

Tal nodded and told them they were too far away to take any action, but in his heart, he was content to ignore them. Today was a joyous day of spiritual commitment. There would be other days to worry about the Shadow People.

★   ★   ★

Many years passed.

Every day he was not hunting, healing or helping his clan, Tal was inside his cave, soaring and painting. And twice a year, before each bison hunt, he summoned the boys who had come of age. There, in the yellow glow of his juniper lamps, the clan would gather in the Chamber of the Bison Hunt, Tal's mystical two-walled mural, where a half man, half bird, stood open-beaked, amongst a herd of charging bison and the chosen beast was felled by a spear, spilling its guts. The chosen boys would chant a prayer to the ancestors. They would call out their pleas in their high sweet voices, and the clan, taking the role of their ancestors, would respond in low, far-away voices.

Tal would then give the boys a long drink of Soaring Water and the clan would watch over them singing until they were able to stand and be led by Tal, trance-like, into the deeper reaches of the cave, past fantastic, brightly painted, lions, bears, red deer, and woolly mammoth. The boys would stare with amazed eyes and from the fire in their eyes, Tal knew they were soaring alongside the creatures, close enough to feel the heat of their bodies, to merge souls. The cave would disappear, the walls would disappear, the boys would pass through them like a man walking through a wall of water to a place on the other side of a waterfall. And later, when their visions turned to anger, the boys would howl at each other and fight for a time, but the Elders always kept them safe.

Uboas gave birth to only two children, both sons, then despite Tal's desires to father a large brood, she became barren. No amount of exhortation to his ancestors would make her womb fertile. Yet, both his sons survived beyond infancy and grew healthy and strong. There were no prouder moments in Tal's life than when he initiated his own sons into manhood and took them into the cave for the first time. His oldest son Mem, was, without doubt, his favourite, and he poured his teachings into the boy the way a woman lavished a newborn with her milk. The boy would be a shaman, the clan's next head man.

Mem was quick to learn and proved to be nearly as fine a painter as his father. They worked together side-by-side, spit-painting beautiful creatures. Day after day, month after month, father and son would build platforms of tree limbs and vines and stand upon them to reach the high walls and ceilings in chamber after chamber.

One day, early in his tutelage, the boy made a mistake. He was spitting a red ochre against his outstretched hand, using the angle between his thumb and wrist to make the gentle curve of a deer's back leg. He was momentarily distracted by the unsteadiness and shifting of his wooden platform and instead of delivering the paint to the wall, most of it landed squarely on the back of his hand, coating it orange-red. When he took his hand away from the wall, there was a perfect stencil of his palm and parted fingers. The boy winced, waiting for the opprobrium of his father but instead, Tal was delighted. He thought the handprint was a wonderful thing and he promptly tried the technique himself.

One handprint became two and in time, the cave would be filled with them, joyful marks of humanity and a father's pride in his son.

And many years later, after Tal had discovered the malachite crystals that he learned how to grind into green pigment, Mem and his other son joined their father in the last chamber. They crawled through a narrow natural tunnel, into the special part of the cave Tal had long reserved for his sanctuary, the most sacrosanct of places, where they would paint the images of the plants that let him soar and connect with the spirit world.

And among the plants, Tal himself painted the life-size bird man, his soaring spirit, his other self.

24

Tuesday

Luc called Sara once, twice, three times then repeated the effort every hour or so. He hammered her mobile with messages. He got her home number in London from directory assistance and tried that. He called her office. When leaving messages got old, he hung up at the beep.

He was back at his flat in Bordeaux, a tidy bachelor pad in a high-rise, minutes from the campus. He was battling a rough sea of roiling emotions, barely keeping his head above the water.

Anger. Frustration. Grief. Longing.

Luc wasn't the type to dwell on feelings, but he couldn't avoid them. They were bashing him in the head, ramming him in the gut, making him punch the furniture, scream into a pillow, choke back the urge to cry.

He ducked calls. If he didn't recognise the number he let them ring through. Reporters, including Gérard Girot from *Le Monde*, called him incessantly but he was under a gag order from the Ministry; press contacts were in the hands of Marc Abenheim.

Who could he talk to — other than Sara?

He would have called Hugo, but he was dead.

He would have met up with Jeremy and Pierre

for a beer, but they were dead.

There were no women to turn to. All his relationships were dead.

His bastard of a father was dead.

His mother was in another world geographically and neurologically, in the first grip of Alzheimer's, and what would be the point of distressing her? And he might have the bad luck of getting the dermatologist on the line.

That left Sara. Why wasn't she picking up the phone or responding to texts and emails? He'd left her in hell at Nuffield Hospital, blazing off in a blind panic, oblivious to *her* needs. 'There's been an emergency,' and he was gone. He alluded to the crisis in his messages. It was in all the papers. Other team members would have surely reached out to her. She *had* to know.

Where was she?

He wasn't one to drink on his own, but he drained a bottle of Haitian rum left over from an old party over the course of the afternoon. In a boozy mist he came to this conclusion: Sara was done with him. This was more than a brush off, it was terminal. The bridge was burned to its pilings. Bad things happened to her when he was around. He'd hurt her once. He'd probably just hurt her again by ditching her in Cambridge. He was toxic. Cars veered at him on the pavement. People died around him. The next time he heard from her would be an email with an attached report on her pollen findings at Ruac, signed, With Best Regards, Sara. Or maybe not even that. Abenheim might have already contacted her and told her to communicate exclusively with him from now on. Maybe he forbade her to speak with Luc altogether.

Abenheim could go to hell. Ruac was *his* cave.

He ran a bath and while he was soaking he tried not to close his eyes because each time he did, he saw the covered bodies on the floor of the Portakabin, or Hugo, crushed in his car, or Zvi, broken at the river's edge. He balled his hands into fists and realised his right hand was getting better, less red and less painful. He didn't much care but he'd keep taking the Asian doctor's pills. The phone chimed a few times. He let it ring.

Wrapped in a towel, he listened to his new voice messages. One was from Gérard Girot again, urgently requesting a comment. The next was from Pierre's father, calling from Paris.

25

Wednesday

Luc had only one suit and fortunately it was dark, appropriate for funerals.

There were two in rapid succession, Jeremy's in Manchester and Pierre's in Paris.

There was an interesting bond between a graduate student and a thesis adviser. Part parental, part filial, part comradeship. It didn't always work out that way. Some professors were stand-offish. Some students were immature. But Jeremy and Pierre were good students and close friends and he thought he would never fully recover from their murders.

That morning, with a thick head, dry mouth and pangs in his chest, he caught one of the few direct flights from Bordeaux to Manchester.

Jeremy's funeral was a rather bloodless Church of England affair. The family and parishioners were stoical. It wasn't clear that the minister, a high-pitched Irish fellow, had ever met Jeremy judging from his generalities and platitudes about a man being plucked from the flock at such a young age.

Outside the church, in a gritty central Manchester neighbourhood, a cold rain was falling and no one wanted to hang about too long. Luc waited for his turn and introduced himself to Jeremy's family, an older couple who had clearly conceived their boy at the edge of female fertility. They seemed confused by it all, almost post-concussive, and Luc didn't put any demands on them. They had heard of him through Jeremy and acknowledged that and his father thanked him for coming all the way from France. Then his mother asked, 'Were you there, Professor Simard?'

'No ma'am. I was in England.'

'What on God's earth happened?' she said. It wasn't clear from the glassy look on her face, she really wanted to know.

'The police think it was a robbery. That's all I was told. They don't think he suffered.'

'He was a good boy. I'm glad of that. He's at peace.'

'Yes, I'm sure he is.'

'He was keen on this archaeology,' his father said, snapping out of his daze, long enough to start crying.

★　★　★

Rather than fly directly back to Paris, he took a commuter jet to Heathrow and jumped in a cab. Sara was still *in communicado*, but he couldn't let it stand. He was in England. He'd exert the effort and try to make amends.

She lived in St Pancras, a stone's throw from the British Library and a short enough walk to her job at the Institute of Archaeology.

At Ossulston Street, he got out of the cab into the driving rain of a muddy-skied evening. He had no umbrella and his suit jacket soaked

258

through in the time it took to figure out which entrance to the block of flats was hers. From the directory, Flat 21 was on the third floor. Its entrance was in a well of sorts, protected from the rain, which was fortunate because there was no answer to his persistent buzzing.

He was about to call it quits when a woman came to the door. It wasn't Sara. The woman, about Sara's age, was stringy-haired and wore no make-up. A long baggy sweater hid her figure.

'I'm sorry, were you ringing Sara Mallory's bell?'

Luc nodded.

'I'm her neighbour, Victoria. The walls are frightfully thin. Actually, I've been worried about her. Do you know where she is?'

'No, that's why I'm here.'

'You're French, aren't you?' she asked.

'Yes, I am.'

She looked at him like a robin about to pluck a worm from its hole. 'Are you Luc?'

★   ★   ★

She took him up to Flat 22, gave him a towel and made tea. She was a freelance writer who worked from home. As she told it, Sara and she had become friends from the day Sara moved in. When Sara was in town, they had dinner at each other's flats or the local curry house once or twice a week. They'd been emailing and texting sporadically during the dig. She was clearly clued into Sara's life and she looked Luc over with knowing eyes that seemed to proclaim: *So that's*

259

the famous Luc! That's what all the fuss is about!

She poured the tea and said, 'She texted me Saturday night from France. She said she was coming back to London Monday night. Now it's Wednesday. I saw what happened at Ruac on the news. I've been frantic but no one's been able to tell me anything. Please tell me she wasn't caught up in that.'

'No, no, she wasn't there when it happened, thank God. She was with me in Cambridge Monday morning,' Luc explained. 'We were visiting a man in hospital when I was called away to deal with the tragedy. I went back to France and left her in Cambridge. I haven't heard from her since.'

'Oh my,' she said, with a look of fright.

'Are you positive she couldn't have come back to London without your knowledge?'

She confessed she couldn't be sure and volunteered that she had a key to Sara's flat. Perhaps they might check together.

Sara's flat was identical in size and shape to her neighbour's but it was a world apart in atmosphere. Unlike Victoria's drab décor of lumpy furniture in greys and whites, Sara's vibrated with colour and energy and he recognised it straight away as a re-creation of sorts of her old Paris apartment he knew so well. They'd made love on that red sofa. They'd slept under that peacock-blue bedspread.

Victoria buzzed around, checking the flat, and announced, 'She's not been back. I'm sure of it.'

Luc had another card in his wallet from the investigating officers in Cambridge.

'I'm going to call the police.'

26

Thursday Morning

Paris looked pristine in the flat cold light of the autumn morning. As Luc's taxi drove from his hotel in the centre of the city, east towards the Périphérique, the neighbourhoods became dingier until they were in the suburbs, in Montreuil, where if you strained your eyes you could just spot the Eiffel Tower glimmering hopefully on the western horizon.

Off the Boulevard Rouget de Lisle, they drove through a section where there were as many black faces as white, and outside an old Catholic church in the middle of a crowded block, black people were streaming up the steps.

Luc had never met Pierre's father but Philippe Berewa obviously had his eye out for him, because the man rushed down the steps as soon as Luc sent the taxi off.

They embraced. As tall as Luc was, Philippe was a head taller and had the same type of athletic physique as his son. His face was creased with age. He was wearing a three-piece suit with a gold watch chain, an elegant throw-back to another time and place. Luc knew he'd been a doctor in Sierra Leone, and that he'd never been able to get his certification in France and had been relegated to more lowly work as a hospital technician. Luc nevertheless, called him Doctor.

261

The church was already packed. Luc was led to the front pew where a seat of honour had been reserved for him, next to Pierre's mother, a heavyset woman in a sombre dress and small black hat, who was weeping openly.

As the Requiem Mass progressed, the contrasts to Jeremy's funeral were manifest. The mourners here were under none of the emotional constraints of Jeremy's kith and kin. There was open sobbing and wailing and the moment Pierre's casket was met by the priest, who sprinkled it with Holy Water and began intoning the *De Profundis*, a tsunami of grief ran through the church.

Afterwards, there were no questions about what had happened, as if God's will was a universal explanation, a completely soothing balm. What his parents and siblings wanted Luc to know was that Pierre had died doing something he loved more than anything on earth and that it had been an honour for him to be the student of the illustrious Professor Simard.

All Luc could do was hold on to them, say a few choice words about how special he was and tell them a plaque with Pierre's name would be driven into the cliffs at the mouth of Ruac Cave.

★   ★   ★

Luc was in a taxi again, heading back into town, limp from mourning. He checked his voicemail; there was nothing, so he called up the detective inspector in Cambridge he'd spoken to the previous evening about Sara. The detective had promised to check accident and other police reports and local hospital admissions for any mention of a Sara Mallory.

He reached DI Chambers on his mobile. The man seemed rushed and distracted, in the middle of something else. He said there had been no police, ambulance or hospital records involving Professor Mallory but he'd be sure to let Luc know if that were to change. Luc couldn't even be sure if he'd done anything. Maybe he was lying through his teeth. And when Luc asked if there'd been any developments in the Science Park explosion, the officer frostily referred him to the Cambridge Police website for information. That was that.

Luc had seen Hugo's people at his memorial service, so when he returned to the office of H. Pineau Restorations on Rue Beaujon there was no need to replay words of grief and loss. The sentiment was on everyone's face — it wasn't necessary to put it on their lips.

Even the effervescent Margot was incapable of more than a wan smile. He followed her past Hugo's office, sealed like a mausoleum, to Isaak Mansion's office down the hall. Isaak was on the way, she told him, and offered a coffee.

When she came back with a tray, he asked how things were going.

'Not well. Isaak can tell you.' She had something in her hand and opened her palm to show it, as if it was a jewel or a relic. Hugo's mobile. Small, thin and modern, just like him. 'The police sent it back. Maybe I shouldn't have but I looked through it. There were some lovely photos of you and Luc with some women.'

'Ah,' Luc said faintly, 'our dinner at Domme. His last night.'

'You all looked so happy. Would you like them?'

He thought about it, the sadness of it all, but said he would.

'I'll email them to you, if that's okay,' and she was off, crying again.

Isaak was a few minutes late. He came striding in, with a troubled look on his face. With a minimum of smalltalk, he launched into an agitated apologia for his foul mood.

'You were his friend, Luc, so I can tell you that it's all going to hell. I had to take over the books, of course, and I can tell you, the business wasn't as good as Hugo made out. He had big loans against the assets, to feed his lifestyle, you know. It was barely profitable and now, without him, business is way down. We're in the red. It's not sustainable.'

'I'm sorry. Is there anything I can do?'

'Other than join me in the restoration business? No, just venting. We'll have to sell it to settle his estate. I'm talking to bankers. This is my problem. You have your own. I'm sorry to equate mine with yours.'

'Don't apologise,' Luc said. 'We'd both be better off if Hugo were still here. Look, it's good of you to make some time. What do you have for me?'

'Like I said in my voice message. More of your manuscript. Hugo's Belgian contact decoded another chunk.'

'Did he say what the key word was?'

Isaak's desk was in chaos, files and papers everywhere. He searched and cursed for a good minute before laying hands on the folder. 'HELOISE.'

'Not a shock,' Luc said. 'It's in Latin, no?'

'It's not a problem. I read Latin, Greek, even a bit of Hebrew and Aramaic. Hugo picked me for my background. He didn't want a guy who only knew spreadsheets.'

'Do you have time to translate it now?'

'For a friend of Hugo's, of course!' He scratched his beard. 'Also, I'm curious, and it's more fun than sorting through accounts payable.'

Luc's phone rang and he excused himself when he recognised the number.

'Luc, it's Father Menaud calling.' There was a tremor in his voice.

'Hello, Dom Menaud. Are you all right?'

'It's a silly thing to be upset about, what with the horrible tragedy of the murders but . . . ' His voice trailed off.

'But what, Father?'

'I've just found out the manuscript is gone! It was in the box on my desk. You recall it?'

'Of course.'

'I opened the box this morning to look at it and it wasn't there! You don't know anything about it, do you?'

'No, nothing. When was the last time you saw it?'

'Perhaps a week ago. Before the tragedy.'

'Could someone have gone into your rooms

265

and stolen it Sunday night?'

'Yes. Nothing is locked here. I and the Brothers were at prayer when your people were attacked.'

'I'm sorry, Father. I don't know what to say. We have a very faithful colour copy of the manuscript, of course, but that's no substitute. You should call Colonel Toucas and let him know. And listen — a little good news, I suppose. Another section has been decoded. I'll send you the information when I have it.'

Luc re-pocketed his phone and saw that Isaak was staring at him.

'On top of everything, Isaak, the Ruac Manuscript was stolen, perhaps the night of the murders. I'm not buying the randomness of all the shit that's happened. Not for a minute. It's more important than ever for us to know what the manuscript says. It has to be the key, so please, let's go.'

Isaak had the lengthy email from Belgium printed out. He put on his reading glasses, and began translating the Latin, on the fly, apologising for his stumbles and wistfully interjecting that Hugo was the superior Latin scholar.

It is a mystery to me how like-minded men, united in exaltation of Christ, could come to opposite conclusions about a shared experience. Whereas myself, Jean and Abélard were firmly of the belief the red infusion we prepared was a path to spiritual enlightenment and physical vigour, Bernard was

266

strongly opposed. Whereas we took to calling the liquid, Enlightenment Tea, Bernard declared it a Devil's brew. Bernard's rebuke was a great blow to us all, but none more so than Abélard who had come to love and respect my brother as deeply as if they were of the same flesh and blood. Bernard took his leave of Ruac and returned to Clairvaux when we three declared we would not forego the pleasures of the infusion. We would not, and indeed, felt we could not.

27

Priory of St Marcel, 1142

For a priory as modest as the one in St Marcel, it was an extraordinary gathering. Well set back from the River Saône and nestled in a dense thicket, the priory was ill equipped to deal with the influx of pilgrims. They arrived from all the compass-points of France, and how such a diverse population had efficiently learned about one man's imminent death, no one could say for sure.

Abélard, the great teacher, philosopher and theologian lay dying.

There were students, disciples and admirers from all the way-stations of his life — Paris, Nogent-sur-Seine, Ruac, the Abbeys of Saint-Denis and St Gildas de Rhuys, the Paraclete in Ferreux-Quincey, and finally, this friendly final sanctuary near Cluny. He had spent his life teaching and wandering, thinking and writing and were it not for the dreaded white plague, the consumption that was eating away at his lungs, he would have continued to attract many more followers. Such was his charisma.

The infirmary was little more than a thatched hut and in the trodden-down clearing between the hut and the chapel, perhaps forty men had pitched camp to pray, to talk and to visit at his bedside in ones and twos.

The path from Ruac to St Marcel had been a

twenty-four year exploration of life and love. Abélard had left Ruac, his health and outlook restored and had travelled to The Abbey of St Denis, where he had assumed the habit of a Benedictine monk, and had begun an explosively rich period of meditation and writing. Not only did he produce his controversial treatise on the Holy Trinity, much to the discomfort of the Church orthodoxy, but he also continued to write letter after letter, ever more passionate, to his beloved Héloïse, still ensconced at the nunnery of Argenteuil.

He was nothing, if not feisty. His inquisitive temperament, rapier intelligence and boundless energy led him to argue and probe and shake established thought from its foundations. And whenever his spirits flagged or his pace slowed, he would set off with his wicker basket into the fields and meadows to collect plants and berries, much to the amusement of his fellow monks who knew not what he did with them.

He had his own personal trinity of sorts that occupied all his waking thoughts: theology, philosophy and Héloïse. Of the first two, few men had the sufficiency of mind to spar with him or share his intellectual proclivities. Of the last, all men could understand his longings.

Héloïse, sweet Héloïse, remained the love of his life, the fiery beacon on a faraway hill that beckoned him home. But she had taken the veil and he had taken the cloth and Christ was their proper object of devotion. All they could do was exchange letters that singed each other with their passion.

Neither he nor Bernard of Clairvaux, would have ever imagined that Bernard's new-found enmity of Abélard would have formed the bridge that would unite the star-crossed lovers.

When Bernard left Ruac, and returned to Cîteaux healed in body but troubled in spirit, he bitterly rued the decision his brother Barthomieu had taken not to forsake the devil brew. On reflection, he blamed no one more than Abélard for the turn of events because among the players in this affair, none was more ample of mind and persuasive than that eunuch. His poor brother was a mere pawn. The true evil-doer was Abélard.

For that reason, he used his ever-widening sphere of ecclesiastical influence to keep tabs on that renegade monk and when Abélard's treatise on the Trinity made it into his hands, he seized on its heresies, as he saw them, to have him summoned before a papal council at Soissons in 1121 to answer for himself.

Was he not proclaiming a Tritheistic view that Father, Son and Holy Ghost were separable, each with their own existence, Bernard fumed? Was the One God merely an abstraction to him? Had the devil brew made him lose his mind?

With no little satisfaction, Bernard learned that Abélard had been forced by the Pope to burn his own book and retreat to St Denis in disgrace. But bitter seeds had been sown. The monks at the abbey saw fit to rid themselves of Abélard and his heresy and he withdrew to the solitude of a deserted place in the vicinity of Troyes, in a hamlet known as Ferreux-Quincey.

There, he and a small band of followers established a new monastery they called the Oratory of the Paraclete. Paraclete — the Holy Ghost. A stick-in-the-eye to his accusers.

The place suited Abélard. It was remote, it had a good spring nearby, fertile soil and an ample source of wood for building a church. And, to his satisfaction there was an abundance of possession weed, barley grasses and gooseberries in the environs.

When the basics of the oratory were constructed and there was a chapel and lodgings, he did something he could not have done had he not been the abbot of this new place: he summoned Héloïse.

She came from Argenteuil on a horse-drawn cart, accompanied by a small entourage of nuns.

Though veiled in the simple habit of a sister, she was as captivating as he had remembered.

Surrounded by their followers, they could not embrace. A touch of hands, that was all. That was enough.

He noticed her crucifix was larger than her companions'. 'You are a prioress, now,' he observed.

'And you are an abbot, sir,' she countered.

'We have risen to high office,' he jested.

'The better to serve Christ,' she said, lowering her eyes.

★ ★ ★

He came to her at night in the little house he had built. She protested. They argued. He was wild-eyed, talking too fast in a dreamy way, cogent but fluid without the starts and pauses of normal discourse. He had drunk his Enlightenment Tea earlier in the evening. She did not need to know that. He was pressed for time. His mood would curdle soon enough and he did not want her to bear witness.

Her wit and tongue were rapier-sharp, as ever. Her skin was as white as the finest marble in her uncle Fulbert's salon. Too little of it showed from under her chaste rough habit. He pushed her down on her bed and fell onto her, kissing her neck, her cheeks. She pushed back and chided but then yielded and kissed him too. He pulled at the coarse fabric that covered her to her ankles and exposed the flesh of her thigh.

'We cannot,' she moaned.

'We are husband and wife,' he panted.

'No longer.'

'Still.'

'*You* cannot,' she said, and then she felt his hardness against her leg. 'How is this possible?' she gasped. 'Your mishap?'

'I told you there was a way for us to be man and wife again,' he said, and he lifted her habit high over her waist.

★　★　★

Hypocrisy.

It weighed on them. She was married to Christ. He had taken the vows of a monk and those vows included chastity. Both of them had towering intellects and full knowledge of the

272

religious, ethical and moral consequences of their actions. Yet, they could not stop.

After Matins, several times a week, Abélard would retire to his abbot house, drink a draught of Enlightenment Tea, and in the middle of the night come to her. Some nights she said no, initially. Some nights she spoke not a word. But every time he came, she would consent and they would lie together as man and wife. And every time, when they were done, he left her in a hail of self-deprecation and tears. And he too, when he was alone, would pray fervently for the absolution of his sins.

Their liaisons could have continued without interference. He was a eunuch. This was universally known. Their relationship, was by this twist of fate, beyond suspicion or reproach.

Yet it could not stand. In the end, Christ was stronger than their lust. Their guilt tore them to pieces and threatened their sanity. Their stealthy practice ground them down. She said she felt like a thief in the night and he could not disagree. He always insisted on leaving her after they made love and warned her of a dark side that had him in its grip, which he would not let her witness. And then he would run off into the woods before the rage overtook him. There, until the cloud passed, he would flail the trees with branches and pound the earth with his fists until the pain made him stop.

Their continual cycles of sin and repentance made them into oxen yoked to a grist mill, turning, turning, going nowhere. Did they not, they asked each other when they were spent from lovemaking, have higher purposes?

In time, despite his overwhelming desire and affection, he bade her to return to Argenteuil and she fitfully agreed.

They continued to write each other, dozens of letters, pouring their souls on to parchment. None affected Abélard more than this missive, which he reread every day for the rest of his life:

You desire me to give myself up to my duty, and to be wholly God's, to whom I am consecrated. How can I do that, when you frighten me with apprehensions that continually possess my mind both night and day? When an evil threatens us, and it is impossible to ward it off, why do we give up ourselves to the unprofitable fear of it, which is yet even more tormenting than the evil itself? What have I hope for after the loss of you? What can confine me to earth when death shall have taken away from me all that was dear on it? I have renounced without difficulty all the charms of life, preserving only my love, and the secret pleasure of thinking incessantly of you, and hearing that you live. And yet, alas! you do not live for me, and dare not flatter myself even with the hope that I shall ever see you again. This is the greatest of my afflictions. Heaven commands me to renounce my fatal passion for you, but oh! my heart will never be able to consent to it. Adieu.

In her absence, Abélard threw himself back into

a world of writing, teaching and fervent prayer. He was always a magnet for students who possessed the finest minds, and they found him at Paraclete.

But Bernard, now entrenched in the role of nemesis, found him too, or at least found his new writings. For several years, he taught and wrote but once again, Abélard's views on the Trinity set him on a collision course with orthodoxy and by 1125, bowing to Bernard's remote but powerful hand, his position at Paraclete became untenable.

Abélard summoned Héloïse one more time to Paraclete, assuring her there was important business, not passion on his mind. This was a half-truth, for his passion had never ebbed.

He told her he had been offered a position as head of the monastery of Saint-Gildas-de-Rhuys in Brittany, and he had accepted it. Yes, Brittany was far away, but he could make a fresh start, further from the sphere of influence of his adversaries. He had much to write and still much to learn and his energy and ambitions had never been greater. And he could visit with their child, Astrolabe, who had since birth lived in Brittany with Héloïse's sister.

And this he saved for last. He placed both hands on her shoulders in a manner both tender and authoritarian and bestowed on her the title of Abbess of the Oratory of Paraclete. The monastery was hers now. He would return to Paraclete only in death.

She wept.

Tears of sorrow for their lost love, for her

daughter who did not know her mother.

But also tears of joy for Abélard's miraculous triumph over her uncle's cruel hand and his indomitable spirit and vigour.

Her nuns were summoned from Argenteuil to join her in this new place. Abélard's brothers would vacate so Paraclete could be a community of women.

In a mass in the church, he formally consecrated her as abbess and passed on to her a copy of the monastic rule and the *baculum*, her pastoral staff, which she firmly grasped, looking deeply into his eyes.

And later, when he rode off to the west, never, he supposed, to see her again, she staunched her tears and serenely walked to the chapel where her nuns were waiting for her to preside over Vespers for the very first time.

★ ★ ★

Abélard's time in Brittany proved short. He directed his sadness and frustrations into an autocratic style and before long had so alienated his new flock, who had expected him to be a lax master. He wrote furiously, prayed with anger in his eyes, cruelly cut the monks' rations and worked them like beasts of burden. His only release was his episodic use of Enlightenment Tea to take him away from his torments and replenish his zeal. But once again, he saw it was time to move on when his brethren at Saint-Gildas-de-Rhuys expressed their displeasure with his autocracy by trying to poison him.

Thus began the last chapter in his life, fifteen peripatetic years which saw him at Nantes, Mount St Genevieve, and back to Paris, where he accumulated students the way a squirrel accumulates acorns. And everywhere he went, he made sure he had a good supply of his precious plants and berries — not a week went by without an indulgence.

By twisted fate, unable to live in matrimonial bliss with his one true love, he felt he had little to lose by freely expressing his views. In tract after tract, book after book, he vented against the traditions of the church with his mighty intelligence and each publication eventually made its way to the desk of Bernard who had bit by bit become a theologian second in influence only to the Pope.

In *Sic et Non*, Abélard almost made parody of orthodox leadership and made it seem that the fathers of the Church could not express themselves clearly. Bernard gritted his teeth but the work was not, in and of itself, actionable. Finally, Abélard crossed the line, as far as Bernard was concerned. He believed that the eunuch's *Expositio in Epistolam ad Romanos*, spat at the feet of the Church by seeming to deny the very foundation of the Atonement. Had not Christ died on the cross as payment for the sins of man by dying in their place? Well, not to Abélard! He maintained that Christ died to win men's hearts by the example of reconciling love.

Love! This was too much.

Bernard threw the full measure of his weight to the task of crushing Abélard once and for all.

277

The time for private warnings was over and Bernard took the matter to the Bishops of France. Abélard was summoned to the Council of Sens in 1141 to plead his case. He reckoned he would have the ability to meet his accuser openly, to debate his old friend and spar with him the way they had done during their convalescence at Ruac.

When Abélard arrived at Sens, he learned, to his horror, that the evening before, Bernard had met privately with the bishops and a condemnation had already been meted out. There would be no public debate, nothing of the kind, but the Council agreed to let Abélard have his freedom for the express purpose of making a direct appeal to Rome.

He never made it that far.

Bernard saw to it that Pope Innocent II confirmed the sentence of the Council of Sens before Abélard made it out of France, not that it would have mattered, because a few months earlier, one of Abélard's students had coughed in his face, and had seeded his lungs with consumption.

Scant weeks after Sens he became ill. First came fever and night sweats. Then an irritated cough which progressed to paroxysms. The green flux from his lungs went from pink-tinged to streaky-red to gushes of crimson. His appetite dried up like a spent well. His weight fell.

He even lost desire for his red tea.

An old colleague and benefactor, the venerable Pierre, Abbot of Cluny, intervened when Abélard passed through his gates, as he persevered in his struggle to venture to Rome for an audience with the Holy Father.

Pierre forbade him from travelling on and confined him to bed. He obtained from Rome a mitigation of the sentence and even got Bernard to stand down when he passed word to him that Abélard was dying. Was not further earthly persecution of the monk pointless and cruel, he asked, and Bernard had sighed deeply and agreed.

Past the new year and into the spring, Abélard grew weaker. Pierre believed a sister house to Cluny, The Priory of St Marcel, was a quieter venue with more tender hands, and that is where Abélard was sent to die.

★   ★   ★

A procession of nuns on horseback snaked into the clearing. It was a windy evening in April. The men in the camp stopped their cooking and rose to their feet. There was a murmur. A gust blew the hood back from a woman who rode straight in the saddle and took the veil with it. She had long grey hair in a single braid.

One monk ran to fetch the veil and helped her dismount.

'Welcome, Abbess,' he said, as if they had met many times.

'Do I know you, Brother?' she asked.

'I am a friend of your friend,' he said. 'I am Barthomieu, of Ruac Abbey.'

'Ah, from years ago.' She looked at him curiously but said no more.

'Would you like me to take you to him?' Barthomieu asked.

She exhaled. 'Then I am not too late.'

A coverlet was drawn to Abélard's chin. He was asleep. Even though the consumption had melted the flesh from his face, Héloïse whispered he looked better than she had expected, then kneeled at his bedside and placed her hands together in prayer.

Abélard opened his eyes. 'Héloïse.' From his weak lips the utterance sounded more like a breath than a name.

'Yes, my dear one.'

'You came.'

'Yes. To be with you.'

'To the end?'

'Our love will never end,' she whispered into his ear.

Despite the whisper Barthomieu heard her, and he excused himself so the two of them could be alone.

Barthomieu waited outside the hut all evening and all night, like a sentry. Héloïse stayed until the first light of morning, excused herself for a short while then returned, as fresh and determined as ever to maintain her vigil. When Barthomieu asked if she needed the assistance of the infirmarer, she brushed him off and said she was perfectly capable of attending to all his needs.

Later in the day, there was a commotion when a group of men, King's soldiers aggressively rode into the Priory. Barthomieu met them, had a word with their captain, and blanched.

'When?' he asked.

'He's not far behind us. Maybe an hour. And you are?'

'His brother,' Barthomieu muttered. 'I am Bernard of Clairvaux's brother.'

*   *   *

A soldier opened the door for him and Bernard emerged from his fine, covered carriage looking pale and drawn. He was fifty-two but could have been mistaken for an older man. The pressures of high office and the years of spartan living conditions had turned his skin lax and sallow and rendered him arthritic and stiff-limbed. He took stock of the ragged conditions of the camp, a pilgrims' enclave, and the assemblage of clerics and scholars, men and women.

Will I engender as much adulation at the time of my death, he thought. Then he called out, imperiously, 'Who will take me to see Abélard?'

Barthomieu approached. The two men briefly locked eyes, but Bernard shook his head and looked elsewhere for a moment before refocusing on the man.

'Hello, Bernard.'

He was momentarily angered by the informality. He was the Abbot of Cîteaux. Papal legates sought his counsel. He had sat by the side of popes and the current Holy Father valued his advice over any man. He was the founding benefactor to the Knights Templar. His name was uttered by Crusaders. He had healed great schisms within the Church. Who was this monk to simply call him Bernard?

He looked into those eyes again. Who *is* this man?

'Yes, it's me,' Barthomieu said.

'Barthomieu? It cannot be you. You are young.'

'There is one, younger still.' He called over to the camp fire. 'Nivard, come here.'

Nivard came running out. Bernard had not seen him for half a lifetime, but his youngest brother Nivard would be well into his forties by now, not this strapping fellow he saw before him.

The three men embraced, but Bernard's hugs were tentative and wary.

'Do not fret. All will be explained, brother,' Barthomieu said. 'But be quick, come and see Abélard while he still draws breath.'

When Bernard and Barthomieu entered the sick house, Héloïse turned to hush the intruders, then realised the great man of the Church had entered.

She rose and made her intentions clear to kiss Bernard's ring but he shooed her back and bade her keep at Abélard's side.

'Your Excellency, I am — '

'You are Héloïse. You are Abbess of Paraclete. I know of you. I know of your intellect and piety. How is he?'

'He is slipping away. Come. There is still time.'

She touched Abélard's pointy shoulder. 'Wake up, my dear. Someone is here to see you. Your old . . . ' She looked to Bernard for guidance.

'Yes, call me his old friend.'

'Your old friend, Bernard of Clairvaux, has come to be with you.'

282

A weak huffing cough signalled his wakening. Bernard appeared shocked at the sight of the man, not because he looked like skin and bones, but because he looked so young. 'Abélard too!' he hissed.

Barthomieu was standing in the corner with his arms tightly folded around his chest. He nodded.

Abélard managed to smile. In order to speak without inducing a paroxysm he had learned to whisper, using his throat more than his diaphragm. 'Have you come to drop a heavy weight upon my head and finish me off?' he joked.

'I have come to pay my respects.'

'I was not aware you respected me.'

'As a person, you have my utmost respect.'

'What about my views?'

'That is another matter. But we are finished with those arguments.'

Abélard nodded. 'Have you met Héloïse?'

'Just now.'

'She is a good abbess.'

'I am sure she is.'

'She is a good woman.'

Bernard said nothing.

'I love her. I have always loved her.'

The abbot shifted uncomfortably.

Abélard asked that Bernard and he be left alone and when Héloïse and Barthomieu withdrew, he beckoned Bernard closer. 'Can I tell you something, as one friend might say to another?'

Bernard nodded.

'You are a great man, Bernard. You perform all the difficult religious duties. You fast, you watch, you suffer. But you do not endure the easy ones — you do not love.'

The old man slumped into a bedside chair and tears filled his eyes. 'Love.' He said the word as if it were foreign to his tongue. 'Perhaps, old friend, you are right.'

Abélard gave him a sly wink. 'I forgive you.'

'Thank you,' Bernard answered with a touch of amusement. 'Would *you* like to confess to *me*?'

'I am not sure I have the time left to confess all my sins. We have not seen each other since that night in Ruac when we drank some tea together.'

'Yes, the tea.'

Abélard had a coughing fit and stained his mouth cloth red. When his breathing was under control he said, 'Let me tell you about the tea.'

★ ★ ★

Two days later, Abélard was dead.

Héloïse took his body back to Paraclete and buried him in a grave on a small knoll near the chapel.

She lived to be an old woman and in 1163, according to her wishes, she herself was buried next to him, certain in the knowledge the two of them would rest side by side for eternity.

28

Thursday, Midday

The taxi ride to the Palais-Royal was a brief one and didn't give Luc much time to reflect on what he had just heard.

Was it possible there was a connection between the Ruac manuscript and the chaos and carnage of the present? How could a twelfth-century monk's fanciful tale of infusions and monastic intrigue ripple through the centuries to affect his life?

When Isaak had finished translating the Latin he became excited, saying, 'You know, Luc, I don't know about this concoction, this brew, Barthomieu keeps writing about, but the independent first-person account of the affair and the coda to the romance between Abélard and Héloïse is priceless. I have to put on my commercial hat. If the manuscript is recovered I'd love to broker the sale to a museum or the State.'

'I hope it is. But anyway that would be up to the abbey to decide. It's their property.'

Isaak nodded and promised Luc he'd contact him as soon as the next email arrived from the decoder. But they'd see each other again over dinner. They would eat and drink to Hugo that night. Both of them wanted that closure.

He tried Sara by phone one more time in what

had become an obsessive and futile routine. The midday traffic was fairly light. The Place de Concorde was wide open and magnificent as always. He glanced absently at his knuckles. They were less red; the new pills were definitely working. He'd almost felt guilty taking them. People were dead. Sara was missing and he was attending to a mundane hand infection. He got angry with himself and in the flick of a physiological switch, the anger turned to melancholy. He put his hands to his face and literally shook his head, trying to shake out the demons. But he couldn't permit himself to wallow. He had work to do.

Maurice Barbier had agreed to see him on short notice. Here was a man who had grown into his affectations. While Einstein hair and a cravat had marked him throughout middle age as somewhat of a dandy, it suited him as an older man. His office too, in the ministry, was an exercise in unselfconscious ornateness, an overstuffed assortment of archaic artefacts and pre-classical art on loan from the storage cabinets of the Louvre, an extravagant spectacle that seemed less ridiculous the older he became.

Barbier was sedate and serious. He guided Luc by the shoulder over to his gilded drinks cabinet.

Luc relaxed when he saw they were going to be alone.

'You thought I'd ask Marc Abenheim to sit in?' Barbier asked.

'I thought you might.'

'I have too much respect for you to play the

tricks of a politician. He doesn't even know you're here.'

'I need your help,' Luc said.

'Anything I can do, I will do.'

'Give me my cave back.'

Barbier took a delicate sip of sherry and looked at an oversized Etruscan urn in the corner as if seeking strength from its spear-clad warriors. 'That, unfortunately, I cannot do.'

Then and there, Luc knew he'd lost. Though saddened, Barbier seemed resolute. But he couldn't just give up, finish his drink and walk away. He had to fight. 'Surely, Maurice, you don't buy into the nonsense that the things which have happened during the excavation represented a dereliction of duty or a failure of leadership!'

'I want you to know that I don't believe that.'

'Then why?'

'Because we have here the problem of perception versus reality. The image of Ruac has been sullied before we can even define it. There won't be a magazine or newspaper article written about it which will not mention the deaths. There will be idiotic Internet postings about the Curse of Ruac. The mishaps are over-shadowing the importance of the archaeology and this is hard for me to bear. The Minister herself has ordered a health and safety assessment of the conditions of the dig and by the way, you will be questioned by more lawyers and functionaries than you can imagine. What I'm saying is that perception has *become* reality. You're in an untenable position.'

'I'm sure Abenheim shaped the discussion within these halls,' Luc said with disgust.

'Of course he did. I won't lie to you about that, and I tell you, whether or not you trust my word, that I fought for you — until the pendulum of opinion had swung too far. So yes, I voted, in the end, for your removal. I'm worried about future funding. The cave is more important than one man, even its discoverer.'

'Let's not confound one tragedy with another. My heart's already been broken. Losing Ruac will tear it out.'

More sherry, then the glass came down hard on the table. 'I'm sorry.'

Luc rose and picked up his case. 'Is there nothing I can do to change your mind?'

'It would take a miracle.'

★ ★ ★

Luc was back in his hotel room with more time to kill before dinner than he would have liked. He sprawled on the bed and pulled out the notes he'd jotted down during Isaak's translation.

The mentions of the red tea.

Gooseberries, barley grass and possession weed.

Over and over.

Like an amnesic coming out of the fog, he remembered the last conversation on Monday morning before his life came completely unglued. In the corridors of Nuffield Hospital, by the Radiology Department. Fred Prentice. They'd been talking about barley grass and some kind of fungus. Then the call from Abbot Menaud. Then hell.

What else had Prentice learned about their plants?

The general number of Nuffield Hospital was on his prescription bottles of antibiotics. He rang through and asked to be connected to Dr Prentice's room. Judging from the extent of his injuries, Luc reasoned that he had to be hospitalised still.

'Prentice, you say?' the hospital operator asked.

'Yes, Dr Fred Prentice.'

'May I ask if you're family?'

He lied. 'Yes, his brother-in-law.'

After a long wait, the phone was ringing again. A woman identified herself as the ward sister in Orthopaedics and asked if he was inquiring about Dr Prentice.

The protective tone of her voice alarmed him. She asked him again if he was a relative.

'Brother-in-law.'

'I see. It's your French accent. We can't talk to just anyone.'

'Of course. His sister married a Frenchman. It happens in the best of families.'

She didn't chuckle at that. 'I must have met you on Monday night when he was admitted.'

'No. I only saw him in Casualty.'

'It's just that there was a French gentleman who came to see him Monday night, that's all.'

'Not me. There's more than one of us. So, may I speak with him?'

'Has your wife not been in touch?'

289

'No. She's in Asia. She asked me to call.'

'Well, I'm very sorry to have to inform you but Dr Prentice passed away in the early hours of Tuesday.'

His mind garbled most of the rest of what she had to say. A suspected pulmonary embolus. Not uncommon in patients with leg injuries and immobilisation. Seemed like a nice man.

He managed to ask if the nurse had seen an American woman named Sara Mallory on the ward, but no, she couldn't recall an American.

He hung up and tried all of Sara's numbers again, punching numbers by memory, he'd called so many times. He felt panic in his throat.

Prentice.

Another death.

Another unrelated, disconnected death?

Who was this 'Frenchman?'

Where the hell was Sara?

He hadn't checked his emails since the morning. Maybe there'd be one from her, explaining everything innocently. She needed to get away. She went to visit her family in America. Anything.

His inbox was bursting with unopened messages, none of them from Sara or her friend from Ossulston Road. Then he saw one from her boss, Michael Moffitt, the Director of the Institute of Archaeology. He opened it excitedly.

Moffitt had received Luc's message. He hadn't a clue where Sara was but had been relieved, no end, that her name hadn't surfaced on the Ruac victims' list reported in the press. He was as concerned as Luc and would make inquiries amongst the Institute staff.

So, nothing.

Luc scanned the rest of his messages. One was from Margot. The subject read HUGO'S PHOTOS. He couldn't bear to click on it.

Or any of them. Except just when he was going to log off, one message line caught his attention in an irresistible way. A BIT OF GOOD NEWS TO BREAK THE GLOOM. It was from Karin Weltzer.

It was about the tiny human bone they had found in the Chamber of Plants. An infant's distal phalanges. They had sent it to a palaeontologist at Ulm, one of her colleagues. She apologised for even writing when the sense of loss was so fresh and great among the surviving members of Team Ruac but she couldn't keep the news to herself, even though she admitted she'd been instructed by Marc Abenheim to communicate official matters directly to him. Professor Schneider had completed his examination and had a most unexpected finding. He was certain, as she put it, absolutely, one-hundred-and-ten-per-cent-certain, that this was not a Cro-Magnon infant.

It was *Neanderthal.*

The rest of the email was Schneider's point-by-point differential between the morphology of phalanges from *Homo neanderthalensis* and *Homo sapiens.* All the check marks from their bone were in the *neanderthalensis* column.

Neanderthal?

Luc was momentarily swept back to the world he loved — the Paleolithic. This was an

291

Aurignacian cave. A Cro-Magnon cave. This was the art of Homo sapiens. What was a Neanderthal infant doing in the tenth chamber?

The two species certainly co-existed in the forests and savannas of the Upper Paleolithic Périgord but there was not one single example of a mixing of their artifacts or human remains in the archaeological record. Could it have been scavenged elsewhere, carried into the cave by a predator, like a bear? All the way into the furthest chamber? Perhaps, but unlikely.

Ruac was unique in many ways. This was another example of its singularity.

A phone call interrupted his musings.

It was Colonel Toucas with his smooth, cultured voice.

'Are you in Bordeaux?' he asked, and seemed disappointed when he heard otherwise. 'I'm in Bordeaux on business and was hoping to drop by to discuss something.'

'I'll be back midday tomorrow,' Luc said. 'I have a dinner in Paris. Can't you tell me what it is?'

'Well, yes, okay, but I'm telling you this in confidence. It's not for others, definitely not for the press.'

'Of course.'

'You know that stick of material we found under Pierre Berewa's body? We had it analysed. It's a material called picratol. It's a military high-explosive. But no one's seen it for years. It's almost a footnote to history. Both sides used it quite a bit during the Second World War.'

Luc felt light-headed. 'An explosive?'

'There's more, I'm afraid. I followed up with the police in England, as you requested. In fact, I've been in touch with Scotland Yard. Your explosion in Cambridge? What would you say if I told you that explosive residue was also found at the bombed building?'

'My God.'

'Not picratol, mind you. Modern material, some variant of military-grade C-4. A very curious development. I think we need to have a more extensive discussion, Professor Simard, about you, about Pierre Berewa, about everyone who has had anything to do with your cave.'

'I'll cancel my dinner and come back to Bordeaux this afternoon.'

'No, no, that's not good for me. I've got to get back to Perigeux for an engagement tonight. Can you come to my office, say, noon, tomorrow?'

'I'll be there. But Colonel, please, one of the professors on my team, Sara Mallory, an American who works in London, is missing. She was in Cambridge with me on Monday morning heading for the building that blew up. We were visiting a victim in the hospital. That's where I left her. No one's seen her or heard from her since. The man we were visiting was connected with Ruac. He died unexpectedly on Tuesday morning after being visited by a man with a French accent. It's all connected, I don't know how but all of this is connected! The Cambridge police know about Sara's disappearance but have done nothing. Please get Scotland Yard involved. Please!'

293

'I'll make a call,' he said, then added sternly, 'Noon, professor. My office.'

Luc closed the phone and stared.

Someone wanted to blow up my cave.

29

Ruac Cave, 30,000 BP

Tal awoke, covered from head to feet in sweat, the taste of Soaring Water still on his tongue. He tried to remember what had just happened but he was unable.

He felt between his legs and stroked his erect member. Uboas was a few feet away, lying on a beautifully lush bison skin, the last beast killed in their bi-annual hunt. She was asleep, wrapped in a reindeer skin blanket, and had not been well. He could have woken her and satisfied himself but he chose to let her sleep till the morning light entered the mouth of the cave.

He stroked himself until he was satisfied then rolled himself in skins to warm himself against the night chill. He ran his hand over his own bison skin which was starting to get thin and patchy. It was from a kill he had made as a young man. Not his first — that trophy had gone to his father, but his second. That was his to keep. He remembered the spear throw that had taken the animal. He could still see the shaft flying fast and straight, the flint tip, slipping perfectly between the ribs and sinking deeply. He remembered it vividly, even though it had occurred a very long time ago.

As he felt the animal's fur bristling between his fingers, suddenly, in a flash of blinding light as if he had looked into the sun, the remembrance of the soaring came back to him. He began to shiver.

He was flying over a herd of bison, close enough to reach out and touch a powerful, muscular shoulder of one of the beasts. He felt, as he always did, the exultation of effortless flight, the honour of moving with the herd, of being one with them. In pleasure, he stretched his arms to their fullest and spread his fingers to the wind.

Then, he was aware of something strange, an alien presence closing in on him. He always soared alone but he sensed there was someone or something else intruding on his realm. He turned his head and saw it.

A long, sleek figure, swooping down on him, like a hawk after prey.

It had the head of a lion but the body of a man. Its arms were tucked against its body, allowing it to cut through the air like a spear. And it was aiming for him.

He flapped his arms to pick up speed but could go no faster. The herd of bison parted, half going right, half going left. He wanted to turn to follow along but he was unable to change directions. He was flying on his own, low, the tall grasses of the plain tickling his bare body. The lion man was getting closer and closer. He could see it open its mouth and snarl, and had a notion how its hot saliva would feel against his flesh the instant before its fangs clamped down on his leg.

The cliffs were approaching and beyond them, the river.

He did not know why but he believed if only he could make it across the river, he would be safe. He had to make it over the river.

The lion man was on him. Its mouth was open, its jaw ready to clamp down.

He was at the cliffs.

There was the river, silver in the sun.

He felt a drop of hot saliva on his ankle.

And he was back in the cave.

He pondered the meaning of the experience. The ancestors were giving him a warning, no doubt. He would have to be on alert, but he was always so. It was the responsibility of the head of the Bison Clan. He had to protect his people. But who would protect him?

He reached over to try to touch Uboas but his fingers could only reach her bison skin. The honour of that bison's death had been given to the son of Tal's son, Mem. This exceptional young man, who bore the name Tala, in honour of his grandfather, was more like Tal than Mem ever was.

Tala took an interest in plants and healing, was a keen flint knapper, and had the same ability as Tal to capture the power and majesty of a galloping horse in a flowing outline of charcoal and graphite. Tal had always loved the boy as if he were his second son, because alas, his real second son, Kek, had gone out hunting one day, on his own, which was the way he liked to venture out, to keep proving his courage to his father. He was perpetually angry and frustrated, given to bursts of pique against his older brother and even his father, lacking the temperament to

297

be a second son. He had never returned. They searched for him and found nothing. Again, a long time ago.

In the quiet of the cave and the deepness of the night, Tal wanted to sleep a dead, black sleep, a sleep without dreams. A pure escape to nothingness, to give himself respite from his fears and apprehensions would have been a gift, but he could not drift off. He would have to leave soon and spare Uboas the rage.

He tried to think about happy things, the pride he had in his son, Mem, his love for his grandson, the certainty that the Bison Clan would be in good hands based on the issuance of his loins. But then, the old thoughts invaded his mind, dark thoughts that began to blacken his mind, the harbinger of Tal's Anger.

It had snuck up on him, the way a man sneaks up on a reindeer drinking from a pond.

One day, years earlier, he realised that Uboas was growing old, and he was not. The notion was easy to dismiss at first, but as time went on, her hair became streaked with white and her skin, once as smooth as a bird's egg, wrinkled. Her breasts, once firm, began to sag. She started to walk with a limp and often-times favoured her knees and took to rubbing them with a poultice Tala prepared for her.

And his son, Mem, was ageing too. As the seasons changed and the years rolled on, Mem began to look more like his brother than his son, and now, he looked older still. In time, Tala and he would appear a similar age, he reckoned.

In fact, all his people grew old in front of his

eyes. The old ones died, the young ones aged, new ones were born. The cycle of life continued for all but him.

It was almost as if the river of time had stopped for Tal but flowed on for everyone else.

The older men of the clan would talk about this mystery in small groups and the younger men would chatter about him when they were out on a hunt. The women would whisper when they were together sewing hides or butchering a carcass or scaling fish.

Tal was a head man like no other. For his strengths and abilities, for his protection of the clan, he was loved. For his power over time, he was feared.

Uboas became sad and withdrawn. She was the head man's mate but her status had waned over the years as she first became barren and later became increasingly decrepit. Younger, unmated women looked at Tal's muscular body hungrily, and she imagined that he might steal off and lie with them.

But no one was more troubled than Mem. It was his destiny to become head man and he desperately wanted that to happen. He had always loved and revered Tal but over time he had become more of a rival. Now, he seemed older than his own father and he imagined dying first and never ascending to head of the clan.

Father and son hardly spoke. A word here, a grunt there. Tal gravitated to his grandson for his want of filial affection and it was Tala who accompanied Tal to paint in the sacred cave. Mem resented this. In his youth, *he* had been the chosen one to paint side by side with his father, and it was he who had made the first of many handprints that had so delighted Tal. Now, it was Tala who was given the honour. He might have been proud, but instead he was jealous.

When the time came for initiation to manhood, the boys of the Bison Clan would still be taken to the cave, given the bowl of Soaring Water and when they could stand, Tal would lead them ever deeper to pay homage to the creatures who deserved their respect.

The bison, above all, their spirit kin in the animal world, their brothers.

The horse, who because of their swiftness and cunning could never be conquered.

The mammoth, who thundered the ground, could destroy any foe with a flick of its tusks and feared nothing, man included.

The bear and the lions, the rulers of the night, who were more likely to kill a man than be killed.

Tal never painted the reindeer. Though they were abundant, they were stupid and easy to kill. They did not deserve his respect. They were food. Nor did he give his respect to the lowly creatures of the land, the mouse, the vole, the bat, the fish, the beaver. They were to be eaten, not lauded.

Tal partook of the Soaring Water regularly, as often as five or six times every cycle of the moon. Soaring gave him wisdom. It gave him comfort. It brought pleasure. And, over time, he reached an inescapable conclusion. He came to suspect it kept him vigorous and young while others grew old. He even grew to like the way he felt during the Anger. When he bellowed in rage he reckoned the ancestors could hear him. He was powerful and he was feared.

He would not curtail his practice and he would not make it universal. He was above all others. He was Tal, head of the Bison Clan and keeper of the sacred cave. As long as the grasses grew, the vines crept and the berries plumped, he would make his hot red water in his mother's bowl. And he would soar.

★   ★   ★

The clan had made a fresh summer campsite by a tight bend of the river where the fish were plentiful and the ground drained quickly after a downpour. It was a spot where the cliffs rose up behind them, protecting their rear from all but the most nimble bears. Their main worries were upstream and downstream, and at night the younger men kept watch. To reach good hunting grounds they had to walk two hours downstream to a point where the cliffs petered out, but all things considered, it was a good location, and not very far from Tal's cave.

The first sign of trouble came when a hawk changed its pattern of back and forth sweeps from the cliff tops to the river, and began to do a compact circle downstream.

Tal noticed. He was hafting a flint point to a length of antler to make a new knife. He put down a strip of sinew to watch the bird. Then, in the not too far distance, a flock of nesting partridges took to wing in a sudden rush. He put down his work and stood up.

In the time he had been head man, the clan had grown modestly. There were close to fifty of them now. He called for the clan to come out of their lean-tos and listen to him. There might be trouble coming. Mem should take a scouting party of the best men and see what he could find.

Mem was almost surprised the task went to him rather than Tala, but he took it as a sign of favour and enthusiastically grabbed his spear. He chose six young men and then his own son, but Tal objected and demanded Tala stay behind. Mem was angered by this. It sent the message to the clan that he was expendable, but that precious Tala was not. Nevertheless he obeyed and left with his warriors.

Tala asked why he was not allowed to go. Tal turned away, refusing to answer. It was his vision, of course. Something was going to happen. He could feel it. He would not put both his son and grandson in danger. The clan would need a head man and to Tal's mind he *must* come from his own lineage.

Everyone stopped their activities to watch and wait for the scouting party to return. The men made spears and axes ready. The women kept the children close. Tal paced the trodden-down grass of the camp, watching the hawk, listening to the bird calls, sniffing the wind.

After a long while, there was a cry. A man's cry. Not one of fear or rage or anguish, but of proclamation. The men were returning. There was news!

Mem appeared first, coming fast with his long-legged run. He was breathing furiously but his spear was at his side, not up over his shoulder offensively.

He called out something that stunned the people and made Tal reel.

Kek was back!

His brother. Tal's younger son. He was back!

The other scouts followed. But their spears were raised and they were looking over their shoulders nervously.

Kek was back, Mem explained, but he was not alone.

He was with the Shadow People.

Tal asked if he was their prisoner, but according to Mem, he was not. Tal asked why had he come back. And what was he doing with the Others.

Mem replied: Kek would tell Tal himself. He had offered to come alone. The Shadow People would not enter the camp.

Tal agreed, and Mem plunged back into the tall grass disappearing from sight.

And a father spent what little time he had to prepare himself for a prodigal son.

When Mem returned, he was with a man whom Tal at once recognised but at the same time did not.

The man possessed the blue eyes, and round forehead, the unmistakable jutting nose which marked the kin of Tal.

But his hair was different, a mass of black, tangled rats' tails, and his beard stuck out long and bushy in all directions, making his face look

303

bigger than it was. And his clothes. The men of the Bison Clan favoured leggings and shirts made of soft red deer hide, stitched with sinew. Kek was wearing coarse reindeer hide, a one-piece garment tied at the waist with a braided belt. His spear was heavy and thick and shorter than the one he had left with so many years ago.

He had become one of them.

There was a story to tell and Kek proceeded to tell it with no acknowledgement of the extraordinary nature of his return. At first he stumbled over his words, a sign he had not used his native language for a very long time. As his tongue loosened, he blurted out the tale in rapid beats, *click, click, click*, like a man bashing flakes off a flint block.

That day, a long time ago.

He was hunting alone.

He was stalking a roe deer while a bear was stalking him.

The bear attacked and began to maul him.

It swatted away his spear.

His knife, the one made of white flint that Tal had made for him, saved his life. He slashed the bear's eye, spilling its juice, and the animal ran off.

He lay wounded, bleeding from the mauling. He called out for help then slept.

Kek awoke in the camp of the Shadow People — he would learn they called themselves Forest People. Their name for the Bison Clan was the Tall Ones. He was very weak. Over many months a young woman stayed with him, feeding him, applying mud to his wounds.

He learned their language and came to understand that their head man and the others had debated whether or not to kill him. His nurse was the head man's daughter and she protected him from harm.

When Kek was stronger, the head man told him he could stay and teach them some of the ways of the Tall Ones, or he could go. They would not kill him. The woman was squat and not as beautiful as those of the Bison Clan but he had grown to love her. And, he was tired of being the second son of Tal.

So he stayed.

They had no children. She was barren, but he remained with her and the forest people, strange as they were. They did not believe their ancestors were in the sky. They died and were no more. They did not respect the bison. They were food, just like any animal, but harder to kill. They did not sing and laugh like some in the Bison Clan. They did not carve little animals from bone and wood. They made fine axes but their knife blades were poor.

They exchanged some knowledge. He taught them how to haft a spear the Bison Clan way, they taught him how to surround and box in a reindeer and force it over the cliffs without throwing a single spear.

He was happy with them and they became his clan.

But now his head man had a crisis. He was getting old. He only bore daughters and feared he would die without a son. But when a boy was finally born, he was glad and the clan rejoiced. A week earlier, the boy became sick and would not get well. Kek told the head man about Tal and the way he could heal people with plants. He told him about the sacred cave. The forest people began their trek to the camp of the Tall Ones. Kek would ask Tal to heal the boy.

Tal listened, chewing hard on a piece of dried reindeer meat. It was not their way to let a tribe of Shadow People into their midst. It was dangerous. And the ancestors would surely object.

But Kek pleaded and called him wise father. He said he was sorry for going off to live with the Others. He said their men would lay down their spears when they entered the camp. He beseeched him to heal the head man's baby.

★ ★ ★

The Neanderthals entered the camp, slowly and suspiciously, whispering to each other in a clipped, unknown tongue. Their darting eyes were veiled by heavy brows. They were shorter than the Bison Clan, with immensely powerful-looking arms, each like a club. Their hair was wild and untamed, their beards uncut by flint. The women were heavy-breasted with broad shoulders and they ogled their taller, leaner counterparts with plaited hair.

Tal had his men assembled in a gauntlet, spears at the ready and nodded when the Shadow People did, as promised, leave their spears in a pile.

Their head man came forwards, clutching a silent infant. The man wore a splendid necklace of bear teeth.

Kek translated. *I am Osa. This is my son. Make him well.*

Tal took a few steps forwards and asked to see the boy. He peeled back the hide blanket and saw a limp, listless baby, several months old, its eyes shut, its smooth chest contracting with each breath. With the permission of his father, he touched the skin — it was hot and dry as an old bone. He saw its bowels were leaking.

He let the blanket fall back. Then the head man took off his necklace and handed it to Tal.

Tal accepted it and put it around his neck.

He would try to heal the infant.

★   ★   ★

Through Kek, Tal instructed the Neanderthals to congregate at the river bank and wait. He had Mem organise the best spear men to keep watch while he and Tala ran off to find the correct plants. When they returned, they had filled a pouch with two kinds of bark, a handful of succulent round leaves and the stringy roots of a tuber. When Tala filled a skin with river water, Tal said they were ready to begin.

Because the boy was very ill, Tal decided to take him into the deepest, most-sacred chamber for the healing. He would need all the powers at his disposal. Osa bore the infant in his thick arms and followed Tal into the cave accompanied by three of his clansmen, brutish fellows who seemed genuinely scared to venture into the darkness with only lamp light. Mem, Tala and one of Tal's nephews represented the Bison Clan. Kek rounded out the party. It was his lot to straddle both worlds and bridge their languages.

The Neanderthals cried out when they saw the painted walls. They pointed and jabbered. Kek spoke in their guttural tongue and tried to soothe them by showing he could safely touch the images without fear of being trampled or maimed.

It took a great deal of coaxing to get the visitors to crawl through the tunnel into the Chamber of Plants. Fearing a trap, one of the brutes insisted on being the last one through. Crowded together in the hand-adorned vault, they murmured and blinked at the stencils and held up their own hands for inspection in the light of the burning fat and juniper.

There, most of the joint party waited, in tense comity, with as much physical separation as the vault would allow. Tal, Mem, Kek, the head man and one of his kin entered the tenth chamber with the boy.

Tal immediately began singing one of his mother's old healing chants and proceeded to prepare the cure. Using one of his long flint blades he cut the succulent leaves and stringy roots into small pieces and when done, he laid the blade on end, propped against the wall. He scooped the vegetation into his mother's stone bowl. Then he added some bark pieces, shredded between his rough palms. Finally some fresh water from the skin. He stirred and mashed the mixture with his hands until it was moss green and added more water to make it liquid enough to drink.

In the light of the flickering lamps, he kept the chant going, sat the boy up and had his father open his parched lips wide enough to pour in a small amount. The boy reflexively coughed and sputtered. Tal waited and gave him some more. Then more. Until the child had drunk a fair measure.

The boy was laid down on the ground, wrapped in his skin and the men stood over him, two species, sharing one earth, united in the common interest of saving one tiny being.

Tal chanted for hours.

Fresh lamps had to be brought.

Throughout the night, word was relayed to the two clans huddled on the ledge on either side of the cave mouth in wary peace. Tala would emerge and tell the Bison Clan that the child was moaning, or vomiting, or finally sleeping quietly. Uboas would press on her son strips of dried meat before he rushed back to be at his father's side.

As the first light broke outside the cave, the infant seemed to rally. He lifted his head on his own to accept water. Tal let it be known they would leave the cave because the healing was working. The child's father grunted his approval.

Then, a catastrophe.

In a wet intestinal gurgle, the chamber suddenly filled with a foul odour as the child suddenly evacuated much of its weight. There was a high-pitched sigh and the little body simply stopped breathing.

The men looked down on the lifeless body in stunned silence.

The boy's father kneeled and shook him, trying to wake. He cried out something and Kek yelled back at him. By his tone, Tal could tell his son was trying to avert disaster.

Osa slowly rose to his feet. In the low light of the hissing lamps his sunken eyes were the brightest objects in the chamber. Then he let out a curdling scream which seemed from another realm, an amalgam of a man's cry and a beast's roar, so loud and reverberating that it froze all the other men into paralytic inaction.

For a lumbering man, he moved like a lion. In a blink he had Tal's stone bowl in his massive hand. Tal, nor anyone else, had a moment to react. He saw a dark blur as the Neanderthal's arm swung in an arc and bashed the bowl behind his ear.

The world became bright for a time as if the sun had moved from the sky and made its way through all the chambers of the cave into the last chamber.

He was on the ground, on all fours.

He was aware of shouts in the distance, the sounds of flint thrusting through flesh, great shouts of pain and war.

He heard the sound of men falling, the thud of death.

He lifted his head.

The bird man was towering over him, his beak proudly open.

I will soar, he thought. I will soar forever.

His head was too heavy to keep up. What was that on the ground? He struggled to see it through the pain and fog in his head and the poor light.

It was the small ivory bison, fallen from his belt pouch.

He reached for it as he fashioned his last thoughts.

Bison Clan.

Uboas.

★ ★ ★

Tala was the only one to make it out of the cave alive. It was he who killed Osa by bashing his head against the wall. Kek was smitten by his own brother and Mem fell to one of the Neanderthals. In close quarters men stabbed and stomped and gouged until there was nothing but a bloody mess of humanity.

Tala's arm was broken, either from a blow that he had struck or one he received, he did not know. He ran into the sunlight crying out in alarm. Tal was dead. The Shadow People had attacked. There must be revenge.

Quickly and brutally, the men of the Bison Clan fell on the frightened Neanderthals. Since they had been obliged to leave their spears at the camp, it did not take long until every one of them, every man, woman and child was run through or thrown off the high ledge.

They had called themselves the Forest People. They were no more.

Tala was head man now. There would be time for ceremony. In the midst of the crisis, the clan simply fell into line and began to obey his commands. And Uboas stoically ignored her own sorrow and busied herself making a wooden and sinew splint for her son's arm.

All the dead and broken men were dragged out. Except for Tal. Tala ordered that the dead infant, the son of Osa, have his hand cut off before he was carried out. One of the clan men used Tal's good blade to separate the small finger bones into a bloody pile and then carefully put the blade back against the wall where Tal had left it. The finger bones would be used to make Tala a trophy necklace, but in his haste one of the tiny phalanges was dropped into the dirt, never to make it around Tala's neck.

The Neanderthals, whether dead or alive, were pitched over the ledge onto the rocks below to join their brethren. The lions, the bears and the hawks would have a feast.

They carefully bore the bodies of their dead down the cliffs for burial in the soft earth beside the river. That was their custom. The clan waited to hear Tala's decision about Kek. Was he of their clan or the Others?

He was my brother, he declared, and one of us. He would be treated in death as a member of the Bison Clan.

The young man's decision was well received and there was a sense of confidence that he would also know how to honour their extraordinary leader's bodily remains. He withdrew back into the cave. He would sit beside his dead

312

father, drink the Soaring Water, and when he was done, he would know what to do.

It was nearly sunset when the clan finished restoring order to their world. They ascended the cliffs one more time and gathered around the cave mouth.

Tala emerged, spoke to them clearly and with resolve, waving his one good arm for emphasis. He had soared with the bison herd and in the distance, he saw the bird man flying into the cave and disappearing.

He had his answer.

Tal would be left in the Chamber of Plants, in the sacred place he had created. He would have his soaring bowl with him. He would have his ivory bison. His best flint blade. His bird man would be his company. No one would ever enter the chamber again.

Whereas the other ancestors dwelled around their camp fires in the sky, the great Tal would forever dwell inside his painted cave.

30

Thursday Afternoon

Luc still had several hours until dinner with Isaak. He lay on the hotel bed, his computer, warm on his belly, ready to doze off and retreat to a sanctuary of oblivion. His email inbox was staring him in the face. He wavered in indecision whether to snap the laptop closed and let it be for now.

Instead, he clicked on the message from Margot.

He had to do it some time, why not now? Take the bitter with the sweet, have a glance at the last happy interlude in a life. The message line simply read: HUGO'S PHOTOS. He took a deep emotion-choked breath and clicked on the attachments.

A series of a dozen jpegs downloaded in a daisy-chain of embedded images.

He scrolled down and took each one in.

Shots of Luc, Sara and Odile, strolling through Domme.

Table shots inside the restaurant — Sara and Luc together, Hugo, with a cheesy grin, his arm slung around Odile, a hand resting casually on her bosom.

Then a group snap of the four of them, taken by the waiter, a selection of house desserts spread on the table. You could almost hear the laughter.

At the bottom of the scroll there was one more photo.

He stared at it. It didn't fit — its presence made no sense.

He clicked to render it full screen.

What the hell?

It was an oil painting, on a yellow wall. A young man, of the Renaissance perhaps, seated and staring suspiciously at the artist. His face was long and effeminate, his hair flowing onto his shoulders. He had a black foppish hat, a white shirt with impossibly puffy sleeves and, most strikingly, his shoulder was draped with a rich fur coat from a spotted leopard.

What was this doing on Hugo's mobile? Did someone use the camera after he was dead? Who would take a dead man's mobile phone to a museum and use it to photograph a painting?

Wait! The time and date stamp!

The date of the photo time marked in crisp digital display: 11:53 p.m.

What was it the gendarme had told him at the crash scene?

'*He didn't make it to the village. If he left your camp at eleven-thirty, the accident must have happened no later than eleven-forty.*'

Luc was sitting on the edge of the bed now, raking his hand through his hair over and over, as if the static electricity would fire more synapses in his brain.

11:53 p.m.! Thirteen minutes after he was supposed to be dead, Hugo takes a picture of an oil painting?

Another conversation came back to him,

flooding into his consciousness with startling clarity, a snippet that was accessible, that his mind must have tagged for future use.

At the welcome party for the excavation, the council president from Périgueux, Monsieur Tailifer, had been gushing over the local lore.

'The Resistance struck the main railway line, near Ruac, and made off with a fortune, maybe two hundred million euros in today's money, and some very famous paintings, let me add, including Raphael's Portrait of a Young Man, all on their way to Goering personally. Some of the loot made it to de Gaulle and was put to good use, I'm sure, but a lot of that money and the art disappeared into thin air. The Raphael was never seen again.'

Luc was breathing heavily now, as if he'd just finished an anaerobic sprint and was air-hungry, repaying his oxygen debt.

He clicked on to Google Images and entered RAPHAEL'S PORTRAIT OF A YOUNG MAN.

And there it was. The same painting, on a website devoted to looted art recovery.

The caption read: THIS MASTERPIECE REMAINS MISSING.

★ ★ ★

Luc was a man who knew his way around museums and what's more, he loved everything about them. In ordinary circumstances he would have savoured the experience of discovering a new museum, particularly one located in a charming nineteenth-century hotel perched on a

316

pleasant knoll on the banks of the Marne. He would have inhaled the mustiness of the exhibit halls and been captivated by the complexities of off-limits storage areas. The Museum of National Resistance in Champigny-sur-Marne, had a collection rather more recent than his usual haunts, but all museums shared a pleasing commonality.

However, this was not an ordinary moment in his life and he rushed through the entrance hardly noticing the environs.

At the ticket booth he breathlessly announced 'Professor Simard for Monsieur Rouby,' and paced while the attendant placed a call.

They had talked less than an hour earlier. Luc had reached the curator after a frenetic series of calls had shunted him from museum to museum, archive to archive, all over France. His request was quite specific, which helped, but he was getting nowhere until a sympathetic elderly woman in Corrèze, at the Museum of Resistance Henri Queuille, mentioned that thirty boxes of archival material pertaining to Luc's topic of interest had been sent to Champigny-sur-Marne for cataloging and preservation.

And fortunately, Champigny-sur-Marne was a scant twelve kilometres from the centre of Paris.

Max Rouby was a charming sort of man, in many ways an older version of Hugo, and Luc had to shrug off the unsettling transference. The curator was more than happy to extend a professional courtesy, one museum man to another, and put his minuscule staff at Luc's disposal. Luc was given a table in a private

317

archives area and a homely young woman named Chantelle began to dolly in the pertinent cardboard boxes.

'Okay,' he said, 'we're looking for any documentation of a Resistance raid against a German train in the vicinity of Ruac in the Dordogne in the summer of 1944. It was carrying a lot of cash and maybe art. Is there an index?'

'That's why it was sent here but unfortunately we haven't got to it yet. It won't hurt for me to thumb through it today. It'll make my job easier later on,' she said helpfully.

They dove in. As they sorted through wartime memos, diaries, newspaper clippings, black-and-white photos and personal diaries, Chantelle told him what she knew about the lending museum.

Henri Queuille was an important post-war politician who had been active in the Resistance in the Corrèze area during the occupation. When he died, his family bequeathed his house to the State for the purpose of remembering and honouring the Resistance efforts in the region, and in 1982 both Mitterrand and Chirac attended the inauguration of the museum. The family archives served as the backbone but over the years the museum swelled with deposits and gifts from other local archives and family estates.

It was slow going. Luc was impressed at how meticulously the Resistance had documented their activities. Whether from pride or a military sense of discipline, some of the local operatives wrote voluminously about plans and results for, what turned out to be, posterity.

The first twenty boxes had no mention of the Ruac raid. Chantelle was going through box 21 and Luc was rifling box 22 when she announced, 'This looks promising!' and took the files over to Luc.

It was a notebook with the seal of a lycée général in Périgueux, dated 1991. It appeared an enterprising student had done a project on the war, interviewing a local man who had been a Resistance fighter. The man, a Claude Benestebe, who was in his late sixties at the time of the exchange, recounted a raid on a German train a mile from the station at Les Eyzies. From the very first page, it sounded like Luc's incident. He began to page through Benestebe's oral history while Chantelle took the lid off the next box.

I was barely seventeen years old in 1944, but very much a man I would say, very adventurous. In truth, the war saw to it I would never have a normal end to childhood. All the frivolous things that teenagers do today, well, I did none of them. No games, no parties. Yes, there was romance and even some flings, but it was in the context, you know, of a struggle for existence and liberty. The next day was never a certainty. If you didn't pack it in during a mission, the boche could have plucked you out of a crowd to be taken a hostage and shot for this or that.

We didn't really expect to survive the attack on the Banque de Paris train in June

319

1944. We knew it was an important raid. We had the information maybe two weeks in advance from a bank employee in Lyon that a lot of French cash and Nazi loot were going to be sent via rail from the main branch in Lyon to Bordeaux for transfer to Berlin. We had the word that the entire train, some six box cars, were chock full, so we had to be prepared to make off with all of it in case we succeeded. We were told that two box cars would contain nothing but objets d'art and paintings looted from Poland, bound for Goering personally, who wanted all the best pieces for himself.

Well, I can tell you that it was a big operation. The maquisard, as you know, were diverse, to use a polite description. Yes, there was central coordination, to some extent, by de Gaulle and his lot in Algiers, but the Resistance was very much a local affair where the maquis were making it up as they went along. And for sure, there was no love lost between one maquis band and another. Some of them were right-wing nationalists, some Communists, some anarchists, everything. My group which had the codename, Squad 46, operated out of Neuvic. We simply hated the boche. That was our philosophy. But for this train job, about half a dozen maquis bands worked together to pull it off. After all we needed a hundred men, many trucks, explosives, machine guns. The attack point was between Les Eyzies and Ruac, so we had to

320

involve the Ruac maquis, Squad 70, I recall, even though no one trusted them. They cloaked themselves with a Resistance banner, but everyone knew they were in it for themselves. They were maybe the biggest thieves in France next to the Nazis. And they were vicious as they come. They didn't just kill the boche. They tore them to pieces when they had the chance.

Usually there were big screw-ups and people got hurt or killed but the night of 26 July 1944 went like a dream. Maybe the boche were too clever by half, deciding that too much security would attract attention, but the train was lightly protected. At 7:38 precisely, we attacked from all sides, blew up the track and derailed the locomotive. The German troops were massacred quickly. I never had a chance to fire my own rifle, it was over so quickly. The Banque de Paris guards who were French employees, gave their pistols to our commander who fired off rounds and returned them so they could say they tried to fight us off. By 8:30, the train was unloaded. All of us formed a human chain up from the track to the road, passing money bags and crates of art to the trucks.

Only years later did I learn that in today's money, that train had tens of millions of French francs. How much of it made its way to André Malraux and Charles de Gaulle? I don't know, but it's said that millions of francs and quite a bit of art never made it

*out of Ruac. Who knows what's true. All I
know is that it was a pretty good night for
the Resistance and a pretty good night for
me. I got good and drunk and had a high
old time.*

Luc looked through the rest of the file but there
was nothing else of interest, nothing about the
Raphael painting. But the discovery of a tangible
link to Ruac gave him the enthusiasm to keep
pressing on to the last box.

In the late afternoon, Chantelle left the research
room to fetch two cups of coffee. The overhead
fluorescents were now brighter than the light
streaming through the windows. There were only
two boxes left and when he was done, he'd get a
taxi back to Paris and meet Isaak. Box 29 was
largely filled with a photo archive, hundreds of
glossy shots printed on the heavy paper of the
day. He moved through them quickly, as if he
was dealing cards at a poker game, and the
moment the girl came back with coffee was the
moment he saw the photo with the hand-written
caption printed in black ink on the white border,
GEN. DE GAULLE IN RUAC CONGRATULATING
THE LOCAL MAQUISARD UNIT, 1949.

De Gaulle towered above the others. He was
dressed in a dark business suit, squinting into the
sun over the photographer's shoulder. Behind
him was the village café looking much the same
as it did now. He was flanked by six people, five
men and a woman and was shaking hands with
the oldest man.

Luc's eye was drawn immediately to the old

man. And then another young man, and then the woman.

'Coffee?' Chantelle asked.

He couldn't respond.

Because Chantelle disappeared.

And the room disappeared.

It was him and the photo. Nothing else.

The old man looked strikingly like the mayor, Bonnet. The young man looked like Jacques Bonnet. The woman looked like Odile Bonnet.

He stared some more, from face to face.

He shook his head in confusion. The resemblance was uncanny.

⋆ ⋆ ⋆

Paris was glowing in the twilight. From Luc's taxi he hardly noticed the Eiffel Tower alight in the distance. With all the rush hour traffic, he had just enough time to get back to his hotel before Isaak came to pick him up but now he wished he hadn't made the appointment.

He had thinking to do, facts to sort through, puzzle pieces to assemble. He didn't need idle chit-chat. He'd be better off sitting in his room with a clear head and a clean sheet of paper. He'd be seeing Colonel Toucas the next day. He wanted to lay out a coherent theory, not ramble on like a nut. He wanted to be back home; if he hadn't already missed the last train he would have preferred travelling tonight.

He ought to cancel.

He called Isaak.

'What are you, telepathic?' Isaak said. 'I'm just

working on a translation for you.'

'You did it earlier. What do you mean?' Luc asked.

'The new one!' Isaak exclaimed. 'The Belgian guy's been busy. He's finished! Margo forwarded his email an hour ago. I wanted to have it ready for you by dinner.'

'Look, about dinner. Do you mind if we postpone? I've got some urgent work.'

'No problem. What about the translation?'

'I'm stuck in traffic. Could you read it to me over the phone? Would you mind?'

'Luc, whatever you want. Let's do it now.'

'Thank you. And Isaak, before you start, what was the last key word?'

'That's what got me excited. It's one of those words that get a medievalist's heart beating. It was TEMPLARS.'

31

Ruac, 1307

Bernard of Clairvaux had been dead for a very long time but a day did not pass without someone at Ruac Abbey thinking about him or mentioning his name to make a point or punctuate a prayer.

He took his last breath in 1153 at the age of sixty-three and in near-record time he was canonised when, in 1174, Pope Alexander III made him Saint Bernard. The honour both thrilled and saddened his brother, Barthomieu, who was still troubled to live in a world without Bernard's weighty presence.

On the occasion of his brother's sainthood, Barthomieu journeyed to Clairvaux with Nivard, now his sole surviving brother, to pray at Bernard's tomb. They did so with trepidation. Would any of Bernard's contemporaries at Clairvaux be alive and remember them? Would their secret be exposed?

They thought not, but in the event some old monk might look them over suspiciously or try to engage them in conversation, they would remain aloof and would keep their heads cloaked in hooded anonymity.

This was an exchange they would not entertain:

'*Good monks, you remind this old man of the*

brothers of Saint Bernard! I met them once, a great many years ago.'

'We are certainly not these men, brother.'

'No, how could you be? They must be dead or if not, they would be in their eighth decade!'

'And as you can see, we are young men.'

'Yes, to be young again. How marvellous that would be! But still, you sir are the image of Barthomieu and you sir are the image of Nivard. My old mind must be playing tricks.'

'Let us get you out of the sun, brother, and bring you some ale.'

'Thank you for that. Tell me, what did you say your names were?'

No, they would not permit that conversation. Their secret was closely held. No one outside the tight confines of Ruac Abbey knew. Over the years, the abbey had involuted, turning increasingly inward, an island unto itself. Partly, this was due to their doctrinal shift towards Cistercianism, in homage to the teachings and filial ties to the ever-more influential Bernard. The outside world held only temptation and sin. Bernard taught that a good monastic community needed only the sweat of its members to tend to earthly needs and heavenly prayers to Christ and the Virgin Mary to preserve them spiritually. But in increasing measure, the monks at Ruac were losing synchronicity with their secular brethren at Ruac village and for that reason, they needed to tuck themselves away.

Once a week, sometimes twice, they would brew their Enlightenment Tea and retire to the solitude of their cells or, if the evening was fine, a blanket of ferns beneath a favourite oak. There they would drift away to another place, another time, another plane, one which they were certain, brought them closer to God.

For a time, Barthomieu had fretted over Bernard's hostility. His distant words were still fresh. *'The Devil visited evil upon us last night. Do you have any doubt of this?'*

He had waggled an accusatory finger. *Wicked! Wicked!*

Bernard was a supremely learned man, infinitely more so than he. With Abélard he shared the honour as the most intelligent man Barthomieu had ever known. Popes turned to him to settle disputes. Kings. But in this matter, as Barthomieu ultimately convinced himself, *he* was in the right — it was Bernard who was short-sighted.

Nothing about the tea robbed Barthomieu of his ardour for Christ. Nor did it sap his resolve to pray and work towards spiritual purity. In fact, it increased his physical and spiritual vitality. He awoke every morning to the timbre of chapel bells with love in his heart and a spring in his step. And they bore their forays into distemper stoically enough, taking the bad with the good, and endeavouring not to cause each other harm.

He and Jean the infirmarer and herbalist preached the virtues of the tea among the abbey's monks and soon it was widely used by all as a vitality tonic and spiritual chariot. The monks did not talk freely about their personal experiences but on the days large batches were prepared, they lined up eagerly for their rations.

Even the abbot held out his personal chalice before scurrying off to the privacy of his abbot house.

And as the years went by, Barthomieu and the others noticed something creeping up on them, almost imperceptible at first but inescapable in the fullness of time. Their beards were remaining black or brown, their muscles stayed taut, their eyesights stayed keen. And in the delicate matter of their loins, despite their vows of celibacy, they retained the extravagant potency of their youth.

From time to time the monks of Ruac had need to do commerce with outsiders or perchance they would meet a Ruac villager out on a ramble. It was during these encounters that the realisation eventually dawned. Time was claiming the outsiders but was not visiting itself upon the monks.

Outside the monastery, people were growing older.

They were not.

It was the tea, there was no doubt.

It became something to be jealously guarded. Nothing good could come from exposing their practice to outsiders. These were uneasy times and charges of heresy flew easily. Yes, there were rumours. There were always rumours about the secretive doings inside an abbey's walls. The whispered speculation from villagers who lived near an abbey usually turned to debauchery, drunkenness and the like, even black arts from time to time. And yes, there were rumours in Ruac about monks who never seemed to die, but they stayed as just that — rumours.

So they hid themselves away, and when that became untenable, as when some of them were obligated to travel to the Priory of St Marcel on the occasion of Pierre Abélard's death vigil, they hid their faces as much as possible. At his deathbed, Barthomieu was forced by dint of his devotion and respect to his brother Bernard, to reveal his secret, only to him.

Bernard once again was furious and in private, railed against the tea and its inherent affront to the laws of nature. But, for the sake of his sole-surviving brothers, he swore an oath to take the secret with him to the grave, as long as Barthomieu and Nivard agreed never to see him again.

And painfully, that bargain was struck. That was the last time Barthomieu saw Bernard in life.

Nivard, the youngest of the six brothers from Fontaines, came to Ruac to join Barthomieu in a circuitous fashion. There were two traditional family paths that he might follow: the priesthood or the sword. At first, he chose neither.

Two brothers, Gérard and Guy had fought for the king. The others, Bernard, Barthomieu and André had donned the habit. André died a young man, struck down by the pox during the first harsh winter at Clairvaux Abbey. Gérard and Guy left the King's arms and came to Clairvaux when it was established. They took the cloth but soldiering never left their spirit. So it was a matter of course that following the Council of Troyes in 1128, they would become Knights of the Church. And when the Second Crusade began, they slipped on their white mantles with red crosses and joined their fellow Templars in the ill-fated raid on Damascus. There they fell under the deadly swarm of Nur ad-Din's archers and were lost in a melee of blood.

As a young man Nivard was pious and hoped to follow his famous brother Bernard to Clairvaux but that was before he laid eyes on a young woman from Fontaines. Anne was a commoner and the daughter of a butcher. His father was livid, but Nivard was so smitten by the shapely, cheerful girl that when he was not with her he could not eat, sleep nor pray in earnest. Finally, he forsook the noble traditions of his family and married her. Cut off from the munificence of his father, he became a lowly tradesman and apprenticed himself to his father-in-law in an offal-filled butcher's stall near the market place.

Three years of happiness was wiped away when the plague came to Fontaines and Nivard lost both his wife and infant child. He became a despondent rover, a drinker and an itinerant butcher and found himself in a godless haze in Rouen where, in 1120, in a stinking tavern smelling of piss, he heard of a position as a butcher on a new sailing ship. It was called the White Ship, the greatest vessel ever built in France. It was deemed so reliable and mighty that on a calm November night, it set out from Barfleur carrying the most precious of cargoes. On board was William Adelin, the only legitimate son of King Henry I of England, and with him a large entourage of British royals.

Navigation errors were made — or was it sabotage? It was never known. Near the harbour, the ship was steered into a submerged rock which tore through the hull. It quickly sank. Nivard was deep in the holds, fortified for his maiden voyage by wine, clad in butcher's ramskins. He heard the cracking timbers, the screams of the crew, the whoosh of the incoming water and the next thing he knew the ship was gone and he was all alone in the dark sea, bobbing in his buoyant ramskins. The next morning a fishing boat plucked him from the channel, the only survivor. A hundred were lost. The heir to the throne of England was gone.

Why was *he* saved?

That question perplexed Nivard, nagged at him, caused him to foreswear strong drink and led him back to God. His embarrassment over his youthful transgressions prevented him from venturing to Bernard's gate at Clairvaux. How could he explain his life and his choices to one so rigidly imperious? He could not. Instead, he made his way to the more forgiving climes of Ruac, where Barthomieu welcomed him with open arms.

'You are my brother in blood and in Christ!' he declared. 'And besides, we can use a monk who knows how to butcher a hog well!'

The years passed. Nivard became an ardent user of the tea, a fellow cheater of time.

The monks at Ruac came to understand that while their infusion could do many things, it was certainly not a shield of invincibility. It was no protection against the scourges of the day: the white plague — just look at poor Abélard — the black plague, the pox. And bodies could still break and be crushed. Jean, the infirmarer, fell off his mule one day and broke his neck. There was a story there. Scandalously, a woman was involved.

But notwithstanding the Devil's evil tricks, most of the brethren lived, and lived and lived.

★ ★ ★

It was high irony that one of Bernard's most famous actions, the one that would resonate through history, would lead to Barthomieu and Nivard's demise.

In 1118 Hugues de Payen, a lesser noble from Champagne, arrived in Jerusalem with a small band of men and presented his services at arms to the throne of Baudouin II. With Baudouin's blessings, he spent a decade of rag-tag service protecting Christian pilgrims on their visitations to the Temple Mount. Then, in 1128, de Payen wrote to Bernard, the most influential man in the Church, the shining star of monasticism, to sponsor his fledgling effort and create an order of Holy Knights to fight for Jerusalem, for Christendom.

Bernard took to the idea readily and penned a treatise to Rome, *De Laudibus Novae Militiae*, a vigorous defense of the notion of holy warriors. At the ecclesiastical Council of Troyes, in his home territory of Champagne, he rammed through the approval, and Pope Innocent II formally accepted the formation of The Poor

Knights of Christ and the Temple of Solomon.

The Templars were born.

Some of the earliest knights joining Hugues de Payen were blood relatives of Bernard, including André de Montbard, his maternal uncle, and his brothers Gérard and Guy. A gaggle of nobles from Champagne took the oath. And from the moment of their inception, the Templars venerated Bernard and were unwavering in their affection — up to the fateful year of 1307.

With Bernard's powerful patronage, the Templars received gifts from the nobility to aid their holy mission: money, land, noble-born sons. They could pass through any border freely. They paid no tax. They were exempt from all authority, save that of the Pope.

Though they were not able to secure a major victory during Bernard's lifetime, and in fact suffered ignominious defeat at Damascus during the Second Crusade, in the years that followed they flourished as a militia. Gloriously, in 1177, five hundred Templar knights helped defeat Saladin's army of twenty thousand at the Battle of Montgisard. One of these knights was Nivard of Fontaines, monk from Ruac, and a man his comrades could count upon to butcher a goat or camel.

Their reputation was secured and over the next century their fortunes swelled. Through a cunning mix of donations and business dealings, the power of the Templars exploded. They acquired huge tracts of land in the Middle East and Europe, they imported and exported goods throughout Christendom, they built churches and castles, they owned their own fleet of ships.

And then, the inevitable: because everything that rises must at some point fall.

The Templars, still exempt from the control of countries and other rulers, in effect a state within a state, were both feared and despised by outsiders. When an animal is wounded, other predators strike. Over the years the Templars were wounded. They suffered military setbacks in the Holy Land. Jerusalem was lost. They retreated to Cyprus, their last stronghold in the Middle East. Then Cyprus was lost. Their prestige waned and lords of the land, powerful foes, closed in for the kill.

Philippe de Bel, King of France, harboured a long-simmering feud against the Order ever since as a young man his application to join them had been rejected. He had also racked up massive debts to the Order, which he had no intention of repaying. The King pounced.

The Church resented the Templar's creed that permitted them to pray directly to God without the need for the Church to act as intermediary. The Pope pounced.

The Templars were accused by King Philippe and Pope Clement, working in concert, of all manners of heinous crimes. They were charged with denying Christ, ritual murder, even worship of an idol, a bearded head called Baphomet. Writs were drawn up, soldiers were readied.

The trap snapped shut.

★　★　★

In the year 1307, during the month of October, the King's men struck a massive coordinated blow. It was Friday the thirteenth, a date that would forever resonate with portent.

In Paris the Grand Master of the Templars, Jacques de Molay, and sixty of his knights were imprisoned en masse. Throughout France and Europe, thousands of Templars and their acolytes were rounded up and arrested. An orgy of torture and forced confessions followed. Where was their immense treasure hidden? Where was their fleet of ships formerly harboured at La Rochelle?

At Ruac, they struck at midday, just as the monks were filing out of the church following their observance of the Sext hours. A contingent of soldiers led by a short pugnacious captain with disgusting breath named Guyard de Charney charged through the gates and rounded up all the brothers.

'This is a Templar house!' he bellowed. 'By order of the King and Pope Clement, all knights of the Order will surrender themselves to our offices, and all Templar monies and treasures are hereby forfeit.'

The abbot, a tall man with a pointy beard, declared, 'Good sir, this is not a Templar house. We are a humble Cistercian abbey, as you well know.'

'Bernard of Clairvaux founded this house!' the captain bellowed. 'By his foul hand did the Templars come into being. It is well known that over the years, it has been a haven for knights and their sympathisers.'

From the rear of the assembled monks a voice was heard. 'Foul hand? Did you say that Bernard, our revered Saint, had a foul hand?'

Barthomieu tried to grab Nivard's robe to prevent him from stepping forwards but it was too late.

'Who said that?' the captain shouted.

'I did.'

Nivard strode to the front standing tall. Barthomieu fought his instinct to cower and followed his brother to the front of the line.

The captain saw two old monks before him. He pointed his finger at Nivard. 'You?'

'I order you to retract your vile statement about Saint Bernard,' Nivard said with an unwavering voice.

'Who are you to order me, old man?'

'I am Nivard of Fontaines, Knight Templar, defender of Jerusalem.'

'Knight Templar!' the captain exclaimed. 'You look like my deaf grandfather!' With that, the King's men broke into laughter.

Nivard stiffened. Barthomieu saw anger turning his face to stone. He was helpless to prevent what happened next, just as he was always helpless to prevent the stiff-necked Nivard from doing whatever he chose to do throughout his long, colourful life. Barthomieu had always been content to dwell within the cloisters of the abbey but Nivard was the restless adventurer, packing supplies of Enlightenment Tea in his chest and disappearing for long stretches of time.

Nivard slowly drew himself close enough to

smell the stink of the captain's rotten teeth. The soldier warily sneered at him, unsure of his next move.

A surprisingly sharp slap from the back of Nivard's hand stung his mouth. He tasted blood on his lip.

A sword was drawn.

The abbot and Barthomieu rushed forward to pull Nivard back but it was too late.

There was a soft sickening sound of punctured flesh.

The captain seemed surprised at his own action. He had not set out to kill an old monk but the bloody sword was in his hand and the wretched priest was on his knees, clutching his middle, staring towards heaven and saying his last words, 'Bernard. My brother.'

In a fury, the captain ordered the abbey to be searched and ransacked. Silver goblets and candlesticks were confiscated. Floorboards were prised up looking for Templar treasure. The monks were subjected to crude epithets and were kicked around like dogs.

In the infirmary Brother Michel shook like a frightened hare as the soldiers tossed the beds and shuffled through the shelves. He had laboured for endless decades as Jean's assistant and when the ancient monk met his untimely death under a mule, he had finally risen to become the abbey infirmarer. A hundred and fifty years was a long time to wait to improve one's station, he had sniffed at the time of his elevation.

Michel tried to ingratiate himself with the

soldiers by pointing out the location of a good jewel-encrusted crucifix and a silver chalice that had belonged to his former master and when they had left, he sat on one of the beds breathing heavily.

When the soldiers were spent by their exertions, the captain announced that he would report back to the King's council. The Abbot of Ruac would come with them and no amount of protestation from the monks would alter his decision. There would be an investigation, of that they could be sure. If this man, Nivard, had indeed been a Templar in his youth, then there would be a dearer price to pay than had so far been collected on this day.

Barthomieu was not allowed to touch his dead brother until the soldiers were gone. He sat beside him, lifted his head onto his lap and stroked his grey fringe of hair. Through his tears he whispered, 'Goodbye my brother, my friend. We have been brothers for two hundred and twelve years. How many brothers can say that? I fear I will join you soon. I pray I will meet you in Heaven.'

★   ★   ★

In the weeks that followed, the occasional visitor to Ruac Abbey reported the same stories. All over France, Templars were being tortured and burned at the stake. There was an orgy of violence throughout the land. Templar buildings and lands were being seized. No one suspected of keeping ties to the order was spared.

In his two hundred and twenty years of life Barthomieu never prayed harder. To the outside world, he looked like a man in his sixth decade, perhaps seventh. He looked as if there was plenty of life within his veins. But he knew this would be his last year. The Pope had set up an Inquisition chamber in Bordeaux and tales of human torches were spreading throughout the countryside. Word came that their abbot had been broken and burned.

What should he do? If Ruac abbey were seized, if the monks were martyred for their allegiance to Bernard, what would become of their secret? Should it die with them? Should it be protected for the ages? There was no one left with more wisdom than he. Jean was long dead. Nivard was dead. His abbot was dead. He had to rely on his own counsel.

Over scores of decades, he had acquired a good many skills, none better than scribe and bookbinder, and he emerged from a fitful bout of prayer with the firm resolution to put these skills to work. It was not for him to decide the disposition of their great secret. It was for God to decide. He would be God's humble scribe. He would write down the story of the cave and the Enlightenment Tea for others to find. Or not. It would be up to God.

Lest it fell into the hands of the Inquisitors, he would cloak the text in a fiendishly clever code that Jean the infirmarer had produced years earlier to hide his herbalist recipes from prying eyes. If his manuscript were found by men whom God wished to discover its meaning, then *He*

339

would enlighten them and lift its coded veil from their eyes. Barthomieu would be dead and buried, his work done.

So he began his work.

By the light of the sun and the flicker of the candle, he wrote his manuscript.

He wrote of Bernard.

He wrote of Nivard.

He wrote of Abélard and Héloïse.

He wrote of the cave, of Jean, of Enlightenment Tea, of Templars, of a long, long life in the service of God.

And when he was done, his true words concealed by Jean's cipher, he used his skills as artist and illuminator to illustrate the manuscript with the plants that were important to the tale and the paintings that first caught the attention, so many years before, of two frail monks taking their recuperative exercise along the cliffs of Ruac.

And to refresh his fading memory, Barthomieu took one last visit to the cave. He went alone early one morning with a good torch in his hand and a heart full of emotion. He had not been there for well on a hundred years but the path was clear in his mind and the yawning mouth of the cave seemed to welcome him like an old friend.

He spent an hour inside and when he emerged, he rested on the ledge and feasted his eyes for the final time on the green, limitless expanse of the river valley. Then he slowly began his journey back to the abbey.

Back at his writing table, Barthomieu drew the

images of the wondrous cave paintings from memory and finished the illustrations with a simple map showing a pilgrim how he might find the hidden cave. The book was ready for binding and he did so with love in his heart for his brothers, and especially Bernard. There was a special piece of red leather stored on a shelf in the scriptorium. He had never found a high-enough purpose for it; its moment had come. Over several days, he painstakingly bound the book and on its cover, he used his awls to carve the figure of Saint Bernard, his dear brother, complete with a heavenly halo floating above his fine head.

The book looked fine. Barthomieu was pleased but not completely so. It lacked a final touch which would make it truly a work befitting its subject. Under his mattress was a small silver box, a family heirloom, one of the few pretty objects not looted on that recent October day.

He melted it down over a hot fire and summoned Brother Michel to assist him.

At a small abbey like Ruac, out of necessity the monks often learned more than one skill. Over his long tutelage to the infirmarer, Jean, he also acquired a metal-working facility from the blacksmith and became reasonably adept at silversmithing. Barthomieu presented him the red-leather manuscript and asked him to embellish it with his precious bit of silver as best he could and left it in Michel's curious hands, unaware that in earlier years old Jean had taught his assistant his method of cipher. Untroubled, Barthomieu had written the key words, NIVARD,

HELOISE, and TEMPLARS in a parchment slipped between the pages on a bookmark.

A few days later, Michel handed the book back with shiny silver corners and endbands, five bosses on each cover and twin clasps holding the covers shut. Barthomieu was well pleased and hugged Michel and kissed him warmly for his splendid work. Aware that Michel was perennially inquisitive about the affairs of other monks, he asked him why he had not inquired about the nature of the manuscript. Michel mumbled he had other matters to occupy his mind and scuttled back to the infirmary.

There was word that a nearby Templar vineyard had been emptied, all the workers turned out and the nobles arrested. It was only a matter of time before the King's men returned, Barthomieu was sure of that. One night, when the monastery was quiet and all were asleep, he chipped away at a wattle and daub wall inside the Chapter House and opened a hole large enough to hide his precious manuscript. Before he inserted it, he looked at the last page, and though it was ciphered, he recalled the words he had written.

To you who are able to read this book and fathom its meaning, I send you tidings from a poor monk who lived for two hundred and twenty years and would have lived even longer had kings and popes not conspired against the good works of the Templars, the Holy Order nobly founded by my beloved brother, Saint Bernard of Clairvaux. Use this book as I have, to live a long bountiful life in service of Our Lord, Jesus Christ. Honour Him as I have honoured Him. Love Him as I have loved Him. May you have a long life and a good life. And say a prayer for your poor servant, Barthomieu, who left this earth an old man with a young heart.

When he was finished putting fresh plaster upon the wall he heard dogs barking and horses whinnying in the stables.

Men were coming.

They were coming for him. They were coming for all of them.

He hurried to the chapel to say one more hurried prayer before being carried off to a certain fate.

★   ★   ★

As the soldiers barged through the abbey gates, one monk was running as fast as he could through the moonlit meadow of tall grass behind the abbey. He had shed his habit and his crucifix and was dressed as a simple blacksmith in shirt, leggings and smock. He would hide by the river and in the morning light he would present himself to the good people of Ruac village as a hard worker and God-fearing man.

And if they were reluctant to take him in, he would reveal to them a secret that would surely interest them. Of that, Michel de Bonnet, formerly Brother Michel of Ruac Abbey, could be quite sure.

32

Thursday Night

Isaak finished reading the last words of the manuscript and when he was done there was silence on the line. 'You still there, Luc?'

Luc was in his taxi, a few blocks from the hotel. The sidewalks were full of people with a purpose, heading home, heading out.

'Yeah, I'm here.'

His mind was spitting out fragments.

The bison of Ruac.

Sara's long neck.

A car hurtling towards them on a dark Cambridge street.

Pierre lying face down on the cave floor.

Two hundred and twenty years.

Templars.

Saint Bernard embossed on a red-leather cover.

An explosive concussion and a plume in the distance.

Picratol.

Hugo, laughing.

Hugo, dead.

Zvi's body broken on the rocks.

Bonnet's sneering face.

The tenth chamber.

Sara.

Suddenly, it all came together. It was the moment a mathematician solves a theorem and

344

writes on his pad with a flourish: QED. *Quod erat demonstrandum.*

It has been proved.

'Do you have a car?' Luc asked.

'Yes, of course.'

'Can I borrow it?'

Luc's phone vibrated in his hand. Another call was coming in. He took it away from his ear for a moment to look at the caller ID.

Sara Mallory.

His heart pounded. He hit *answer* without warning Isaak he was dropping off.

'Sara!'

There was silence. Then a man's voice. An old voice.

'We have her.'

Luc knew who it was. 'What do you want?'

'To talk. Nothing more. Then she can go. And you too. There are things you need to understand.'

'Let me speak to her.'

There were muffled sounds. He waited.

'Luc?' It was Sara.

'Are you all right?'

She was frightened. 'Please help me.'

The man was back on the line. 'There. You spoke to her.'

'If you hurt her I'll kill you. I *will* kill you.'

The taxi driver shot a look at Luc in the rear-view mirror but seemed determined to mind his own business.

The man on the phone had a mocking tone. 'I'm sure you will. Will you come and talk?'

'Has she been hurt?'

345

'No, only inconvenienced. We've been gentlemen.'

'I swear. You'd better be telling me the truth.'

The man ignored him. 'I'll tell you where to go.'

'I know where you are.'

'Good. That's not a problem for us. But here's the thing. You've got to come alone. Be here at midnight. Not a moment later. If you bring the gendarmes, the police, anybody, she'll die unpleasantly, you'll die, your cave will be destroyed. There won't be anything left. Don't tell anyone about this. Please believe me, this is no idle threat.'

★　★　★

Isaak left Luc alone in his study for a half hour while he helped one of his children with a homework assignment. Isaak's wife poked her head in to offer coffee but Luc was writing so furiously he hardly had time to say no. It wasn't a polished letter, more of a rough sprawl with partial sentences and abbreviations. He would have liked to consolidate his thoughts into a well-reasoned piece but he was frantic for time as it was. It would have to do.

He used Isaak's printer/copier to run a duplicate and also made duplicates of the Isaak's colour copy of the Ruac Manuscript. He stuffed his letter and manuscript into the two blank envelopes Isaak had given him. On the first he wrote, COLONEL TOUCAS, GROUP GENDARMERIE OF DORDOGNE, PÉRIGUEUX, and the other M. GÉRARD GIROT, *LE MONDE*.

He pressed the sealed envelopes into Isaak's hand and told him if he didn't hear from him within twenty-four hours to see to it that the letters were delivered.

Isaak rubbed his forehead in worry but wordlessly agreed.

Isaak had a good car, a Mercedes coupé. Once Luc was free of the Périphérique Intérieur and onto the A20, he began to gun it and eat up the kilometres. The car had a GPS with radar. It told him he had 470 kilometres to go and gave his arrival time at 1:08 a.m. He'd have to make up more than an hour.

Every time the radar detector chirped he let up on the accelerator and took it down from breakneck to legal. He didn't have time for a chat with the gendarmes. A half hour of road-side nonsense could mean the difference between life and death. These people in Ruac were operating with a kind of ruthlessness he'd never experienced.

He'd never been in the military. He'd never even been in the boy scouts. He didn't know how to box or flip a man over his hip. He had no weapons, not even a pocket knife. What good would they do? The last time he'd been in a fight was in a schoolyard and both boys wound up with equally bloody noses, he recalled.

All he had to fight with were his wits.

★ ★ ★

He was in the Périgord again. Familiar ground. He'd made up most of the time he needed but

347

not all of it. He'd have to push it on the smaller roads, but it was late and the traffic was sparse.

He still had time to make a call to Colonel Toucas. Maybe that was the smarter play, to leave it to the professionals. It was the countryside but an RAID team could probably muster in an hour. He'd seen these guys in action on TV programmes. Hard young men. What was a middle-aged archaeologist doing storming the ramparts?

He shook off this line of thought. He'd got Sara into this. It was up to him to get her out of it. He gritted his teeth, pushed the accelerator and the car responded to his emotional tone.

★ ★ ★

He arrived at the outskirts of Ruac at 11:55. For better or worse, he wouldn't be late. He instinctively slowed at the curving hill where Hugo met his end, then guided the Mercedes into the deserted main street of the village.

It was a cloudy night, with a whipping wind. The village had no street lights and every house was dark. The only illumination came from the bluish halogen of the car's headlamps.

Down the street, a single house lit up in stages. First the upper floor, then the lower floor. It was the cottage three doors from the café.

Luc slowed and pulled to the kerb.

Instinctively he checked the rear-view mirror. He could make out two men in dark clothes taking up positions on either side of the street. Through the windscreen he saw the same thing

348

playing out down the road.

He was boxed in.

He got out of the car, shaking the pins and needles from his legs.

The front door of the lighted cottage opened. He stiffened. Maybe he'd be met with a shotgun blast. Like his diggers. Maybe this was how it ended.

She was dressed for a party with a festive blouse showing cleavage and a clingy black skirt, tight to mid-calf, almost vampy. She looked like she'd spent a lot of time on her make-up. Her lips were very red, aiming for luscious.

'Hello, Luc,' she said. 'You're on time.' She was purring and friendly, as if he was expected for dinner.

He felt a deep queasiness, the kind that ripples through the gut when the first wave of flu hits home.

He forced himself to talk and the words came out strained and dry. 'Hello, Odile.'

33

Friday, Midnight

Her sitting-room cushions had absorbed decades of fireplace and cigarette residue. Above that smoky staleness Odile's own sweet perfume hung heavily in the air.

They were alone. She gestured towards a wing chair by the front window. It was upholstered in damask with pink roses and green thorny stems, old-fashioned, like everything in the room. Luc half-expected a grandmother to dodder in on a cane.

'Where's Sara?'

'Please sit. Would you like a drink?'

He stood his ground, arms folded. 'I want to see Sara.'

'You will, believe me. But we need to talk first.'

'Is she safe?'

'Yes. Will you sit?'

He acquiesced, his posture rigid, a stony anger on his face.

'Now, a drink?' she asked.

'No, nothing.'

She sighed and sat across from him on the matching sofa. She pressed her legs together and lit a cigarette. 'You don't want one do you? I've never seen you smoke.'

He ignored her.

She dragged deeply. 'It's a terrible habit, but it's done me no harm as far as I can tell.'

'What do you want?' he asked. 'It's Sara I'm interested in, not you.'

If she was stung, she didn't show it. 'I want to talk about Hugo.'

What did she want, he thought. Absolution? 'It wasn't an accident, was it?'

She fiddled with her cigarette. 'It *was* an accident.'

'But he didn't die in his car.'

Her black eyebrows arched in sharp surprise. 'How did you know?'

'Because he took a photo with his mobile *after* he was supposedly dead.'

'What photo?'

'A painting.'

'Ah.' She exhaled a cloud of smoke that obscured her face for a moment. 'When you get involved with this kind of thing there are so many details. It's too easy to miss one or two.'

'Is that what Hugo was? A detail?'

'No! I liked him. I really fancied the man.'

'Then what happened?'

'He came here, unexpectedly. He let himself in. He was about to see things he shouldn't have seen. Jacques hit him. Too hard. He hit him too hard — that was the accident. I liked him. We could have had a good time together, a few laughs, maybe more. I had hopes.'

'So you put him back in his car and ran it into a tree.'

'Yes, of course. Not me, the men.'

'You murdered my friend.'

351

She let the words slide off. 'He didn't suffer, you know. If you're going to go, that's the best way. Cleanly, without pain. I really did like him, Luc. I'm sorry he's dead.'

Luc reached into his jeans pocket. She closely followed his hand perhaps expecting a knife or a gun. It was a piece of paper, a Xerox. He unfolded it and smoothed it on his knee, then half rose to hand it to her.

She stubbed out her cigarette and studied it carefully, her eye roaming from person to person, soaking up each image, seemingly lost in memories.

'She looks a lot like you,' Luc said pointedly, bringing her back.

She smiled. 'Look how tall de Gaulle was! What a man. He kissed me three times. I can still feel his lips. They were hard.'

Luc leaned forward. 'Okay, let's stop playing. How old are you?'

Her response was to light another cigarette and to watch the curling smoke rise to the beamed ceiling. 'You, know, by years, I'm not so young. But age is how you feel. I feel young. Isn't that what counts?'

He asked again. 'How old are you, Odile?'

'Luc, I'll tell you. I'll tell you everything you want to know. That's why you're here. To make you understand. We've done some bad things, but out of necessity. I'm not a monster. It's important for you to see that. We've done great things for France. We're patriots. We deserve to be left in peace.'

She began to ramble, chain-smoking and

talking in spurts. After a while, she offered him a drink again and this time he accepted, numbly following her into the kitchen partly as a way to satisfy himself they were still alone. She didn't object. Over the kitchen table there was a large clean rectangle, where something had hung on the wall for a long time. She caught him staring at the blank space but offered no explanation. She simply poured two brandies, took the bottle with her and led him back to the sitting room. Back in the wing chair he kept up his guard and started on the drink only after she drank hers first.

Before she was done talking, he'd allowed his glass to be refilled.

★ ★ ★

Her first strong childhood memory, the earliest one that really stuck, was toddling into her father's café from the living quarters above.

The stairs connected the kitchen of their flat to the kitchen of the café. She always remembered the magical feeling of having two kitchens because it made her feel special. None of the other children in Ruac had two kitchens.

She was upstairs in her bedroom playing with a family of rag dolls when she heard two sharp bangs that frightened but also beckoned her. She was a sprig of a girl, a little black-haired beauty, and none of the men spotted her in their midst before she'd spent a fair amount of time mutely studying the scene.

She'd seen many dead animals, butchered

animals, even put-down old horses with their brains blown out. So she approached the bloody sight on the café floor more with curiosity than revulsion.

She was mainly drawn to the young blond man, whose face was untouched owing to the trajectory of the bullet. His eyes were open and still glistening blue, retaining the last vestiges of life. They were friendly eyes. He had a kind face. She would have liked to play with him. The other man looked old and rough, like the men in the village and besides, his face was grotesque with a nasty exit wound through the eye socket.

Her father saw her first. 'Odile! Get the hell out of here!'

She stayed put, staring.

Bonnet rushed forward and scooped her up with his thick arms and calloused hands and carried her up the stairs. She remembered the way his pomaded black hair smelled and the curve of his long black sideburns. He threw her down on her bed, slapped her hip with the back of his hand hard enough to hurt and called for his wife to take charge of her.

It was 1899. She was four years old.

★　★　★

She remembered being taken to visit the cave soon after the strangers were shot. Her father and some of the others had already been there, and while guards stood along the cliffs in case a walker happened by, the villagers were given the chance to see it one time.

Her father toted her on the steep parts of the climb, but he was holding her more tenderly than before, talking to her along the way, telling her she was going to see pretty pictures in the dark.

She remembered the hissing sound of the kerosene lamp and the colourful animals prancing in the darkness and the huge bird man who the grown ups said would scare her, but he did not.

And she remembered her mother holding on to her dress to prevent her wandering off the edge while the men built a dry wall of flat stones to hide the mouth of the cave and close it for ever.

★ ★ ★

She was a rebellious child. Some girls easily fell into the rhythms of village life and went with the flow without question. Not Odile. Early on she discovered books and magazines, one of the few village children who took to the printed page. There were snickers about the black-haired Canadian who had wandered into Ruac some nine months before Odile was born. Hadn't he been some kind of professor? What ever happened to him? At that, the men would make snorting sounds and turn the conversation to Duval's fat pigs and Canadian-flavoured rashers.

When she was eighteen, just before her initiation was to occur, she ran away to Paris, to live, to be free. She had a strong sense that once initiated, freedom would be as elusive as a butterfly winging over the cliffs. Her father, Bonnet, and his best friend, Edmond Pelay, the village doctor, went looking for her, but the city was too vast and they had no firm leads. Besides, trouble was brewing and they had to suck up their worries about Odile's loose tongue and return to Ruac to deal with the coming storm.

Nobody knew exactly where the fire would spark, but all of Europe was dry tinder, with shifting alliances, land grabs, boiling anger and mistrust. As it happened, on 28 June 1914, Gavrilo Princip, a Bosnian — Serb student assassinated Archduke Franz Ferdinand of Austria in Sarajevo. If that hadn't started the war, it would have been something else. There was a sad inevitability to it.

Odile fell in with a bohemian crowd of artists and writers in Montmartre and when the young men in her circle went to war, she moved into the grimy studio of an older painter with a bad leg and a worse drinking habit who supported himself fitfully by driving a taxi. It was a time of danger and foreboding. The Germans were on the offensive and Paris was in their sights. Still, for a country girl from an insular village in the Périgord, the urban chaos was exhilarating and she drank the excitement like wine.

By the end of August 1914 the French Army and the British Expeditionary Force had been forced back to the Marne River on the outskirts of Paris. The two main German armies that had just polished off Belgium were advancing towards the capital.

On 6 September, the Germans were on the

356

verge of breaking through the beleaguered ranks of the French Sixth Army. The word went out to the garrisons of Paris that reinforcements were needed at Marnes. The 7th Division was at the ready but all military transport vehicles had been pressed into service and the rail system was choked to the point of paralysis. Then the military governor of Paris fatefully declared, 'Why not use taxis?'

The call went out across the taxi ranks of Paris and within a few hours a convoy was forming at the Esplanade des Invalides. Odile heard the call. Her boyfriend was in the midst of a bender, blind drunk at the time. She jumped into action; the hell with him! The Germans were coming and she knew how to drive a car — that much she'd learned from her miserable beau. The red Renault taxi with its yellow-spoked wheels, one of the more beaten-up specimens on the streets of Paris, was at the ready so she jumped behind the wheel and joined the convoy.

She may or may not have been the only female driver that day; she liked to think she was an army of one. The column of taxis made their way empty to Dammartin where at dusk, at a railway siding, they met the infantrymen reinforcements who clambered five at a time into each taxi and took off in the dark without auto lights.

The boys who pulled Odile's taxi, hooted and hollered at their good fortune all the way to the front. She kissed each one goodbye, let one of them squeeze her breast and began to turn back for another round trip when a volley of German artillery shells rained down.

357

There were ear-splitting booms and flashes of light. A spray of wet dirt landed in her open cab, covering her clothes and hair with a sticky mess. She looked down. There was a bloody palm in her lap and when she picked it up it was like holding a boy's warm hand on a date. She threw it onto the ground, prayed it didn't belong to one of the lads she'd just dropped off, and headed back to Paris for a second run.

That night, the taxis of Marnes delivered four thousand reinforcements who turned the tide and saved Paris and, for all anybody knew, France.

Odile wanted Luc to know.

★ ★ ★

After that night, Odile stayed at the front for weeks, helping the nurses, doing whatever she could for the wounded boys. She stayed until some kind of fever almost killed her. Exhausted and shocked by the calamities of war, she limped back to Ruac and allowed her mother to tuck her into her old bed, where under the soft covers she sobbed for the first time in years.

Her father came to talk to her when he was assured she wouldn't break down. He wasn't one for feminine emotions. He had only two gruff questions for her: 'Are you ready to join us now? Are you prepared to take the initiation?'

She'd seen enough of the outside world to last a lifetime. Ruac was far from the madness of the trenches.

'I'm ready,' she answered.

★ ★ ★

War came again soon enough.

This time the Germans were more successful invaders and as occupiers of all of France the villagers of Ruac couldn't avoid them. Bonnet was now the mayor. His father, the previous mayor, had passed away as the Second World War began.

The new mayor wrote out his father's death certificate with the old man's thick fountain pen, falsifying the date of birth, as the previous mayor had done for generations. And his father was duly buried in the village plot, which had surprisingly few stones considering its antiquity.

Furthermore, comporting with their custom, the stones had the name of the deceased only. There were no chiselled dates of birth or death, and since the plot was tucked away, down a lane through a private farm, no one seemed to notice the oddity.

Ruac village formed its own maquis group, which was under the Resistance umbrella but loosely so. De Gaulle's staff in Algeria tried to inject some order into the effort and assigned the code name Squad 70 to Bonnet's gang and passed coded messages to them from time to time. In the dead of night, they would meet in their underground hideout where the mayor would preside and Dr Pelay would act as his deputy. Bonnet would always repeat: 'These are our priorities: Ruac first, Ruac second, Ruac third.' And one person would always draw a laugh by concluding, 'And France fourth.'

359

Odile's experience in the previous war put her in good stead with the maquisard and her father reluctantly allowed her to participate in some of their raids alongside her brother, Jacques. Both of them were strong and healthy, quick and athletic. And if Bonnet hadn't given his permission, Odile would have run off and joined another maquis band anyway.

Bonnet and Dr Pelay made a good pair. Bonnet was a man of few words, but decisive. Pelay was more of a talker, and the people in the village knew that when they went to his surgery he'd chew their ear off. Their maquis soon had a reputation for effectiveness and complete ruthlessness. They were said to engage the *boche* with an almost superhuman ferocity and cruelty. Squad 70 was known to turn their Nazi victims into unrecognisable hunks of bloody flesh and the SS Panzer Division Das Reich, which was tasked with suppressing the Dordogne, feared this particular maquis group above all the others.

In one of their more notable escapades, Bonnet got it in his head that his band would be responsible for the retaliation for a massacre of French civilians from the nearby village of Saint-Julian. A Panzer unit had surrounded the town looking for maquis elements suspected to be hiding in the surrounding forests. All the men in the village were rounded up and gathered into the grounds of the village school. Information on collaborators was demanded. When none was given, all seventeen men, including a fourteen-year-old boy holding his father's hand, were executed with bullets to the back of their heads.

Two weeks later, a group of eighty-two Germans was captured by the maquisard fifty kilometres west of Bergerac and was transported en masse to the Davoust Military Barracks in Bergerac, a Resistance stronghold.

On a Sunday, Bonnet and Pelay entered the barracks and under false pretenses took seventeen German prisoners from their cells. They were loaded into trucks driven by men from Ruac who snarled and verbally tortured their prisoners with what was going to happen to them during the trip from Bergerac to Saint-Julian.

By the time the Germans were assembled in the same schoolyard where the civilians had been massacred, the prisoners knew their fate and were incontinent with terror. The presence of Odile, a pretty woman, did nothing for their spirits because she was, like the men, wielding a long-handled axe. Bonnet personally addressed the condemned men, raging at them for their crimes and told them they were going to suffer before they died.

And in an orgy of axe blows, starting with arms and legs, all seventeen men were summarily hacked to death.

Word eventually came to Bonnet that Squad 70 had attracted the attention of the leadership of the Free French Army and General de Gaulle himself. A personal audience was desired. Bonnet hated to travel. He sent Dr Pelay to Algiers and the man spent a giddy time being feted by the co-presidents of the French Committee of National Liberation, Generals de

Gaulle and Henri Giraud, who lauded the work of the Ruac Squad, the fiercest of the maquisard in France.

Pelay came back with a medal, which Odile thought ought to go to her father, but instead Pelay wore it proudly on his vest every day of his life.

In July 1944 Bonnet and Pelay disappeared for a week to liaise with a group of maquisard commanders in Lyon and when they returned they informed the group of a big action planned for the night of 26 July. If all went well, a lot of *boche* would be killed and a lot of money could be made.

First Bonnet told them what their role in the attack was supposed to be.

Then he told them what they'd be doing instead.

Odile and the Ruac gang hid in the woods by the railway track. To this day she remembered the pounding in her chest as the train approached. It was only early evening, still light. She and everyone would have preferred the cover of darkness but they had no control over Nazi train schedules.

Ahead, sixty kilos of picratol had been placed under an aqueduct. The Ruac squad had one machine gun and two automatic rifles among them. Everyone else, including Odile, had pistols. Hers was a Polish Vis, an old nine-millimetre handgun that jammed with regularity. Her father and brother had grenades.

The locomotive, on its way from Lyon to Bordeaux, passed their position and Odile started counting box cars. She got to five when the explosion ripped through the locomotive. The train came to a macabre halt, cars buckling against each other. A sliding door opened in front of their position and a trio of dazed German soldiers, bruised and confused from the impact, stared into her eyes. She began to fire her entire eight-shot magazine at them from no more than ten paces. She saw her bullets strike home and felt a frisson of excitement each time an exit wound splashed blood.

She heard her father say, 'Good work.'

The Ruac squad secured the last two box cars while other bands hit the front cars. The plan was to offload all the contents to heavy lorries standing at a lay-by which would transfer the loot to Resistance headquarters in Lyon.

Bonnet had other ideas. The Ruac box cars were filled with bank notes, gold bars and one thin crate stencilled with a provocative notation: FOR DELIVERY TO REICHSMARSCHALL GOERING.

He and Pelay lobbed grenades into the woods to give the impression there was a pitched battle going on at the rear. In the confusion, every blood-spattered box and crate from those two cars found their way to transport vans driven by members of the Ruac maquis.

In under half an hour, all the loot was in Ruac, the Resistance leadership none the wiser.

In their underground chamber, Bonnet took a crowbar to the crate and splintered the plywood. Inside was a painting. A beautiful pale-faced young man draped in fur.

'Fat-arsed Goering wanted this,' Bonnet announced spreading his arms wide, holding it up to the villagers. 'Probably worth a lot. Here, Odile, this is for you, a pretty boy for you to look at. You earned this tonight.'

She instantly fell in love with the portrait. She didn't care if it was valuable or not. The young man in the painting was hers now. She'd put it on the wall over her kitchen table to have breakfast, lunch and dinner with him.

He *was* a pretty boy.

By the light of bare bulbs, they counted the cash and stacked the gold bars into the night. Giddy with victory and drink they listened to Bonnet's final tally, which he punctuated with the following proclamation: 'There's enough here to set us all up for life.' He raised his glass. 'My friends and family, here's to long lives!'

★ ★ ★

It was after one in the morning. Despite the endless day, Luc wasn't tired. Numb, but not tired. The woman he was staring at was one hundred and sixteen years old. But she looked sultry and supple, like a dishy forty-year-old.

'Since the war, we've lived peacefully,' she said. 'We don't bother anyone, nobody bothers us. We want to live our lives. That's all. But then you came here and everything changed.'

'So this is my fault?' he asked incredulously. 'You're saying that I have the blood on my hands of the people you killed?'

There were heavy steps coming from the

kitchen. Luc turned quickly at the sound. Bonnet filled the doorway with his bulky frame. He hadn't shaved in a while and his cheeks were white with stubble.

'We have a right to protect ourselves!' He was almost spitting. 'We have a right to be free. We have a right to be left alone. I will not permit us to be studied and poked and prodded and treated like animals in a zoo. All that will happen if you continue with this goddamn cave.'

His son was behind him, the sleeves of his T-shirt stretched tight over his bulging biceps. Both men strode into the sitting room. Their boots were muddy.

Luc stood and faced them down. 'Okay, I've listened to Odile. I have some understanding of who you are. Fine. Now let me see Sara and let me bring her home.'

'We need to talk to you first,' Bonnet insisted.

'About what?'

'About who else knows? Who else did you tell about us?'

If they were intending to intimidate him with their glowers and their body language, they succeeded. Luc was large but he wasn't a fighter. These men were capable of extreme violence, that much was clear.

'No one else knows, but if anything happens to me, everyone will know. I've left a letter to be opened if I die or disappear.'

'Where's this letter?' Bonnet demanded.

'I've got nothing more to say. Where's Sara?'

Jacques was sneering now. 'She's not far. I've had my eye on her.'

That big oafish face oozing with sexual innuendo set Luc off. It didn't matter that he was going to get the worst of it. It wasn't a rational move, but he lunged forwards and caught Jacques firmly on the cheekbone with his clenched right fist.

It seemed to hurt his hand more than the man's face because Jacques was able to shake it off and deliver a hard knee to Luc's groin, dropping him on all fours and submerging him in a deep pool of pain and nausea.

'Jacques, no!' Odile screamed as her brother swung his leg back to kick him in the crotch again.

'Not there!' Bonnet ordered, and his son backed off. The mayor stood over Luc and smashed his fist down onto his neck with a hammer blow. 'Here!'

34

Luc awoke with a dull throbbing in his head and a sharp pain in his neck. He squeezed the spot that hurt. It felt tender and bruised but his fingers and toes were moving so nothing was broken, he reasoned. He was on his side on an old musty camp bed facing a stone wall. Cold grey limestone, the backbone of the Périgord.

He rolled onto his back. Above him was a bare bulb hanging from its cord. He rolled again, this time onto his right side, and there was that face.

His skin was so white and pure it almost seemed ghostly. The young man was staring back at him every bit as steadily as the Mona Lisa stares down her admirers in the Louvre. It was the Raphael. The *Portrait of a Young Man* rested on a crate with German stencilling, propped against the damp stone wall as if it were a worthless canvas awaiting the dumpster or a yard sale.

He swung his legs and sat up. His head was pounding but he was able to stand. The room was about the size of Odile's sitting room, cluttered with crates, rolled carpets and a hodge podge of bric-a-brac: candle sticks, vases, lamps, even a silver tea service. He picked up a candle stick and it was awfully heavy.

Christ, he thought, solid gold.

There was the clunk of a bolt unlocking and the door creaked open.

Bonnet and his son again.

They saw he had a candlestick in his hand. Bonnet pulled a small pistol from his pocket. 'Put it down,' he demanded.

Luc snorted at him and tossed it hard on the floor, denting it. 'There goes half its value.'

'Who has this letter you say you wrote?' Bonnet asked again.

Luc thrust out his jaw. 'I'm not saying anything else until I see Sara.'

'You need to tell me,' Bonnet said.

'You need to screw yourself.'

Bonnet whispered into his son's ear. Both men left and locked the door again. Luc had a better look around the room. The walls were stone, the floor concrete. The door was a solid-looking affair. The ceiling was plastered. Maybe there was an opportunity there. It wouldn't be hard to climb up onto the crates and poke around. Then in the corner behind some cardboard boxes he noticed a jumble of hardware and cables. He swore out loud. His computers!

The door opened again.

This time Sara was there with Odile behind her. 'Ten minutes, that's all,' Odile said, giving Sara a small shove. The door slammed again and they were alone.

She looked small and frail but at the same time she beamed at the sight of him. 'Luc! My God, it's you!'

'You didn't know I was coming?'

She shook her head and lowered it to hide her tears.

He moved forward and pulled her to his chest

so she could cry against it. He felt her sobs with the palms of his hands pressed against her shuddering back. 'It's okay,' he said. 'It's going to be okay. You're not alone anymore. I'm here.'

She pulled away to dry her eyes and managed to smile again. 'Are *you* okay?' she asked. 'Did they hurt you?'

'No, I'm fine. Where are we?'

'I'm not sure. I haven't seen anything but the inside of a room like this one and a tiny loo. I think we're underground.'

'I've been sick with worry about you,' Luc said. 'You fell off the face of the earth. I had no idea what happened. I went to your flat. I called your boss. I tried to get the police to investigate.'

'I never made it out of Cambridge,' she replied weakly.

★   ★   ★

She'd stayed at Fred Prentice's side in the bustling corridor of the Nuffield Hospital. Luc had told her there'd been an emergency back in France. Something bad, nothing more. He had to go, he was sorry. He'd call when he knew the facts, and then he was gone.

Fred saw she was shaken, and in his fractured state, *he* was the one consoling *her*.

'I'm sure it'll be all right,' he said.

'Fred, for God's sake, don't worry about me!'

'You look upset. I wish you had a chair. Maybe they can bring one.'

'I'm fine.' She leaned over his railing and patted him on his only uninjured limb. 'Why don't you tell me what you found?'

'Yes,' he said. 'It'll do us good to distract ourselves with a bit of science. Have you ever heard of the FOXO3A gene?'

'No, sorry.'

'How about SIRT1?'

'Not in my lexicon, I'm afraid.'

'Not to worry. It's a bit specialised. I'm not an expert either, but I've been reading up since your sample lit these targets up on our test panel like Piccadilly Circus.'

'You're saying there was additional activity beyond the ergot alkaloids?'

'The ergots were only the beginning. Your broth has quite a few interesting properties. I'd describe it as a cornucopia of pharmacology. Had that phrase on one of my PowerPoint slides, actually. Thought it was apt.'

She wanted him back on track. 'The genes . . .'

'Yes, the genes. Here's what I know. They're called survival genes. SIRT1 is the Sirtuin 1 DNA-repair gene. It's part of a family of genes that control the rate of ageing. If you activate it by revving it up with a chemical activator or, curiously, by calorie-depriving an animal, you can achieve remarkable longevity results. They work by repairing the damage done to DNA by the normal wear-and-tear of cellular processes. You know how it's said that red wine makes you live longer?'

'I'm a devotee,' she chuckled.

'There's a chemical in red wine, especially Pinot Noirs: resveratrol.'

370

She nodded. 'I've heard of it.'

'Well, it's an activator of the SIRT1 gene. Hard to do the experiment in humans, but give enough of the stuff to mice and you can double their life spans. And it's not even all that potent a chemical. Presumably there are better ones waiting to be discovered. And by the way, as a plant person, you'll be interested in knowing that the Japanese knotweed root is a richer source of resveratrol than wine.'

'I'll stick with my wine,' she scoffed, but he had her attention. 'And the other gene, FOX something?'

'FOXO3A. It's another member of that family of survival genes, maybe a more important one than SIRT1. Some describe it as the holy grail of ageing. There aren't too many known activators of FOXO3A other than polyphenols in green tea extracts and N-aceytlycysteine so there haven't been any direct experimental studies done manipulating the gene. But there's some interesting epidemiology. A study of Japanese men who lived to ninety-five or over compared to chaps who popped off at a normal age showed that the old boys had extra copies of the FOXO3A gene.'

She squinted in thought. 'So if you could boost this gene artificially, you could achieve longevity.'

'Yes, perhaps so.'

'Could a man live as long as two hundred and twenty years?'

'Well, I don't know. Maybe if he took your broth!'

'Okay, Fred,' she said with rising excitement. 'What makes you say that?'

'As I told you, the broth lit up these genes on our screens. It's not like I'm a genius for testing for SIRT1 and FOXO3A. Our robotic screens test hundreds of potential biological targets all in one go. Once I had that result, I did serial dilutions of the broth and retested for activity, and this is the really exciting thing, Sara: whatever chemicals possess the gene-activating properties, they are extremely potent. Many, many times more potent than resveratrol. And forget about green tea extracts. Not in the same league. Whatever's in the broth is really extraordinary.'

'You don't know what it is?'

'Heavens no! Our screens only detect activity. It will probably require a small army of smart organic chemists to identify the chemical or chemicals responsible for activating SIRT1 and FOXO3A. These structural elucidations can be devilishly difficult but the academic and commercial interest will be immense. What I would have given . . . ' His voice trailed off.

She stroked his good shoulder again. 'Oh, Fred . . . '

'My lab, gone. Everything, gone.'

She fished a tissue from her handbag and he daintily dabbed his eyes with it.

'Do you think it's coming from the redcurrants? The bindweed?'

'There's no way of telling without an awful lot of grunt work. Maybe there's one compound activating both genes. Maybe two or more compounds. Maybe the molecule or molecules don't come from either plant but from a chemical reaction involving heating all the ingredients in the soup, as it were. Maybe the ergots from the *Claviceps* play a role too. Really, it might take years to sort it all out.'

'So let me understand all this,' Sara said. 'We've got a liquid rich in hallucinogenic ergot alkaloids which also has unidentified substances which could cause extreme longevity.'

'Yes, that's right. But there're other wrinkles. Two more of my screening targets lit up.'

She shook her head and cast her eyes upwards as if unprepared to absorb any more information. 'What were they?'

'Well, one of them was the 5-HT_{2A} receptor. It's a serotonin receptor in the brain which controls impulsivity, aggression, rage, that type of thing. Something in your broth was a very potent agonist, or stimulator of that receptor. Not much positive to say about the medical uses there. You might make someone quite nasty with that kind of pharmacology. The other target was rather more salubrious.'

'And that was?' she asked.

'Phosphodiesterase type 5,' he said with a glint in his eye, as if she'd get his drift.

'Sorry,' she said, 'and that does what?'

'PDE-5 is an enzyme involved in smooth muscle activity. Something in your broth was an exceptionally powerful PDE-5 inhibitor, and you know what they're good for?'

'Fred, this is so not my area.'

He grinned like an embarrassed schoolboy. 'It

would be something like a super-Viagra!'

'You're joking!'

'Not at all. This broth of yours could conceivably make you higher than a kite, turn you into a sex machine with a very bad temper and make you live for a very, very long time.'

* * *

Luc watched her channelling Prentice's pithy summation. An image of the priapic bird man in the tenth chamber flashed in front of his eyes, replaced, with a sad pang, by the thought of the gentle scientist who wouldn't live to see another morning. He didn't have the heart to tell her that Fred was gone. He needed her to stay strong.

'And then you left?' he asked.

'Not right away. I stayed until they found a bed for him in the wards, then went back to the hotel to collect my bag. There was a knock on my door. I answered it and two men rushed in. I wasn't even able to scream. One of them choked me.' She started crying. 'I blacked out.'

Luc held her again while she sobbed and told the rest of the story heaving into his chest.

'I woke up in the dark with tape over my mouth. It was hard to breathe. I must have been drugged because time was way off, all screwed up. I think I was in a car trunk. I'm not sure. They could have taken me on one of the car ferries. I don't know how long it took but when I got here I was a mess and I was dehydrated. Odile was here. She took care of me, if you want to call it that. It's a prison. What do they want,

374

Luc? They won't tell me what they want.'

'I'm not sure.' He held on to her shoulders at arm's length so he could look her squarely in the face. 'If they wanted to kill us, they could have done it already. They want something from us. We'll see, but you've got to believe me, we're going to be okay. I'm not going to let them hurt you.'

She kissed him for that. Not a passionate kiss, a thankful one. She held both his hands, then inspected his left arm. 'Your infection's improving.'

He laughed. 'What a small thing to notice.'

'I was worried about you,' she clucked.

He smiled. 'Thank you. The tablets are working nicely.'

The bolt clunked and the door opened. Bonnet was there with his pistol again. 'Okay, it's time,' he said.

Luc moved Sara behind him and took a truculent and threatening step forwards. 'Time for what?' he said. 'What do you want from us?'

Bonnet's eyes were dull. He looked like a man who was tired and weary but determined to stay awake. 'You'll see.'

35

They were in a cool windowless chamber the size of a primary school gymnasium or a town cinema. It was far too large to be the simple basement of one of the cottages. If they were still in the village, as Luc suspected, then the chamber had to be under the street, an excavation accessible from several cottages. It appeared that a number of corridors ran off from various points along its perimeter and he thought it possible that each might lead to a cottage.

The walls were the ubiquitous limestone block, but the floors were wood planks, smooth with age and covered with a patch-work of rugs, most of them large, fancy orientals in various shades of greens, blues, reds and pinks. The room was lit with cheap industrial fluorescent fixtures affixed to the plaster ceiling. Copper water pipes ran down the walls.

Luc and Sara were seated beside one another on wooden chairs up against one of the long walls. His right wrist and her left wrist were handcuffed to a couple of the copper pipes.

On the opposite wall a vintage phonograph was turning a vinyl record. The room was filled with tinny, old-time *bal-musette* — dance-hall, accordion music with an urgent tempo.

In the centre of the room there was a sturdy folding table. Bonnet and Dr Pelay were fussing over a huge aluminium pot on a large electric coil that glowed red-hot. The pot was the kind of model an army cook would use to make stew for two hundred men and the ladle was also out-sized. Steam was rising from the vessel filling the room with a sweet, almost fruity kind of fragrance.

Luc and Sara had smelled it before in the kitchen of their campsite.

Bonnet kept up a slow-paced monologue, talking loudly across the expanse of the room, over the music. The scene had the incongruous air of a chef doing a cooking show before a hand-cuffed audience.

'I don't have to tell you that these plants aren't available all-year round,' Bonnet said. 'We have to harvest them when they're abundant and store them for the winter months. It's nice and cool down here so they keep well as long as we keep them dry. The berries and the bindweed, they're dead reliable. Never a problem. It's the barley grass that's tricky. If they don't have those black or purple lumps they're no good. What do you call those lumps? I always forget.'

'Sclerotia,' Sara replied automatically, her voice dry with fear.

'I can't hear you. Speak up,' Bonnet said.

'Ergot bodies,' Pelay told him.

'Yes! That's it, ergot bodies,' he replied. 'Without those, it's rubbish. Unusable. So we've got to find the grass with the purple lumps on their spikes. Then we're in business. You've got to cook it through and through but not to the boil. Simmer it, like a good cassoulet. You do it for as many years as Pelay and I have, you get a feel for it so it comes out perfect every time.'

Luc called out, 'How old are you, Bonnet?'

The mayor stopped stirring and rubbed at his stubble. 'I always have to think,' he replied. Pelay chuckled at his show. 'I'm not the oldest, you know. That fellow Duval, the pig farmer, he's the oldest. I'm two hundred and forty-two but my wife says I don't look a day over one hundred and eighty!' Pelay found this hilarious and cackled like a woman. 'I learned how to make the tea from my father, Gustave. He learned from my grandfather, Bernard. And he learned from my great-grandfather, Michel Bonnet, who, I'm told, was a monk in his younger days in Ruac Abbey before he left monastery life in 1307, the year the Templars were wiped out. That's not bad, eh? Only four generations of Bonnets in seven hundred years!'

There was a plastic carrier bag on the table. Bonnet removed a red-leather book, the Ruac manuscript.

Luc shook his head at the sight. 'Having trouble reading that, Bonnet?'

'As a matter of fact, yes, except for the little Latin passage the fellow wrote in 1307, which goes with the family date I just mentioned. Maybe we'll persuade you to tell us what it says. But never mind if you don't. I think I know well enough what's in it. The pictures tell a thousand words. This Barthomieu who was two hundred and twenty — I expect he and my great-grandfather were well acquainted.'

'How often do you drink it?' Luc asked.

'Our tea? Once a week. Always late, in the middle of the night, when we won't be disturbed by some idiot wandering through the village. Maybe we could take it less often but it's a tradition and frankly we enjoy it. I've used it well over ten thousand times and it doesn't get old. You'll see.'

'There's no way we're going to play along,' Luc said.

'No?' Bonnet responded, shrugging. He dipped a finger into the pot and it came out red. He licked it clean and declared, 'There, it's ready. Proper Ruac tea. What do you think, Pelay?'

The doctor tasted some from the ladle. 'I can't remember a better batch,' he laughed. 'I'm sorry I have to wait.'

'Well, you and me, old friend. We're the keepers tonight. Special keepers for special guests.' He looked around the chamber. 'Jacques!' he yelled. 'Where the hell are you?'

His son appeared from one of the corridors.

'We're ready,' Bonnet told him. 'Let them know.'

Luc and Sara held each other's free hands. Her hand felt limp and cold. There was little he could say to her except, 'Everything will be all right. Stay strong.' Soon, there was the muffled sound of a clanging bell. It persisted for no more than half a minute then ended.

The villagers began to arrive in knots of threes and fours.

None younger than twenty or so, by appearance. Mostly men and women well on in

379

years, exactly how old, Luc could only guess. Odile arrived, looking guiltily at the handcuffed pair along the wall. There were maybe thirty or forty people her age. People tended to congregate with their peer groups, milling around, whispering, seemingly uncomfortable with strangers in their midst. All told, there were at least two hundred people but Luc lost count as the room filled.

Bonnet banged the pot with the ladle to get everyone's attention. 'Good people,' he shouted. 'Come and be served. Don't be shy because of our guests. You know who they are. Don't pay them any mind. Come on, who's first tonight?'

They lined up orderly and each, in turn, received a paper cup, filled to the brim with hot red tea. Some sipped at it, savouring it as one might a good cup of ordinary tea. Others, especially the younger villagers, gulped it.

They struck Luc as some kind of ersatz parishioners queuing to receive holy communion. But Bonnet was no priest. He grinned and joked as he dolloped out the brew and seemed amused whenever he accidentally sloshed some onto the table top.

When the last villager, a heavy-haunched old woman with long grey hair knotted into a bun, had received her ration and whispered something to him, Bonnet replied loudly, 'No, no. For me, later. I've got to do something tonight. But come with me, let me introduce you.'

Bonnet led the woman to Luc and Sara. 'This is my wife, Camille. These are the archaeologists I told you about. Isn't the professor a

380

good-looking fellow?'

The mayor's wife looked him over and grunted, and with that, Bonnet swatted her on the rump and told her to enjoy herself without him. He pulled up a chair and sat himself down, just beyond Luc's reach.

'You know, I'm tired,' he sighed. 'It's late. I'm not as young as I used to be. Let me sit with you a while.'

Sara's eyes wandered around the room. People were finishing their tea, tidily disposing the cups in a bin, all very neat and civilised. There was a din of conversation, some polite laughter, all very banal.

'What happens next?' she asked.

'Wait, you'll see. It takes fifteen minutes for some, twenty for others. Watch. It won't go unnoticed.' He called for Pelay who approached from the folding table with two more cups of tea in his hands.

Sara looked at them and began to cry.

'No, you'll really like it!' Bonnet insisted. 'Don't make a fuss. Trust Pelay. He's a good doctor!'

'Leave her alone,' Luc threatened. He rose from his chair and strained against his tether, causing Bonnet to reflexively lean back even though he was a safe distance.

Bonnet shook his head wearily and pulled out his pistol. 'Pelay, hand her a cup.' He stared at Sara and gave her a little lecture, as if he were a headmaster and she were a schoolgirl. 'If you throw it down, I'll shoot the professor in the foot. If you spit it out, I'll shoot him in the knee.

I'm not going to kill him because I need his help but I will spill his blood.'

'Sara, don't listen to him!' Luc shouted.

'No, Sara,' Bonnet said. 'You should definitely listen to me.'

She took the cup in her shaking hand and started to raise it to her shaking lips.

'Sara!' Luc cried out. 'Don't.'

She looked at him, shook her head and drank it in a series of gulps.

'Excellent!' Bonnet said. 'See, tastes pretty good. Now, professor, it's your turn.'

'I'm not going to do it,' Luc said firmly. 'Sara, if I drink this I can't protect you.'

'Look, this is tiresome,' Bonnet said, turning the gun towards Sara. 'Now I'm going to have to shoot her if you don't cooperate. Just drink the tea and get it over with.'

Luc grimaced in his anguish. How did he know that Bonnet wouldn't pull the trigger? He was certainly capable of violence. But if he succumbed and drank the tea, he'd be abandoning the only weapon he had, his mind. He cursed himself for coming without the gendarmes. It was turning out to be a tragically bad decision.

Sara reached for his free hand and he let her take it. She squeezed his fingers tightly and suddenly looked up as if startled by something. 'Let me talk to him,' she said to Bonnet. 'I'll persuade him. Just give us a moment alone.'

'Okay, a moment. Why not?' He got up and took a few steps back and stood next to Pelay who was leering at Sara lasciviously.

She leaned in trying to get as close to Luc as possible but whatever she said was going to be overheard.

'What are you doing?' Luc asked her.

'Go ahead and drink it,' she whispered.

'Why are you saying that?' he whispered back.

'Do you trust me as a person?'

'Yes, of course.'

'Do you trust me as a scientist?'

'Yes, Sara, I trust you as a scientist.'

'Then *drink* it.'

Pelay crept close enough to hand Luc the cup and quickly backed away.

Sara nodded her encouragement and Luc threw his head back and chugged it down.

'Okay, Pelay, go watch over the flock. I'll stay here with our friends.'

He sat back down and Luc also crumpled onto his chair with a look of defeat on his face.

'You know it's funny,' Bonnet said. 'We had to force you to do something we do ourselves, willingly and gratefully. It's a strange world, no?'

Luc was bristling with contempt. 'What's strange, Bonnet, is how you can pretend to be civilised when you're nothing more than a murdering piece of garbage.'

The old man arched a brow. 'Garbage? Me? No. What I do I do to protect my family and my village. I've lived a very long time, monsieur, and I've learned something important along the way. You take care of your own. If that means pushing others out of the way, then that's the way it is. Ruac is a special place. It's like a rare, delicate flower in a hot house. If the thermostat is

383

disturbed, if the temperature goes one degree up or one degree down, the flower dies. You come here, with your scientists and your students and your cameras and your notebooks and really what you're doing is turning the thermostat. If we let you do that, our way of life will die. We'll die. So, it's a matter of survival for us. It's kill or be killed.'

'Christ,' Sara murmured in disgust.

'These were innocent people,' Luc hissed.

'I'm sorry. From our side, each one was a threat. That one from Israel, he surprised us when we were checking to see what kind of locks you had on your precious cave. That guy Hugo, he had the balls to break into my daughter's house and come down here on a tea night! What did he expect? And the ones at your camp ground last Sunday night? We had to take your computers and destroy your files. We had to blow up your cave to stop you people once and for all from coming to Ruac and we would have if that black bastard hadn't killed my demo man.'

'Pierre's dead?' Sara asked pathetically.

'I'm sorry,' Luc said. 'And Jeremy. And Marie. And Elizabeth Coutard. And — '

She burst into tears and whispered, 'Horrible, horrible,' over and over.

'And what was your justification for raping the women?' From the look on Sara's face, he wished he hadn't said that. He told her the rest of the story, 'The gendarmes said the rapists had immotile sperms.'

Bonnet did his usual shrug. 'Boys will be boys.'

Luc simply said, 'You're a piece of shit.'

That only stoked Bonnet's fires. He became animated, waving his arm. 'Pelay said it would have been better if my men had flattened you two like bugs in Cambridge! I say what's going to happen to you tonight is better.'

'And the company?' Luc asked. 'You blew that up too?'

'Nothing to do with us,' Bonnet shrugged. 'A happy coincidence. We were after you. What do we know about blowing up buildings? Pelay persuaded me we had an opportunity to get rid of you before you could do us more damage. If it happened in another country, it wouldn't track back to us. So I said, why not? When they failed and the two of you split up the next morning, we decided to take her to get you to come to us. What a load of trouble you've caused us!'

Luc wasn't sure if he believed him about their lack of involvement in PlantaGenetics. His water-tight theory was leaking.

'And Prentice? You didn't kill him?'

'Fred's dead?' Sara cried.

'I'm sorry,' Luc said. 'He died in hospital.'

'I don't know anything about that either,' Bonnet barked, 'but you know what?' he continued. 'None of your people would have died if we'd shot you and your chum Hugo the first time you set foot into my café. Just like we did when two jackasses found the cave for the first time, back in 1899.'

Sara curled her mouth into a smile of pure contempt. 'You've got another secret, don't you?'

'Oh yes? What's that?'

'You're infertile, aren't you? All of you men are infertile sons-of-bitches.' She laughed at his hurt expression. 'Luc, it's got to be a side-effect of the tea. They all shoot blanks!'

Luc managed a smile too. 'I don't think I've seen children in Ruac. How many children are there?'

Bonnet stood up, spouting a look of discomfort. 'Not many, not enough. It's a problem, it's always been a problem. The men make the tea for a year or two and our little fish stop swimming. But we get by. We make it work.'

Luc thought for a moment. 'You're matrilineal, aren't you?' he asked.

'We're what?' Bonnet challenged, as if someone had insulted his mother.

'The men can't reproduce,' Luc said. 'Your bloodlines go through the women. So you've got to bring in outside males to keep the maternal bloodlines going. Who fathered your own damned children, Bonnet? Do you use stud service, like horse breeders?'

'Shut up!' Bonnet shouted. He pulled his gun again and waved it at Luc.

Luc taunted him; he had nothing to lose, 'Does your little pistol shoot blanks too?'

Bonnet was shouting now, drowning out the incessant musette rhythms. The villagers stopped talking, turned, and watched him. 'You think you're so damned clever. You come from Paris, you come from Bordeaux, you come to our village and try to destroy our way of life! Let me tell you what's going to happen to you tonight!' He pointed his gun at Sara. 'My son is going to screw this bitch good, then he's going to put a bullet in her head! And she won't even care because she's going to be in love with the tea in a few minutes. And you, you're going to be the stallion. You're going with Odile. You're going to be high as a paper kite and you're going to give me a grandchild, thank you very much. Then I'll personally put a bullet in *your* head! Then I'm going to march up to the top of the cliffs and set off the charges we planted tonight. With all the fancy new gates and locks and cameras they installed we can't get inside it but that doesn't mean we can't blow the cliff up from above and collapse it into the cave! And then I'm going to burn this goddamned manuscript! And then no one else is going to ever know our secret! I don't believe you wrote a letter to anybody. It's a stupid bluff. No one else will ever know! And then I'm going to go back to my café and my fire brigade and my pile of Nazi gold and my quiet village and my tea and my good times and I'll keep on living for so long I might forget that you bastards even existed!'

He was blue from the tirade, puffing and wheezing.

But Luc wasn't looking at him, he was looking at the villagers. It didn't matter whether they were young or old. They were beginning to ignore their mayor's rant. They were gyrating to the music, grinding themselves against each other, pairing off. Clothes were shed. Moans and grunts. Rutting sounds. Older couples were heading into corridors, away from the main room. Younger ones were falling to the carpets, laying into each other with abandon out in the open.

'That's what we do,' Bonnet said proudly. 'And we have done it for hundreds of years! And, Professor, look at your friend!'

Luc looked over and shouted, 'Sara!'

Her eyes were rolling. She was limp in her chair, making short breathy moans.

Bonnet unlocked her handcuff and pulled her upright onto unsteady feet. 'I'm taking her to Jacques now. By the time I come back you'll be ready for Odile. Make me a granddaughter if you're able. Then go to hell.'

36

Bonnet led Luc by the hand. He had no need for weapons or protection. Luc was shuffling like an automaton, distant, eyes searching, passive and compliant.

'There you go,' Bonnet coaxed, as if addressing a dog. 'This way, follow me, good lad.'

Bonnet headed down a corridor off the main chamber. He opened a door.

It was one person's idea of a fantasy.

The windowless room was lined in heavy apple-red and gold matelassé fabric, giving it the appearance of an Arabian harem. The only light came from two standing lamps in the corners glowing with low-wattage bulbs. Gauzy peach-coloured fabric billowed from the ceiling, covering the plaster. A large bed took up much of the floor, its box springs lying on a rug, the bedspread orange and satiny. Shiny red pillows everywhere.

In the middle of the bed, Odile was naked and slowly writhing like a snake looking for a place to bask in the sun. She was creamy and voluptuous, a good, tight body, her pubic hair as black as her long tresses.

'Here, Odile,' her father said proudly. 'I've got him ready for you. Stay with him as long as you like, have him as many times as you can. I'll be back to check.'

She appeared too dreamy to understand, but when her eyes found Luc she began touching herself and moaning.

Bonnet pushed Luc forwards. 'Okay, do a nice job. Have some fun then *bon voyage*. Enjoy the Ruac tea, Professor.'

With that, he shoved both of Luc's shoulder blades hard and sent him flopping onto the bed.

Odile reached for him, grabbing at his clothes, popping the buttons off his shirt with uninhibited force, working on his jeans.

Bonnet watched for a few moments, laughed heartily and left. He checked his wristwatch and went back to the main chamber to change the record on the phonograph, sit and watch the carnal nakedness of the couples who chose the basic comfort of rugs on the floor.

In about an hour he'd finish off Luc and Sara and lay them out for Duval to reward his pigs in the morning. Where *was* that old codger? Bonnet searched the floor, looking for a particularly wrinkled, skinny nakedness. He wasn't there. Probably went into one of the private rooms. And where was Bonnet's wife? He scanned for a big pink rump with long grey hair down to her keister. 'Don't tell me she went off with Duval!' he said to himself, laughing. 'That old man's a scoundrel!' Then he spotted the wife of the village baker, a redhead a hundred years younger than himself who looked a bit like Marlene Dietrich in her prime.

She was astride one of the men, a farmer by trade, who'd done the botched car job in Cambridge then kidnapped Sara. He was a hard man Bonnet trusted for hard jobs. He'd killed more Germans during both world wars than any man from Ruac. Now, his eyes were closed and his teeth gritted. Her breasts were bouncing up and down to the beat of the musette drums.

'Hey, Helene,' Bonnet shouted to the redhead over the music. 'Later on. You and me! I'll find you.'

★ ★ ★

Odile was alternatively clawing at Luc, stroking him, moving her hands over the broad expanse of his back down to his waist, trying to wriggle off his tight jeans.

Her eyes were glassy, her lips moving as if talking, but nothing was coming out. Then a word formed, and another, '*Cheri, cheri.*'

Luc's eyes snapped open.

He looked around the room then took her head in his large hands and said, 'I'm not your *cheri*, and I'm not going to screw a great-grandmother.'

He tried to shake her off but she grabbed him tighter, her nails digging into his back.

'I've never done this before,' he said angrily.

He scowled and slammed his fist into her jaw.

Thankfully, she went limp immediately so he didn't have to pummel her to unconsciousness.

He lifted himself off the bed and rearranged his clothes, watching the naked woman quietly breathing. 'You look pretty good for one hundred and sixteen,' he said. 'I'll give you that.'

He fished inside his pockets for his mobile and

as expected, it was gone.

He twisted the door knob open. Bonnet had thought his daughter was enough of a honey pot to keep him in an unlocked room, Luc figured.

The corridor was empty, the music wafting from the large hall.

His head was perfectly clear. It was clear when he drank the tea. It was clear twenty minutes later. It was clear now.

He'd put on an act. He'd faked being zoned. He watched Sara and the villagers and did his best imitation. Bonnet had been fooled, that's all that mattered.

Why wasn't he affected?

No hallucinations, no other-worldliness, no nothing. Just a headache.

Sara was convinced he'd be immune? How did she know?

Sara.

He had to find her. The thought of Jacques pawing her body made him sick with rage.

He started twisting door knobs.

One after another, the same thing: old, overweight people having it on, oblivious to his intrusion. It was beyond unappetising.

After he tried all the private rooms off that corridor, he crept to the main hall. Bonnet was sitting in a chair on the opposite side of the room, resting drowsily. There was no sign of Pelay. There was enough floor-squirming going on between him and Bonnet to make him think he could slink low and make it to the next corridor.

He dropped down, frog-walked along the wall.

He was level with the tea-service table. The Ruac Manuscript was so close.

He didn't even think. He just acted, dropping to his belly, starting to crawl.

He was swimming in a sea of naked bodies who were oblivious to his presence. He gritted his teeth and kept going.

He looked over for Bonnet.

He wasn't in his chair.

Christ, Luc thought. *Christ*.

In one more second he was under the table.

He reached up and felt his hand close around it.

Sara, I'm coming.

He quickly wriggled back to the wall. Bonnet was nowhere to be seen so he boldly rose and sprinted to the next hallway, shoving the manuscript into his shirt.

He opened the first door he came to.

An old couple sweaty and panting.

Then, the second door.

On the bed, was a man with a hairy back and unbuttoned trousers. Jacques was awkwardly trying to peel them off with his free hand. The only part of Sara he could see, hidden underneath the beast, was tan silky hair, cascading onto the pillow.

There was a standing lamp, a heavy iron affair.

He felt a kind of murderous rage he'd never felt before.

It made him grab the lamp, snapping the plug from the wall.

It made him swing it like a pick axe, bringing

the base crashing down onto the man's thoracic spine.

And when Jacques arched his back in pain, raising his head off Sara's chest and baying like a wounded dog, it made him swing the base of the lamp hard into his skull, crushing it like a walnut, and driving his body halfway off the bed.

Sara was moaning. He held her naked against him and told her she was going to be all right. Her eyes wouldn't focus. He kept speaking to her, whispering into her ear which felt cold against his lips. And finally he heard a tiny, breathy, 'Luc.'

There wasn't time to try to dress her. He pushed Jacques' corpse off the bed and wrapped her in the blood-splattered bedspread. He was about to lift her when he had a thought. He dug into Jacques' pockets. The hard edge of Jacques' mobile felt wonderful against his fingertips. He glanced at it.

No bars. Of course. They were underground.

He pocketed the phone, bundled Sara up and carried her in his arms, pushing the door open with his knee.

The corridor was empty.

He started to run with her, away from the music.

He felt strong and she felt light.

The hallway was darker the further he got from the main hall. He strained to see what was ahead.

Stairs.

★ ★ ★

Bonnet checked his watch again, lifted his heavy hips out of the chair and plodded back to Odile's room to see how she was getting on with her paramour.

It had been four years since the birth of a new child in Ruac. They needed to pick up the pace if they wanted to sustain themselves. Odile was too picky for his liking. A women as attractive as her should be pumping out babies like a machine.

But she'd been pregnant only three times in her long life. Once during the First World War, where she lost the baby to a miscarriage. Again, right after the Second World War, a boy sired by a Resistance fighter from Rouen, who'd died of an infant fever. And again in the early sixties to a Parisian lad back-packing through the Périgord, a one-night stand.

This time a girl was born. She grew up young and pretty and carried the hopes of Bonnet and the entire village on her little shoulders. But she died in a freak accident down in the basements. She had been climbing on the old German crates, trying to scramble to the top of the box mountain, when one of the crates toppled and crushed the life out of her.

Odile had sunk into a depression and despite her father's pleadings, lost interest in the pursuit of men from the outside.

Until the archaeologists came to town.

The only bright spot in a nightmare as far as Bonnet was concerned.

Bonnet opened her door, expecting to see two beautiful people making love, but she was alone, snoring, with a puffy jaw.

'Jesus Christ!' he exclaimed.

There wasn't any need to search the room. There was no place to hide.

He rushed out and ran as fast as his arthritic hips could carry him towards Jacques' room.

There he found a profoundly worse scene. His son, bashed, bloody and most certainly dead, Sara gone.

'My God, my God, my God!' he muttered.

Something had gone terribly wrong.

Where was Simard?

'Pelay!' he screamed. 'Pelay!'

★　★　★

Luc carried Sara up the dark stairs. At the top there was an unlocked door.

They were in a kitchen, an ordinary cottage kitchen.

He carried her through into a hall and a sitting room, dark and unoccupied, the layout similar to Odile's house. He placed Sara onto a couch and adjusted the sheet to cover her properly.

He parted the curtains.

It was the main street of Ruac.

Isaak's car was parked across the street in front of Odile's house.

All the houses *were* connected. The underground hall was, as he suspected, an excavation under the road.

He quickly checked Jacques' phone. There was a good signal. He punched up the recent call list.

Father — mobile.

Good, he thought, but no time now.

The keys to Isaak's car were long gone.

He had a quick rummage; he tried to be as quiet as he could, assuming the occupant of the house was somewhere underground, but he couldn't be sure of that.

In the hall he found two useful items; a set of car keys and an old single-barrelled shotgun. He broke the gun open. There was a shell in the barrel and a few more rounds in a pouch.

★ ★ ★

Bonnet waddled through the underground complex, screaming for Pelay. In the clutches of the tea, none of the other men would be functional for a good hour or more. The fate of his village was riding on him.

I'm the mayor, he thought.

So be it.

Then he found Pelay in one of the corridors, slipping out of one of the rooms.

'Where the hell were you?' Bonnet screamed.

'Checking. Watching. Keeping the peace,' Pelay answered. 'Like I'm supposed to be doing. What's the matter?'

Bonnet yelled for Pelay to follow him then told him what had happened through breathless gasps as the two old men began to run.

Bonnet found the light switch for the corridor. Nothing.

At the next corridor he again switched on the lights.

He pointed. 'There!'

There was a streak of red marking the floor

where Sara's bloody bedsheet had dragged. The corridor led to the baker's house. He drew his pistol and both men made for the stairs.

* * *

Luc awkwardly bundled Sara into the cramped back seat of the baker's Peugeot 206 parked in front of the cottage. The car had obligingly chirped and given itself up when Luc pressed the unlock button from inside the sitting room.

He started it, put it in gear and sped off.

In his rear-view mirror he saw Bonnet and Pelay emerging from the baker's front door. He heard a shot ring out. He shoved the Peugeot into second and floored it.

* * *

Bonnet ran back to his café to get his own car keys.

They had to be stopped.

They had to be killed.

He screamed these mandates at Pelay.

* * *

Luc was talking fast and loud and pushing the little Peugeot to its limits on the dark empty country road. He was brow-beating a low-level emergency services operator to push his call higher. He needed to speak to Colonel Toucas in Périgueux.

The colonel had to be wakened!

He was Professor Simard from Bordeaux, goddamn it!

He had the Ruac Abbey murderers in sight!

★ ★ ★

Bonnet had his keys in hand and was about to shut the café door when his mobile rang.

Luc was shouting at him. 'It's over, Bonnet. It's done. The gendarmes are on the way to Ruac. You're finished.'

Bonnet's rage spouted like lava. 'You think it's done? You think it's done? It's done when *I* say it's done! Go to hell and say goodbye to your goddamned cave! Come on, try to stop me! Come on! Try!'

Bonnet's car was at the kerb in front of the café. He folded himself into the driver's seat and Pelay climbed in beside him as fast as an old man could.

'My rifle is in the boot,' Bonnet said.

'I'm still a good shot,' Pelay grunted.

★ ★ ★

Bonnet pulled the car over to the side of the road at a point he knew, closest to the cliffs. Pelay retrieved the rifle and gave it a perfunctory check. It was an M1 carbine with a sniper scope, liberated from a dead US soldier in 1944. Pelay had been there. He remembered the day. He and Bonnet also took the young man's wallet and boots. It was a good gun that they'd used to kill a lot of *boche*. Bonnet kept it clean and oiled.

The two men ran into the woods, the branches whipping their faces.

After a while, they separated.

Bonnet made straight for the cliffs. Pelay took an oblique path through the dark.

★　★　★

Luc drove to the dirt road leading to the parking area above the cave. He didn't want to run the car all the way. Whatever happened, Sara had to be safe, so he parked a quarter mile away and leaned over the seat.

She was gradually coming out of it.

'I'm leaving you here, Sara. You'll be safe. I've got to save the cave. Do you understand?'

She opened her eyes, nodded, and drifted off again.

He wasn't at all sure she did understand but it didn't matter. Hopefully he'd be around to explain it to her later.

★　★　★

Bonnet could hear his feet pounding and rustling on the forest floor and the wheezy bellows sound his heaving chest was making. There was a clearing ahead, the gravel parking area which the archaeologists had laid down. He was close.

The big oak tree was across the gravel lot, the landmark he'd chosen, and he was glad he'd picked an easy one to spot in the dark.

The gravel sprayed under his heavy fire brigade boots.

Luc wished he had a torch to light his way. It was pitch black but he kept to the lane. It was a chore running with the shotgun. Sara had felt lighter in his arms.

Ahead was a band of grey, the horizon over the cliffs.

Something was silhouetted in the grey, moving.

Bonnet.

* * *

Bonnet was at the base of the tree. A metre away from the trunk was the pile of rocks which he and Jacques had piled up to mark the spot.

Bonnet fell to his knees and began to remove and scatter the rocks. The leather case was just below the ground in a shallow hole.

He slowly lifted the case out, careful not to disturb the copper wires that ran to its terminals. It was a Waffen-SS M39 detonator, liberated from a division of combat engineers in 1943. It was pristine and efficient-looking, a heavy brick of cast alloy and bakelite. Bonnet was confident it would work perfectly.

It had been a tough job but he was confident his old demo men had done it properly, auguring into the cliffs in a half-dozen spots, stuffing picratol, lots of it, deep into the ground. A huge swathe of the cliffs would crumble into the river taking the cave with it.

The cave that had brought his village to life

401

and threatened it with death would be dust. If Pelay did his job, Simard would be dust. He'd find Sara and she'd be dust.

He cranked the wooden handle and heard it ratcheting. When he couldn't turn it anymore he would put his thick thumb on the knob that said ZÜNDEN: ignite.

He heard the footsteps first then, 'Stop!'

Luc was ten metres away, creeping forward on the gravel. He saw Bonnet hunched over something, doing something.

Luc lifted the shotgun to his shoulder.

Bonnet looked up and grunted a simple, 'Go to hell!'

Luc could hear the sound of ratcheting.

The ratcheting stopped and Bonnet moved his hand.

At that moment, Luc's head completely filled Pelay's sniper scope, perfectly contrasted against the grey horizon.

Pelay was in low brush, on one knee. His hands were steady for a man of his age. Luc's head was in sharp focus.

Luc screamed at Bonnet, 'Not my cave!'

Pelay heard the shout and through the scope saw Luc's lips moving. The cross-hairs were planted on his temple.

The trigger was digging into his forefinger. He began to squeeze it.

Luc reeled when he heard the shot from behind.

He expected to feel some kind of searing pain but there was nothing.

He turned back to Bonnet. The old man was

only five metres away now.

Bonnet looked into Luc's shotgun. He shouted, 'Pelay! Hurry!' His thumb was on a knob.

Luc shouted. But it wasn't a word. It was a primitive roar, a primeval death cry that came from somewhere inside of him.

The shell from his shotgun exploded and flashed the darkness.

There was a *thwacking*. Wood, stone, flesh. It was bird shot.

Luc slowly moved forward, straining to see what he had wrought.

Bonnet was lying on his side, bleeding from his face, his eyes still searching. His right thumb was on the ignition button. His left hand was moving. It was grasping the copper wire that had been sheared off the detonator by shotgun pellets.

Bonnet was going to touch the wire to the terminal.

It was a centimetre away.

Luc didn't have time to reload. He didn't have time to smash Bonnet's head or arm with the butt of the gun.

He was out of time.

Then, another shot rang out.

37

Luc was disorientated.

His shirt felt wet. He instinctively touched the fabric. Blood and bits of gelatinous material.

There were men surrounding him, pointing automatic weapons and roughly shouting at him to drop his gun.

Bonnet's head was half gone. The detonator wire remained a centimetre from the terminal.

Luc let his hands go limp. The shotgun fell at his feet.

From the circle of men, one came forward. He was tall and erect, unarmed, dressed in dark civilian clothes, a black commando-style jumper with epaulets.

'Professor Simard,' he said, in an upper-crust type of accent. 'I've been wondering when we'd meet.'

Luc gave him a once-over. He certainly wasn't from the village. 'Who are you?'

'General André Gatinois.'

Luc looked quizzical. 'Military?'

'Of sorts,' was the enigmatic reply. Gatinois came closer and inspected the mayor's corpse. 'Bonnet had a long run at the tables. It had to end sometime. Even for him.'

'You killed him,' Luc said.

'Only after you failed.' Gatinois observed the peppering Bonnet's body had received. 'Bird shot is not an efficient way to kill a man.'

'It was all I had. He was going to blow up my cave.'

There was a commotion as two men in black dragged a moaning body inside the circle of protection their comrades had created.

It was Pelay, bleeding from a chest wound, gasping for breath. One of Pelay's handlers gave his M1 carbine to a shorter man who had appeared at the General's side. It was his aide, Marolles.

'He had you in his sights,' Gatinois said, adding matter-of-factly, 'I saved your life.'

'Are you going to tell me what's going on?' Luc demanded.

Gatinois paused to think. 'Yes, I don't see why not. Do you, Marolles?'

'It's entirely up to you, General.'

'Yes, I suppose it is. Where's the American?'

Marolles spoke into a walkie-talkie pinned to his vest and a static reply followed. 'We're bringing her in,' he told Gatinois.

Pelay let out a pitiful, gurgling cry.

'Are you going to get him a doctor?' Luc asked.

'The only doctor he's going to see is himself,' Gatinois replied dismissively. 'He was valuable, but I never liked him. Did you, Marolles?'

'Never.'

'His last useful act for us was letting us know you were coming to Ruac tonight.'

The baker's Peugeot pulled onto the gravel, driven by another of Gatinois's men who helped Sara out of the car draped in her bloody sheet. She looked confused and wobbly but when she spotted Luc in the centre of the circle, she had the strength to slip the light grip of her guard and run to him.

'Luc, what happened?' she asked weakly. 'Are you all right?'

He put his arm around her. 'I'm okay. These men, I don't know who they are. They're not from the village.'

She saw Pelay who was curled into a fetal position on the ground, making low, horrible sounds. 'Jesus,' she said.

'No, we're not from Ruac,' Gatinois said. 'But Ruac has consumed us for many years. We are devoted to Ruac. We owe our existence to Ruac.'

'What are you?' Luc asked. 'What do you do?'

'We're called Unit 70,' Gatinois said.

Marolles looked down and shook his head. It was a gesture that caught Luc's attention and alarmed him. This man, Gatinois, had apparently crossed some line. Some dangerous line.

'You know, during the war, the Resistance leadership, as loose as it was, gave the Ruac maquis a code for the purpose of their communications. They called them Squad 70. They were a particularly ruthless and effective group. The Germans feared them. The other maquisard distrusted them. When our unit was set up in 1946, our founder, General Henri Giraud, one of de Gaulle's inner circle, chose the name. Not very creative, but it stuck.'

'I know about Ruac's role in the Resistance,' Luc said. 'Tell me something I don't know.'

'Yes, I'm sure you know quite a lot. We're going to find out how much.' He pointed to

Pelay. 'How much do you know about this man?'

'Nothing,' Luc said.

'He's an old bugger, this Pelay. Maybe two hundred and thirty, two hundred and forty years old. Even he isn't sure exactly. He became a doctor in the 1930s. They sent him to Lyon for training. They needed one of their kind. They'd never allow an outsider to treat them, of course. But Pelay's always been a drinker and a talker. During the war, he was Bonnet's number two in Squad 70. Giraud invited him to Algiers for a sit-down. He got good and drunk one night and spilled the beans to de Gaulle and Giraud! Hundreds of years of secrecy, and this buffoon gets drunk and blows it. Their longevity, the tea, the reasons they're so aggressive. Everything. So, after the war, de Gaulle remembers this, of course, and decides Ruac needs to be watched, to be studied by the best minds.'

Sara's head seemed to be clearing. She stood straighter, her eyes were more focused. 'And *that's* what you do?' she asked. There was a bite of anger to her tone.

Gatinois nodded. 'Yes, for sixty-five years we've been studying the Ruac tea. It's remarkable really, Professor Mallory, and a testament to modern science that in a very short time you were able to learn many of the features of the tea, things that took us decades because we had to wait for the science to catch up to our needs. So, for example, I believe Dr Prentice would have told you about the activity he found at these so-called longevity genes, the serotonin receptors, the other effects.'

407

'And that's why you killed Fred?' she asked angrily.

'Well, we didn't really have a choice.' He was casual about it, completely casual.

'Christ!' Luc exclaimed. 'You blew up the lab in England! Over forty people were killed! This was a state-sponsored act of terror!'

Gatinois sighed. 'I wouldn't characterise it that way. We have a remit to protect France's greatest secret. Our methods aren't subject to review and clearance. Nothing is known higher up. Nothing is official. As long as we are absolutely discreet, all is well.'

Luc felt his fear mounting. This man was telling him too much. The implications were clear enough but still, his desire to know more pushed him on. 'And you had Bonnet kill my people, and try to kill Sara and me in Cambridge.'

Gatinois laughed at that. 'Did you hear that, Marolles! That's a good one! No, Professor. Bonnet didn't even know we existed. None of them did, except for Pelay here. Pelay was our man. Our informer. Giraud and de Gaulle turned him after the war, after they controlled the government. They gave him money. They gave him secret medals and all the status he never got under Bonnet's thumb. They buttered him up good, and then they threatened him. They threatened to let Bonnet know he'd talked. He knew Bonnet would carve him up and feed him to the pigs. That was his greatest fear. We've used the same approach with the good doctor ever since. So Pelay's been giving us information for sixty-five years. Every time one of the villagers saw him for a problem, we got a sample of their blood, their urine, their swabs, whatever. We got regular reports. That's all. What Bonnet did — these murders — he did on his own.'

'You let him!' Sara screamed. 'So you're responsible too!'

Gatinois shrugged it off. 'Maybe. In a legal sense, who knows? But this is never going to a court of law. What we do is very secret and very protected. It's probably easier to get France's nuclear launch codes! But, yes, we let Bonnet be Bonnet.'

Sara stiffened and leaped forward. Her slight body turned into a weapon, and letting loose a blood-curdling, 'You fucking bastard!' she closed the gap between herself and Gatinois, her sheet falling away, and naked she began clawing at his face, his eyes.

Gatinois was too caught off guard to defend himself well so Marolles pulled her off. Others subdued her while Marolles pointed his pistol at Luc and warned him to stay put.

Luc was stunned by Sara's action, the way she was kicking and screaming at her subduers with wild abandon. 'Don't hurt her!' he shouted.

Gatinois blotted a streak of blood on his cheek with a handkerchief. 'You see, Professor. That's a graphic example with one of the problems with the drug. It's a delayed effect, maybe an hour or two after the high wears off. I'm told it's the action on the 5-HT$_{2A}$ receptors.' He guffawed. 'You know, this job has turned me into a scientist, what do you think, Marolles?'

His aide grunted and told the men to cuff her wrists and ankles, cover her back up and put her inside the car until she calmed down. She yelled and swore at them ferociously but they managed to remove her from their midst, all the while pointing rifles at Luc and threatening him not to intervene.

'Good,' Gatinois said. 'Much quieter.'

'You've gotten a drug out of the broth?' Luc finally asked.

'Not one. Three, actually. We've had them since the 1970s but, as I said, it's taken until now to begin to understand the biological characteristics of the most important compound, R-422. These longevity genes, SIRT1 and FOXO3A were only recently discovered. There will undoubtedly be other important things scientists will come up with in the future. Eventually we'll understand how 422 works. The other ones are easier, better-defined. The main ergot drug, R-27, makes you high as a kite. It's quite the hallucinogen, really sends you on a trip. The drug R-220, that's an interesting one. It works on potency and libido. In fact, we had a bit of a scandal on that one in the late 1980s. We had an outside contractor working on the compound, a university chemist who didn't have a clue where it came from — that's the way we like to work — and he apparently passed some information about the chemical structure to some guy he knew at the pharmaceutical company, Pfizer. That, apparently, was how Viagra was invented, so I think we've given back to society, wouldn't you say? But our drug,

R-220, though it's even stronger than Viagra, has a nasty side-effect. It shortens and paralyses the sperm tails, makes the men infertile.'

Luc nodded knowingly.

'And this you were aware of?' Gatinois asked.

'Yes, I knew. From the rapes.'

'Ah. But from our perspective, R-422 is the real gem. That's what all the fuss is about. That's what Unit 70 is about. Imagine! The genuine fountain of youth! Live for two hundred years! Three hundred! In good health! And where are the heart attacks? Where are the cancers? What can this do for mankind, eh? Think about it.'

'But,' Luc said emphatically.

'Yes, but,' Gatinois agreed. 'That's the problem. That's why there's secrecy. The violence, the aggression, the impulsivity. These are not trivial effects. The drug can turn a man into a wild animal, a killer if the circumstances are right. And what about other long-term effects on personality, the mind? With Pelay's help, the people of Ruac have been our guinea pigs for sixty-five years. There's a mountain of data to sort out. The epidemiologists call it a longitudinal study. But most importantly, we've been working very hard to get the scientists to modify the drug, to change its structure to retain the longevity effects and eliminate the serotonin effect. So far, no luck. You lose the rage, you lose the longevity. It's more complicated than that but anyway, it's how a layman understands it. So you see?'

'I see that Sara and I have been inconvenient for you.'

411

'Inconvenient. Yes, a good word, but somewhat understated,' he said, waving the hand clutching the blood-stained handkerchief. 'Your discovery of the cave was a *disaster* for us, and maybe for mankind. Can you understand this? These plants are everywhere. Anyone with a saucepan can make the tea. Can you imagine what would happen if thousands, hundreds of thousands, millions of people started taking the Ruac tea? For the sake of your little sliver of prehistory study, you wouldn't want to bring chaos to the world, would you? Millions of stoned, licentious, violent characters, creating havoc? It's a scene from a horror movie, no? So we kept it contained within Ruac. Imagine if the genie were out of the bottle for ever. No, it's up to us to protect the world from this.' His voice rose. 'Once we've found a safe way to exploit R-422, then *France* will own it, *France* will control it and *France* will do what is right for mankind.'

Luc went silent.

Gatinois stooped over the detonator and pulled the broken wire through Bonnet's dead fingers. 'They gave you the tea tonight?' he asked Luc.

'Yes.'

'You've shown no signs of it. Why?'

'I don't know.'

'Maybe we should study you too,' Gatinois chuckled. He told one of his men to shine a torch on the detonator while he carefully inspected it.

'What are you doing?' Luc called at him.

Gatinois stood and rubbed the dirt off one of

his knees. 'It should work well. Bonnet had some men from the old days, good munitions men. If they said they could blow up the cliff, then they could blow up the cliff. We'll see.' He called one of his men forward by name. 'Captain, get everyone back a few hundred metres and set off the charges.'

'You can't do that!' Luc screamed. 'This is the most important cave in the history of France! It's a crime of immense proportions!'

'I can do it,' Gatinois said evenly. 'And I will do it. We'll blame it on Bonnet. By the time the sun rises we'll have a credible story for everything that happened tonight. Bonnet, the dealer in stolen Nazi loot. Bonnet, the protector of Ruac's war crimes. Bonnet, willing to murder to keep the archaeologists and tourists out of his hair. Bonnet, the hoarder of huge quantities of old unstable wartime picratol. It will be fantastic, but partially true and the truth makes for the best stories.'

Luc challenged him. 'What about me? What about Sara? You think we're going to go along with this?'

'No, probably not, but it won't matter, I'm sorry to tell you. But you knew that already, didn't you? We've got to finish the job Bonnet started. That was always going to be the way this ended.'

Luc lunged forward, determined to try to smash the man with his fist. He wouldn't let them do this to Sara. Or to him. Not without a fight.

A rifle butt struck his back. He felt a rib snap

413

and he collapsed in agony, struggling to catch his breath. When he was able to speak again, he felt the edge of the manuscript through his shirt, the silver corners biting into his skin. 'And what about the Ruac Abbey manuscript?' he asked, wincing through the pain.

'I wanted to ask about that,' Gatinois said. 'We looked for that in Pineau's factory but never found it. What was it?'

'Nothing important,' Luc grimaced. 'Only the entire history of the tea and its recipe, written by a monk in 1307. It makes for fascinating reading.'

Gatinois's confident expression sloughed off his face. 'Marolles! Why don't we know about this?'

Marolles was tongue-tied. He wilted under Gatinois's withering gaze. 'I'm at a loss. We monitored, of course, all the communications between Pineau and Simard, between Mallory and Simard. Nothing. We saw nothing about this.'

Luc smiled through the lancinating pain. 'The manuscript was in code. Hugo had it broken. If you'd been looking at his *incoming* emails you'd have seen that.'

There were sirens in the distance.

They all heard them.

'I called the gendarmes,' Luc said. 'They're coming. Colonel Toucas from Périgueux is coming. It's over for you.'

'I'm sorry, you're wrong,' Gatinois said with some strain in his voice. 'Marolles will have a word with them. We're on the same team as the gendarmes, but somewhat higher on the feeding chain. They'll stand down.'

Pelay, who had been quiet for a time, began loudly moaning again, as if he'd lost, then regained consciousness.

'My God!' Gatinois said. 'I can't even think with this noise! Marolles, go and finish him. Maybe you can do *that* properly.'

As Luc propped himself onto his knees, he saw Marolles march over to Pelay, and without a second of hesitation fire a single round into his head. When the percussive sound of the shot faded, the circle was quiet again — except for the sirens in the distance.

'You're nothing but a murderer,' Luc hissed at Gatinois.

'Think what you like. I know I'm a patriot.'

Luc got himself upright and used the solidity of the hidden book to splint his chest by pressing it against his ribcage with his elbow. 'I'm not going to debate you, you son of a bitch. I'm only going to tell you that you're not going to kill Sara and you're not going to kill me.'

'And why not?' Gatinois asked defensively as if sensing Luc's confidence.

'Because if something happens to me, the press will get a letter. Maybe it won't have anything in it about you, but everything else is there. Ruac. The tea. The murders. And a copy of the Ruac manuscript with its translation.'

The sirens were getting closer, piercing the air.

'Marolles,' Gatinois ordered. 'Go and deal with the gendarmes. Intercept them. Keep them well away from the village. Go, and don't screw up.' Gatinois slowly walked to Luc, close enough for either man to strike each other. He stared at him for a full fifteen seconds without uttering a word. 'You know, I've read your profile, Professor. You're an honest man and I can always tell when an honest man is lying. I believe you're telling me the truth.'

'I believe I am,' Luc replied.

Gatinois shook his head and looked skyward. 'Then I suggest we find a solution. One that works for me, works for you but most importantly, works for France. Are you willing to do a deal, Professor?'

Luc stared back into the man's cold eyes.

Gatinois's phone rang. He pulled it from his trouser pocket. 'Yes,' he said. 'Yes, on my authority, proceed.' He pocketed the phone and addressed Luc again. 'Just wait a moment, Professor.'

First there was a flash.

It was so bright it was as if day had come to night, a premature sunrise, blazing and incandescent.

Then came the sound. And the rumbling sensation.

The shock-wave travelled through the ground, rattled the gravel and for a second made everyone sway.

Gatinois said simply, 'It's always been a contingency. Now was the time to end it. Our work continues, but Ruac is gone.'

38

In the morning drizzle, the crater that had been Ruac village reminded Luc of pictures he'd seen of Lockerbie after the Pan Am crash.

There was no main street. There were no cottages, no café, only a vast black, rubble-strewn, car-filled chasm, weeping charcoal-coloured smoke. The firemen were spraying their hoses down onto flaming spots along the length of the trench but due to fears of instability, they weren't permitted to get close enough to be effective. The fires would have to burn out on their own.

A good proportion of the emergency services capability within the Dordogne was at the site. Access points into the village were choked with gendarmerie vehicles, police cars, ambulances, TV vans and fire brigade equipment. Ordinarily, Bonnet would have been there, tramping around in his heavy boots and tight-fitting uniform ordering his men about, but they had to make do without him.

Colonel Toucas was in charge of the operation, growling at the news helicopters which were thumping overhead and making it difficult to use his mobile phone.

At the dawn's first light he had told Luc he reckoned that some of the Second World War-era explosives, picratol, more than likely, stored in a cellar by Bonnet and his fellow scoundrels, must have accidentally gone off and started a chain reaction with other caches of explosives hidden in other cellars.

He added in a hushed voice, that he had it under good authority that Bonnet was a trafficker in old stolen goods, that certain clandestine government agencies had him under surveillance. There was talk of hundreds of millions of euros of gold and Nazi spoils that might be found under the rubble.

Luc looked at him blankly, wondering if he fully believed the story that Gatinois had fed him.

Toucas couldn't imagine there'd be any survivors; the mangled and charred state of the corpses that were readily retrievable seemed to bear this out. But it would be days before they could reasonably change the mission from rescue to recovery.

Toucas framed the catastrophe with his own point of view. 'This will be my entire existence for the next year, maybe two,' he told Luc. 'You and I will be spending a lot of time together. Of course, by your own admission you killed two men last night, but I shouldn't worry. You'll come out clean. These men were trying to keep the outside world out of Ruac, out of their business. They resorted to murder. They intended to eliminate your cave. You were protecting yourself, protecting a national treasure.'

Abbot Menaud arrived at mid-morning to offer up the abbey grounds for whatever purpose the authorities saw fit but Toucas didn't have much time for him.

The cleric spotted Luc near the mobile command centre and spent a few minutes commiserating. With all the loss of life, it seemed trivial that the Barthomieu manuscript was likely in ashes somewhere deep within the crater, but the fellow did seem wistful anyway.

Luc drew him aside and partly unbuttoned his shirt.

'You have it!' the abbot cried.

'And you'll have it back soon enough,' Luc assured him. 'As soon as I know it will be safe.'

★ ★ ★

Luc borrowed a mobile phone from an ambulance driver. He'd probably never be able to make a call again on his own phone without wondering if Unit 70 was listening in. He apologised to Isaak for losing his car. Then he asked him to tuck away the unopened envelopes somewhere safe. He'd figure out what to do with them later.

Luc borrowed another car from an archaeologist friend at the museum at Les Eyzies. He drove to Bergerac to collect Sara from the hospital where she'd spent the rest of the night.

She was waiting for him in the casualty ward when he arrived, wearing the spare clothes of a nurse who'd taken pity on her. She looked pale and weak, but when they hugged he felt the strength of her young arms around his neck.

They went to the cave.

Munitions experts from the army had worked

all day clearing explosives from auger holes in the cliff-top and the area was declared safe.

Maurice Barbier had arrived in a Ministry of Culture helicopter to personally meet with Luc at the old abbey camp site and hand over the new keys and security codes. He mumbled something about Marc Abenheim's lack of availability, but anyway, he was sure that pending an investigation, Luc would be reinstated as Director of the Ruac Cave.

He listened in a fatherly way to the story Luc and Sara chose to tell, an official version hastily cobbled together with Gatinois in the dead of the night. When Barbier had heard enough to brief the Minister, he kissed Sara's hand and flew off into the steel-grey sky.

At the cave mouth, Luc pulled the gates open and switched on the master lights. 'No protective suits,' he told her. 'Special occasion.'

They walked slowly through the chambers, hand-in-hand like kids on a first date.

'How did you know?' he finally asked.

'That you wouldn't be affected?'

He nodded.

'Your pills for your staph infection. Rifampin. It boosts an enzyme in the liver called CYP3A4. You know what that enzyme does?'

He looked at her, lost.

'It chews up ergot alkaloids. It inactivates them. If you were being a good boy and taking your pills like you said you were, I knew you wouldn't be affected by the ergots in the tea. Or maybe the other chemicals too.'

'I'm always a good boy. Well, usually. But let's

talk about you. You're a clever girl, aren't you?'

'I know my plants.'

Then he got serious. 'So what was it like?'

She held her breath while she thought then exhaled completely. 'Look, I know what happened to me, and what didn't happen to me. The doctors told me there was no rape. Thank you. And mercifully, I don't remember any of that part. What I remember was glorious. I was light, I was floating, I felt I was on the wind. It was intensely pleasurable. Surprised?'

'Not at all. I figured as much. Would you take it again?'

She laughed and said, 'In a New York minute,' then gripped his hand tighter. 'No, probably not. I prefer an old-fashioned natural high.'

He smiled.

'Luc, I feel so bad about so many people — Pierre, Jeremy and the rest — and Fred Prentice's death is so profoundly sad. That dear man would have had a field day working out the chemistry and everything to do with survival genes.'

'It's awful that it's up to Gatinois to take the science forward,' Luc said. 'I have no trust he'll do the right thing.'

She sighed heavily. 'Did we do the right thing?' she asked. 'To trade for our silence?'

'We're alive. The cave is still here. We can study it in peace for the rest of our lives. They would have killed us, Sara, blamed it on Bonnet.'

'But we can't study everything,' she said. 'We have to play dumb about the plants, suppress knowledge of the manuscript, be a party to a cover-up. All those murders in Cambridge and Ruac are going to go unpunished.'

He said it again, squeezing her arm. 'Look, I don't feel clean, but *we're alive*! And I hate to agree with Gatinois about anything, but it *would* be terrible if the recipe for the tea got out. We had to make a choice. We did what we had to do. We did the right thing.'

She sighed and nodded.

He took her hand and tugged. 'Come on, you know where I want to go.'

⋆ ⋆ ⋆

In the tenth chamber, they stood in front of the giant bird man and embraced. For the first time, Luc imagined the bird man's beak was open in a triumphant laugh, a very human expression of joy.

'This feels like our place,' Luc said. 'I want to keep coming here forever to work and learn. I think it's the most amazing place in the world.'

She kissed him. 'I think so too.'

'I'll be good to you this time,' he promised.

She looked up into his eyes in an effort. 'Once burned, twice shy. Are you sure?'

'Yes, I'm sure. I'll be good to you for a very long time. As long as I live.'

From her wry smile he wasn't sure she believed him.

Epilogue

Rochelle, Pennsylvania

Nicholas Durand dried while his wife washed.

He'd faithfully helped with the dishes ever since they were first married. Creatures of habit, they always did them by hand. He couldn't recall ever using the dishwasher their daughter had bought and installed for them. Husband and wife were white-haired, stooped with age, moving through their chores slowly and deliberately.

'Tired?' his wife asked.

'Nope. I feel good,' he replied.

It was night-time. They'd had a late supper following an afternoon nap, their usual routine on barn nights.

Rochelle was a speck of a town in central Pennsylvania, a farming town nestled in rolling hills. It was founded in 1698 by Huguenots, French Protestants who couldn't abide the Catholic Church. It was off the beaten path, just like the founders had wanted. There'd never been more than a few hundred residents, then or now.

Pierre Durand, the town's founding father, had left his own village in France for the Huguenot hot-bed of La Rochelle on the Bay of Biscay back in the 1680s. He hadn't wanted to leave his village in the Périgord but there'd been a terrible dispute involving the village's leading family over money and there was violence in the air. Although he'd never been religious, he settled upon a Huguenot woman in La Rochelle and she wound up turning his head and his beliefs. They set sail for North America in 1697.

The couple finished stacking the plates and returning the cutlery to the drawer. They sat back at the kitchen table and watched the clock tick for a while. There was an *USA Today* newspaper half-folded on the counter. Nicholas reached for it and put his reading glasses on.

'I still can't get over it,' he said to his wife.

The front page of the paper was mostly devoted to the explosion that had destroyed a place in France named Ruac. 'Are you sure your father was from there?' she asked.

'That's what I understand,' the old man said. 'He never wanted to talk about it. He had a blood feud with a man in Ruac named Bonnet. Bonnet apparently got the best of him and that was that.'

'You think they were our sort of people?' she asked.

The man shrugged his narrow shoulders. 'According to the paper, there's no one left to ask.'

Through the kitchen window they saw head lights in the distance coming down their mile-long lane. One car, then two, then a steady stream.

'They're coming,' he said, pushing back his chair.

'How's the tea tonight?' she asked.

'Good and strong,' he said. 'It's a good batch. Come on, let's get up to the barn.'